RISE of the GRISYM

DISAVOWED BIRTHRIGHT BOOK 1

BRITTON BRINKLEY

Rise of the Grisym

Britton Brinkley

Landingham Stanley Press

Copy Edits: Ashley Wessel

Cover Design: Isabelle Olmo

First Edition

Author's Note

I learned a valuable lesson when I agreed to this book: Never let my friends ask for something ridiculous because it will become this living, breathing thing I will obsess over and have to bring to life. That happened here with Rise of the Grisym. Jordan came to me and said I want a why choose, fantasy, dark academia with rivals to lovers (I failed that one) with dragons (also failed) and spell work, a professor has to be part of the choose and ghouls (no sex with ghouls unless it furthers the plot)—that one I made happen. Add in CNC (consent non-consent—that's for book two). That ask became this book, and I loved every second. This is only the first installment of this series and I can't wait to continue developing this world and finding out what type of shenanigans these characters get into.

A few things to note as you're reading this. The setting is a partially fictionalized version of the world. Country names and the United States are named the same but may be described differently. Some of the cities are made up and others are real. References to topics like government are mostly true to how our government operates now. Other than how we live modernly now, any correlations you may find to other people or places are coincidental. This book is whatever fell out of my twisted head on the day I wrote it.

Okay, I am just going to put this out there before someone does it for me. Yes, this is a magical school, like a certain series many of us grew up reading and watching. This book is not that. If you're just looking for an adult version, you will not find that here. There is so much more and there's spice too.

Trigger/Content Warnings:

- The chosen one/most powerful
- Why Choose Romance
- Dark Magic
- Divide Between Magical Beings (Similar to discrimination)
- Extreme violence
- Death threats
- Assault between opposite sexes
- Explicit language
- Explicit sexual content
- Sex with non-human creatures
- Sex with multiple partners (individually and in group settings)
- Necromancy (mentioned)
- Student-teacher relationship
- Betrayal by family
- LGBTQ+ side characters

For the most up-to-date list of trigger and content warnings:

Prelude

Some are born with magic. Some must borrow it.

Many descend from the light. More crawl their way out of the dark.

I am both.

The light.

The dark.

The center of it all.

I am the blanket of gray that will swallow us all whole.

But I am also the only being standing between us and destruction.

1

BRYONY

I AM THE LIGHT. I am the light. I am the light.

The timeless mantra plays through my mind as I waltz through the onyx-wrought iron gates of the Beauxgraton School of Wielding. The oldest school for dark magic still standing in our country. A monstrosity of what once was a family home is now mine for the next three years.

I've witnessed many castled institutions throughout my life. Every shade and every finish. Every design and every luxury. An eyesore of wealth signifying a common corollary of those belonging to a family of importance. I have followed my dad through the halls of schools all over the world. The story never changes. Each institution and every group of administrators acts thrilled to have you around, but it's all a farce. It's nothing more than an opportunity for them to recruit new students who bring with them the power of a strong wielding name and the magical gifts to match.

Roman Avalon is a man of purpose. One with prestige and honor behind his name. My father has held his position for the past thirty years as the Director of Education under the Wielding Council. He was quick to snatch that position of power the moment it became available. The man who holds the director's seat controls every wielding institution in the world.

For the first time, I am venturing into a magical school without his hand on my shoulder. The distinct lack of comfort from his gruff laugh and twitching walnut mustache add to the unease brewing in my gut. The tickle that started as butterflies is now tightly corded into knots.

I asked him not to come today. It's bad enough that I'm part of the first light class entering Beauxgraton, an institution that has historically only educated dark wielders. To everyone around me, I am nothing more than another student with light gifts. Just the same, having the director walking in beside me would bring unnecessary attention.

I did what I could to hide myself over the years. Made myself invisible to everyone but my closest friends, so that when I did attend school, the other students wouldn't gawk at me, fear my abilities, or think I'd received privileges courtesy of my father's power and influence. I'd hoped no one would recognize me, a stupid notion based on delusion.

There are other reasons for trying to remove myself from notice. Reasons no one can ever know.

With a deep sigh, I press my hand to the invisible barrier just beyond the first gate. My magic signature recognized by the wards allows me to step through the intangible shield.

To the human world—and anyone without permission to enter—the large gate seems as though its only purpose is to guard an abandoned castle of mixed gray stone. Humans only know this place for its tragic past. They believe an old lord once came here looking for a new way of life, only for his entire family to pass. The deaths of the family members are believed responsible for the estate falling into disarray. The abandonment of the property was a perfect opportunity for the Wielding Council to purchase the land from a distant relative of the original owner.

The story is partially true. True enough that when asked about it, it's not a lie.

There are humans out there who know about us wielders. They still call us witches. Many of their ideas about us are based on movies and cartoons. But you can't educate people on something they don't understand, especially when they don't *want* to learn.

We are wielders. Those that possess and can use magic for good, or evil; anything we want, really.

In the human world, we hold jobs and live in homes like everyone else. Those that know about us are on either side of a tall fence. The humans either accept us or would rather cast us away.

I'd prefer non-magical beings leave us be altogether.

For most of our lives, we follow the normal progression of any human child. Daycare, elementary, middle, and then high school. Some of us choose higher learning with college and graduate degrees, but even more don't bother knowing that at age twenty-five when we mature into our powers, we are mandated to attend wielding schools.

My mind coasts back to those days as I continue down the path, hoisting my leather backpack up my shoulder. In high school, there was a girl obsessed with learning to do spells. She would find me daily asking about random junk she found on the internet, begging me to tell her if it was real and how to conjure magic to perform said enchantments. I swear I wanted to turn her into a toad most days. But the Council frowns upon that type of spellcraft. One of the few rules for us wielders:

Wielders may only cast spells on humans when innumerable damage would be caused by said human. A spell may only be cast as a defensive measure against a human.

My thoughts continue to wander as I make my way up the curved pathway toward the main residence. Taking in the colossal structure of this manor, it's hard to believe that it once housed a single family. I simply can't imagine what four people would need all this space for. It is absolutely beautiful though. A work of art meant to be gawked at. The breathtaking architecture speaks of a long history fashioned after the French man who built it with massive bastian corner towers that stand taller than any other peak. Several smaller towers cluster toward the center at the rear of the residence, only slightly shorter than the corners. The asymmetrical chimney tops along the roofs appear more like spires than their intended purpose. Then there's the tiny tower dead center toward the rear of the structure housing five small bells that chime hourly. It's the only part that seems out of place.

Students stomp past me, not much distinguishing the light from the dark. Only a few are identifiable because of their influential parents. Some in the magical realm, some in the human. For instance, the daughter of one of our country's government officials just strode past me typing away at her phone. She is a dark wielder with power-hungry parents. A common story for that half of our community.

Then there's the son of some king in Europe. The young man's eyes are so wide with fear, that I can't fathom why anyone in his family thought it would be smart to send him to our country. It's not like there aren't hundreds of schools overseas. I wonder if he too had no choice.

"Students, please make your way to Buckingham Proper. Our opening assembly begins in ten minutes," a projected voice states, drifting over the campus. The disembodied voice draws many of our gazes up to the sky—giving a clear picture of which of us are new to Beauxgraton.

Beauxgraton always fascinated me when I was young. Not just because of the dark magic, but the culture and simplicity of it. Where most schools have a dozen or more buildings for their student body, Beauxgraton has only ever had three. The main residence is where classes, sleeping quarters, and a grand dining hall are located. Buckingham Proper holds the assembly hall, where they have added additional amenities such as a gym in the basement. Then there's, Beechum, which holds, the faculty quarters—former living space for the help when this place was first constructed. It's the smallest structure of the three, set off far enough from the residence that it's easily forgotten.

From the outside, it would be impossible to tell that these buildings hold thousands of students and faculty. Only a select group of staff members are permitted to live in their own homes off-campus. The headmistress, of course, is one of those individuals.

That woman often embodies the definition of terrifying. Her features are sharp and unforgiving with brows that arch toward her low hairline and hair so perfectly white that many have thought it colored. She wears a scowl that never seems to leave her face. Yet, I know she is the sweetest woman this world has ever known.

As a synchronized mass of mixed students, we enter the auditorium. The rows of seats are reminiscent of those found in old theaters. That same gray of the outside carried within. The monotone coloring showcased by the charcoal-flecked chairs. The squeak of their hinges reverberating through the room as bodies settle into each one.

I do my best to stay close to the middle of the auditorium. My only goal is to remain within the center of anonymity. Lost in a sea of bodies in hopes that no one notices me, especially on the first day. Fortunately, no one I know from my personal life is attending Beauxgraton as a student. But that doesn't change the fact that for years my family's notoriety has brought my face before the eyes of millions.

Sadly, the light wielders I knew from back home chose to attend the last few light schools still open overseas. The same friends I've had since middle school. Not a single one looked back when they left for their institutions before I did the same to come here. Not a single call or text once they ventured off to the next chapters of their lives.

Tucking my backpack under the seat at my feet, I lean back. The press of the metal sides into my full hips is irritating, but nothing new for me. With a subtle shift, my rear pressed to the back of the chair, I know this is as comfortable as I am going to get. Ready for an hour-long lecture on school rules and how things will be different this year. I'd been briefed on it before coming here, so I'm prepared to listen to the lies they will tell about the exponential number of light schools closing when not a single dark school has. The mixing of our different types of magical skills is an experiment that few have tried at this level.

My dad assures me all will be fine, but I've seen that glazed look in his eyes. The one that tells me he's doing his best to hold it together. Fighting like hell to understand what is happening in our world. Even as the director, he holds little influence over the decision to close schools. His power lies in sculpting the curriculums and execution of duties by the administration. Ultimately, that power sits with the Wielding Council. Their closed-door discussions do not reach anyone else's ears until the damage is already done. By then, there's no undoing their decision.

"Welcome students," Headmistress Milgren broadcasts to the room. She looks just as she always has as she approaches the edge of the stage. There's no microphone in front of her. Nothing to suggest her voice is being artificially magnified. Her natural-born gift is amplification. An innate gift. She is a wielder similar to me in that way.

"This year will be the start of a new era. One where the light—" her right hand gestures to one side of the auditorium, "and the dark—" the left hand following the same gesture in the opposite direction, "—can come together and forge new bonds."

Several students snicker at the front of the room as two guys bump fists.

I know exactly what they are thinking and it's illegal—sort of.

"And this year, we have someone special amongst us." Her eyes lock with mine and my stomach drops. *NO. No,* I internally plead. *Please don't do what I think you're going to do.*

It's not possible to sink any lower in my seat. The girls on one side of me point their glares in my direction. Expressions of annoyance and confusion utterly transparent on their faces.

"If you'll please stand, Bryony Avalon, our Director of Education's youngest daughter."

Headmistress Milgren begins clapping enthusiastically. The scowl she wears is still in place, but a bit of pride shines behind her eyes, too. It makes me question if she understands what she's done. If she is ignoring what is most important. *My secrets.* Secrets I will have to keep close to me.

More applause echoes out from about half of the room. It's the light half, always eager to cheer on one of their own.

Or so they think.

All I want to do is drown in the dark.

2

Bryony

I WOULD FIND IT nothing short of fantastic if the floor would just open up and swallow me whole this instant. My fingers itch to call those dark tendrils of glittering magic to my palms, to simply cut a perfect sphere around my feet—a silent wish for any escape as I slowly stand surrounded by my peers.

But, I can't do any of that.

Just like all the other first years here, I'm supposed to be a novice. Brand new and coming into the maturity of my powers. A change all wielders undergo at twenty-five. Their next stop is a wielding institution. Similar to applying to human colleges, we must do the same, waiting for an acceptance letter that serves as a binding contract once acknowledged.

Briefly looking down at my palms, I remind myself I'm not supposed to have this much control over my power. I shouldn't know the spells to bring their worst nightmares and best dreams to life.

My fingers curl into tight fists at my side. My weight quietly shifting from foot to foot. I'm uncomfortable having every pair of eyes in the room focused on me. The rigid smile tugging at the corners of my lips sure to make me appear demented.

One guy with a messy bun at the back of his head stares more intently than the others. A familiar face, but I can't place it. His seat is only a few rows ahead of mine. A vicious, dark gaze so focused on me, that sweat begins to trickle down my spine. It's as if the fix of his eyes is undressing me.

I want to run. Anywhere but right here, in this moment, will do.

The applause finally dies down, my classmates righting themselves in their seats before I finally drop back into mine.

"Camilla Van Buren," the woman to my right greets me as she stretches out a palm. We shake casually before she faces forward once more. Her smile bright and never leaving her face.

"Bri Avalon," I whisper back, internally chastising myself for adding my last name like it wasn't just announced to the room.

"Thank you all for welcoming Bryony so warmly. I expect each of you to treat her the way you would any other." *Terrible wording.* The desire to roll my eyes is overwhelming. She pretty much just gave them all an order to do the exact opposite of what she asked.

Any chance of me blending in now is no longer a possibility. Even if the intent was just to include me; I'll find myself singled out. It's not like I'm not "other" enough as is. There will be those—staff and student alike—who exclude me for fear that I am a spy for my father—not wrong. Those who cozy up to me will hope that befriending me equals better opportunities once their schooling is done. However, my favorites will be those that say fuck behaving and the implied expectations of being my father's daughter.

"Due to the influx of students this year, first-year students will share living spaces. Come second year—should you live to see it—you'll have earned your own space." She pauses for effect. The press of her mouth thinning her lips into a lethal line as if daring my classmates to complain or challenge her. "For my next announcement, as you all know we are only a few weeks away from a Red Moon. Students are prohibited from venturing to the restricted area of the property to participate in the festivities without written permission from myself and Assistant Headmaster Mighel Schouten."

Groans filter through the room. I perk up. I've never been to a Red Moon Festival, only heard about them. I've dreamed of going to one for as long as I can remember. Just one chance to tap into the side of me I've been told to pretend doesn't exist.

A Red Moon marks the release of ghouls into the mortal world. Just eight nights a year. That one weekend each quarter, reserved for them to escape their caverns below. Occasionally outside of a Red Moon, a ghoul may escape, wreaking havoc on the area they've wandered into. Ghoul hunters—*creative, I know*—are then dispatched to bring those rogue ghouls back to their underground dwellings, or kill them if they don't cooperate.

Red Moon Festivals are special to dark wielders, especially those without innate magic. Though historically every dark wielder would partake in these festivals, for many it has become more of a symbolic celebration versus actually partaking in the debauchery of ghoul pits. For those who do indulge, siphoning dark magic from ghouls is the most efficient way to gain a significant amount of power at once. Just a few minutes of animalistic sex with one of those gnarled beasts can give a dark wielder enough magic to hold them until the next moon—at least—from what I've read.

Though it's common knowledge it's by no means the only way to gain that level of power.

I fail to hear the rest of Headmistress Milgren's speech. Every previous image I've seen of ghouls floods my mind. Most humans who know they exist think of them as the ghosts you see in movies. Nothing more than a white sheet draped over a transparent body. Just an entity of nothingness floating through the air. *Wrong.*

Ghouls are anywhere from seven to ten feet tall. Their long stretched bodies have withered, leathery skin. Full rows of teeth as sharp as mini daggers and tongues the length of my arm. The tip of that disturbingly long tongue can fork apart should they choose. But their eyes are the feature that unnerves people the most. No pupils or irises the way we have them, only filmy white orbs that allow them to see within an individual. This is how they choose whether to share their power with a wielder.

I should stay away. A Red Moon Festival is sure to land me in more trouble than my father would care to clean up. But that curiosity still lingers. A tempting burn brewing inside me.

The girl next to me nudges me hard. *Camilla, was it?* An interruption that brings my thoughts to an abrupt halt. "Where's your room? We can walk together if you wanna."

Her sweet voice and thick accent grate on me. She has an innocence to her that I feel I've never gotten a chance to know. I have a feeling she's the type who loves everyone and refuses to cuss because someone once told her that it's not ladylike to use foul language. Further, judging by her modest attire, she either still lets her mother dress her or she's one step away from becoming a politician's wife.

"Yeah. Sure," I shrug, pulling my backpack from beneath the seat.

She might be the type to drive me crazy, but I'm not sure I am going to be anyone's fan favorite here. Might as well take advantage of those willing to talk to me after that unwarranted introduction.

"Okay, so my mobile says room thirty east," she recites with a huge grin plastered on her face.

Snatching my phone from my jacket pocket I scroll to the email that has all the prep information. I'll be damned. Thirty east.

"Looks like we're roomies."

She giggles loudly clapping her hands together and we're off.

This place is a labyrinth of halls and short flights of stairs intermingled with long, curving staircases that seem like they shouldn't be there and probably lead to nowhere. I would give anything to teleport right now, but Dad warned me I couldn't in front of others. It's not ... common. Guess I'll just end up with toned legs and a great ass. Well, greater ass. Something my genes gave me ample amounts of.

We turn down a hallway following the masses of students heading toward the housing wings of the residence. Many of the women in front of us converse animatedly. Wielders that are already friends. A sudden burst of loneliness leaves me rubbing at the ache under my sternum. I miss my friends, but it doesn't change that I've still always been pretty isolated. I know I should keep things that way here, but I don't want to.

It takes me a moment to recall why no men are walking in our direction. It's no surprise they've worked so hard to keep the men and women separate. Sure, this is technically still a boarding school, but we're all adults. More than likely the change has more to do with keeping the opposite sexes of light and dark wielders from mixing. From what I recall the wings used to be separated by year and chosen track of study. Now it's simply the women to the east and men to the west.

Our room is easy enough to find. Camilla lifting her hand reciting the code word we were given before throwing the door wide open. Her giggle leaving me with a quirked brow.

I walk in expecting dark and gloomy, but the room feels like an angel's dream. Light airy colors accented with a variety of whites and silvers that touch every surface. The blue is so pale it could be mistaken for frost. Our entire room places us in a winter wonderland. Light wooden desks and bed frames complement every hue. Gossamer curtains frame our windows, dimming the little sunlight this part of the country gets.

Nestled in the mountains of the mid-west, Beauxgraton is a place with serene settings and snowcapped hills almost year-round. Endless forests that transition into the most beautiful array of colors in the fall. But it can be a dreary place too. The cold comes in full force quickly. Rain and clouds are often the backdrop on any given day.

"Well, this is just delightful," Camilla squeals, falling back onto the bed at the far end of the room with her arms spread wide.

Immediately she jumps back up smoothing her basic cream blouse and slim-fit camel-colored skirt hitting just below her knees. "I'm so sorry," she belts. Her shoulders curl forward, hands braced in front of her like she's offended me beyond fixing. "I had no business staking claim to the bed you may have been eyein'. I-I can clean that blanket if that's the one you want."

A laugh barrels out of me. Her posture frozen and her short fingers spread apart as her hands remain in front of her face, eyes wide with confusion.

"First off, take whichever bed you want. I don't care. Second, please, please, please do not kiss my ass. I am just like every other student here." *Biggest lie known to man.*

It takes a moment before she relaxes and realizes I mean what I said.

"Oh," she gasps. "You really are just as sweet as pie. I heard you were." Her arms wrap around me, my taller frame dwarfing her petite one. "We're going to have an amazin' year."

I smile back at her as she finally releases me. I sure hope so. I can only pray my classmates don't learn the secrets that could make that statement the furthest thing from the truth.

"Let's unpack." I take a step away from her, hoping she doesn't hug me again. It's not that I'm not an affectionate person, I would just prefer strangers keep their hands to themselves just in case. That single step signals the both of us to take in the pile of luggage deposited in the center of the room.

Our belongings were gathered from our homes last night, transported here through a series of spelled systems. All four of my ebony suitcases and person-sized mahogany trunk sit at the center of the room atop the white and gray marbled area rug. Camilla's neon green cases are blinding in comparison. The placement of our belongings feels strategic. As if the neutral position will allow us to make our first choice since arriving here—even though it's something as innocent as which side of the room we'd like.

With a heavy sigh, I snatch the handle of the first case tugging it up onto my bed. I hate unpacking. I always have. It was the worst part of going on trips with the family or traveling the world with my dad. I've also always been one to pack so much more than needed. My brothers and elder sister hated it. I always took up more space, so they couldn't because I refused to leave anything behind. This is no different.

I will spend the next three years here. The general innate wielders program is the shortest by far. I'd begged my dad to allow me to do spellcasting instead—a five-year program—as I thought that a better way to shield my capabilities, but he insisted the longer I was here the more likely it was that my secrets would come out.

Daddy knows best.

3

VALEN

THE DANK SCENT OF aged water and mildew wafts up my nostrils as my best friend, Pierson Flaggstaff, and I wander down to the subterranean levels of the residence, the main building here at Beauxgraton.

The Vault is where our group meets every Sunday night. A predetermined and secure location per our liaison here at the school. There are six of us who remain loyal to something greater than ourselves. Including myself and Pierce, there's Damian, Sean, and the siblings Kaia and Kormoran.

Pierce and I are third-years. We both only have two years left of our respective programs of Ghoul Studies and Spellcasting before we can make our mark on the world. We've been best friends since we were in diapers. Families like ours are destined to run in the same circles. The human elementary school we both went to had their hands full with us from day one. I can't say anything has changed since we've gotten older.

The rest of our group is already waiting when we slink into our chamber hidden behind a movable stone wall. A steep flight of stone steps beyond it leads straight into the private room. That mobile wall is only one of the countless hidden doorways and passages the original owner, David Hamilton Beauxgraton, had built into this place. The many less-than-legal operations he led needed to be concealed somehow.

Kaia and Kormoran—the most devilish twins you'll ever meet—Damian, Sean, Pierce, and I are the only ones who come here now. The Vault is ours to use at will. We spelled the entrance to only allow certain individuals unchaperoned into our domain.

We're originals to Beauxgraton. We've been here since our first years, unlike all of these new transfers. The fact that none of us are innate wielders only further strengthens our friendship. Our lack of ability to wield magic without siphoning or channeling puts us in the category of extrinsic. On paper, we're nothing more than a different type of wielder. Yet we're treated as inferior. We always have been.

Our position grates on us. Burns within us. Our gifts are exceptionally powerful when we can channel them properly. Though we're not considered the most powerful or prestigious of wielders our gifts are just as necessary as theirs. A balance. Give and take between the two sides innates don't like to acknowledge most days.

"Took you long enough," Kormoran grunts, tucking his phone back into his cargo jacket pocket.

"So sorry that the top-floor bedroom I've been assigned to for the past two years forced me to shove my way through a bunch of light wielders, which in turn took up too much of *your* time." The corner of my lip trembles as it curls. I can't stand being challenged.

A growl vibrates through his chest. No one hates those who wield light magic more than Kormoran and Kaia Vue. Their mother—one of the most proficient innate dark spellcasters—left when they were twenty. Even her husband was too dark a demon for her to live beside anymore. She waited until the kids were adults and out of the house, then told them she'd been having an emotional affair with a light wielder on the other side of the world and she was leaving to be with him.

Shit didn't go down well.

We'll be lucky if Kaia or Kor doesn't kill one of those light pricks this year.

It's funny. For all the rules we have here, death by magic isn't one of them. Should a classmate fall to a bad spell, or lose control of their gifts and kill another student it means nothing. As long as it doesn't appear deliberate, all you get is a shrug of the shoulders and a sigh knowing the outcome was inevitable.

The majority of us dark wielders are less than thrilled to have light wielders here. It changes our curriculum. Forces us to learn both sides, even though light and dark will never conjure gifts the same way.

Those who are excited about our new classmates are weak. They refuse to embrace what it means to summon from the dark, in my opinion. Spineless dicks, afraid to take all that the world has laid out for us. Power left for us to claim as ours, manipulating and molding it into our vision.

Like the other dark schools around the world, we've gained light wielders from all years—first through seventh. It's a pain in my motherfucking ass. I can't help but roll my eyes at their bright smiles and wide eyes as they take in the perceived eccentricities of this place. Not to mention they're in my way, especially *her*.

All the newly matured will be a problem. Our first few years after maturing into our powers are something like a supernova. Some of us can gain control quickly. We can hone what we are born with or mold what we borrow. Others become lost to the magic raging within. A force far too powerful for what these mortal shells can hold.

Wielders like me and my friends are naturals, always have been, and always will be. As extrinsics we must borrow. We use what we can siphon or channel in very different ways. The control we've earned over our unique and powerful gifts is what sets us apart from the average extrinsic.

"So, what's the plan?" Damian questions, his jaw working heavily as he chews his gum. A habit I wish he'd lost years ago. The bastard always has his mouth open with a wad of gum working between his teeth. That wet clicking making me twitch. Fortunately, this is his fifth and last year, so soon, I'll no longer need to deal with it.

"Same as always. We all have permission to be out there for the Red Moon Festival. We grab some extra relics from the archives and be done with it. Try to stick to the ghouls that cater to your gifts. Get in. Get out."

I shoot Kaia a look. She's always too eager to take too much. Her impulsivity threw us headfirst into several situations I would prefer never to repeat. I'm expected to keep my friends in line, which is exceedingly difficult when Kaia decides to go on a rampage.

It's not the first time we've done this, yet the stakes are a bit higher this year. The inner workings of our society are crumbling before our eyes and we have a role to play. The more magic we can harness the better. Hence the additional relics we'll swipe from the library and archives beforehand, only to be returned once we've used what power they hold.

I can only hope a Nigeros—a ghoul draped in skin of obsidian—will be present this time. They are rare. The darkest bastards around. Yet they cater to my particular gifts. I can't outright kill someone per se, but I can force their insides to eat away at them. Their flesh necrotizing with time as their bodies eat themselves. The most direct path to the type of magic I need is those black giants.

"Can you believe that girl is here?" Kaia's snort draws my attention to her. She walks around like tough shit, but somehow still snorts at all of her own jokes.

The answer is *no*. Of all the schools they could have sent her to, they put her here. *Here*, where her presence could ruin everything.

It was impossible to look away from her at the assembly today. That pouty mouth and those dark eyes. The coloring way too dark to be a light wielder, but anomalies happen, I guess.

I can tell she's going to be a problem. She pretended like she hated being called out in front of the whole school, but secretly I bet she reveled in it. Stood tall knowing that we would all have to *behave* or she could report us back to Daddy. That man is yet another powerful player standing directly in our way.

"She won't be a problem." I don't know why I say the words when I don't believe them. When I know she's going to have to be one of those magical deaths and somehow I am going to have to ensure it appears as an accident.

A sudden idea comes to me. With the Red Moon Festival coming soon it might be enough time for a ruse of friendship to put me in her good graces. An opportunity to make her believe she could be one of us. We sneak her out there, get her to have sex with a ghoul, the animal freaks, and she's dead. Simple. Clean. And no one could pin it on me. Even better.

She may have a banging body with those voluptuous curves—such a waste—but I'll do what needs to be done. Ridding the world of the Director of Education's daughter is as good a plan as any. There's no way she would survive a raging ghoul attack. My work would be done. My place amongst the greats solidified.

A light wielder can't siphon dark magic. They'll die if they do. The incompatibility of our essences is too much for a body to handle. Like an autoimmune disease, the body rebels on itself, resulting in insanity and warped organs. The result is always the same. Always a slow, painful death as the body fights what it doesn't understand, assuming the siphoning was successful. Yet, we only allow light wielders to know a portion of the truth.

"What are you thinking, Val?" Sean asks, his stare drilling into the side of my skull.

I shake my head. "Nothing. I'll catch you guys later."

Patting Pierce on the back, I jog up the steep flight of stairs, leading me back to the doorway that seals off the Vault. If I'm going to make this plan work, then I need to get a move on. Fortunately, it's still the middle of the day so as men we can wander over to the female side without a second glance.

Not that anyone is going to adhere to this separate shit. We're all in our twenties and early thirties. Adults in our own right. It's ridiculous that they expect a bunch of grown, but still young, people to follow a curfew mandate. We're going to fuck, commingle, and do whatever we want with the opposite sex. The administration can just accept it—or not.

My strides are long as I make my way down Bryony's hallway. I know every room for every student. Perks of having a solid relationship with Professor Rupert Blanc, one of our on-site administrators. He's a friend of the family and therefore helps me out when needed. He's been the one to slip me the necessary information for my crew to carry out our plans these past few years. One that puts dark wielders right where they should be. Where they *deserve* to be.

A grin pulls at the corner of my mouth as I feel my prized tattoo tingle across my back.

Darkness will reign.

Scrolling through the list on my phone I confirm Bryony's room number. My knuckles quickly rap against the dense wood. The ward that allows only her and her roommate entrance pushes back against my foreign signature. The biting sting draws out my grimace, only to curve into a charming grin the moment I hear a hand on the doorknob.

A petite woman greets me. Her hair so blonde it's almost white. She'd been sitting next to Bryony in the assembly, but otherwise, I know nothing about her.

"Can I help you?" her accent tells me she's straight from the southeastern portion of America. The lilt so delightful my grimace returns.

"Yeah. Is Bryony here?"

She yanks open the door, revealing her body. A body I helplessly imagine naked just for me. Thick thighs barely hidden in loose cotton shorts, draw my attention downward, before trailing back up. Her long hair sits tied up in a knot at the top of her head, her bun definitively bigger than my own.

"Who are you?"

I expected a nicer welcome. Just like we have to watch ourselves around her, I'm sure her father gave her a speech about doing the same for others. Warnings hammered into her, emphasizing the importance of making the right impression.

My mouth opens, ready to spew some bullshit that would make any woman kneel at my feet, only to be cut off.

"Right. Okay." Her eyes roll. "Don't care."

The door slams in my face. My body instinctually jumping back to avoid it smacking me in my pronounced straight nose.

What the actual fuck just happened?

4

Bryony

It's been a week of acclimating to life here. Classes don't officially start until tomorrow. The beginning of a new chapter. It is as exciting as it is daunting.

It all boils down to three consecutive years. Three years of living here. Three years of being away from my family. Three more years of watching my back, pretending to be someone I'm not. It's the only way I'll survive.

Three additional years of ensuring I don't slip up because the consequences aren't something I can come back from. Neither could my parents or my siblings. Our safety in this world is dependent on me protecting our secrets.

It's a burden and an exciting challenge all at once.

Camilla is everywhere all the time. I finally had to tell her I was going for a run—her least favorite activity—to get some alone time. She's a riot, but quiet isn't something she knows how to be and sometimes I just want the silence while my fears pummel me. I honestly don't run. I am a thick girl. This booty was made for lounging or looking cute in my favorite high-waisted jeans, not for running.

All of my siblings and my mother are tall and slender. I got the tall part, but slender drove right on past me. My mom says she has no idea where I got this body, and I don't have an answer for her. Skinny is something I have never been.

My only assumption is it comes from my biological father's side, but I guess I'll never know for sure.

A breeze kicks up as I near the lake behind the main residence. A copse of trees almost obscures the center from view. I'm grateful I brought one of my athleisure wear jackets with me as my chilled fingers sink into the pockets. The rounding of my shoulders giving me just a fraction more warmth in seconds.

I may not want to be here at this institution, but nothing beats the scenic view. Beauxgraton sits atop a forested mountain. The downward panorama seemingly endless and lush.

Pinks that shift to purples set off the sky as the horizon begins to darken. The haze of color still reflecting off the surface of the lake would instantly convince a nonbeliever that magic exists.

Drawing my hand from my pocket, I allow swirls of black essence to seep from my fingertips. Yet, I will the light into them, forcing my essence to become a pale gray as the tendrils dance forward brushing across the surface of the water. The coloring is a unique hue I've only ever seen from myself. I've never thought it might be because of what I am, but rather what an essence most resembles. Each one has a unique combination created solely for its wielder, like a fingerprint or DNA.

"Cute," a voice drifts from behind me.

Instantly, I yank my magic back. My fist returns to my pocket as I turn to find Valen Greer. He has been on my ass all week too. Somehow he always finds me during meals or while wandering the halls with Camilla. He's only come to the door one more time. Camilla shooed him away, since I was only in a towel. My savior.

I pretended not to know who he was the first time. His identity eluded me as we sat in the auditorium and then found me in the fifteen minutes it took for Camilla and me to find our room. That feeling of knowing a face but struggling to place it is enough to drive me crazy every time. The work his father does is in direct opposition to the matters handled by the Council and ghoul hunters. When your parent is a name of note in the wielding world, there's no way to stay completely unknown.

Seeing him standing here now, that same bun atop his head sends a shiver through me. I'd taken the time to look up more about him. Both he and his best friend Pierson Flagstaff are bad news. Actually, all of his friends seem to be. Although Pierson doesn't look it, everything I've seen says they're all the epitome of dark and dangerous. Ambitious men, and that one woman, I need to stay far away from.

Oddly enough when Valen and Pierson found us roaming the halls a few days ago I didn't mind talking to Pierson. His sense of humor is a dark wave of sarcasm similar to mine. Then Valen opened his mouth and I was done.

"Do you need something?" I snap my hip cocked to the side, punctuated with enough emphasis that the damn thing might dislocate.

"No," he replies with cool nonchalance as the corner of his mouth slightly quirks.

"Then disappear." I turn my back on him again, making my way around the edge of the lake. Night creeps closer with each passing moment. I can't imagine I would want to be caught out here in the dark. These woods are dense. The trunks thick and spaced closely enough in some areas I wouldn't be able to get through them easily.

My teeth grind as he falls into step beside me. His long legs keeping time with my quickened pace. The silence isn't awkward, per se, but I don't need him around right now. I came out here to release my essence, the build-up from keeping it contained beginning to wear on me, but I can't have anyone witnessing it. Yet, I don't force him to leave. Camilla talks nonstop so it's nice having some company that welcomes silence.

"Are you excited for classes to start?"

I stop to face him, my lips pursed in annoyance. "Really? You came out here to ask me about classes?"

"No."

I move again, determined to be on my own. "I came to ask you if you were going to sneak out to the Red Moon Festival next week?"

Spinning to face him again, I'm sure disbelief shadows my face.

"You do know who I am right?" The question is not one of arrogance but a lack of understanding of how he thinks someone like me is going to sneak into an occupied ghoul pit. It's the last place I need to be. Since I entered this school as a light wielder, he definitely knows what contact with a ghoul would do. What he doesn't know is that my dark wielding powers could react much differently.

I worry I may lose control. That the draw toward the ghouls could be too much for me to resist should I be near one compatible with my essence signature. From my research, I believe it would be a Viynuum. Their skin is the deep maroon of a rich red wine. Their eyes are just as white as any other.

"I can help you sneak out." He quirks a grin that's sure to make other girls swoon but churns my stomach, vomit threatening to shoot up my throat.

Why would he think I would go anywhere with him? His reputation wasn't hard to discover. He's the king of assholes, taunting and torturing others that don't bend to his will. It's no secret his father doesn't agree with the way light wielders preside over us, so why would he want to help me sneak out to a ghoul pit if he knows I'm one of them?

"No thanks."

Shoving past him I finally get that run in. My sneakers pound into the soft grass as I sprint back toward the residence. Back to my bedroom. As far away from Valen Greer as possible.

If I let him, that man will destroy everything.

5

BRYONY

I'VE ALWAYS BEEN A competitive student. An unmatched dedication to outperforming my classmates. Honors and specialty awards line the walls of my bedroom at my parent's home from my elementary through my college years. My parents insisted human college wasn't necessary. It serves us no purpose after we've graduated wielding school, that is, unless we choose to hold positions of prestige in the human world. Very few of us do.

Unlike most wielders, I matured early. Another unique feature that sets me apart from everyone else. Another secret to keep close to my chest. It didn't matter that I was fifteen, with more power than I could control, I couldn't attend a wielding school until now, ten years later. I needed to satisfy the overachiever in me, so against my parent's wishes, I attended the most prestigious university in our corner of the country. I'd begged for New York, but Maine was the only compromise they were willing to make.

It was a no-brainer choosing to study criminology. The minds of the dangerous are a fascination I've never been able to ignore. Maybe it's because we share a kinship of darkness living within us. It was a pointless major. One I will never be able to use outside of watching crime documentaries with my elder brother, Merrick. There's just something about solving a good mystery that floods me with adrenaline. It's impossible to ignore that I'm an unsolved enigma, too. It's no wonder I need to decode what puzzles I can, a substitute for failing at figuring myself out.

Despite my additional education and attending school here at Beauxgraton, the map for my future is already set in stone. It won't matter what I have already achieved through academics. I will still need a profession that allows me to stay hidden. My dad already has things lined up for me. I suspect as a way to stay under his watchful eye, while he claims it's to do meaningful work. If only he would tell me what "meaningful work" actually is.

The natural hue of my essence determined how I've had to live my life. Hidden and in fear. Existing as a lie to every individual I meet. It will forever determine life for me and there is nothing I can do about it. An accepted fact that drags down the corners of my mouth into a deep frown just as the doorway to my classroom comes into view.

The moment I cross the threshold into the room, it feels like home. A deep breath fills my lungs as a small smile begins to spread. This is my comfort zone. Learning is the one thing I can't get enough of, and it would be foolish of me not to enjoy it while I'm here.

Professor Johanna Pollin is already in the room when I enter. Light wielders fill only half the desks as fellow first years. Each of us on the innate, and possibly charter, wielding tracks. It's only when the bells chime that the other half enters. Their determination to stay on a single side of the classroom setting the precedent for what this year will be.

Light versus dark.

Always us versus them.

"Right, class," Professor Pollin suddenly booms. "Welcome to *Wielding Basics*. You will likely hate this class if you already have control over your essence." She purses her lips hard, her hand flips, brandishing her palm. "Yet there's always room for improvement." Her wrinkled face scrunches as her lips thin further, tar gerbil-like eyes meeting each of our own as if daring us to riot against the mundane.

I sit straighter. I'll need this class to help with control, just not for the reasons others will. I've had a lot more time than my classmates to master the basics. Countless hours with my family and other influential wielders who know I matured early, all working to shape me into their creation. Dad says it's to protect me, but I know that's not entirely true.

I am loyal to my family. I am special. I am meant to be a specimen they can learn from behind closed doors. Dad says it's vital for them to understand me since no one knows of others like me who have matured. It's something I accepted long ago because playing by their rules keeps me alive.

Professor Pollin rattles off the rules of the classroom and her expectations for each of us in rapid succession. My pen scratching across the paper as I scramble to write fast enough. I am by no means perfect, but I need to be. I can't afford a slip-up. Not here. Not in front of anyone.

Professor Pollin pulls out a chest from under her desk. The textured carvings mold the rectangle into an abstract shape, transforming the ordinary into a stunning piece of art. Cracking open the lid with a loud creak, a soft glow colors her sallow cheeks.

Emari Orbs glow brightly as she turns the open trunk to face us. Each is a seamless mixture of greens and blues with flashes of soft yellows. The colors moving past each other like storm-driven clouds in the sky, entrancing us.

"Right, so we will start with something rudimentary. You will use your inherent gifts to manipulate foreign magic your body doesn't recognize. Who would like to start?" She clasps her hands in front of her thighs, peering out at the faces that fill the room. Not a single hand raises to volunteer as her eyes narrow.

It's interesting to me that she didn't use the term "innate". Even charters, a subset of innate wielders, fall under the same category. Where an innate like me can wield on a whim, a charter usually cannot tap into their essence at will and needs to siphon or channel from external sources. Using a strong source, charters can sometimes temporarily restore their internal essence levels. In those cases, for brief periods, they can wield the same as any other innate wielder would.

A tall man dressed in wrinkle-free slacks and a button-down with the neck open stands from his seat sauntering to the front of the room. A confidence in his stride that no newly matured wielder moves with. He grabs a globe without hesitation, lifting it in front of his face to observe the contents at eye level. The eerie swirls deepen to a violent haze, shifting the color of his sandy, blondish-brown hair to a shade of amethyst.

Many of the students stare, transfixed by the power contained in front of them. Others appear bored, doing their best to pretend they are above something so simple. None of us are. Not even the most experienced. Foreign magic can either be an exceptional compliment or your destruction.

"Great work. Now allow it to touch you," Professor Pollin instructs.

The man places his palm dead-center at the top of the glass sphere. The solid orb, then metal base, quickly fade away, leaving the rolling mass in his palm. A perfectly shaped sphere of unknown power.

At first, it seems to contract away from him, then loosens, the tendrils beginning to creep through his fingers and then up his forearm. In no time they've expanded covering the majority of his body before hiding him from view.

Several gasps fill the room. Others beg Professor Pollin to do something with their bulging eyes.

Amateurs.

I only stare. A gut instinct reassuring me the man has nothing to fear. That this is all a part of a demonstration. Pollin stays perfectly still as my classmate allows a violent tornado of eggplant clouds to surround him.

"Now," she commands.

In an instant, his hand stretches through the vortex, palm face up. It only takes seconds. Just a few short moments before it all fades, revealing him to us just as he was. Not a single hair is out of place. The miniature storm returned to a lightly churning pool of violet in his palm. Every bit of that magic centers in his outstretched hand as the original orb reforms around it. The showman nailing his finale without a bit of effort.

"Well done, Graham." Professor Pollin carefully takes the orb from his hands before he returns to his seat. He never says a word. Never looks at anyone in the room. His chin held high as he slips into his chair. This guy must be one of those pretentious pricks who have to be great at everything.

Well, so do I.

He will be the greatest challenge I've ever had.

The urge to aggressively rub my palms together, grinning wickedly like a cartoon villain, has me shifting the edges of my hands beneath my thighs. Their weight enough to keep them tucked in place. No need to act out my weird fantasies on day one.

Professor Pollin calls for the next volunteer, my arm involuntarily shooting into the air. She gestures me forward, my shoulders square until she cradles a different orb into my waiting palms. The glowing ball is warm in my hands. The magic within calling to me. A whimsical voice singing my name for only me to hear.

Dad's words suddenly work their way to the forefront of my thoughts. That song's crescendo aiming to block out his warnings.

"Don't show off," he'd warned me. *"Don't give away too much of yourself. Make intentional mistakes. Be sure that you don't catch on too quickly, but don't perform sluggishly. No one must know that you mastered your basic powers long ago."*

Seven years ago to be exact. Yet it's been ten long years of holding this secret. Lonely years of having to separate myself from my peers. A decade of pretending I was nothing more than an immature light wielder.

"Proceed," Professor Pollin flicks her wrist. I slowly turn to face the class. A group of dark-wielding guys in the back snickering as they watch me. The glint in their eyes sparking with life as they silently hope for my failure.

Fuck. Them.

With a deep breath, I will myself to calm down. To do just as Graham had done before me. But the whispers distract me. The part of me I have to hide slithering to the surface. In an instant, the orb shatters. Glass shards shooting in the direction of those who so rudely made their comments. I do what I can to reel those tiny pieces of glass back in, but only succeed in stopping them from impaling their fear-stricken faces.

Professor Pollin gasps behind me, shuffling around her desk, likely thinking I'm in danger of losing control of the magic held between my palms entirely.

I'm not.

But I am pissed.

Just as the coloring changed for Graham it does for me too. The gorgeous hue of purple he'd achieved more along the lines of a midnight blue under my control. Stars twinkle within the swirling tendrils leaking from my fingertips, quickly dispersing to blanket the room in my shadows.

"That's enough Miss Avalon."

A grin marks my face. One that's tied to the part of me no one can know about. With an exuberant exhale, I let the tendrils free. The dark curves fill every crevice of the room. The students begin to scream. Professor Pollin's black essence fighting to pull back what she must think is only the foreign power. But she can't. I am stronger than her. My wielding is more raw, more unique. It will only bend to my will.

For several minutes I let the intensity grow. Let those who thought it funny to crack jokes at my expense witness what they are up against.

I count to seven. One second for every year that I've had to live like this. My clap is sudden and thunderous, instantly brightening the room. Every particle of magic riots, trapped between my slightly quivering palms. There will be no reforming my orb, so I turn to Professor Pollin. That same grin stretches my lips as I flash all of my teeth.

"I'll need something to put this in."

6

Graham

The first day of classes became an exhausting combination of me killing myself to prove I was the best, only to find myself sulking when Bryony Avalon continued to show me up. I've never been a competitive person. Never felt the need to prove my academic prowess or intelligence to anyone because everyone knew they couldn't touch my skill.

Until Bryony.

She's been in every class of mine except *Essence Manipulation: Tier One*. A class our professor didn't even show up for. An assistant simply dropped in to tell us we'd start next week. It's the only identifying mark that we're on different schooling tracks. With what she did in Pollin's class today, there's no doubt she is an insanely powerful innate wielder. Her power and control are impressive for someone our age. Dare I say, unheard of.

I was technically born innate, but with such a weak affinity for using my essence, I do better with borrowing magic. Somewhere along the way, we became known as charters. Those born innate but without the ability to use our internal essences at will. Initially, the only known charters were light wielders, until a large population of dark wielders in South America popped up. Now, it's well known any wielder, anywhere, can be any combination. Doesn't matter if you're light or dark, you can be innate, a charter, or extrinsic.

It's been a long day and all I want to do is consume an endless amount of food and then collapse into bed.

I've just sauntered through the floor-to-ceiling double doors of the dining hall. Obsidian metal latticework covers both sides of the massive wood panels. Our preparatory literature mentioned that the heavy doors remain open during designated meal hours. A small mercy. I couldn't imagine having to shove one of those open.

It only takes me a moment to spot my roommate, Tiernan McDeigh. He's already deep in conversation with several other guys from our hall when I slump down onto the long bench. There's not a single individual chair in the monstrous room, only these long planks of solid wood that threaten to trip you every time you get up or down. Your ass is set to ache by the time you get up again. So, many of us limit how long we lounge here.

"Hey man, what took you so long?" Tiernan nods my way.

"Last class let out late," I shrug. "Professor Caulder is way too enthusiastic about spellcasting, but they say he's one of the best."

He might be. For now. There's no doubt I want to surpass him in talent. Truth be told, I want to surpass everyone at everything. But for today I'm just hungry, tired, and annoyed.

My thoughts drift to all the times Bryony outshined me today. I guess I better get used to it. Something tells me that what I saw from her today wasn't the full extent of her capabilities. But then again, there's a lot that can be done when you can use what you were born with at all times.

Innate light wielders and extrinsic dark wielders, who perform best by siphoning ghoul magic, are the most powerful wielders in this world. Innate lights can take the power they were born with and manipulate, or even use foreign magic, to enhance their own essence. Whereas dark extrinsics who respond better to siphoning, simply take. From what we're taught, only certain ghouls can give them such potent levels of borrowed magic. For me, though, it's a terrifying thing to think about being intimate with a ghoul regardless of the breed.

The mercurial beasts have always fascinated me. My desire to see one up close sometimes consumes my thoughts. As a child, I'd asked my parents about ghouls. My young mind wondered if I could use them the same way. Even as a child, I wanted to be important, and power was the way to ensure that I achieved that status. As a charter, I wanted only the strongest magic as my essence's source of power.

I still remember the day I asked. Arriving with a notepad full of questions, with spaces left for me to jot down the answers, I slid into my seat at the breakfast table. Even though

I was only ten, I'd made sure to look my best, dressed in slacks and a suit jacket. I knew it would impress my father and it did. His compliments on my initiative to always present myself perfectly left me beaming with pride. Yet, my parents didn't answer my initial question about my ability to use a ghoul to siphon from. They didn't have to. Their eyes told me everything I needed to know.

My father's cerulean blue stare beside the sea green of my mother's conveyed the danger of what I was asking. Their mouths tense with fear, likely wondering if I was daring enough to give it a try. Necks taut with tension until I laughed it off, insisting it was nothing more than self-led historical research on magical siphoning I was conducting. Playing it off as the reason for my question.

I would later learn it wasn't fear I saw but their version of disgust for the acts that go along with siphoning from ghouls. "*It's despicable how those darks degrade themselves by fornicating with animals.*", I'd once heard my mother snarl at my dad. The heated conversation that followed enough for me to never bring up my dark curiosities again.

"Be right back," I mumble to no one in particular.

I'm quick to trek over to the food line eager to fill a tray with whatever tonight's hot and steamy choices are. The aroma of a variety of dishes hitting me hard, my stomach loudly growling in response. I'm too far back to see the options, but that doesn't stop me from salivating.

My nostrils flare in recognition of the familiar scents. Some sort of pasta. Fried chicken, maybe. Sauteed vegetables of some sort.

Knowing it will be a while before I reach the front, I allow myself the distraction of my phone. My pulse kicks up as I check the latest news feeds broadcasting the three additional light school closures in Asia. None of us understands what is happening. Director Avalon's declarations are vague at best. I honestly believe he doesn't know why our schools are the ones abruptly closing, either.

It makes no sense to force us to learn alongside the dark wielders as if we have a similar focus. As if we stand for the same things. We don't. Our ancestors drew the line between light and dark long ago.

"You did so good in class today," an accented voice rings from behind me. I'd heard it all through three of my classes today. A twang reminiscent of strumming on guitar strings wrong. Camilla Van Buren. I believe she's roommates with my newly minted nemesis, Bryony.

"I did not, but I appreciate the compliment," Bryony's coarse response carries to me. There's a husky, rasping quality to it. It's almost as if her throat is dry or as if she just woke up. Odd for a woman to sound the way she does. A deeper part of me hopes she continues to talk so I can hear its hoarseness some more. It's as if something inside me feels drawn to her.

I glance over my shoulder. The two of them stand separated from me by another woman who looks utterly terrified to be here. It's an expression many of the light wielders carry. Especially those that transferred in from recently closed light institutions as opposed to this being their first year. They desperately cling to their expectations of what a wielding school should be. Those same expectations are likely nothing more than disappointments now that they're here. Our two schools—the light and the dark—are nothing alike.

"Where did you learn to wield like that?" The question slips out of me. I didn't mean to break into their conversation, but I'm curious how Bryony got so good, so fast.

I'd taken it upon myself to look her up on social media. She's the same age as me. Her birthday was only two months ago, just before the cut-off to allow admittance as a new student this year. In her profile picture, she seems so different. There's a carefree nature to her that has not been on display here.

Here she carries herself with her chin held high, almost with arrogance. She knows she's badass, and wants to make sure we all know it too. If my daddy was Roman Avalon, I'd likely walk around the same way. Taking a longer look now, I study her face. This version has a dark edge to her. One so sharp you're sure to get sliced open if you frolic too close.

"Dad." Her answer is curt. As if answering with that one word was the biggest inconvenience to her. A twitch of a smile there and then it's gone.

"Of course." I turn back around shuffling several steps forward in the line. That same husky timbre ringing out behind me, stiffening my spine and knotting my intestines.

"How about you, Graham? It's Graham right?" she adds as I let the terrified woman go ahead of me.

"Spent a lot of time with family these past six months." It's the truth, but maybe not quite all of it. But it's enough to share with a stranger, my rival no less.

"Aw, look at you two, just lovin' your family support so much." Those little hands of the woman next to her clasping in front of her body as she bounces on her heels. The both of us tossing a wry look her way.

"Really, Camilla?" she chuckles with a snort.

Camilla's grin only spreads as she throws Bryony a cartoonish wink. This girl is so damn cheery and optimistic all the time. I'm generally an optimist too but she takes it to a whole other level.

"Um, do you want to come eat with my friends and me?" I point a thumb behind me. They shrug. Bryony sticking her hand out in greeting as we move a few inches forward.

"Bri," she introduces herself with a warm smile.

"Graham Mayer."

"And y'all already know I'm Camilla. Hi. Hello there."

I give an awkward wave, lips sucking into my mouth. Neither woman says anything else to me as we make our way through the line. All three of our trays piled with more than any of us should be able to eat.

Everyone gives introductions as Camilla and Bri take seats across from me. The guys immediately launch into a conversation, tossing out questions and asking who did what in class. Bri tossing out her own nonchalant comments and inquiries when topics concerning the school closures come around. I would think she would know more than any of us.

Camilla is a riot. Her high-pitched laughter and weird phrasing leave us with aching stomach muscles and sore cheeks. I think I'm going to like her.

"So Bri," Collin Pecket, a dark-haired guy with his hair shorn so short you can see his scalp, blurts, his jaw working hard to chew on the hulking chunk of pizza he just bit off. "Do you have a date for the Red Moon Ball?"

She lets out a laugh as if to say *nope,* and *not with you,* but answers with a reversed question. "Do you?"

The guys all *ooh* as if she just knocked him down several pegs. I am totally missing what is happening in this interaction here as my focus darts between their faces. Camilla's eyes are wide as she takes it all in. Her hands cupped in front of her as if waiting for the answer to her best friend being proposed to. Eagerness brightening her small features as we all sit in silence.

As if realizing she missed something, Camilla blinks several times. "Wait, what's this ball thing?" She chews loudly, as she takes in each of our faces, waiting for yet another answer.

"How do you not know what the Red Moon Ball is?" Collin snickers.

"We're light wielders," I grunt. "It's not our tradition." He only nods as if he's willing to accept the explanation, but doesn't seem pleased with my answer.

"It's a post-Red Moon Festival party, pretty much. We get dressed in our finest and celebrate the Red Moon and siphoning from ghouls." His shrug is nonchalant as he stuffs a handful of fries in his mouth before pointing a finger at Bri. "And to answer your question, I was going to ask you."

Our table goes completely silent. Again.

"Aww, that's sweet." She takes a drink of her water, pointedly catching my eye with a wink. What is it with these two, and winking at people? "But Graham already did."

Water shoots from my mouth, covering the contents still on my tray. *I—What?* Eyes wide to match Camilla's, I stare at the woman in front of me. I wasn't even going to go to this ball. It's something the dark wielders celebrate, Collin being one of them, not me.

"Damn you move fast man," Collin claps me on the back.

"Uh, yeah. I guess I do," my words mumbled in confusion.

Bri throws me yet another wink before she grabs her half-empty tray and stands. "Catch ya later, boys," she calls before adding, "Graham, come by later."

Our table hoots and hollers as she retreats with her roommate. Their rambunctious laughter drifting back to us until she disappears through those same immaculate double doors.

I'm not sure what just happened or even if it's a good or a bad thing.

I guess I'll just have to wait and see.

7

Bryony

I HADN'T PLANNED ON putting Graham on the spot. But he was there, so I used him. He could have denied it, but he didn't. That's interesting.

More importantly, I noticed how he attempted to probe about my abilities. It didn't escape my notice that his eyes stayed firmly focused on me in every class as we took turns showing our professors various uses of our magic and control. I can't have people asking questions, so what better way to learn what he knows or what he thinks he knows than cozying up to him?

It doesn't hurt that he's gorgeous. Those light mint greenish blue eyes with the outer ring of gold are unique, despite the blended colors being common ones for light wielders. Most tend to have eyes on the paler side. Even those with brown tones exist as hues of soft amber and honey.

A tentative knock sounds at the door. Hopping off the bed, I'm quick to answer. I've dressed the part for the walk I have planned. Fitted skinny jeans and flat-heeled boots, with a cute lightweight jacket that accentuates my waist. Graham seems to appreciate appearances, judging by the way he dresses himself, so I made sure to do the same.

"Uh, hi," he mutters lowly.

Cute. The poor guy is nervous. If he stays out of my business, then he won't need to be. But why would he know that?

This will be a piece of cake. Merrick taught me how to talk to men in power through my teenage years. A precarious method of prying the information I want out of them, so I always have the upper hand. Graham exhibits every attribute you find in the ones that are easy to bend. And then break. Their secrets slithering past their lips with little more than a flutter of my lashes.

"Hey, I thought we could go for a walk. Get to know each other." I bat my lashes now as I look up at him. His Adam's apple bobs as he stares down at me. He hadn't seemed so tall earlier. But my focus was on those bright eyes and the sloped bridge of his nose.

He nods, stepping aside so I can exit. My call back to Camilla goes ignored as she works through a hundred brush strokes of her near-white hair. Some country tune hummed to herself.

Neither of us speaks as we make our way through the endless hallways. My gaze eagerly wandering to the many paintings and tapestries pregnant with the history of dark wielders. For the first time, I can openly believe it is my history too. Graham follows in silence as I lead us toward the rear double doors of the residence, the exit route I have been using for the few ventures I've taken out to the lake.

The chill is worse than I thought it would be. The school grounds nearly empty as we make our way down the gray stone path toward the lake directly in front of us. The abnormally shaped body of water backs up to a stone wall only a couple hundred feet behind the residence. A man-made barrier meant to add to the beauty of the home and nature beyond. That same edge of the lake sits nearly straight before curving around a bend shadowed by towering, lush green trees.

"Where are you from?" I ask. A question I don't actually care about, but we need to start somewhere.

"Tycoh." That single city's name is all the information he surrenders. No further explanation or talk about his home life comes to the surface as we continue along in silence for several moments.

"Ahh, opposite side of the country."

He nods. "I know." Of course he does. Everyone knows where Director Avalon and his family live.

Seela is one of the richest cities in the country. Its location strategically tucked into the upper right corner of the states just along the shoreline. An over-the-top suburbia with ten-thousand square foot homes and vibrant green gardens bordering properties decorated with flowers clustered into complementary color schemes. Wrought-iron gates with complicated passcodes sit at the end of every half-mile-long driveway. No doubt a family like mine would live there.

"Right. Anyhow, what do you think of classes so far?"

This is by far the most awkward conversation I've ever had. He has me pulling at teeth to get answers. This was supposed to be easy, but I'm having to work too hard to get even a fraction of something worthwhile out of him.

Maybe this plan wasn't such a great idea.

"I enjoyed them," he sighs. "Believe it or not I've always loved school."

My insides warm. Another overachiever like me. Someone who values learning and the importance of knowledge. A stupid thought comes to mind: maybe instead of trying to show him up, I can just be his friend. The friends I did have back home could never relate to my nerdiness.

The lake sparkles in the moonlight. Little flecks of starlight dancing across the surface. A reminder of the essence that lives inside me. A reminder that I must hide my true power.

My fate for the remainder of my life.

Sitting at the edge of the water, we finally fall into conversation. Stories about nothing and everything. Where we've struggled with wielding. The areas where we can help each other. A possible alliance beginning to blossom, and a connection I hadn't planned on. I didn't expect Graham to be funny or charming. I hadn't expected him to be a warm presence, a person I could converse with for hours.

I came to this school believing what my dad told me. That my peers would leave me standing alone. There wouldn't be help waiting for me no matter where I turned. I convinced myself it was because somehow my classmates would be able to sense that I'm different. But now I realize it's because my last name is more likely to ostracize me than earn me genuine friends. I've spent much of my life in that kind of isolation. In front of others, I can only be a light wielder. I can only be an Avalon. Nothing more. Nothing less.

Footsteps sound from the trees behind us. The both of us gaze over our shoulders to see a tall thin-framed man waltz out of the tree line. The outline of the bun atop his head reveals the last person I want to see.

I'm quick to hop to my feet, Graham doing the same, as we dust grass and dirt from the backs of our thighs.

"Ahh, getting in some alone time, I see."

"Fuck off, Valen."

"Now that's not nice, Bryony," he wickedly admonishes. His steps slowly bring him closer. Close enough that his sharp features come into focus. His eyes are darker than they were when I last saw him several days ago. Black as the night or the pits of Hell. That same Stygian hue of his hair shadows his face and matches the thin mustache and short beard.

"Can I help you with something?" His grimace deepens at my tone.

I stand taller before performing an exaggerated curtsy for effect. As I blow him a sarcastic kiss, a dark eyebrow hitches higher.

"Better?" I ask with icy sarcasm.

"Not at all," he sneers. "I came to have a word."

"Well, you've had several."

"Don't be a smart ass."

"I was born this way. If you don't mind, we were having a conversation."

Valen smirks at me, his eyes trailing Graham up and down. "Is that all you were doing?"

My insides boil. No matter how much I have tried avoiding Valen and his friends, the bastard just keeps popping up. I don't trust him. That dark gleam in his eyes would send anyone with sense running in the opposite direction. Yet, that tiny curious seed within me wants to see how close I can get before I'm burned. The weed already blooming, internally stamped on repeatedly, with my proverbial boot.

What the hell is it going to take for him to leave me the fuck alone?

A bad idea sparks within me and I can only hope that Graham will just go along with it. Yanking him to me, I press my mouth to his. His body goes rigid against me. Eyes likely wide open as I press mine shut.

Why I thought this was the only way to get Valen to go away is beyond me. This is *not* something Merrick taught me.

Then his lips move. A slow wave that mine follow. His hand gripping my waist, pulling me that much closer, the other cupping the side of my face.

Is he ... enjoying this?

Am I?

I keep my hands fisted in his shirt as Valen fake snores behind us. Yet it doesn't distract me from the fire burning between Graham and me. It's been a long time since I've kissed anyone. My last boyfriend broke my heart. Now I keep it from everyone so it never gets shattered again.

When he finally breaks away his gaze slowly lifts to mine, clearing his throat violently. I nearly pat his back, hoping he's not choking on his own saliva.

I'm slow to face Valen once more, my arms crossed at my chest.

"So—if you two are done—Bryony, we need to talk."

With a roll of my eyes, I make my way halfway around the lake with Valen. Clearly, hearing him out will be the only way to get rid of him. My brow furrows with frustration, knowing my little show didn't do the trick. "So talk."

"The Red Moon Festival is next week."

"And?"

"And I think you would rather be there than cooped up in your room."

I hate to admit that he's right. Why is he right?

I'm fascinated with the activities that accompany the Red Moon festivities. Particularly the process of magic siphoning from ghoul to wielder. I always wondered if someone like me could use them the same. If so, what would be the impact of that? Would I survive it? Would it affect me less or more?

I'd read books, studied scholars, and even dared to ask my parents. Not once have I ever gotten a straightforward answer. Mostly because someone like me isn't supposed to exist. Wielding law states harboring a Grisym is illegal. No exceptions. There are those who would see a Grisym as a commodity, but they'd never openly say so. To them, I'd be a prize to test the limits of what someone like me might be able to do.

As far as I can tell, there's not much special about me other than occasionally losing control and the coloring of my essence. So far I've shown no real affinity toward a specific gift other than teleportation. Supposedly, it should reveal itself in time. Meaning with bloodlines like mine I should have known by the time I matured.

"Ah, she's interested." Valen's grin pulls higher. The shining silver moonlight reflects off his dark hair. Hues of blue intermingle with the black more vividly against his pale skin. An eerie but perfect combination.

"And if I am?"

He steps closer, our chests almost brushing. His hand rises to tuck a stray strand of hair behind my ear, face dropping close. *Shit, please don't let this man kiss me, too.* Well, not "too" seeing as how I all but forced Graham into making out with me.

Not the point, Bri.

"Then I'll gladly sneak you out with me and my friends."

"I'll think about it."

"No," he says coolly. "You won't." He eyes me up and down before stepping back, the curls of his bun bobbing with his movement. "I'll be by your room Friday night at eleven. Don't have that roommate of yours around when I show up."

Then he's gone, disappearing into the woods at the far end of the lake.

I stare after him, anticipation filling me.

Am I really going to do this?

Hell yes, I am.

This is likely the dumbest thing I've ever considered, but maybe it's time I embraced my dark side. Even if it's just for a night.

Sorry, Dad.

8

VALEN

IT WAS EASIER THAN I thought it would be to catch her attention. I knew I would find her out by the lake. There have been enough nights I've watched her sit by the edge alone, tendrils of her essence dancing at her fingertips as I watched from the trees. From so far away, clouded by the darkness, I was sure her essence looked almost as black as mine. But we all know what tricks the dark is capable of playing on our minds.

I've never interrupted her. Only watched with curiosity. Mesmerized by those floating black tendrils. Fascinated by her otherness. Even her eyes are dark for a light wielder. It's rare, but not unheard of. Bryony is an enigma to me. A puzzle I am determined to solve and then eradicate.

I question if she is more than she says she is. I'd heard about her display in Pollin's class. Others recounting how she'd had enough control to turn that essence into a swirling midnight mass around the room, the rotation so violent tornadoes appear calm. But only after she lost it shattering her Emari Orb.

I tell myself it's just that she's powerful. The bloodlines of her mother and father are both strong. Her mother, Geneva Avalon, is one of the most proficient transport wielders in the country. Her expertise would be useful at any institution or organization around the world but instead, she works for the Office of Artifacts, procuring objects meant for storing foreign power. A position of prestige for our kind most deem much more important than teaching newly matured wielders. As if an ancient being herself she has a way of manipulating how each unique item can control their storage of magic. That ability is a wielding gift on its own, so for her to have two strongly distinct gifts is odd, but it seems that family has a lot hidden beneath the surface.

I should care about all their secrets. That family could be a problem for what me and my crew need to do. A meticulously laid out plan led by the one man our world would rather see burn.

Bryony was never supposed to come here. Not now. Not when we're so close to creating a world that caters to a different agenda. She could ruin everything. Hence my plan to get her to fuck a ghoul. Sure, her death will create an uproar, but that will only aid us that much more. Distract the masses from the actual goal. Hide the true mastermind behind it all in plain sight. The man I answer to.

My alarm blares in my ears, signaling me to climb out of bed. I have a free period on Tuesdays, so I returned to my room to think. A chance to ponder the things I've noticed about Bryony other than her deliciously curvy body and that pouty mouth. Clearly, I need to get a good fuck in on Friday night. Kill two birds with one stone. I get a wet, well-used night of pussy and siphon enough power to make me near invincible.

That's the interesting thing about ghouls. They hold no gender, but rather the ability to accommodate their wielder's opposite sex. The transaction between wielders and ghouls is based on nothing more than trading power.

I can only hope a Nigeros decides to grace us with their presence this time. There aren't many of them left these days, so it's always hit or miss on whether they show at any particular pit. If I have to siphon from other ghoul breeds, I'll need at least three to reach that same level of power.

There are limits to what we can take. Yet, I've never adhered to the rules, pushing every boundary that I can. Life's more fun that way.

It's a quick walk to my next class taught by Professor Knox. He is one of my least favorite in the school. Yet he's one that every student has each year of their respective programs. His specialty of wielding manipulation of foreign magic is essential to every wielder. A universal requirement across every wielding institution in the world. A mandate from Director Avalon himself during his second year sitting atop his prestigious pedestal.

Due to the nature of the material, a wielder may be at a different tier than their year in school. For that reason, it's not unheard of for Knox's classes to have a mixture of years.

It's the only class based on the ability of the student and lacks a sequentially linear course of study.

If you can't manipulate foreign power, either for your defense or to gain the upper hand, you're fucked. The Council considers you useless. Our kind can be very unforgiving to those deemed too powerful, or those considered unusable.

I'd started at an introductory level and progressed as I should have each year. Just a cover-up for the strength of my real capabilities. It's better not to stand out in that way. Especially when you hold one of the darkest gifts a wielder can be born with.

Death by my hand is not one anyone would ever beg for. It's a specialty you keep tucked in close; hidden if possible. Ready for use when the time comes. Then they never suspect until it's too late. Their last breath stolen with a twitch of my brow.

Just the same, I can't stand Professor Wynston Knox, Headmistress Milgren's golden boy. He's young for a professor but gifted in his abilities. Yet, he rides us harder than the more tenured professors do. Especially those like me that he feels aren't showing their true potential. That's what I hate most; he can see right through me.

I stroll into class, sitting in the same seat I've sat in for the past three years. Pierce plops down next to me, phone in hand as he laughs at whatever video he's watching. If I hadn't grown up beside him, I would swear he was a light wielder. A sunny disposition always shining out of his ass. Not that all of us dark-wielders are broody assholes like me, but his temperament fits better with them.

Leaning toward him, I'm trying to catch a glimpse of what dumb shit he's got pulled up now. My body just getting close enough to see the screen when *she* walks in.

We just started wearing our uniforms this week and this is my first time seeing her dressed like one of us. Typically, uniforms are required from day one. A way to put us on a level playing field. It doesn't do shit in the face of reality, though.

Thanks to the light wielders joining us, they made updates. Lightening the gray of the jacket. Switching out the opaque black button-downs for crisp white ones. Luckily, we got to keep black bottoms. Each alteration was meant to blend us into a new student body.

I'll say overall it worked. All the high tension many of us expected having light students here is almost non-existent. Groups of commingled friends are already forming. I have no personal issues with light wielders as long as they stay out of my way. My perpetual scowl has been enough to make that happen. This united front thing is bullshit. But it's also part of the plan, so who am I to go against it?

She opted for the pants that fit her perfectly, the fabric molded to her figure as she edges her way to a desk in the second row. Dead center. Her starched white shirt is unbuttoned one too far, giving me a glimpse of cleavage. Exposed golden-brown skin I wouldn't mind running my tongue over.

Fuck, she's hot. It'll be a shame killing her.

Then it hits me. She's a first-year walking into a third-tier course. *What the actual fuck?* She shouldn't be here. Jumping up a level is extremely common, but not two. Two is almost unheard of.

She slips into her seat, back ramrod straight, and I know without a doubt her last name got her into this class. *Fucking Avalons*. She's here to show off. To rub it in all our faces that her father's position can open any door. Too bad she'll be dead by the end of the weekend.

Knox enters moments later. Tossing his backpack under his desk he keeps his back to us, a deep inhale before he exhales as if steeling himself for some big reveal.

He slowly turns, scanning his new prey, and pauses when he spots her. Her body stiffens in her seat as swirls of dark essence leak from her fingers. The shade I convinced myself I was imagining all those times watching her by the lake is clear as day. She shakes her hands as if trying to put out a match. Several moments passing before she breathes deeply, the tendrils reluctantly seeping back into her skin.

Odd. What are you hiding Bryony Avalon?

From what I've heard and seen she is generally completely in control. It does not make sense that a single look could unnerve her like that.

"Okay class, two volunteers."

Two classmates I've seen over the years step forward; third and fourth years eagerly making their way to the front. A snort escapes me. *Damn overachievers.*

"You'll each wield. Your job is to capture the other's essence so they cannot retrieve it," Knox deadpans.

This is the first lesson Knox always does. His way of determining where each of us stands. A gauge for the work that needs to be done. Who will be a waste of his time? Who will be his next shining star?

If you show no promise, he will not put a nuanced effort into you. To me, it's smart. He could hold several powerful positions in this world, but he's here. Why is he wasting his time as a professor? Like Bryony's mother, he should put his gifts to better use.

It never made sense to me. Too many things don't make sense to me.

"Pierson. Bryony. You're up," Knox calls.

She shrugs out of her uniform jacket, quickly moving down the steps to the front of the room. I admire her profile as she angles her body sideways so she can squeeze through the desks.

Pierce takes his time making his way to her. His hands shaking uncontrollably as they square their shoulders, his eyes darting everywhere but her face. This is not his forte. He can spellcast extremely well but manipulating other wielder's essences has always given him trouble. Where I did not need this class and soared through each year, he struggled to progress. No amount of help I've given him has done anything to improve his skill set beyond the minimum.

Those tendrils sneak from her fingers once more. Small at first, until they lighten before my eyes. The near-black shifting to a softer gray. *Interesting.* I've never seen anyone do that. Light wielders tend to have a white or faint gray essence. On multiple occasions, I've now seen hers release a shade of black as dark as mine, never this shade of pale iron I'm seeing now.

Pierce immediately shoots his essence her way, roping her body with his strands of magic. Her face doesn't change as the short spirals of her essence loop around her fingers. Her eyes appear dead as she just stands there. She should be fighting back but does nothing to even attempt to wrangle free of his hold.

The minutes tick by. Knox remaining seated on his walnut-washed desk, thick arms crossed over his chest as he waits.

In a flash, she unleashes her essence. Swirling gray tearing through Pierce's and engulfing it. His signature black disappears, face scrunching tight as he fights to regain control. None of his essence filters back to the surface until she chances a small glance at Knox. Her nose twitching several times as a small tendril of dark essence shoots up her nostril, her focus broken.

The hue changes again, back to a black so dark it's unfathomable. Twinkling specks of glitter sparkle throughout, lighting up her essence as it engulfs her and Pierce. His screech vibrates through the room as the rotating cyclone barriers them off from the rest of us. Something I will make fun of him for later.

"Enough, Ms. Avalon. Mr. Flaggstaff," Knox warns.

But the tendrils only grow thicker. The swirls moving faster and faster with each passing second.

"Enough!" Knox bellows.

"I can't—" Panic muffles her voice. She's lost control. She isn't doing this on purpose.

In a second, both sets of essences dissipate. Her body lurches forward into Pierce's arms as Knox snatches the power within his fist. His muscles strain to hold on tight, as veins pop along his exposed forearm. He will hold it until it calms, and he can release it back to the both of them. If need be, he will discharge their magic into a containment object. A task he has had to perform countless times in my years as a student in his class.

"Class is over," he barks. "Everyone out. Ms. Avalon, you stay."

The class empties quicker than I thought it would. The twins snickering as they bolt from the room. We all know Knox has a temper. No one is willing to test it their first week with him. The administration canceled our first class, last week, due to him not being back on campus yet, so he's likely already pissed we're behind.

Pierce slowly releases her, his head ducking to check her face. Her gaze casts downward, darting back and forth in question. She hadn't expected this and I want to know why.

Gently, Pierce's essence leaks through Knox's slightly loosened fist, seeping straight into Pierce's waiting palm.

"Let's go," I snap as I grab his arm, tugging him behind me.

I'm quick to come up with an excuse to go back into the classroom as we make our way down the hall. I need to know what the fuck I just saw. What better way to hold leverage over the Avalons than learning Bryony's secrets?

"Shit, I forgot something," irritation thick in my tone as I groan loudly. A reaction I know Pierce won't question, as practically everything annoys the fuck out of me.

He shrugs, continuing toward the dining hall, his focus on that same hand that just reabsorbed whatever siphoned power he used for today's class. Turning back down the empty corridor of richly-toned wood and walls lined with historic photos, a grin pulls at the corners of my mouth. Peering through the glass window of Knox's door, I'm just in time.

Good.

9

Wynston

Panic flows through me. I couldn't have witnessed that. I am fighting myself, trying to convince my mind that it was nothing more than my imagination. But as my fist strains to contain Bryony Avalon's essence, I know it wasn't. Slowly, I uncurl my fingers, allowing it to flow back to her.

She can't be.

"What the hell was that?" I bark at her. My butt collides with the edge of my desk again, my hands curling over the lip as I grip on tightly. I don't trust my knees not to buckle from the anxiety running wild through me. If I stand my heart is sure to give out from the speed with which it's currently pumping the blood through my veins.

I wait for an answer that may or may not come. Wonder if she will have a solid explanation. Or maybe she'll attempt to lie to me.

Slowly, she faces me. A stoic expression locked back in place, as she shrugs into her uniform jacket. "I apologize. I lost control. I—" she cocks a single shoulder as if she doesn't know what happened. "Well, you know how it is. I'm newly matured. It's only been a few months."

For any other newly mature wielder, that would be the explanation I expected. But I saw her essence shift color. There's only one type of wielder that can do that. One that shouldn't exist. I have an up close and personal relationship with that type of wielder, so there's no fooling me on this particular topic.

"Care to tell me how you shifted the color of your essence?"

Her eyes go wide as her steps recede away from me. A yelp escaping her when her feet trip over the legs of one of the desks. The piece of furniture unyielding under the spell welding it to the floor. Much safer to have desks that can't move when you have young wielders throwing their powers around. "I didn't," she pants.

"You did." My tone is menacing as my gaze narrows on her. "And *you* better hope like hell no one else saw it."

"You didn't either." Her voice changes, that faked nonchalant confidence slipping back into place. The transition is so seamless I know she's practiced it a million times. "You must be seeing things."

"Bryony, don't fuck with me."

"Professor Knox, I can't be sure how you dark-wielding professors normally speak to your classes, but I can assure you my father would not appreciate you being so aggressive with your students."

"Is that a threat?" I seethe. Hopping down from my desk, I am nose to nose with her. Entirely too close for a professor to be to a student, but the pull of what I know she is holds me close. Someone else who might understand me within reach. Someone who might ruin everything.

"No. It's not. If you'll excuse me, I'm starving."

She grabs her shoulder bag from the seat she'd been in, making her way toward the door.

"You shouldn't be alive. Grisyms are illegal. That's what you are."

She spins to face me again. Her face calm, but her eyes give her away. Tendrils dance at her fingertips again. Long waves growing with each passing second. I take my chance, storming toward her, snatching her hand in mine.

Her head flies back, waves of dark essence flowing free of her mouth, swirling around us. Her whimpers drowning out the whoosh of the waterfall of black power leaking free. The rear of my neck gripped tightly with her free hand, but I shuck it off. The murky swirls darken further, keeping us chest to chest, narrowing its tornado-like rotation around us. As I'd done before, I snatch them back. The muscles in my arm ache from having to fight her volatile essence twice now.

"I—" she croaks.

"You are a Grisym."

It takes several deep breaths for her rigid composure to find her again. Her fingers yanking at the hem of her jacket as she straightens it. Eyes narrowed in my direction, acting as if nothing happened.

"Prove it."

Then she's gone, leaving me with a quivering fist. Her essence slithering through the creases between my fingers, following her from the room. An effortless slip beneath the door, only to disappear from view along with her.

This cannot be happening. The Director of Education has a mix for a daughter. How has he kept her hidden? She's clearly quite powerful. The way her magic reacted with another's proves it. The way it waited to strike, grabbing hold and refusing to release. Even I had to fight to secure it that first time. I'm sure I only accomplished capturing her essence because she allowed me to that second time. It was almost like it had learned. A newfound determination ensuring only its owner would keep it in the end.

Looking down at my hand again I almost expect to see her essence floating in my palm. The unique shade of black with those twinkling stars. A combination I've never seen before.

I've never met another Grisym. Never encountered another by touch. The way her essence released from her in a torrent of volatility the moment I did makes me believe if I ever had touched another Grisym, the same would have happened. When hers met with Pierson's essence, it defended and then conquered. That's not what it did when I touched her. Me touching her was like awakening a beast that had been waiting for me, not for destruction but for consumption.

I need her out of my class.

If she's still alive, that means her true identity is a secret, and I refuse to put another Grisym to death by revealing it. Further, I refuse to expose myself only to die for another.

Not bothering to think about the consequences of others witnessing me jogging through the hallways, I take off for Milgren's office. I know better than to disturb her unannounced, but this isn't something that can wait.

Her door flies open as I wave a blast of magic at it. I'd been moving with such purpose there's no way I would have had the time to stop my momentum to use a doorknob. Anger, excitement, and fear wash through me. My body uncontrollably vibrating unsure how to respond to the onslaught of emotions coursing through me as I let myself into her office.

"Hello, Wynston," she drones. Her eyes don't leave the scroll of parchment before her. Typical when she wants to be left alone.

You would think the woman ancient. Where the rest of us use regular paper, she insists on still using parchment. Her quill stays dipped in ink. Her lectures on the preservation of tradition never adopted by the younger staff like me. A gut feeling tells me there's something more than just tradition to the things she does. Regardless, it's not the reason I'm here.

"Bryony Avalon has to be removed from my class." My chest heaves with my words, fingers curled over the back of the leather chair that sits directly opposite her.

"No. You are the only professor that teaches *Essence Manipulation*."

"Then hire another. There are countless light-wielding professors out there that can teach."

"I said no."

"You don't understand! I cannot have her in my class." I hate the desperation in my voice. Hate the panic brewing in my gut. Hate that I am begging anyone for anything.

I've never been one to plead, but for this, I will. I will get down on my knees to keep that woman as far away from me as possible. It's the only way to protect both of our identities.

"Wynston. I said *no*. I don't know what you are so up in arms about, but she will stay in *your* class. You will take the gifts she has and mold them. She needs someone like you to watch out for her and guide her through her ... gifts."

My skin tingles. She can't be inferring what I think she is. That she knows what I just witnessed. It can't be true. My pulse races. The implications of what she is suggesting nearly make me run, pack my shit, and disappear.

"Headmistress, are you saying what I think you're saying?"

My eyes narrow, scrutinizing the tiny changes in her facial features. The twitches of movement are enough for me to discern there's plenty she isn't willing to say. A morsel of hope lingers in my gut. Hope that I am misreading the situation. I must be imagining correlations that are the opposite of the truth.

Having Bryony here puts us in danger. Having her near me could ruin everything I have built over a lifetime. A defense mechanism that has kept me alive for the past thirty-seven years.

I can't let that happen.

"I can't be near her. You didn't see—"

I've always been one to dive into a panic quickly. It's easy to see why with the life I've had to lead. Hiding in plain sight waiting for the reaper to come take me away. It makes it easier to be a grouch to everyone around me so they stay away. But that doesn't change the anxiety constantly coursing through me as I keep one eye trained over my shoulder.

Milgren finally looks at me for the first time since I walked into her office. Her glare a darkening storm filled with anger as she steeples her fingers on the surface of her desk, leaning forward, her stare enough to make me cower away from her.

"Wynston, you will do as I tell you to. You will keep your composure. You will watch her and report back to me. Help her. Don't help her." She shrugs as if she truly couldn't care either way. "Do as you choose, but she stays in your class. That's the end of the discussion."

She lowers back into her seat. Her way of dismissing me from her presence.

Running my fingers through my thick hair, I stomp from her office. Away from the admin wing and straight toward my living quarters on the fourth floor of Beechum. I need to be away from everything and almost everyone.

Beechum is relatively quiet as I make my way up the stairwell. The soles of my shoes clap against the metal steps, echoing around me. Stopping at one of the doors, I pause for a brief moment before knocking loudly. My colleague coming into view as it swings wide, her thin frame leaning against the doorframe of her apartment. Hair dyed a deep wine, brushes over her protruding collarbones. Thin pink lips curling into a welcoming grin. Simple deep brown eyes, large and doe-like hungrily taking me in.

"It's been a while, Wynston."

"Yeah. It has." My trembling hand runs through my hair, my glance casting downward. Something like embarrassment courses through my chest, knowing I am here to do nothing but fuck my thoughts away. For the first time, guilt creeps through me. For years, I have used this woman with no intention of giving her any real part of me.

"Come in." She flags me inside, her robe billowing out behind her.

"Fiona, I—"

"Shut up and strip. That's what you came here for, isn't it?"

I do, throwing my clothing onto the floor before tackling her to the couch. Its coloring and three sections are an exact match for the one in my apartment two doors down.

A sigh finally uncoils my shoulders as I sink into her. This is exactly what I came here for.

A distraction.

A chance to forget.

10

Bryony

The remainder of my day can't pass fast enough. I feel the eyes on me. Those who were in class and saw me lose control and those who have heard the rumors. The hardest part about boarding schools is that everyone will know everything. There are no secrets. No places to hide.

Most human boarding schools have built-in breaks to return home providing an opportunity to escape the stagnant environment and their classmates. Not wielding schools, though. It takes special permission from your parents, headmistress, and the assistant headmaster to be granted permission to leave campus for multiple days, even holidays. Lucky me, I have personal access to two-thirds of those individuals.

Our only reprieve is the lack of restrictions on day trips into town. I have no doubt most of us will take advantage of that freedom, frequently.

It gives the sense of being trapped with no way out. Nowhere to turn, but your room. A place that might not even be a sanctuary for us first years if we're not acclimating to our roommates. I adore Camilla, but she's also like a stretch of Velcro. Bound to me day in and day out, unless I can find a way to tear myself free.

As much as I enjoy her company, I'm in desperate need of some peace and quiet more and more these days. A luxury that doesn't come as part of Camilla's friendship package.

I cross my fingers that she's not there as I pull myself up one of the side-spiraling staircases nearest the women's wing. My feet drag, thighs burning from constantly having to go up and down these stairs every day. It's barely been three weeks, but I can already see my body taking shape under the strenuous exercise. I would kill to use my teleportation gifts here, but I think I've "shown off" enough.

It's a guarantee that once Dad hears about my blips in class so far, he will have plenty to say. The same lecture he fed me for months before I came here. Harley, my eldest brother, was not satisfied until he also threw in his two cents about how I was destined to be the destruction of our good family name. His attempts at keeping me from attending Beauxgraton petitioned directly to the Council. A request they denied in less than twenty-four hours. It was the only card Harley had to play to keep me out of the public and it failed.

For the Council, it's an honor that the Director of Education would pick the oldest dark-wielding school in the U.S. for his daughter to attend. It shows that we value tradition and history. Two things the Council holds in the highest regard.

If only they knew one of the reasons my father sent me here was simply to be his spy. A way to funnel information to him that he believes the Council is keeping from him. Beauxgraton a prime place to potentially gather that information with this being one of the premier institutions wielding "royalty" send their children to.

"Hey, Bryony," a male voice calls from behind me. I turn to face Valen's supposed best friend. The same one whose essence mine attempted to devour in front of the entire class. Maybe I should apologize or better yet pretend it never happened in the first place.

There's no tearing my gaze away from his unforgettable face. Denim blue eyes, heavily pigmented with flecks of silver that seem to sparkle in the light. Each spot is reminiscent of the glittering stars that mark my essence. Staring into his eyes now, all I see is the night sky, my neck aching as it cocks back to look up at his face. One I hadn't given myself a chance to memorize in our previous interactions.

This guy is the typical type I'm attracted to. Big smile. Caring eyes. Tall with a slender but muscular build. A shade of brown hair so dark when wet it's mistaken for black, the ends curving into wide arcs as it lies to one side.

"It's Bryony, right?" he questions when I don't answer. I search my mind for the moment we'd first met. Surely we've introduced ourselves when Valen has come around, but I quickly realize we never actually did.

"Uh, yeah. Bri, actually. You are?" The question spewed so quickly, I didn't have time to stop it. But all I want to do is slam the heel of my hand into my forehead. I know exactly who he is.

"Oh, right." As if reading my mind he slaps the heel of his hand against his forehead. A gesture indicating he was stupid to forget I might not know him, despite previous brief conversations. "Pierson Flaggstaff." He sticks out his hand, mine clasping around it as we shake. "You know, the one you made look terrible in class?"

I wince. He said it with a light enough tone, but just the same, no third-year wants to be shown up by a first.

"Sorry, I know who you are. Is there something I can help you with?" I don't mean for my attitude to be so harsh, but I'm tired and simply want to be alone. I also don't want this guilt that's burrowing deep from his light-hearted comment.

"Uh, well, Val mentioned you were going to sneak out with us Friday night. I'm the king of getting in and out of this place undetected, so I figured I would introduce myself." His smile widens as he looks down at me, gripping the straps of his backpack tighter.

"I never said I was going to the festival."

"Oh, I—"

For a guy who hangs out with Valen, he seems so unsure of himself. As if he is nervous to be speaking to me at all. The same confidence Valen exudes clearly ran right past this guy.

He adjusts his grip on his backpack straps again. Students filing past us down the ornately carpeted hallways of the dormitory. Each one taking a glimpse our way before continuing on.

Just twenty more steps to go, Bri.

With a sigh, I apologize. "I'm sorry. I didn't mean to be so rude. These stairs are just killing me."

He laughs. A rich, deep sound that shoots straight to my lower belly. A feeling I haven't had for a while. "You'll get used to it in no time."

"Right." I begin to climb again. "Meeting someone in the lady's wing?"

"No."

He doesn't say anything more. Instead, he keeps his pace even with mine. His fingers lightly dance as he grips the straps of his pack. Long digits releasing and then curling back inward every few seconds. A nervous tick if I've ever seen one.

"You don't seem like the type that would hang out with someone like Valen," I say. Anything to break up the silence with the attractive man next to me.

"Yeah, a lot of people say that. We grew up together. Best friends since we were in diapers." There's pride in those words and the slight upward tilt of his chin. This guy must see something in Valen the rest of us missed.

"Ahh, that explains it. You know you don't have to stay friends with him out of pity." My eyes shoot to his with a glimmer of humor and I give him a not-so-subtle wink, just in case my dry humor didn't translate. The little butterflies in my stomach putting me on edge as I wait for his response.

That same laugh burst from him. My muscles tightening just a bit lower this time.

"Well, don't tell him it's out of pity. It would break the guy's heart."

It's my turn to laugh as we weave into the hallway that leads to my room. Each hallway has the same stone walls. The grayish-tan is an interesting color that you simply don't see in architecture anymore. I run my fingers along the uneven surface now. A way for me to feel like I'm part of history in a good way.

Matching carpets cover the floors of the men's and women's wings, whereas the rest of the main building mostly remains bare. The original stone floors are somehow preserved despite the millions of steps that have traipsed over them through the years.

"Why are you still walking with me?" I ask, confusion thick in my tone.

"Two reasons. One: I need to know which room is yours. Two: I always walk a woman to her door when I want to get to know her."

"Wow, cheesy much?" The corner of my mouth quirks into a grin, one brow raised in surprise that he would try a line on me.

Just as we stop in front of my door, the two of us facing each other in silence, Camilla swings the thing wide open. Her hand latching around my forearm and pulling.

"Excuse me, Cute Boy, I need to discuss a very important matter with my roommate."

Before I can even wave goodbye to Pierson, Camilla slams the door. Her petite frame facing me head-on with hands on her hips.

I think she's glaring at me, or attempting to give me a stern look, but I can't tell. It almost feels like a child trying to scold me. Her near-white thick brows shaded with taupe—maybe so they don't blend in with her nearly translucent complexion—pinch together in a firm look of disapproval.

"What's up, Cammie?" The nickname I'd given her a few days ago when she said she'd never had one. Even then I could tell she only wanted to belong, so why not do some good while serving out my time here?

Surprise, surprise, Camilla hadn't been the most popular back home. Coming from a city where every facet of life was about being beautiful at all times she didn't fit in. She dressed too conservatively, covering too much skin. Her hair was nothing more than a long sheet of white. Her face free of makeup, instead speckled with tawny freckles that darkened with even a short duration in the sun. She was more interested in historical books, reciting every major event across the ages. Poor thing had been an outcast from the day she could read.

She said she had a close-knit group of friends back home—all humans—but even they didn't always include her. Sometimes it was just easier to leave the brainiac who was super sweet and had an answer for everything at home. The boys liked them better that way. There were more party options when she wasn't there to clap and cheer at every moment.

"When were you gonna tell me you locked lips with Graham Mayer?"

I'd honestly forgotten about it. Not that the kiss wasn't memorable, my thoughts were just more preoccupied with school and Valen's proposition for sneaking out to the Red Mood Festival. Graham never brought it up, so it was easy to put it out of my mind. Our friendship had blossomed since the first week of classes. The two of us often cozied up in the double-wide suede chairs in the back of the main library to study each day. But it was all innocently platonic.

My thoughts suddenly change direction. A visual of the brightness of a Red Moon steals my focus. Why do they even call it a festival? As if it's some event where children run and play and eat sweet treats. I always thought it odd, but after I first asked Dad about being able to use ghouls, I never wanted to bring up anything to do with Red Moons and ghouls again.

Much like my true identity, it became forbidden territory. It simply joined the list of topics better to pretend didn't exist to keep tension out of the home. My parents have always accepted what I am, but that doesn't change the fear that must live within them. Being a Grisym could mean death for us all if it gets out. My blood and magic, an intricate mix of the light and dark, the potential downfall of us all.

That weight hangs over our heads, my parent's and mine, precariously dangling from a taut rope. The likelihood that it will snap sooner rather than later always looming.

"It was nothing," I brush past her, toeing off my boots and then socks. I wiggle my toes against the plush area rug at the center of the room, a wide grin pulling at the corners of my mouth.

"Excuse me miss, have you seen his face? And the clothes he wears outside of his uniform?" Her small hands fan her cheeks as her eyes roll in the most exaggerated way. "That boy is a steamin' buttered biscuit."

A laugh bubbles out of me. "Yes, he is good-looking. Pretty sure that's what you were trying to say." The loud *thunk* of my bag into my chair makes me wince. "If you're interested, I can introduce you. We've been studying together this week."

"Oh, goodness no. I would never presume to think I could steal your handsome fella. "

"Cammie," I laugh as I throw her a warm smile. "He's not my boyfriend. Or anything other than a new friend. I'll introduce you."

"No, really, that's alright." Her hands are up in front of her as if pleading for me not to.

Throwing sharp, narrowed eyes her direction, she buckles, curling into herself as she sinks onto her bed. "I prefer the lady variety."

Oh. Oh. Well, that was unexpected. I've known my fair share of those interested in the same sex, or even any sex, and quite frankly they make life much more entertaining. There's a freedom that lives within them. A greater desire to live life to the fullest.

"Okay! So, no Graham. Do you have your eye on anyone else?" I ask.

She blows hard, shifting her long straight strands out of her face. Her hands knot in front of her belly, focusing anywhere but in my general direction.

"I'll let you know," she mumbles.

"Deal," I wink at her.

"Now, back to your kiss with Graham."

A groan escapes me. I would rather think about Pierson—and his kind eyes—than Graham right now. "Nothing to talk about. I, uh, have my eye on someone else, I think."

She smiles at me knowingly. Her small head bobbing as if she knows all my secrets.

"Well, you can tell me all about him at dinner."

Absolutely not!

11

BRYONY

THIS FRIDAY, CLASSES LET out early. A tradition across the globe that aligns with the Red Moon Festival weekends. Businesses close. Families take the few days away to venture to their favorite pits. For many dark wielders, these four weekends a year are sacred. For light wielders, they are scandalous events that many turn their nose up at with disgust.

The rules are the same for every school campus with an onsite ghoul pit. Each pit is an expanse of cleared ground warded off with spells that keep the beasts contained. Those that have approval and choose to participate, will go out there and fuck ghouls for the night, drinking in their power so they can either funnel it into the magic objects for storage or hold it within themselves for at-will use.

It varies across the board depending on a wielder's gifts and ability to channel or siphon. Siphoning is a process that can only occur between living creatures—ghouls and a few other magical beings that hold small amounts of essence. Channeling is different, requiring inanimate objects or the earth to obtain the power held within.

Friday night is the festival, while Saturday serves as an opportunity to indulge in booze and dancing in celebration of the new power dark wielders obtained from their ghoul partners. A chance for men to dress their best and women to flaunt an array of gowns in shades of crimson. It's so weird to me. Why have a ball? It's something I hope to understand during my time here.

The tradition extends to the homes of dark wielders with parties. An experience I never got a chance to have in my own home. From what I've heard and seen in pictures, the same black-tied tuxes and luxurious ball gowns are the attire for these in-home soirees. Everyone is just as glamorous as I expect us all to be tomorrow night.

Beauxgraton houses students who tend to be from rich or influential families. It's safe to say I expect the level of glamour to be eons above what average families may wear for attire or the extravagance of their parties. I can only assume since I have no first-hand experience and my family won't tell me the truth.

I am not one to pass up an opportunity to wear a custom gown, though. I've always loved them. My father's position and my mother's reputation earned us lots of invitations to dinners, fundraisers, and parties around the world. My collection of formal attire grew quickly enough by my teen years, that my parents installed a secondary walk-in closet with a motorized rack full of nothing but the gowns I've worn. I only ever wore each dress once. My mother's rules. I may be a fan of elegant gowns, but that's really where my desire to acquire the finer things ended, unlike the rest of my family.

Despite the dark half of me, my parents never allowed me to attend a Red Moon Ball. They are light wielders so that's all I'm allowed to be. Light wielders don't celebrate anything to do with the Red Moon. So, my excitement at finally getting to partake in that part of my identity left Dad's bank account just a bit emptier and my trunk full of six new gowns of varying shades of ruby. It's the closest my parents have even allowed me to get to that side of my roots other than attending school here. I had no choice but to take the sliver of a slackened leash and run with it.

Checking my phone for what must be the hundredth time, my thoughts shift back to what I plan to do tonight. A stupid plan.

It's past eleven. Seventeen minutes past eleven to be exact. Valen is late. Pierson is a no-show, too. Unease settles in my gut. Paranoia kicking in. My mind becomes convinced that this was some sort of trick or plot against me. Rivulets of sweat stream down my back as I rub my clammy palms on my jeans, terrified I'm seconds from exposure.

I know I shouldn't trust going anywhere with Valen, or any dark wielder for that matter. I don't trust him; I'm sure of that. I've given no indication I want any sort of friendship with him, and he doesn't seem the type to actively seek out new ones. Still, I'm quite aware it's no coincidence he keeps showing up everywhere I go. There's nothing but trouble hiding behind those ebony eyes. But my curiosity wins. It always does.

The real reason I excitedly dressed for tonight, going against all logic, is this single chance to live as my other half. I can ignore the danger of going out to this ghoul pit with strangers who might hold malicious intentions against me, though, I shouldn't. My curiosity overpowers the caution I've always cowered behind. I've spent my entire life told to keep my dark side and questions to myself. For the first time, I'm in a place where no one would question my desire to learn. It's a chance to get to know myself and I can't pass that up.

I take another look at the time on my phone. I'd wholeheartedly expected Pierson to show. The man has become my second shadow behind Camilla. Appearing out of thin air countless times since Tuesday to walk me to classes, or my room, or the library, or the dining hall. He always deposits me safely at my destination but never sticks around. It's odd, but cute.

Unlike Valen, he seems to be a kind soul. He loves his family but hasn't given any details about them and aspires to be a Potion Master, short for a mad chemist for wielders. It's been fun talking with him and making a new friend, but I haven't missed the dirty looks of the others in his group. The worst of those burning stares coming from that twin brother and sister who look like they want to tear my head from my shoulders. Those two are terrifying.

A knock sounds at my door. Perfect timing. Camilla will be back from her quest to the library at any moment.

I open the door to find Valen. His black long-sleeved tee and snug black jeans do nothing to hide the slim tone of his body. His bun sits in the middle of the back of his head, the curls still wet from a shower, I presume. The darkened hue of raven hiding the hints of rich royal blue until it dries.

"Let's go," Valen grunts.

I close the door behind me, following him silently down the hall. The carpets that hold no historical significance muffle our steps. I wasn't entirely sure how to dress for this, but figured a loose sweater and jeans would work. It's not like I have to take them off. I won't be fucking any ghouls tonight. It's too risky for a first time, especially in front of everyone.

He turns a corner, pressing his hand to the wall. The stones slide aside with scratching groans to reveal his group of friends. Pierson at the front with a wide grin on his face. Before I can even speak strong arms pull me into a hug, pressing our bodies together, mine celebrating at the sensation of our fronts flush against one another. I can't help my inhale. *Damn,* he smells so good. I relax into the soft curves of his muscles and luxuriate in the scent of cedar wood that surrounds us.

A gagging noise comes from behind Pierson. "Let's go," a woman's voice drones. There is so much violence in the female twin's sneer that it unnerves me. I'm actually nervous I might shit my pants if she looks my way again.

I get it. She doesn't want me here, but I'm not the one who invited me. Any issues she has, she can take up with Valen. He's the one who insisted I couldn't resist sneaking out, which is the truth.

Fucking Valen.

We creep through a series of tunnels forming their own labyrinth behind the walls and down several sets of stairs. Our endpoint, a generous jump off a small ledge that puts us at the rear side of the residence, hidden by an alcove created by the trifold corner.

An immediate chill sends a violent shiver through my body. The winds toss my newly straightened hair out behind me. Shadows drape over us, concealing us from the moon's glow. Its sinister coloration twisting my gut into knots of anticipation.

The moon always seems like this far-off distant globe of beauty until it glows bright red. A brilliant illusion of its surface floating within an arm's reach. The circumference undergoing a continuous growth for two nights. This masterpiece shining bright for wielders around the world to view.

I've seen a Red Moon. We all have. They come like clockwork every quarter.

My room at my parent's home sits in the back corner. One my dad picked out for me, so his little girl would always have a balcony to look up at the stars that shone like the ones in my essence. It's one of my favorite places to be alone. Just me and the night sky, wondering what was happening out in the world. On the nights of the Red Moon, I would fantasize about watching the ghouls crawl from their underground caverns and into the mortal realm. One meant just for me, finding me in the crowd so it could share its power.

"Can you actually walk in those?" Pierson slides up next to me. His hands are tucked in his pockets, those thick brows angled high.

Looking down, I realize he's referring to my heeled knee-high boots. I'd even picked the chunky heeled ones to give myself more support for however far the pit is from the main residence.

"You just watched me jump off a ledge in them."

"Fair point."

"Shut it," Kaia snips from ahead. I only know her name because Valen asked her and her twin to go wild with him tonight. A request that seemed to give the both of them pause.

That girl really doesn't want me here. And I have no intention of pretending like I want to befriend her. However, she catches an attitude with me again and I might let my essence choke her ass.

Frankly, I don't want to befriend any of the dark wielders. They're too close to my secret for me to embrace their friendship. Yet I am out here because Valen made too enticing of an offer to pass up and Pierson elicits sensations within me I haven't felt in gods knows how long.

Our walk through the woods stretches on. For once, no life-altering thoughts flit through my mind. I keep my eyes trained above, watching for the moments when the moon peeks through the treetops bathing us in its red glow. It's by far the most beautiful thing I have ever seen. Its pull drawing me closer and closer to somewhere I shouldn't be.

The trees begin to thin, and the soft glow of a yellow light mixed with the red casts the space in a burnt tangerine as we clear the tree line.

My eyes bulge at the sight before me.

I'd known that ghouls were large, but these creatures are like small giants. At least seven feet tall, some larger. The orange haze further highlights their gnarled skin. Several already engaged with other dark wielders. Their white eyes focused on the body they're fucking. Grunts and moans and roars of pleasure filling my ears.

Oddly, I hadn't heard a single sound until we crossed the tree line. Someone surely placed a type of shield around the area, keeping the events of the evening away from prying ears. But why, when this is a natural way of life for those who come from dark bloodlines?

"Which one calls to you?" Valen whispers in my ear making me jump away from him. His soft chuckle is enough to make my lips curl. I'm on edge enough as it is, I don't need him driving my anxiety any higher.

"Uh ... No thanks." Not at all the answer to the question he asked me.

The twins are gone in a flash, both finding two deep-green ghouls—Virideists, I think—at the far edge of the open area.

It's known that ghouls will form the appropriate anatomical parts needed for the partner that takes them. For the first time, I am watching it happen as Kaia strips out of her clothing. Her small breasts lightly bounce as she impales herself on the massive dick that literally just shot out of the ghoul's body. It roars as she seats herself, riding it with an enthusiasm that makes me wildly uncomfortable, but turned on at the same time. A dampness beginning to coat my panties driving the soft shift of my hips to alleviate the ache.

Her head falls back, nails digging into the arms of the creature. Her mouth willingly opening as swirls of black leave her, the same as when Knox touched me the other day. Long auburn hair touches the curve of her ass, the perfectly styled curls bouncing in time with her tits.

It's fucking erotic as hell to watch.

I'm mesmerized by the confidence with which her body moves as she siphons from the beast that now has her thrown onto her back. Her cackling laughter so at odds with the moans of pleasure surrounding us.

Her brother is right beside her. Rippling muscles flex as he thrusts into his ghoul. The thing dragging its claws down his sculpted back before digging into the meat of his rounded ass.

This is fucking insane.

"Crazy right?" Pierson shoulders me. A jolt of electricity shoots through me at his touch. The shock pulling me out of my daze.

"Uh, yeah," I mutter moving closer to him. Out of comfort or fear, I'm not sure which.

Pierson just as soon saunters off, leaving me alone with Valen, as the other two guys also drift off into the sea of writhing bodies. His choice is an excessively large brown ghoul. Their breed currently escaping me. As if the creature knows him, it drops to all fours as he approaches. His hand runs down the shoulder and across the flesh of its back before he unbuttons his jeans, letting them drop. Unlike Kaia, he only removes what's necessary. Even his boxers remain in place as he lines himself up between the butt cheeks of his pick.

Unlike Kaia and her brother, he takes his time. Pierson caressing the bumpy, leathery flesh. The ghoul meets him thrust for thrust as he drives into it from behind. Where others have given themselves over to pleasure, his eyes stay locked with mine. A connection between our gazes forcing the shift of my hips once more.

Pierson's eyes only drift downward when Valen snakes an arm around my waist, his large palm resting on my hip. I'd forgotten he was the only one still standing next to me. An expression I can't quite place at this distance crosses Pierson's face. Only to turn into one of boredom as he continues to drive into his ghoul.

Valen leads me forward, through the throng of ghouls and wielders fucking. Countless naked bodies grinding into leathered flesh. Roars of—I'm not sure what—releasing from the ghouls as the wielders shove them away having had their fill.

Several wielders switch to other ghouls of different coloring. The genitalia changing to accommodate the new wielder that approaches. My pussy aches, taking in the size of these ghoul dicks. No way that shit would fit.

Thankfully, the professors we do pass are so lost in what they're doing that they don't notice me. Eyes pressed shut, mouths open as they take, and take, and take. Mercifully, most aren't ones I have to look in the eye come Monday morning, so this is slightly less awkward.

Valen stops at the opposite edge of the horde, his eyes scanning until he spots a black ghoul. A Nigeros—a rare breed, if I recall correctly. It's alone, as if waiting for the night to end, back flat to the cold ground beneath it. It's still, except for the rise and fall of its chest, completely uninterested in this scene of debauchery and power siphoning.

Valen immediately heads toward it dragging me behind him.

The moment we've reached the ghoul, it sits up, eyeing the both of us with those bright white orbs. They are unnerving so close to me, only inches from my face as a wide grin unfurls. Sharp, jagged teeth snap at me, before it sniffs at my hair, one clawed hand pulling me forward.

I fight for it to release me. I can't have sex with a ghoul. I have no idea what would happen if I did. Anxiety builds in my chest as I fight to keep my essence tucked beneath the surface. Fear that Valen brought me here to expose me drives my bounding pulse. The burn up my throat and in my lungs evidence I can no longer hold my breath.

The ghoul releases me suddenly as if it could hear my thoughts loud and clear, but its skeletal nose continues to run through my hair. A weird lapping noise rattles from it like a snake rapidly moving its tongue in and out of its mouth. The white eyes changing slightly, appearing to roll into the back of the ghoul's head. *Fuck, it's terrifying.*

Valen quickly strips the way the others have. His lean muscles illuminated by the glowing moonlight. Tattoos cover the entirety of his arms, torso, and back. Intricate designs that almost seem otherworldly. Fuck me, does the sight of him get my panties wet, too. My core pulsing in time with my rapid breaths.

He moves toward me, removing my sweater over my head in a single swift movement. I can't say why I don't stop him. I should object.

His mouth is so close to the skin of my throat that it warms me. A chill snaking through me as he pulls back.

"Do you want me to go first?"

I nod. Unsure how else to keep him from pushing me to fuck alongside him and his friends.

The ghoul falls to its knees in the dirt, legs spread wide before falling flat to its stomach as Valen shoves inside it. His head drops forward, then flies back, his hair tie releasing long dark curls that billow in the wind as he pumps into the ghoul that's roaring beneath him.

His pace is punishing. No mercy. Dominance bleeding out of every pore.

Dark eyes find mine as he beckons me forward.

As if under a spell, I move to him, my hand running along the ghoul's thigh. The flesh is as awful as I expected it to be. But somehow, it calls to me, too. A familiarity pulsing beneath the surface as energy buzzes under my palm.

Just as quickly as I'd touched it someone rips my hand away.

"What the hell are you doing here?"

12

Wynston

Only a few moments after I finish fucking the Kirbon—a charcoal gray ghoul—I feel her presence.

The Kirbon is known as a breed with the calmest of temperaments. Their passive nature integral in keeping my light characteristics hidden and the dark from becoming vicious.

I'm always the first out here. Ready to take my fill of what I need to control my light side. Controlling that part of me is a battle I mastered long ago. Anyone who knew me since my teenage years would never suspect me as anything other than a dark wielder.

I had to choose which half I would embrace at a young age. I chose the dark. Became it. My parents never knew the resentment I held for them because of the position they left me in. I wanted to be able to bring down anyone that came for me. To defend myself against those who would hunt me down. Their only objective my death. In my mind, the dark was my way to do that.

Yet all I did was panic and obsess over it, but at least on the dark side, I could blend better. My essence, even as a young boy, was that same eerie cloud of opaque smoke it is now. Light wielders appear so much purer than I will ever be. It was something I knew I could never fake every day of my life.

I don't come out for every Red Moon Festival. I don't need to since I'm innate, but it helps my dark side remain dominant. I'd counted on the daily fucks with Fiona this week to calm me until tonight, but they've done nothing to tamper my nerves. Not a single ounce of impact to help shut Bryony Avalon out of my mind. That woman is just like me, but living here in the opposite role of what I chose.

It doesn't make sense. Both of her parents are well-known light wielders. How can she be a Grisym? And why did it seem like Milgren knew about the both of us? Regardless of how or why, Bryony chose to show her light side. Although with influential parents like hers, I'm not sure she ever would have had a choice. If they were going to hide her she would have to look like their offspring.

I haven't been able to calm down since the interaction last week. And other than sex, nothing calms me when I get this worked up. I tried drinking once. Hated it. Loathed drugs and smoking even more. But a tight pussy usually does the trick at reining in my paranoia. My stepbrother calls me a sex addict. I ignore it.

I was steps away from the far edge of the field, ready to make my way back to my apartment and finally sleep soundly for the night when I sensed her. Something tugging inside me as if I'm drawn to her by some invisible string. I spin in all directions until I spot her, not far from me. Her hand extended toward the only Nigeros to appear at this pit in almost a year, Valen fucking plowing into it from behind as he calls her forward.

Before I can change my mind, I'm sprinting for her. My arms pump furiously at my sides. A single hand wrapping around her wrist just as I get within reach, yanking her away.

She can't be here. Isn't supposed to be here.

If she's never fucked a ghoul there's no telling what response she'll have. My own first experience was an absolute disaster. Not only had my stepbrother picked the wrong ghoul for me, but he left me there in the pit as a joke for him and his friends to laugh about. The idiots didn't know what I was.

My essence released from me in a violent storm, shifting between shades of gray and black uncontrollably, enraging the ghoul that nearly took my head off before my stepmom found me naked and blubbering on the ground. My body curled in on itself like a thirteen-year-old baby. Like I said, not good.

"What the hell are you doing here?" I growl in Bryony's face.

The only words that have time to escape me as her essence breaks free. It swirls around our feet and then splits to drift up the skeletal nostrils of the ghoul. Its snort of air in response thunderous.

That's odd.

The Nigeros immediately shoves Valen away, his bare ass landing in the dirt, lunging for her. The swirls darken, then begin twinkling glowing white, then silver, then blood red.

What the fuck?

"Mine," the ghoul growls. The single word garbled but understood.

Most can't speak, but the few that do can't say more than a few words. The message always delivered as if from under water. Underground, the ghouls communicate with their eyes, any verbal communication is reserved just for us wielders.

"Run!" I roar, tugging her behind me.

The cloud of her essence continues to thicken and darken around us, distorting my vision as we break for the trees. The nine-foot ghoul easily chases on all fours. A predator seeking its prey.

I push harder, pulling her behind me, actively ignoring her angry dark cloud swirling around us. The barrier at the edge of the pit throws the ghoul back, but I don't stop running until we're deep into the woods. Her yelp startling me as she stumbles. A forceful jerk of her arm backward, trying to break free of my grip. Instinctually I grab hold around her waist, linking her to me before we both plummet to the ground. Our bodies flush as we suck in precious air.

Gradually, I release my hold on her. The swirls of her essence softening into a translucent haze before seeping back inside her.

My hands grip my knees as I bend over, panting. A soft thud sounding beside me as she collapses against a tree, chest heaving up and down.

"What the hell were you thinking?" I cough.

"You—" she grunts as she points my direction. "You. What are you doing?"

"I'm a professor engaging in the Red Moon Festival. You shouldn't be here."

"You don't get to decide that."

Why the fuck is she so damn difficult? In an instant, I'm in front of her. My hands braced on either side of her head against the tree trunk, our chests brushing with our heavy breaths. My face dips close to hers, so close my lips almost brush the soft flesh of her mouth. I have no idea what I'm doing, but I know I couldn't pull away if I tried.

Every logical part of me screams to back away from her. Yells at me not to pull this I'm-the-boss-of-you act, but my essence holds me in place. Anchors my body right where it is, leaving minimal space between Bryony and me. It wants us here. Just like this.

I'm careful not to bring my skin to hers. Until I can figure out why she reacts to me the way she does, touching her bare skin more than I have already, is out of the question. She clearly can't control it. And I can't have anyone finding out about her, because then they will find out about me, too. As much as I want to protect another Grisym, I'm not dying for her.

"You should be in bed." My snarl is raw. Guttural.

"Then put me there."

Fuck.

Her words go straight to my dick. The bastard kicking to life as I press my body flush against hers. Our clothing a necessary barrier. I tell myself this is just the after-effects of the lust-dump from fucking ghouls. It has nothing to do with this gorgeous, voluptuous woman pinned between my body and this tree, her sparkling eyes gazing up at me through her lashes, daring me to discipline her.

Libidos are high. I can see in her eyes how affected she was by the ghoul. My logic reminds me there's no way it could have been the ghoul. She didn't fuck it—I don't think. Maybe it's me she's affected by. Part of me wants to find out.

My smarter part says to run. Anything to put as much distance between me and this woman before I do something stupid.

Dipping my head so my breath sweeps across her ear, a shiver runs through her, as her hands tangle in the thin fabric of my shirt.

"Don't. Tempt. Me." The words delivered low and husky. I shouldn't have said it, but my insides forced me to. Each one vomited before I could stop them.

Her face pulls back just enough to look into my eyes. There's want there. That pull between us is almost too much to ignore. My face dips that much closer until a branch snaps behind us. The spell we'd been under, broken.

Immediately, I jump back from her. I had no business getting that close to her. Talking to her like that. Not out in the open like this.

No, Knox. Not at all, you dirty bastard.

For the first time, I realize she's not wearing a shirt, just a lacy bra that's completely see-through. Her peaked dark nipples on vivid display for me. The tip of my tongue darts out to wet my bottom lip, wanting to suck the pebbled nub into my mouth.

She's a beautiful full-figured woman. Dark eyes that shine despite their deeper shade. In any other world, I would want her. Hell, in this world I think I want her.

Fuck! Stop it, Knox.

Shaking my head, I clear every inappropriate thought of Bryony Avalon. No one knows what two Grisyms together would do. I won't risk it.

I won't risk my life for her.

Removing my shirt, I toss it to her. If she doesn't cover herself up, I might not stop myself from yanking those cups down, exposing her bare flesh to me. There will be no stopping me from indulging my lust-filled body.

"Put it on."

She tosses it back. "No thanks, Dad."

She is testing every bit of resolve I have right now. The calm I'd found after fucking that ghoul fading quicker than it should. My panic and my desires mix, so I can't parse out which is driving my actions.

"Fine. Let's go."

I escort her back to the main building, keeping to the shadows as much as possible. The last thing I need is for someone else to see me with a half-naked student, on our way back to the residence, in the middle of the night. Not just any half-naked student, but the Director of Education's daughter. A woman who I know for a fact doesn't have permission to be out here.

I refuse to say a word until we crest the few steps at the front of the residence. "I expect you in my office, Monday morning, before classes. We need to talk."

"Aye, Aye Captain." She salutes me before slipping inside. The silhouette of her figure fading from view as I adjust my hardened dick in my pants.

I stare at those sealed double doors longer than I should before jogging back in the direction of Beechum as fast as my feet will carry me. All while filthy thoughts of the many things I would have done to Bryony tonight threaten to consume me.

What the fuck are you doing, Knox?

13

PIERSON

I'D HOPED TO SPEND more time with Bryony last night after I did what I needed to with the ghoul. The same one I've been fucking since I started school here. Consistency ensures each outing makes for a more efficient exchange. But also a predictable one.

Where many of them enjoy the pleasure that comes from fucking ghouls, I just want the power. I take what I need and I'm out. Frankly, I am rather disgusted that as an extrinsic dark wielder, this is how I have to accumulate power most effectively at school. But it is what it is. Technically, I do best channeling from the earth, but with the campus wards, there are restrictions on when and how frequently students are allowed to do so.

Extrinsics are considered the weakest of the wielders unless you can channel earth power as I can. Then you're bumped up to a level considerably lower than an innate wielder, but still third in line, with proficient ghoul siphoners in a close second.

Unlike many dark wielders who will siphon from living creatures, extrinsic and charter light wielders refuse to. They will only channel earth magic or from objects claiming taking anything from the living is despicable.

I've never disliked being what I am. Sure, it's inconvenient to have to borrow power from other sources and then store it. Somehow, that's made me feel more comfortable, knowing I couldn't just easily use my gifts on someone else unless I had a store of magic inside me to draw on.

I searched for Valen and Bryony for a while last night. I found him, pounding into a teal ghoul, but not her. When I asked where she went, he shrugged and continued with his business.

He and Kaia are the two that love this shit the most. Reveling in what they can take and then what they can do after they've had their fill. Where Valen holds death in his veins, the twins create it with spells curated from plant and herb life.

A gut feeling tugged at me. A thought telling me he hadn't invited her out here to just be friendly. Worry began to consume me, but I stamped it down, shuffling back to my room to stare at the ceiling for hours. My insomnia is always worse after siphoning ghoul magic. An inconvenience I've learned to live with.

Heavy disappointment from not seeing her again or at least getting to say goodbye, lingers. I haven't had many crushes since coming here to Beauxgraton, but I definitely have one on her. I'm hoping maybe I can snag a dance at the ball tonight. I know she'll be there with that Graham guy. His tailored dress pants and button-downs always present him as a picture of perfection. Never missing an opportunity to roll up his sleeves to reveal his collection of expensive watches. A flashy way of showing off how high the pedestal light wielders put themselves on sits.

According to Camilla, they are nothing more than friends. It took too much self-control not to cheer with Camilla's assurances. Those delightful words were quickly followed by a warning that Bryony already had her eye on someone. Other than the guys at her dining table, I haven't seen her talking to anyone. My insecurities left me wondering if it was Valen; it wouldn't be the first time. It was him she agreed to sneak out with, not me.

I figure tonight's ball is as good an opportunity as any to see if there's anything there. The pep talk I gave myself in the mirror was enough to convince me she'd want to give me a chance. A confidence that only grows as I turn into the hallway leading to the raucous celebration.

Students and professors already fill the grand ballroom. The walls are the same stone that lines the rest of the residence. Three-story high ceilings with exposed wooden beams support the twenty-two chandeliers that hang above. Each one dimmed so low tonight, they might as well have left them off. Above those beams is a glass ceiling, each piece a scalene triangle revealing the night sky. The dim lighting and glowing Red Moon draping the room in a beautiful shade of rich wine.

From where I stand at the second-story entrance, there's a full view of the room. Each longer edge is bordered with clusters of circular tables along the perimeter. All evenly spaced, many of the wooden seats positioned between tables that sit side by side, merging two groups of conversation and laughter.

Peering down from the grand staircase, the center of the ballroom now boasts a wooden floor. The flooring, overhead beams, and chairs are all a perfect match for these events.

Students fill almost every square inch of the dance floor. Writhing bodies, sweating through their formal wear. One of the younger professors moving to the beat just above them as he plays DJ for the evening.

The line for the buffet near the back wall is exceptionally long. It will be for at least another few hours until the bar becomes more important than nourishment. That same bar is the only spot in the massive room where only a few patrons linger, leaning against the shined mahogany surface.

It's a sea of red. Tradition states that women wear gowns that honor the moon on these nights. The men usually clad in dark colors to match the magic that lives inside us. However, this ball is the first I've heard of us altering that tradition.

A sudden need to include the light wielders in the festivities meant altering the fashion for men to include crisp white tux shirts with blood-red ties of some sort. While the women now have permission to substitute pearls and diamonds as their white option over the traditional use of rubies.

It's as close to wearing uniforms to a ball as you can get. Our individual stylized choices a reminder to everyone we are not the same.

My eyes scan the room, searching for her. I know the rest of my friends won't be here for at least another hour. They've never been a fan of this but know they must make an appearance, too. This is one of those events you only miss if you're on your deathbed as a dark wielder, an expectation hammered into us from birth. Regardless of whether you choose to siphon from a ghoul or not, the tradition of the celebration on Saturday night holds.

I finally spot her twirling in circles with Camilla and a few other girls who are also light wielders. Her gown doesn't leave much to the imagination. The corset of her dress fits every curve of her body, a small bell toward the bottom almost hiding her bare feet. The cups of the bodice eagerly display her ample cleavage. Thin straps taut against her soft brown skin threatening to break with each twist of her body.

In these few weeks, I've rarely seen her smile or laugh so freely. I can sometimes get her to chuckle at my odd humor, but there is something guarded about it. Almost like she can't stand to give a part of herself over to anyone. Yet, here she is, as carefree as ever. That boisterous laugh given willingly to those surrounding her.

I'm only steps away as the music abruptly changes halting my progression. Foot hovering midair, I suck in a sharp breath. A ballad fills the room through the hidden speakers as Graham taps her on the shoulder and she quickly falls into his arms. Her eyes sparkling as he says something that has her tossing her head back in laughter, her palms flattening on his chest. Hands I wish were on me instead.

I shouldn't be jealous. There's no reason to be. Just because I've developed a slight obsession with her, doesn't mean she even sees me like that. Okay, I-would-murder-someone-for-her type of obsession, but that doesn't matter. Straightening my jacket, I turn away, heading straight for the bar at the rear of the room.

The best part about attending wielding school is that the rules are much more lax than the traditional human schools we attended in our youth. Our parties have ample amounts of booze. Professors don't treat us like children as long as we're not endangering everyone unnecessarily. Debauchery is expected and encouraged. The more the better.

The only rule at balls is no spellcasting once we've been drinking. It's much easier to count how many times that rule hasn't been broken. Zero, to be exact. Without a doubt, there's always some idiot pissed or wanting to show off, that poorly tosses out some spell they barely know how to use. While no one is usually hurt beyond fixing by these poor attempts, it does usually leave the responsible wielder with a disastrous night.

The bartender pours me a swirling monster-green something. Glittering flecks of gold floating throughout as I lift it to eye level to watch them twirl around. I have no idea what it is but I tip it to him before throwing it back. The confidence I'd walked in here with is suddenly gone. I'll need more than a little liquid courage if I'm going to say what I want to her tonight.

I spend the next hour doing pretty much the same thing. The booze flows through me, mixing with my newly acquired ghoul magic. I can't safely transfer it to my preferred storage objects until tomorrow. Some wielders don't need time to let the foreign power stabilize, but without the wait, both my natural abilities and the foreign magic will force horrendous things out of me. My body will turn me into pure violence for anyone who crosses my path.

A warmth fills me as I slump back into my chair, legs spread wide. Whatever the couple at my table is bickering about has become nothing more than blurred words to me. My focus solely reserved for the beautiful woman I would give my last breath to have.

The crew arrives just as Bryony is finally alone. Fanning herself she makes her way to the exits at the rear of the ballroom. Likely to get some air or to find the bathrooms. No one follows her. *Perfect.* Ignoring Valen as he sits down next to me, I storm after her.

My fingers run through my hair. The hours I spent attempting to style it for her likely ruined as I find her leaning against a wall around the corner. Thick lashes flutter against her cheeks, her eyes remaining closed as I approach. The softest hint of rose coloring her skin giving her the appearance of an ethereal being.

"Want some company?"

She cracks an eye. "If it's just you, then yes." *Not into Valen then. That's good. Very good.*

Hope swells in my chest as I lean my shoulder against the uneven stone wall next to her, my body squarely facing her side. "Looks like you've been having a good time."

"I have. You?"

She turns to face me now, her eyes gazing up into mine. "Much better now," I smile, my eyes drifting down to her throat before finding her eyes again.

My fingers curl around her hip, pulling her to me. The pounding of my heart thunderous in my ears having her so close. I wait for her to pull away, but she takes a step closer, our eyes searching one another. Her palm falls flat against my chest, head tilting to the side.

"Why now?" she all but purrs.

I answer with my lips pressed to hers. A forwardness finding me that I've never had. I probably should have asked or some shit, but I couldn't pass this up. Couldn't exist next to her for another moment without tasting her.

I wait for her to break away, but she pulls me closer, her body curved against mine. There's no stopping my growing erection or the groan that leaves my throat when I let her tongue into my mouth. The taste of cherries and vodka mixes with that monster punch I've been consuming like water.

Just as she tugs me closer, I turn us, her back against the unforgiving rock. Her laugh caught in my mouth.

"Touch me," she breathes.

Only then do I pull back, eyes searching hers. A quest to determine her level of seriousness is my only concern. There's no humor behind her stare this time. Just smoldering heat that I would allow to burn me alive if it meant getting this one night with her.

"Or don't." Her gaze shoots downward as if embarrassed, hands retracting from my body as if burned. I think I've ruined the moment, but for only a few seconds before my mouth is back on hers. Her fingers instantly tangling in my hair as she rolls her hips against my rock-hard cock.

"Touch me," she croons again. Her normally husky voice dropping an octave lower this time.

I lift her under the ass. Her body stiff and straight against mine, that sultry dress limiting her ability to bend or arch freely. Those full lips leave mine as I turn the corner into the first room we stumble into.

Of course, it would be one of the small libraries. The dark wooded interior draping us in a gothic scene. Old leather chairs and sofas, with small circular side tables to cordon off the segregated sitting areas. Built-in shelves line the walls, reminding me this place is meant for learning and knowledge, not the things I want to do to this woman. A list of explicit ways I want to worship Bryony's body playing on an endless loop in my head.

I hope to intimately learn every curve before we exit this room.

Lowering her onto one of the small couches, I unzip her dress, our eyes locked. She does nothing to stop me as the fabric falls and pools around her waist.

Palm in the center of her bare chest I force her to lie back, shimmying the rest of the dress down her body, fingertips grazing along her soft skin. My dick twitching in response as she moves beneath my touch.

She's beautiful. Exquisite even.

A single finger trails down the center of her torso, stopping at the edge of her lace panties.

"Touch me." A dare this time.

Removing the damp panties, I shove them into my pocket. A reminder that this happened. That for one night, this woman wanted me. If this is my one chance to touch her, I'm taking it.

Staring down at her, all I want is to taste every inch. It won't be enough for me to run my finger through her soaked folds. Sinking to my knees in front of her, I drag her to me, lining her pussy up with my face. Her giggle riling up my insides, my dick aching to get free.

There's no taking my time as I bury my face between her legs. Her hips bucking and rolling against me as her fingers dig into my hair. At this point, there will be no fighting it back into submission when we exit this room. I don't care. I want her. I want this.

"Fuck, Pierce."

The sound of my name on her lips encourages me, so I let my tongue slip inside her as my fingers pinch at her taut nipples.

The taste of her is better than anything I could have imagined. The constant upward tilt of her pelvis forcing me to abandon her full breasts. Each hand curling around thick hips to hold her in place.

I only release one hand when her rotations soften. Two fingers replacing my tongue, teeth nipping at her swollen clit as she groans loudly. The taste of her is potent on my tongue. An exotic dessert I'll never get enough of.

"Pierce, I'm going to—" her words cut off by her boisterous moan just as her release bows her spine off the sofa. My tongue sneaking back inside her just in time for every drop to coat my taste buds.

Strong thighs squeeze against my temples, thick tendrils of my essence drifting free to force them back open.

I could get addicted to this. To her.

I think I already am.

She pulls me up to her, our mouths crashing together, my hips grinding into hers. I want nothing more than to be skin-to-skin with her but I've never been the type to just expect sex or jump right into bed with a woman.

My approach to dating and sex is so unlike Valen and our friends. They always made fun of me for it. Laughed that I didn't have any balls. As my best friend, Valen is the only thing keeping me tied to the group, despite not being the ruthless fuck boy they expect me to be.

Until now, I'd nearly forgotten just how much I never blended with them. How much I don't belong.

"Bryony ..."

She hums a response, keeping my face close to hers. Our bodies roll and dip into each other, the leather groaning beneath us.

"Bri," I whisper before she pulls back, her eyes searching for some sort of answer written across my face. The number of times she's told me to call her "Bri" over the past week and all I could do was use her real name because I love how it rolled off my tongue stops her now.

Just staring down at her beautiful face the leash wrapped around my restraint is barely holding, but I hang on tight. When I take her. *No*, if I get another chance to be with her, I'm going to do it right. "I, uh. I'm not having sex with you in the history library."

She laughs, a loud, rambunctious sound that vibrates through us both. "Why do you look like I'm going to be pissed?"

"Well, most girls are when you tell them no. Or their feelings are hurt."

"Pierce." Her hand finds my cheek, her swollen lips briefly pressing to mine. "I'm neither. This was fun, but I have no desire to be caught in the middle of ya know," her tongue clicks twice, "by the staff or another student." Of course, she doesn't. Word would certainly get back to her dad and she's already told me how much she "loves" the extra attention due to them sharing a last name.

Slowly I climb off her, picking up her dress from the floor before helping her step into it.

She turns her back to me, her long hair no longer in the intricate bun she'd had it in, but now falling in waves over her shoulder. She pulls it to one side, allowing me to pull the zipper up. My knuckles grazing over her flushed skin for those brief seconds, fingers trembling wanting to unzip her dress again, just to get another taste. God, she feels amazing in every sense of the word. Better than I could have ever dreamed.

When she turns to face me again, her palms on my chest, she pauses. Wordlessly, she straightens my tie and jacket, before properly tucking my shirt back in the way it was. A final pat to my lapels before she grins up at me with a wink.

"Perfect," her smile wide as she places a quick peck on my lips. "I better get back. The girls will wonder where their dance partner wandered off to."

With a nod, I follow her from the room, my hand on the small of her back. She keeps close to me as she hums to the beats of the music drifting down the hall. The soft bob of her head evidence of her joyous mood.

The moment we enter the ballroom, we separate. Not a word spoken, as if we never knew each other at all. She immediately runs up to Camilla, hugging her from behind.

The poor girl's head rests just above the boobs I'd just been fondling. An emotion like jealousy at even the most innocent of things brewing inside me.

"Have fun?" Kaia scoffs, as I sink into the lone chair at our crew's table.

"Huh?"

"Oh please, you were off fucking that girl Bryony," Kaia says her name with such venom that there's no holding back the sneer I throw her way. I know the twins have their reasons for not liking light wielders, but that doesn't mean Bryony isn't a good person.

That's what I hate most about the division between light and dark. We cast each other as the worst mankind has ever seen. We are eternal enemies. To the light, the dark can't be good, and to the dark, the light is evil for casting such stigma on us. It's a cycle that never stops. Stereotypes and discrimination that will never end. Add in, Grisyms ordered to death at birth just for being a mix of the two and you've hit the trifecta of conflict.

It's funny. There's a law against those babies living, but not against the couples coming together that made them. Date, marry, or fuck who you want, but just don't procreate with a wielder opposite of you. It's fucked up. Archaic even.

"I wasn't fucking her," I mumble.

"Right," Kaia snorts. "Just don't let Val find out. He'll flip his shit if he knows you've switched sides." Kormoran nods beside her. A similar gesture that both of them do when one gives any sort of warning.

"I've not switched anything. I don't even know what his plans are for her. Do you?"

She shrugs before pushing away from the table, leaving just us guys alone. The others snicker in my direction. Damian shaking his buzzed head with a sigh. Sean and Kormoran taking deep pulls from the bottles of beer in front of them as if waiting for the shit show to begin.

Kaia is right. Valen isn't going to be happy I'm hooking up with Bri, even if it's just one time.

14

BRYONY

I'M COMPLETELY DISTRACTED FOR the remainder of the ball. I do my best to keep my eyes off Pierson. No, not Pierson. *Pierce.* After what we just did, there's no need for formality.

My ability to solely focus on my friends is a lost cause. The memory of his mouth on my body and the press of his pelvis into mine fueling the buzz zipping through me. My fingers itch to sink between my legs where he'd just been, determined to continue where he left off. Eager to pull another orgasm out of me as his name passes between my lips.

A ballad blares through the speakers. Its soothing beat is just enough of a damper on the heat coursing through me that I can finally look away. Graham is there to sweep me into another slow dance before I have a chance to register his presence. Yet, it does nothing to alter the direction of my wayward thoughts.

I meant what I said. I didn't want to get caught having sex in the library, but if we'd been somewhere different, I might have. It's been a long time since a guy has looked at me the way Pierce does. As if he actually cares about what I have to say. As if my happiness holds genuine significance and my words mean more than my looks or last name.

I've known many dark wielders. Young and old. Charmed and sinister. Many fit into the boxes I would put Valen, Kormoran, and Kaia in. The stereotype of an evil villain or his henchman aligns with the persona that keeps many dark wielders alive. Whether that is who they truly are, most of us will never know.

That's not Pierce. He may have fucked that ghoul last night, but thinking back to the glint in his eye, I don't think it was lust for the beast he plowed into. There was nothing but stone-cold determination to do what needed to be done, not actual enjoyment. I should have noticed it then.

No, Pierce is different. He's kind and thinks of others. I would likely think he was born of the light if I didn't know he was a dark wielder.

The song comes to a haunting end as Graham pulls me into him with a side hug. Headmistress Milgren taking the stage where the band and DJ have taken turns playing all evening. She gracefully spins to face us as her crimson velvet and black lace gown clings to her thin frame, an effortless elegance surrounding her.

I stare up at her fondly reminding myself that here I can only think of her as the headmistress. Nothing more.

"Students and staff, please join us on the patio as our night draws to an end."

I hadn't even realized how quickly the night flew by. The ball's ending aligns with the descent of the fading Red Moon transitioning to the rise of the sun. It's the same for every Red Moon party across the world.

Every wielder in attendance seems to move as one, as the wall of glass French doors swing open with the presentation of Headmistress Milgren's arms. Most wielders have the ability to open doors or summon an object within their eyesight with a simple spell. The headmistress is just more proficient than most, yet another product of being an innate wielder.

Chilled air smacks me in the face. The sweat dampening my skin responsible for the goosebumps lining my bare arms as violent shivers work their way through the length of my body. Chest caved inward, I run my hands up and down my triceps as if my clammy palms will make an impact. My shoulders hover so close to my ears that they bunch my dangling jeweled earrings. The warmth I'm working so hard to bring back into my body not finding me until I notice Pierce staring in my direction. I'm quick to look away as if keeping my focus on him will reveal everything we shared tonight.

An expanse of lush grass spreads beyond the patio. The space is more than large enough for us all to crowd in close, heels clacking against the slated stones. In the glow of the fading luminescent moon, the lake shimmers beyond. Tiny rivulets of waves shift in a mixture between the black waters and soft red hues. The refuge for my mind and my magic alive before me.

Even now, completely abandoned and ignored, it sparkles in my presence. As if it knows I am near. Likely nothing more than my imagination, but I am determined to go with it.

Red Moons only last for two nights. Two nights a quarter, we welcome ghouls into our world so that dark wielders can siphon from them. Two nights where the need for power outweighs civilization's constructs. The lust that comes with a ghoul's presence is nearly impossible to resist. Even tonight I have no doubt it was alive in us all.

My sister, Sicily, always tried to explain as much as she could to me. That the erotic pull of the Red Moon affected those with dark blood. The energy akin to ghoul pheromones. They want to copulate as much as dark wielders do. What they get in return has never been clear.

It's another reason I'm relieved Pierce and I didn't sleep together. I tell myself that the emotions I experienced with him were an effect of the moon. I can confidently say I am attracted to him. What's not to like, other than him being best friends with Valen and Kaia? The woman looks at me as if she's constantly ready to slit my throat. Instinctually, my hand rubs up the column of my neck. A small comfort against my current intrusive thoughts. Her brother is honestly no better, but I think I'm more afraid of her.

"Come on," Graham pulls me by the wrist, yanking me free of my contemplation over sex, and moons, Pierce, and my inevitable death at the hands of his friends.

The deep, blood-red glow of the moon has already begun to fade. The softening of the shade coating the outside world in a warm hue as the intensity dims. Camilla loops her arm through mine on one side. Another girl, Whitney Montenygro, does the same on my other side. Graham at my back. So close that, as we breathe, my bare shoulder blades brush his chest, my ass flush against his crotch.

I say nothing.

Graham and I are friends. We'd talked about the kiss and decided there were only two options for us. Rivals or friends. Our brief liplock had no bearing on which we chose. Friends won in a rock, paper, scissor match. The most juvenile suggestion Camilla could have made, but we had a good laugh. The kind where your stomach muscles ache and tears spring from the corners of your eyes. A moment I won't soon forget.

"It's stunning," Whitney breathes beside me, her head dropping to my shoulder.

Each chin lifts toward the sky as we watch scarlet become crimson become rose. A grayish hue slinking around the edges, transitioning into the common silvery blue haze the moon always holds. A pitted sphere slipping behind the tree line just before the sun rises.

The midnight sky simultaneously shifting through purples, pinks, and peaches, blending into the cloudless sky blue that will remain in place for the day.

A yawn escapes me as we shuffle back into the ballroom and down the previously empty halls. The women with heels clutched through their fingers by thin straps. Men with jackets draped over their shoulders and ties loose around their necks.

I will admit, this was one of my favorite balls to attend. I'd spent time with new friends and made memories that we will laugh about long after we leave this place. For once, I'd just felt normal. As if I belonged exactly where I was, in that moment, with those people. A kinship I've never felt before.

I'd kissed a man who finally made me feel something other than indifference. One whose eyes sparkle when he catches a glimpse of me.

"I'll walk you guys to your room," Graham announces, draping an arm across mine and Cammie's shoulders. She leans her head into him, a series of heavy yawns popping her jaw. The crown of her head grazing against his rib cage as her mascaraed lashes slowly beat against her flushed cheeks.

There's no rush to our steps. My entire body aches. Dance parties alone in your bathroom mirror are nothing like those amongst friends. Even if we could walk any faster, the cramped stairways and student-thick halls prevent it. The one downside to everyone leaving a location simultaneously and returning to the same spaces in unison.

The side stairwells are where the crowds begin to thin. Camilla finally dipping from under Graham's hold, beelining for our door, only two down from the top step. Graham and I chuckle at how swiftly she's suddenly moving when she'd been seconds from sleepwalking moments ago.

Camilla places her palm on the door, reciting our code word. An advantage over having to keep track of a key. Our touch and spoken phrases, in our voices, are specifically required for entrance. A measure that makes it quite difficult to break into someone's room—or so we were told in our welcome emails.

"Good night ladies," Graham waves as Camilla shuffles into the room.

Thank you, I mouth to him as he backs away with a crooked grin and an awkward salute. Our Prince Charming for the night.

I've only just slumped onto the bed after fighting my way out of my gown when a rough knock cracks against the door. Camilla lasted all of two seconds before she fell fast asleep, her child-like frame still draped in the gossamer gown, face down. The knock is loud enough that she mumbles for the intruder to go away, but makes no effort to lift her head from her pillow.

With a groan, I throw my feet over the edge of the bed. Scratching at the new bun knotted at the top of my head in annoyance. I release a yawn, my sleep shorts hiked up higher on one side than the other as I shuffle to the door, but I refuse to fix them. Whoever it is better be ready to see this gross version of me.

I edge the door open, a very angry Valen there to greet me. Softly closing the door behind us, I slink out into the hall with him. The last thing I need is him throwing a temper tantrum and waking Camilla. Her southern will come out and I don't need any of that at six in the morning. Rousing that girl out of her sleep is like asking to be mowed down by an eighteen-wheeler.

"What d—" My words are cut off as his hand latches onto my throat shoving me into the wall just outside my door. Jagged stones dig into the bare skin exposed by my tiny tank top as I twist to break away from him. My entire body painfully vibrating from the impact of him slamming me back a second time.

My brain whirs with panic. The constant beating of my essence against the underside of my skin stealing all my focus. Only determination and gritted teeth keep my essence from attacking him in return. Slow methodical breaths expanding and compressing my chest as he squeezes tighter and tighter. A top row of straight white teeth bared at me in threat.

My focus darts to the side as I think I hear my door handle jiggle. Camilla's tiny form doesn't charge out into the hall, so I'm hopeful she didn't hear our commotion. A small mercy—maybe. No doubt her high-pitched screech would wake the entire floor.

Perhaps I'm simply imagining things as my air supply is further obstructed. Or maybe wishing for a tiny savior. It's unclear which as I claw at Valen's sleeve.

He only presses in harder. His arm extending nearly straight as he stares me down. Pale upper lip twitching with whatever emotions are driving his behavior.

Anger. Disgust. Hatred. Disdain. Jealousy.

I see them all. Flashes of each one in his demonic eyes.

"I won't tell you this again," his snarl throws spittle into my face.

Long fingers flex against my skin, his grip so tight not even a sliver of oxygen can pass through. The edges of my vision begin to go hazy. A wall of charcoal closing in. My desperation only seems to fuel the fire raging within him. That wolfish grin spreading as dots funnel into my vision.

The tingling in my lips and the lightheadedness are just the start of me losing consciousness. But I fight it. I hang on, because I'll be damned if I let Valen Greer get the best of me.

"If you go near Pierce again you'll regret it. Fuck someone else." One more squeeze as his thumb digs into the side of my throat. "So much as think about him, and I will rot you from the inside out, you worthless excuse for a wielder."

He tosses me to the ground as he releases my throat. My cheek scraping along the coarse carpet, as the soft thud of his boots strolling down the hall fades. His retreat louder than the hushed whimper I release.

I'm left there, tears streaming down my face, choking on breaths. Not even enough energy to flip myself to my back so I can see the ceiling.

My favorite quote runs through my head: "If you can look up, you can get up."

Those nine words repeated are the road map to my resolve. They are the strength I need to push to my knees and then to my feet.

Valen Motherfucking Greer will regret the day he ever put his hands on me.

15

BRYONY

THE DAWN OF A fresh Monday morning came like an assault on my senses. There's no question I would have preferred to stay snuggled under my powdery blue comforter when my alarm buzzed at four-fucking-o-clock.

No one should be out of bed this early. If a morning person like me says so, it must be true.

Yesterday passed in a lazy whirlwind of movies, ice cream, and chips from the dining hall. Graham, Whitney, and Collin joined Camilla and me in the sanctuary of our bedroom from sun up to the wee hours just before sunrise. Together we'd camped out on our beds, and then the floor before several more of our schoolmates heard about the movie marathon. Each one showed up with their comforts spread out across the expanse of our room. Each new face bringing me a bit more joy than I would have thought.

Our cheers and screams at the selection of horror movies likely carried down the hall for the entirety of the day. Those that weren't closed in behind our door were either annoyed or unaffected by our commotion.

I needed the relaxation. My feet still ached as did my vagina. Not because of the hot sex I wish I'd had with Pierce, but because I couldn't stop thinking about the encounter. Every thought of him brought my body to life and made me throb with need for him. Made me want to explore just how attentive of a man he is. Hopefully, he can turn off the gentleman next time I have him alone.

Next time?

Stop it!

There won't be a next time. There can't be. The closer I get to anyone, especially intimately, the more likely my secrets will surface. I can't let that happen.

It was better to convince myself it was only the after-effects of the Red Moon. It would pass. I reminded myself that tomorrow, I wouldn't feel any of this for him. We could just be friends again. Friends who are wildly attracted to one another.

Ugh, I'm so fucked.

With a deep sigh, I exit my bedroom. The sun remains hidden behind the trees as I trudge to Professor Knox's office. I'd debated for a solid five minutes on skipping this sure-to-be lecture about my stupidity but decided it best not to test the broody professor so early in the school year. I may be suddenly acting like a rebel without a cause, but I can't forget the last name I carry and those who are depending on me to do the right things.

It's not about fearing my father or even the administration, but rather not wanting to be an embarrassment when he gets a call that I've been doing exactly as I please. My family's reputation means as much to me as keeping my identity as a Grisym private. Maybe more.

A soft knock on the professor's office door has it creaking open. The space dimly lit with dark mahogany wood lining the wall behind him, each shelf stuffed with books, random artifacts, and even sports paraphernalia.

His large frame leans over an object that might be an Egyptian scepter. Oversized headphones hugging his ears as he dips his face just a bit closer to his project. Beats of what I would only describe as soothing and sultry music blanketing his silence. Other than the meticulous movements of his hands he remains perfectly still. His focus solely on the perfect alignment of the metal piece he's setting back into place with massive tweezers.

I rap my knuckles against the dark wood once more. Louder. More insistent. I hesitate to repeat the action, as I do not want to startle him from his work. I'd watched my mom with her objects my entire life. The concentration needed for inspection and restoration is not something to be interrupted. One misguided step and disaster could ensue.

He doesn't acknowledge me at all. My knuckles now tapping at the edge of the desk.

His strong hands rearrange the pieces of the scepter that have broken apart. The jagged edges tell a story of its forceful rupture. Maybe the power it held was too much to contain once joined with the wielder who tried to take it. Just as likely, age and use warped it with time. Many scenarios could explain it, so there's no point in burrowing down that rabbit hole this early in the morning.

A tiny bottle, no larger than a quarter of an ounce, with glowing yellow fluid, sits just beside the tweezers he just set down. As he secures another broken piece, I'm taken by the dexterity contained within such large hands. Massive palms and long fingers shouldn't be able to handle such delicate pieces. One of the many reasons many of the wielders that do restoration tend to be on the petite side.

As a child, I'd watched my mother refurbish extraordinary old pieces for hours. Years of taking antiques and making them like new. It was always a fascinating process to witness. Many of them required her analysis to determine if they were still fit to serve as objects that could hold the magic they were compatible with. Whether it be your own or borrowed from ghouls or the earth or someone else, every object has a finite set of signatures it aligns with.

If misidentified, or placed into the wrong hands, a piece could wreak havoc. Should the pieces lack the appropriate reinforcement to hold the power poured into them, the magic could rebel. The ancient relic could shatter beyond repair, lost to any possibility for future use. Sometimes leaving nothing but glittering dust behind. No chance of revival on the table.

I take in the shimmering jewels as they sparkle in the dim lighting. The sheen of the ancient metal is now dull, but hopefully restorable. A technique my mother once attempted to teach me, but I was too inept to complete properly. The force of my essence was too potent for the delicate touch needed. That was when I knew I would never be my mother's legacy. I knew I would never follow in her footsteps and do as she did. Internally, I smiled wide, hoping I was one step closer to living a life I could choose for myself.

Only when I place a palm on Professor Knox's shoulder does he look up at me. A jolt sending his tiny bottle flying across the room. But I'm quick to call it to me. The cool glass settling in my palm before placing it back on his desk. Interestingly, it didn't shatter and none of the contents spilled.

Spelled.

"Good morning," I say, my voice filled with faked cheer. I hope that if I put forward a pleasant demeanor, this will be quick.

"Sit," he gestures to one of the chairs on the other side of the desk. The plush leather refuses to give as I sink onto the cushion.

Sensing the tension in the room, I leave behind my forced smile. I set my mouth in a straight line as I lean back into my seat with annoyance lacing my voice. "What did you want to discuss?" It's clear pretending to be the upbeat woman the public knows me as won't win me any favors with the professor.

As I made my way here this morning, I made the decision to leave the snark behind. The silence of the school around me taken as an agreement as I nodded to myself. My big mouth is sure to get me into trouble at some point, despite every warning from my parents. They may have taught me to smile and show respect, but they also taught me I'm an Avalon—although by blood I can't be—so I'm not to take shit from anyone. My problem is leaning to the correct side of those two parameters without involving my emotions. Professor Knox's greeting with indignation makes me forget he's a figure I should obey.

"Are you ready to tell me the truth?" His hands clasp together atop his desk, fingers slipping past one another as he stares in my direction. His eyes never leave mine. Dark pine irises staring through instead of at me, attempting to view my very soul. There's no perusal of my body the way he'd done Friday night when we'd been alone under the cover of the trees. That chiseled jaw so tight that the muscles appear as if they may snap with one more flex.

"I'm not sure what you're talking about." Rivulets of sweat begin to run down my spine. Followed by beads of perspiration slowly forming at my temples as my breaths steadily quicken. The same nervous response I've had since I was a child. The desire to fan my armpits, stiffening my body as I shift in my seat.

He can't know.

I am perfectly aware of what he is talking about. He'd seen what I am, but I won't confirm my secret so easily. I won't just bare myself to him unless I have to. I won't die for him or have my parents imprisoned for harboring me all these years. They sacrificed too, and I refuse to forget that.

"Bryony now is not the time to play games." His jaw works. The cleft in his chin is smooth from this morning's shave, unlike it had been nights ago, making him somehow appear more menacing.

"Professor Knox, I promise you I do not know what you are talking about. I am not keeping anything from you. Plus, my entire life is pretty much a public record." Another shift of my hips as his gaze bores into me.

"Something like this never would be." His gaze narrows and I fight not to squirm in my seat, again.

"Professor—"

My words stop as a tendril of magic streams from his pointer finger. The swirl is dark like mine, slowly shifting to steel, then to a soft dove-gray.

I watch in amazement. His small show of faith is more significant than anyone else could understand. In this moment, I understand why he so adamantly declares his knowledge of what I am.

We are the same.

We are Grisyms.

"How?"

"Not important. But what is important, is you controlling your essence. I don't know why it reacts to me. And to be frank, Ms. Avalon, I am not dying for you, so we need to figure this out."

I nod. Unsure what else to say. I've always been so careful. Been so mindful of ensuring no one knows what I am and a motherfucking week into school, someone else found out.

Thinking on it now, I'm not sure I could have ever hidden what I am from him. We are alike. He must sense that. Maybe my essence does too.

"Have you told anyone? About me, I mean?"

"No, but it seems as though Milgren knows about the both of us," he harrumphs leaning back in his chair.

"She does." I swallow loudly. The painful lump forced down making me wince. I know I have no choice but to be honest with him after he'd done so with me. "I mean, about me."

His eyes bulge as he stares at me. Disbelief contorting his features. His palms slam flat onto the surface of his desk, his spine snapped so rigidly straight that mine aches just from observing his posture.

I give a little more truth, but only partially. "That's why I was sent to school here."

He runs his long fingers through his hair. The thick waves unruly, sitting at odd angles. A loud sigh releases from him as he runs a hand over his face. The thick-rimmed glasses he'd been wearing discarded next to the abandoned scepter.

"Anything else I should know?"

Plenty more to know. None of which I'm willing to tell. I've let this secret go, but I won't release any more.

Not to him.

Not to anyone.

16

GRAHAM

Disappointment dug into my chest as I watched Camilla and Whitney enter the dining hall without Bri in tow. The trio's usual animated laughter was not there to steal everyone's attention; that raspy quality of Bri's laugh always a touch louder than the squeal of Camilla and the cackle of Whitney.

We'd texted late last night after we'd all filed out of Bri and Camilla's room. Our plans to review notes at breakfast an unnecessary preparation for the surprise test Pollin has threatened to spring on us at any time. Pollin's taunts of all the convoluted scenarios she could throw our way left us with sweaty palms and throbbing temples. But Bri and I have worked through every single one. Memorized, every fact, rule, and caution. An additional study session isn't needed, but neither of us would leave it to chance.

It is so much easier being her friend than her rival. Her mind works in ways mine doesn't. She takes me outside of the contextual box I've always lived in, allowing me to explore wielding in a more tangible way. A more exciting way.

I admit part of choosing friendship was that whole "keep your friends close and your enemies closer" mantra. She's the one who will keep me from living up to my family's expectations of me. She's the only one who can steal the top spot in our class from me. We may be friends now, but I still can't let that happen.

Her last name alone will open any door in the magical world. No one will think twice when she applies for a job or expresses interest. Not that she hasn't earned that type of convenience. But others, like me, who don't have parents ruling the wielding world don't have the same luxury. My parents are nobodies compared to hers. They worked their asses off to provide the rich lifestyle we have. Still, my last name means nothing.

It was never enough to just be *good*. I must be *great*.

Some kids would buckle under that pressure or rebel against it; I chose it. Dived headfirst with every bit of me to become "someone."

I've always loved academia, especially history. Understanding where we've been and how it has molded us as a society is a continuous journey that will never end. Taking that knowledge and sculpting it into a future that's brighter than any we've ever seen is what has driven me. Ultimately, I hope to work my way to a professorship specializing in the history of spellcasting. My chest swells at the thought of how rewarding it will be to educate young wielders. Wielders who will hopefully be as eager as I am to learn the ways of our world.

Meeting Bri and experiencing her brilliance coupled with the way she can predictably control her essence, burned me from the inside out. I needed to know how she got so good. Newly matured wielders shouldn't be capable of releasing the way she did, just to pull it all back as if nothing ever happened. Was it all for show or an understatement of her capabilities?

Turns out she truly does have capabilities beyond what we saw. Her placement in *Essence Manipulation* with Professor Knox at tier three is a clear indicator. It's rare a first year makes it into his class outside of their tier. The time spent honing your powers that first year is either a success or in need of more individualized attention.

For second years and above it's common to move into a tier that doesn't correlate with your school year.

Although it's a course based on skill levels Knox fights to keep each year with their appropriate tier. First years, tier one. Second years, second tier, and so on. From what I've heard, he only loses the battle when the administration forces him to.

Bottom line, it made me suspicious. Made me want to get closer to her to learn what she was hiding. Then we started hanging out. At meals and the library or even out on the lawn. There's nothing dark or dangerous, or even maliciously secretive about her. Realizing I was jumping to conclusions about her riddled me with shame. My parents taught me to be the best, not to cast judgments.

We'd made the right decision when we chose friendship over rivalry. Why fight one another when together we can be unstoppable? It doesn't mean it won't sting every time she outdoes me, but I figure friendly competition will only make me that much better. Make me that much stronger. More formidable. Destined to remain top of our class for the five years of my chosen path here.

Breakfast moved quickly enough. My ass aches as it always does from sitting on those benches. I admit it was funny to watch as Collin threw innuendos at Camilla. It surprised me the first time since he'd asked Bri to the ball, but a week later, he admitted he had a thing for Camilla. She plays along. Throws him a wink or a coy look. The whole show is nothing more than a joke to her. A way to be part of the in-crowd. An expectation her friends back home had of her if they were hanging out or at parties. Collin is sure to have his heart broken when he finally realizes she's not into him that way. We can all see it. It's a shame he can't.

Per usual, I'm the first to slip into my seat in *Wielding Basics*. Bri's seat to my left remains empty, even once the bells chime. The wild chatter that previously filled the space immediately ceases. Camilla shrugs only a seat away from me as my brows scrunch in question, waiting for Bri to walk through the door.

My focus stays glued to the door for countless minutes. I might hear what Professor Pollin is saying, but I'm definitely not comprehending it. Her lecture continues as if she isn't missing one of the best students in her class. When I finally turn back to look at the professor, there's not a single sign she has noticed.

Her gray tweed Jackie dress eclipses her thin frame as she paces the front of the room. Her focus is solely on the lesson as panic begins to knot my intestines.

"Excuse me," I call as my hand shoots up into the air. The slim-fit uniform jacket pulls taut against my shoulders. Whoever designed these didn't have fashionable comfort in mind.

Professor Pollin slowly turns to me, removing her focus from the text sprawled open in her palm. Those thin crinkled lips purse further, her dark beady eyes staring right through me.

"Mister ...," the two syllables seem to endlessly drift from her mouth while she does her best to remember my name. It makes me bristle. Graham Mayer isn't a name she should ever forget. Not in the classroom, at least.

I've *never* been forgettable in an academic setting. Teachers fawned over me and my intelligence every chance they got. From my well-thought-out answers to my test scores. My competency with any material presented to me has always made me stand out. Even my meticulously chosen attire usually earned me points with the academic faculty. Even now, each outfit I wear is a notch higher than the basic uniform my classmates don daily.

I do my best to hide my irritation. The muscles of my jaw ticking wildly, as my back straightens in my seat.

"Bathroom," I mumble.

She cocks her head to the side signaling me to go with an eye roll and a sigh. "Where were we?" My molars grind at her flippant dismissal. The sound of pages turning follows me as I squeeze past the door.

I don't have an exact plan to find Bri. Once I confirm she's okay, I'll be fine. It seems unlike her to miss class and not say a thing to any of us. But what do I know? I've only known the girl for a few weeks. Who knows if she's the person I think I know? She's charmed quite a few people, and I admit I'm intrigued by her bright smile and sassy attitude. But what if it's all a front?

I storm past classroom after classroom, peeking through the small glass windows in each door. Bri isn't in a single one. Several times desks creak as a student turns, catching me attempting to get a full view of the room through a four-by-four pane of glass, but they quickly forget my momentary disturbance.

Next, I make my way to her room. My knock reverberates off the stone walls of her empty hallway. My knuckles rap so fiercely and for so long that another woman seven doors down pokes her head out to tell me to shut the fuck up.

"The girl doesn't want you, *obviously,*" she sneers before slamming the door.

Ouch.

But way off base.

Finally, I loop back to the administrative floor. A maze of hallways lined with the offices for every professor here. The doors are a match for the ones guarding the classrooms. Solid planks of wood, a burnt brownish black with handles of intricately carved brass. That same brass encircles the cut-out windowpanes of glass that's not quite clear but has a slight tint of teal to it.

I've traveled down half of the hall, and most of the offices sit empty. I'm ready to turn back, to give up the hunt for her, but my feet won't stop pressing forward. I feel as though she's bruised my ego, assuming she is somehow avoiding me. Maybe something personal came up. An emergency she didn't have time to tell us about. Maybe I am being paranoid and putting my nose where it doesn't belong. It wouldn't be the first time.

When I reach the final door on the right, I peer into the square of glass, only to find something I probably shouldn't see.

Bri and Professor Knox stand face-to-face, their hands linked together at shoulder height. Their eyes linger, locked together as black tendrils of essence glacially swirl around them. Nothing like the violent storm she'd set loose on the first day of class or several since. This is different. Intentional.

Dare I say intimate?

It's unheard of for a light wielder to have an essence the shade of night, but maybe what I'm seeing is his essence overpowering hers. Maybe it's creating an illusion, and it's really his essence appearing to seep from her fingers. Maybe the tendril creeping out of the corner of her mouth is actually creeping in.

A trick of the light. Or the mind.

He steps closer, their noses only centimeters apart before he opens his mouth. A deep wave of his essence drifts free. Hers follows, that same twinkling black mixing with his.

There's no denying what I'm seeing. The dark fog emanating from her is no trick. His essence is an opaque ebony. Hers, like a hazy night sky. The spaces in between the stars are as black as midnight. There is no mistaking her essence as his. An essence completely wrong for the type of wielder she claims to be.

Their gaze never breaks. Nor do their fingers as they continue to emit the darkest swirls of magic I've ever seen. Multicolored waves ooze from both of them shifting to lighter grays. The same gray she's always had in class. I hadn't noticed that those twinkling stars were there. Now I do.

Bri is not as innocent as she seems. That's clear by the closeness of her and Professor Knox's bodies to one another. The caress of her gaze upon his face. Technically, we are all adults. Professor Knox is one of the youngest on staff. It's no wonder she's attracted to a man like him. No surprise, a firecracker like her would want a dark and mysterious, ruggedly handsome man instead of someone her age. It does nothing to explain away the power coursing between the two of them, though. Whatever their essences may be is a mystery I will have to solve another day.

As much as I want to think about something other than Bri having an inappropriate relationship with a professor I can't. Something like disappointment settles in my chest. Whether it's disappointment she wants him or that she's engaging in an inappropriate relationship is something I refuse to analyze.

It's hard to believe Bri is hooking up with a teacher, but I saw it. I don't know what to do about it.

My body picks just this moment to release a cough. The bark crashes out of me, breaking their eye contact just before the swirls of magic change color once again. A violent storm weaves around them as if in protection from an enemy.

With my back to the wall, just outside the door, my chest heaves. I saw so much more than I was supposed to. Worse, they may have seen me too.

Before they can come out and catch me, I take off, sprinting around the closest corner. Another cough lodged in my throat, threatening to choke me. My feet only stop once I've reached the main staircase that connects each story.

That cough breaks free, my hands on my knees as I fight to suck in air.

My breathing normalizes, but my pulse refuses to slow. A constant thrumming reminding me I know things I shouldn't.

Shit. This is bad.

17

Bryony

The session with Knox went much longer than intended.

Our bodies touched in tentative, then more intimate ways. His intention, testing my reactivity to his essence. Unease fluttered around my belly as he first took my right hand then the other. With the slightest grip, he held my hands in one of his. Then he gently cupped his warm palm at the side of my neck.

Only when he held me in balance did the violent storm cease to rage around us. It didn't matter if it was just the pad of his finger or the whole palm. He needed both hands to keep me from tipping over the edge. An edge my body and essence seemed all too eager to tumble over just to get close to him. To explore the essence that lived within his shell.

Though my essence responded to him, his rarely did to mine. Only when my swirling waves reached out with soft touches, probing to be let in, would his grow curious and explore me too. It was odd and miraculous to witness. The sensations within something I'll never be able to adequately put into words. A comforting combination of home, calm, and warmth. Familiarity that's only found with time. Peace. Wholeness. All of it in one rotating fog occupying my insides.

He concluded his essence's lack of reactivity was due to him having matured into his power a long time ago. His essence tamed against behaving as impulsively as mine did. I want to believe that, but there was something much more intense about the way I responded to him. The way my magic tore through my body to surround *us*—not just me.

We're not supposed to exist. The combination of our gifts and the unique ways they come to fruition when wielding are a threat to the Council. The reason none other than they don't understand us. They cannot control what they do not understand.

The texts say that the single "birth defect" of our blended essences is what makes us unpredictable. That blend makes us more powerful. The Council will never allow another being to sit above them in power, especially a Grisym.

Defect. The common term used as if there's something wrong with us. With my kind. From what I can tell, we are no different. We're still wielders. But we will always be the "other." A threat to the power of both dark and light, and their single-sided strengths.

My question is: how would they really know? We're not allowed to live.

Centuries ago, the Council decreed that Grisyms threatened the stability of our world. Ill-made creations meant to be put down like rabid dogs. I'm sure some have slipped through the cracks over the years. Successful in hiding what they are their entire lives, like Knox and me.

There was a time when we weren't killed at birth. The information found in the many books I've studied over the years is the only source of understanding what a Grisym might be capable of. Even with that literature, there's very little to go on.

Locked in this room with Knox, I began to see what we could be capable of. Connections between our like but different selves forming a tether that only death could break.

Dramatic, yes. But there's no other way to describe how my insides come alive with his touch. The tiny sliver of his essence I inhaled settling into me as if it always belonged there. That's not normal. Light and dark wielders *don't* and *can't* do that. Every wielder's essence is their own. It will only ever permanently inhabit their bodies, never someone else's.

Those who can temporarily hold foreign magic inside them must release that power with time. Yet, even now, I can feel Knox's essence burrow deeper into me. That single tendril embedded into my very being.

Intentionally touching was his idea, hands clasped together as my essence rioted for almost an hour. The fight to reel it in was exhausting. At his suggestion, and later, his plea, I allowed his essence to enter me. And only when I allowed his essence in did the fight begin to ease within me.

"Relax, Bryony," he breathed, on a long, deep exhale. "Stop fighting me. Let me in," he'd pleaded.

"Yes, sir." The words involuntarily released in submission to his request.

I'd been fighting my essence—fighting his—but the moment I'd let them mingle a calm washed over me. I saw it in him too. The way the cut of his jaw relaxed. Those broad shoulders rolled away from his ears in relaxation. Maybe his essence had been fighting to get to me too. My essence behaved as long as we remained evenly linked. Bound in sight and by our hands.

Break any part of that connection and both our essences went haywire.

We stayed like that for who knows how long, testing the connection and the limits of control. A raise of the heel of a palm or even a finger jolted my essence back into a frenzied state of varying degrees of violence. His differed each time. The mixing of our essences teetered on a precipice of calm that quickly devolved into a raging vortex.

Something like euphoria flowed through me in those moments when my essence started to change color. Knox's eyes dilated as if he felt the same within him. The high of a drug I never wanted to come down from.

This small experiment of mingling our essences solidified what I suspected to be a unique connection between Grisyms. Or maybe only Knox and I. Something that only we would share. Feelings I can't wait to overpower me again.

There are at least two major reasons to run away from these feelings.

One, it's wildly inappropriate to be locked away in an office with your hot professor.

Two, the more people see us together the more they may suspect.

It will only be a matter of time before someone learns what we are. Days—if we're lucky—once they do, before the executioners are at our doors.

A cough sounds outside the door. The connection breaks as both our heads swivel to the small glass pane. Nothing but the tapestry of warriors fighting lions that hangs on the opposite stone wall in view. Just another weird piece of art from the man who originally built this monstrosity.

My essence once again swirls wildly around us, filling the room. A tornado pushing our bodies flush. My breasts pressed into his torso with each panicked breath. The storm grows angrier as it surrounds us so tightly claustrophobia begins to overtake my mind.

"Control. It."

"I—" I grit my teeth fighting to wrangle my essence back to a manageable swirl. "Can't …"

"Figure. It. Out," he growls through the haze. His features are impossible to focus on as chaos rotates around us at a quickening pace. Varying thunks sound from around the room as my storm wreaks havoc on his space.

A hand finds the side of my neck, the other following suit, mimicking the first. I'm suddenly jerked forward as our faces collide. Our noses painfully scrunched as we pant together. His hands still cup the curves of my jaw. A single thumb brushing over the arch of my cheekbone. My mouth goes dry watching his tongue sweep across his full bottom lip before his gaze finds mine.

In an instant, my essence calms. His does the same. It's the first time today that his essence responded with fervor. That his magic lashed out to join in the chaos created by my own.

"What was that?" I pant out as I plant my hand on the corner of his desk. My body doubles over as I do my best to catch my breath while his hands still cradle my face.

"I don't know. I've never lost control like that. Even when I was younger." His eyes rapidly blink as he searches for an explanation. "Open your palms," he breathes.

I do. He nods only seconds before he releases me. The both of us quickly pulling our essences back inside before they have a chance to build momentum again. My body convulses as my essence fights to break free. Fights to get back to him. My eyes scrunching shut as I resist with all I have left.

"Hold it," he commands. His voice is low but comforting. My chin rises a fraction as I internally whisper for my insides to calm. For my magic to trust that it can slumber once more.

Once it has, I nod, unsure what to say next. Sinking into the chair, brushing my now wild frizzy hair back from my face, I take several deep breaths. Moments like this make me wish I would just wear my hair naturally instead of straightening my curls. Then I wouldn't care that I likely look like I stuck my finger in an electrical socket.

Mom is the reason I spend countless hours working to press my hair into straight sheets of silk. She ingrained a sense of perfectionism in me that made my natural curls feel somehow less than.

"The world will judge you on name and appearance first, Bryony. Never forget that."

Thanks to our vortex of essence there will be no saving the perfectly styled strands. Luckily mom isn't here to see me in public like this. Her grimace would be enough for me to return to my room just to start the straightening process all over again.

"We need to keep practicing," I mutter.

He doesn't respond as he sinks into his chair. His hands sift through his thick strands before they stop at the rear of his neck. He still breathes heavily as his head remains bowed.

"Bryony, this is dangerous. We—"

"What?" I interrupt as I lean forward. There's no way I can get this under control without him. I can't go about losing my shit every time I'm in his presence. And who knows, maybe similar reactions could happen with others and I don't know it yet. I need to be able to keep a low profile here.

He doesn't get it.

Not all of it.

"It's not safe to do this here," he sighs.

I'm not willing to back down. Not willing to let him back out of his original idea. "Do you have another place in mind?"

"I do," he nods. "For now you need to get to class."

Pulling the scrunchy from around my wrist I tug my long hair up into a messy bun. The weight adds to what I've been carrying on my shoulders. Dense stone blocks, heavier still, as the truth of what took place in this room presses down on me. Knox's identity is now just one more thing to bear.

Grabbing my bag from the floor, I make my way to the door.

"Bryony," he calls after me. A brief glimpse over my shoulder stays my retreat. A plea echoes from his downward expression.

"I won't say anything. We both have the same burden to carry. I'd never wish this on anyone," I mumble, grabbing the handle and yanking the door open.

The silence of the hallway does nothing to calm my nerves. My eyelids flutter in rapid succession, trying to hold back the tears. It's the same fear I normally carry, but it's something else, too. It's the first time in my entire life I haven't felt alone. That warm glimmer of relief dances around my chest as I finally walk away from Professor Knox's office, determined to go about the rest of my day like nothing happened here.

My first class is nearly done, so I make my way to the second. *History of Antiquities: Tier One*. One I rather enjoy thanks to all my time with my mother. There's always a newly discovered object. Fresh and exciting just waiting to be explored. Answers ready and waiting to be revealed to those who want the knowledge.

I'd been itching to make it out of the initial class just to call Mom. Her excitement matched mine that night. If there's anything that can get my mother to turn into a verbose giggling school girl it is magical antiques. Especially those that are less than perfect.

Before that night, last week, I can't tell you the last time my mom and I just sat and talked for hours. I hadn't even realized such a distance had grown between us over the years until then. I miss her.

My mother is an artist in her own right. A self-made touch to the way she can manipulate almost any antique back into working order that is nearly impossible to duplicate. The classification to follow is as involved as the restoration. The Council requested that she produce an entire spell book and manual crafted just for the purpose. Those resources may exist because of her but she doesn't need them. The words on those pages were embedded into her soul a long time ago, Geneva Avalon's very being intertwined with her one true passion. Her greatest love.

The halls are still empty as I wait outside the room. I am overcome by the awareness that this used to be someone's private residence, but now houses classrooms.

Back against the wall, I pull my phone from my jacket pocket. I've always been one to keep it in my pants, but when you're wearing a miniskirt that's not exactly an option. If I had just performed a cleansing charm on my pants last night, I wouldn't be wearing it at all. Camilla insisted I let her do mine, but after she accidentally burned a hole in the crotch of hers last week, I had to pass. I have no shame over my body, but this particular skirt wasn't made for a woman with thighs and an ass to match.

I scroll through my media pages, checking for updates from my friends. Smiling when I come across silly photos of them at school together. My thumb idly rubs over their lit-up faces. I miss them, too. I miss that little piece of my life that was full of laughter only a few months ago.

I had no choice but to attend Beauxgraton. Headmistress Milgren has known my family since before I was born. She knows what I am and has been integral in keeping my secrets. Not once has she ever asked how I came to be. The question she wanted to know was who my real father was. A secret my parents keep tucked close. Even I don't have the slightest idea.

My mother's only clue is the distant glaze of her eyes when I've asked who he is. The tears building held back. Geneva Avalon doesn't cry in front of anyone. Ever. But her subtle reaction tells me everything I need to know. He was not just some random man she screwed to pass the time. Something significant existed between them. She may have even loved him once.

My parents pretend as if my dad is the one who fathered me. But he isn't. Two light-wielders can't produce a Grisym. A mixed copulation is the only way. Roman may be my dad in all the ways that matter, but he's not my biological father.

My shoulders roll uncomfortably against the stone wall. A torturous ache pulling at my limbs from the hours of practicing with Knox. No doubt I am going to pass right out this evening. Dinner can kiss my ass.

The doors creak as the swarms of students funnel out of their classrooms—a dull roar of voices drifting in and out of focus as they pass me. The room I am about to enter does not house as many as some of my other entry-level courses. A small mercy, since I am dying to sit down.

Kormoran spots me as he hustles through the doorway of the room I am supposed to enter. His abnormally large body ominously blocking the light from the room behind him. He stares down at me, the upper corner of his mouth violently twitching as he fights back a snarl.

"What are you looking at?" he barks.

"Not a damn thing," I spit back at him. My patience for his rudeness was lost days ago. I did nothing to him. Nor do I know him. If he thinks a woman like me will just stand by to be tormented by him, he is going to be in for a rude awakening.

"Use that mouth with Pierce?" he taunts.

Fuck.

Did he tell all his friends about what happened between us? It's not that I'm ashamed or whatever. But damn, can a girl get a little privacy?

Rolling my shoulders back, chin cocked a little higher, I put it out of my mind. *Pierson* and I can talk when I'm not ready to punch him in the throat for telling my business to all his friends.

"Didn't think so." His upper lip curls in victory.

He saunters off, his wide back shrinking as he makes his way down the length of the hallway. Valen exits another room, clasping hands with him. They both look back at me. Hatred and something so much darker in their glares.

Then Valen grins, a dark, salacious stretch of his mouth.

I barely have time to register the dangling knife between his fingers before he launches it down the corridor in my direction. None of the other students move an inch as it whistles through the air, missing each one of them with ease. The blade burrows into the stone a millimeter from my head. I barely have a chance to blink or process what just happened as the handle lets out a faint buzz from toggling back and forth.

By the time I look back down the hall to where they were, they're gone.

Fuck today. Just fuck it straight to hell.

18

Valen

I had my chance, and I should have taken it. I should have willed that blade straight into her chest. Using my gifts to guide it, there's no way she would have survived. Sharp metal buried between bone and tissue. Willed by my mind to twist just a fraction more to ensure her death. By the time anyone noticed she was unconscious on the floor, there would have been no saving her.

A grin pulls at the corner of my mouth as I picture the scene I wish I would have brought to life. Crimson blood pooled around her body, staining the floor. Our classmates standing by while she took her last breath.

But no, I held myself back.

A simple warning was enough for now.

Stay the fuck away from my friends.

If she wants to lurk near me, fine. Let her dance around the fire, hoping she won't get burned. I may not seem as ruthless as the most notable dark wielders in history, but why would I have been recruited for this assignment were I not at least comparable?

Let her fuck with me. All it takes is an "accidental" death due to our magic reacting and I can go about my business. No one will be the wiser to the intentionality behind it.

There's too much that still needs to be done to let her stand in the way. Too much at stake to let the Avalons and families like them continue to loom over the wielding world like gods.

They are not gods.

They are not above us or even smarter or more gifted.

They are not as special as they deem themselves. Soon they will find out. Soon, they will know that others lurk in the shadows, dismantling their stages piece by piece. And there is nothing they can do to stop it.

Part of me wonders if she will actually pose a threat. If her being here will do anything to keep our plans from moving forward. She doesn't seem to give a shit about me or whatever dark corners I prefer to linger in. Just the same, the daughter of the Director of Education can't be trusted. We can't trust any of the influential light-wielders. Their pedestals sit too high. The allegiances are too strong.

Anyone who aligns with the Council and the light order of things can't be trusted.

I sink into my seat. *Spellcasting: Tier Three.*

I hate this class. Have always hated spellcasting.

Learning combinations of words to recite in my mind, out loud, or over an array of dusty-ass objects doesn't interest me. Sure, my spelled daggers are what they are because of spellcasting, but it's the only set of spells I need to know.

A laugh puffs out of my chest. I don't even spell my daggers. Pierce does. The little fucker is a natural at it.

I prefer the gifts I excel at. The ones that bring about the demise of others. Where I can watch my victim lie there writhing in pain for minutes, hours, or days, knowing I can stop it. I could steal your last breath with a single twirl of my index finger, but I won't. I never do.

Death is a beautiful thing until you're hunted for being the one that caused it.

"Hey man, what's wrong with you?" The back of Pierce's hand slaps against my arm. His whisper is just loud enough that several of our classmates can hear it. Their brows quirk high, bodies angling just a little closer to hear what might have me feeling anything other than venomous murder. It's what they all think of me, so I let them.

I may not give a shit about this class, but Pierce does. He needs to excel in this course, with the field he is looking to immerse himself in. Once we finish school, anything less than top marks cost him the position of Potions Master.

Wielders like Pierce will go on and make great lives for themselves. Others like me will continue to serve those like the man I answer to now. Our version of making an impact on the world leading us down different paths. I won't settle for a cushy life over my values.

My worth as a wielder and follower of the cause is so much more important than a wad of cash in my pocket and a mansion with a sports car. I'm fully dedicated to bringing down our modern iteration of the world order.

Wielders may have many, many things that separate us from the human world, but the desire for fame, fortune, and expensive materialistic possessions is the same.

"Other than the usual shit bothering me?" I scoff, slouching down into my seat, legs spread wide.

"If you have something to share with the class ..." Professor Zoreidan quips as he looks down his nose at me before continuing in a deadpan, "please do." His beefy arm drifts out across the space, knocking into today's supplies on the table at the front of the room. The assistant hastily steadies several glass vials and flasks at once, her teeth digging into her bottom lip in concentration. The woman settles back onto her bench as the table's contents finally stop rattling. A deep breath released as she swipes her brow with her sleeve.

The man has to have an assistant come in and help him because he's too large to do the bending and organizing himself.

Professor Z sucks in several deep breaths before preparing to resume whatever bullshit he was rambling on about.

To call this man rotund would be an understatement. His short stature and wiry auburn mustache, offset by his graying tuft of hair at the center of his head, ruin any chance of him being a decent-looking man. I'm convinced, even in his younger years he was the same sloppy guy whose shirts pulled at the seams and whose pants bisected his midsection into two monster tires.

"Apologies, Professor."

He grunts my way before continuing his overview of what we are to do today.

A binding spell.

They come in many varieties. Lovers. Souls. Proximity. Minds. You name it, it's possible. Generally, they won't teach anything stronger than the simpler charms that cling to the limitation of physical distance.

Love can become a dangerous obsession.

Souls, a likely death.

The mind, a surefire way to lose your own.

Spellcasting can be messy, with too many possibilities of something going wrong. A responsibility I have no desire to make mine.

Proximity bonds are easier to break than the ones that take pieces of each party involved and weave them together with your essence. Incorporating your essence with another is more invasive than a blood transfusion. There must be compatibility, at least at the most basic levels, so your body doesn't rebel. It takes time to find that in another or to earn it.

The thought of using a mind-reading spell on Bryony brings a slight grin to my face. It would be the perfect way to keep tabs on her. Just in case my death threats and choke-outs weren't clear enough. I refuse to believe her presence here is mere coincidence.

I've pondered the reasons most nights, lying awake in bed, stroking my dick. The thought of actually hurting, preferably while fucking her, arouses me every time. The answers to the probing questions in my mind tortured out of her. I've considered her family, or the Council, planted her at Beauxgraton, knowing there were those here working to dethrone men like her father. That her "attraction" to Pierce was only a ruse to get close to us. All because the wrong someone knows. What better way to infiltrate a circle of traitors than sending a newly matured student to school with them? The forced proximity makes it entirely too easy.

The possibility taunts me so much that I know there's no way I can let her live. Visions of the many ways I can tear her apart make me come in violent spurts before I finally drift off to sleep at night. A habit since the Red Moon Ball. Fury raged inside me knowing she would fuck my best friend right in front of me. That deep-set anger fueling my bloodthirsty and lust-filled thoughts about her.

Fucking Knox ruined everything. The bitch would be dead if he had just showed up ten minutes later. By then I would have had her switching places with me, holding her against the enlarged dick of that ghoul. But no. Knox barged in the rule follower that he is. *Bastard.*

Most ghouls don't take well to light-wielders, even if it's just that they are coincidentally in proximity. Especially a vicious one like the Nigeros. The moment it felt her, sensed her essence, it would have rebelled. Mauling her until she bled out from countless wounds, no magical healer or human surgeon would have time to fix.

I'd finished my fuck, but I'd seen them, too. The length of his body pressed up against her in the woods just before he threw his shirt at her. I'd seen the rise and fall of their chests and the intent looks in their eyes. Palpable tension between them that should've been nothing more than the lust of the Red Moon. No doubt Knox had done his business well before we students got out there. He always does. That lust drew him to Bryony. It's the most logical explanation.

I kept her sweater. A keepsake should I ever need to use it against her. There are countless spells I could cast on it to make her do as I please or to harm her. That simple camel knit sweater could serve as my endless connection to her.

The flush of Pierce's cheeks and muss of his hair the night of the ball comes to mind. My boy faking as if he hadn't just been with that whore. I knew in a moment that he'd coated his dick in her sweet cum from that sure-to-be delicious pussy. I might want her dead, but I'd still fuck her. Drive my dick deep inside her as my daggers thrust into her flesh in unison.

I hadn't told him about my encounter with Bryony outside her room yesterday morning. Seems like she never told him, either. Had she, he would have been down my throat all, "Val, how could you?" *Boo-hoo.*

Maybe there was nothing to break up. Just two good-looking young people getting it in. That better be all it is. She's not a complication we need.

"Mr. Greer, your attention should be up here."

I groan, sinking lower in my seat, but will my eyes to stay trained on the table at the front of the room.

The assistant swirls ingredients together. Some solids, some liquids, and a few herbs, forming an enchanting and dangerously ominous mixture. Then, taking a length of rope, she binds two objects together. A bracelet and some small trinket. Items no one would look twice at.

"Ms. Dally, please exit the room," Professor Z instructs.

Savina Dally, the slut of the school, stands from her seat. Small hands smooth the skirt that barely covers her white thong as she makes her way toward the front of the room. The sharp, dirty blonde bob she dyes regularly shifts with her every step.

Suddenly she stops with a foot in mid-air as she fights to push forward. She releases a small grunt as she tucks her enhanced lips into her mouth, trying harder. If she wasn't on our side, I wouldn't waste another brain cell on her. That sweet smile and pink shit she accessorizes every outfit with is a front for the sinister demon that lies beneath.

"Ms. Dally, meet Mr. Brett. You two are now bound until we unbind you. No more than ten feet can exist between you two."

William Brett. One of the new light-wielding third years. He's a quiet one. Keeps to himself. I haven't seen him hanging with anyone else, but I also don't give a fuck. I have my shit to deal with and it doesn't involve knowing every fucking student that goes here. Especially those with light magic in their veins.

"Mr. Greer!"

An audible groan leaves me, again. "With all due respect, Professor, please pick on someone else. I swear you've said my name more than any other word today."

Snickers sound from around the room. Pierce's eyes narrow at me. Fucking goody two shoes.

As I said, he takes this shit seriously, and being friends with someone like me who doesn't care how their education goes, I'm making him look bad.

What seems like a lifetime later, the bells finally chime. Professor Z respected my wishes and ignored me for the remainder of the class. Pierce, Kaia, and several others willingly volunteered to demonstrate their ability to replicate the same spell. Pierce nailed it, showing off by binding five of us together at once. Kaia somehow worked her way around the spell, binding a classmate to the wall, laughter breaking out from everyone, but Professor Z. Others blundered the whole thing worse than a first-year would.

Pierce jogs to catch up to me, but I shove away from him, mumbling some bullshit about needing alone time. I have somewhere to be.

I'm quick to exit the main building, making my way to Buckingham Proper. The school renovated this building about a decade ago, unlike the residence. The auditorium is the first thing you see when you enter. Six sets of double doors always set wide open unless an actual assembly of some sort is taking place.

Stairways on either side of the entryway lead down to the sub-level. The walls lined with walnut strips of wood to match the main lobby and auditorium. This section also houses a state-of-the-art gym and soundproof rooms, which none of us know the purpose of. Rooms I slide past to shift open a secret doorway in the wall.

"You're late."

I slide the moving wall back into place. My handler waiting for me as I turn with a smirk on my face.

"Fuck off, Professor."

19

Bryony

I'd finally escaped Camilla again. A stream of nonstop chatter between her and Whitney drove me to the point of near insanity. I love them both, but I'm the type that can usually only take upbeat personalities in doses before my people battery completely dies. A curiosity those who knew me before coming to Beauxgraton would never understand, because I've always had to play that upbeat woman for the public.

I needed to get some history reading done, so I ran for the library without so much as a "see you later" as I slammed the door behind me.

It's almost as if what they teach here differs from the knowledge I consumed at home. Details and significant dates I never learned until I stepped through those Beauxgraton doors. Thirteen hundred pages of an alternate story to devour. Pieces that make me feel more like myself than I ever have.

My upbringing was a product of living in a light-wielding home. The nuances of the dark kept from me because I was never supposed to acknowledge that half. I was supposed to hide it. I still am.

I have no choice but to.

The loneliness of that reminder settles over me as I make my way to the main library. Alone.

No matter how often I walk these halls, they seem to change. A labyrinth meant to confuse. Endless paths that allow me to get lost in the portraits of significant figures in our history—both light and dark—line the walls. It leaves me wondering if the portraits of the light-wielders were always here. Captured in time and remembered for their contributions to our kind.

My fingers brush over a few of the frames, not a speck of dust transferring from them. The entire school is like that. Never a particle of dirt to be found. Likely some sort of cleaning charm to keep it that way with so many bodies moving about.

Many of the faces captured in these portraits are ones I only know from the books I've read. Fractions of their stories captured in ink on a few pages. Partial truths delivered by my parents and a society that continues to choose to overlook the parts they didn't want us to focus on.

It's not until I wind down another hallway of the same gray stones that my eyes find a face I haven't seen since I was a child.

My grandmother was an odd woman. A black sheep to the light-wielding community. A bright light to my younger years when she was still with us. So many had labeled her a kook. Her theories on ghouls rising to overrun our world, decidedly ignored. Brushed off as a side-effect of her mind fracturing, leaving her with nothing but nonsense to speak about.

Yet every time one broke into our world, our officials and ghoul hunters alike would come to her with questions. They would ask her what she knew and how she knew it. Her knowing smirk was always in place, anticipating those moments would continue to come, more and more frequently with time.

I don't recall much of this firsthand. The diary she left behind and Milgren, having been my grandmother's best friend their entire adult lives, have been my greatest sources of information when it came to her. Many of the stories she told me as a child were thought to be nothing more than fiction until I began to witness her predictions firsthand.

Only the night before her death did she reveal to me she was clairvoyant. That she had seen so much of what would become of our world. How much she feared for young wielders like me. I never found out if she meant Grisyms or just young wielders, but I guess in the grand scheme of things it doesn't matter for me. I fall into both buckets. My double-edged sword is destined to find its mark no matter what.

Grandma Avalon begged me to keep my eyes and ears open. To use my gifts to guide me. I never truly knew what she meant by that, but it sparked my curiosity.

I was eight when she passed. Her suicide remained a secret until I was an adult. The story my family chose to tell me was always that age took her. The woman was the clone of those crusty witches they always put in movies, with wrinkles and warts. Turns out Grandma Avalon had a potion made that would take her from this world to the next. Her body laid to rest alongside the other wielders who had left us.

She no longer wanted to be in a world where everyone thought of her as a raging lunatic. Where others couldn't appreciate her for what she was. *Brilliance.*

In the end, only Milgren and I were faithfully standing by her side.

My heart broke when I lost her, but I listened. I read every historical text I could. Wrapped myself up in Mom's work as time allowed. Listened to the words that passed Dad's lips. I fought hard to internalize it all. Even kept a diary with invisible ink so I could remember every bit of knowledge I'd pieced together.

Through it all, I'd found that she may have been right. Over the years, more and more ghouls have appeared outside of the Red Moon. They're deemed rogues. Those that either break through the gates that normally hold them or possess a difference within that allows them to pass through at will. Some do nothing more than seek the dark wielders around them. They fuck and move on.

Others wreak havoc. Destroying property and taking lives. Those are the ones ghoul hunters take down—all of them light-wielders. Dark wielders view the efficient killing of rogue ghouls by the light wielders as a form of gearing up for war. Drawing a more defined line in the sand between the two opposing sides.

I run my fingers over the painted, wrinkled hand of Davora Avalon, my grandmother—not by blood, but in every way that matters. A woman I miss dearly. One I wish I could see again and who could guide me through all this shit. I know she'd be able to tell me why I respond to Knox the way I do. She was the only one who ever had answers for me.

But she's not here; I'm on my own.

The library door swings open just as I approach, a small group of students filtering out. One of them holds the door for me to enter. Their eyes quickly averting when I flash a smile of gratitude. My internal groan wants to break free, knowing this is Milgren's fault, mostly. She first shined the light on me, but I lit the torch with the displays in class.

The first time I entered the main library, I was in awe. Where many of the worldly libraries I've seen present gilded ornate designs, this one is nothing but obsidian wood shelves. Metal reinforcements serve as the edges and hinges holding pieces of the ceiling together. Those same metal sculpted pieces are the infrastructure for each shelf. Every surface holds intricate designs, some I recognize as ancient, while others elude me completely.

Each one is a story to tell. My fingers are desperate to run over the grooves as if their stories will miraculously reveal themselves to me. Whispers of moments in time only these structures still know.

I sent photos of a few to my mother. Her nonchalant response was meant to paint them as insignificant. Until then, it never felt like she was truly hiding something from me. But I know my mother lied to me as my fingers trail over the cool wood-carved symbols that I can only hope to decipher someday. We all have our secrets, don't we?

Picking a table in the back corner, I spread out my notebooks, pens, and books. Unlike many in my age bracket, I don't prefer digital electronics while reading or studying. Old-school paper and pen do it best. And not the spelled ones that dance across the pages for you. Their function based on you reciting the words you want written. Not ideal for a near-silent library.

I'm chapters into the volume our professor asked us to work through by the end of the week, my eyes darting across the pages with fascination. My mind is so lost in the war that has been raging all these years, only the body dropping into the seat next to me pulls me out.

"Hey," a familiar male voice makes me stiffen.

The bass in Pierce's voice warms me in all the places he can't give attention to. Sure, we'd messed around in one library, but there are too many other students here for me to let him lay me out on the table right now.

My pulse races, imagining the dark wood digging into my back and ass as I let us take the plunge. Partially because I want to, but also as a big "fuck you" to Valen for thinking he can tell me what I can and can't do.

I'm not scared of Valen. Not really. He can go fuck himself. And he better damn sure hope I don't learn a death spell after he put his hands on me.

But I am still thinking of my dad. Of me. And now of Knox, too. I need to keep a low profile.

"Don't make waves or enemies, Bryony."

I need this to be an easy stop on my road to moving into whatever role my dad has conjured up for me.

"Are you avoiding me?" Pierce leans close, his breath brushing over the shell of my ear. I roll my neck and shoulders, but it does nothing to work the draw of his voice from my system. Instead, the knot in my lower belly tightens as it flares to life in his presence.

"You should ask Valen." I hadn't meant to say the words out loud. Hadn't meant to cause a rift. Hell, I have no idea if Valen told Pierce what happened.

"I'm asking you." His fingers lightly cup my chin as he forces my gaze to meet his. "I thought—You know, the other night was ... nice."

I release a sigh, dropping my head so my chin leaves his fingers. "Pierson, just go hang out with your buddy. I have studying to do."

"Only if you answer me." His voice is soft. There's no demanding tone or expectation. Just a genuine want to understand what went wrong between the two of us.

Another sigh escapes me as I slam down my pen. Each student in the room whips their head to see what's going on before I throw them an apologetic glance, their focus quickly returning to their tasks.

"Yes, I am avoiding you." I take a deep breath, attempting to calm the building rage. "Because if your asshole of a best friend comes for me again—" I clear my throat, "puts his hands on me again, I can't be held responsible for what I'll do."

Pierce leans back in his chair as if I slapped him. His hand cups his mouth and then pulls straight down as he stares at me in disbelief. A slight shake of his head, like the movement will reverse the truth.

"That's not funny, Bri."

I throw my hands up in surrender before slapping them against my thighs. Shaking my head in exasperation, I'm quick to shove my things into my pack. Of course, he would think I'm just some girl who would make up stories about his best friend acting violently toward me. That's what women do, right?

"Bri." His hand lightly rests on my thigh, freezing my movements.

"Pierson, I'm not joking. Go ask your *best friend,*" the title spewed like a curse.

Truthfully, I hate Valen right now. More than I've ever hated anyone, simply for making me emotional. For drawing a reaction out of me at all. One I can't afford. Lately, my essence seems more determined to respond to extreme emotions, and that leaves me entirely too vulnerable in front of these people.

Pierce allows me to finish packing my things, waits for me to stand, and then grabs my wrist before pulling me behind him.

He drags us through the hallways of history, and down others draped in colorful tapestries—the most color this place has. Depictions of everything from mythology to nature to war blur together with our quick pace.

Suddenly, we stop at a solid wall. His muscles bulge as he pushes, causing the door to release as it slides open.

Does this man know every secret passage in this place?

He yanks at my wrist again, pulling me down the stairs at a quick enough pace that I worry I'll trip and fall to my death. Just a single catch of the toe of my boot and we're both going down. I have no idea why we're headed down here until a chamber opens up before us, large boulders strategically placed throughout. The stone walls give the impression of time passed in a way those upstairs do not. It's as if these hidden passageways didn't receive the same manner of care as the rest of the building.

Pierce's friends come into view. The twins first to notice me.

"Oh. Fuck!" Kormoran groans, rubbing his hands together with a wicked chuckle.

Two other guys pretend as if they didn't just hear us bolting down the stairs. And Valen stands dead center. His expression is blank as his gaze drifts down to where Pierce still has his fingers wrapped around my wrist. A deep frown pulls at the corners of his mouth, that calm demeanor shattered in mere seconds.

He storms forward, his fists tangling in Pierce's shirt. "Why the fuck did you bring that bitch here?"

20

PIERSON

I WASN'T SURE WHAT I was going to say when I confronted Valen. I only knew that my anger raged deep in the pit of my stomach, rising as billowing flames the closer we got to the Vault. The exact spot I knew I'd find him. Mostly because I was supposed to be there, too. But I'd gone to see Bri first, hoping to understand what went wrong between us. If only so I could make it through another one of our group meetings without thinking about her non-stop.

Only our inner circle meets in the Vault regularly. Everyone else we need to communicate with as part of our assignment, we either reach through voice calls or spelled communication channels. Operations are cleaner that way.

Honestly, I would be perfectly fine being left out of all of this. I don't let our purpose or dedication to the cause rule my life. For Valen, it's in every breath he takes. For me, it's nothing more than supporting my best friend in something he is passionate about. But at this moment, with my anger flaring, I am on the brink of walking away from it all.

Rarely do I let negative emotions take hold of me. An optimistic disposition serves me best. Not to mention when my emotions turn negative, mixing with the dark power that lives in my veins, my gifts tend to break loose if I am holding any borrowed magic. It's the number one reason anything I acquire from the earth, ghouls, or objects, gets used almost immediately or stored. I've never been able to control myself when the dark creeps in.

Today, I let it fuel me, small tendrils of essence poking to get free. Those tiny bits of magic wanting to choke the life out of him alongside my bare hands.

I've always known what type of person Valen was.

A bastard.

Cold.

Calculating.

He was a cool kid in school. A bully to some, a hero to others. To me, he'd always just been the best friend I've ever had. My privilege was always getting to see the few redeeming qualities he possesses.

Fierce loyalty.

Commitment.

Dedication.

He's always just been the guy who saw me and knew my secrets, but this was different. It doesn't matter that I'm borderline obsessed with Bri. It doesn't matter who her father is. There is no excuse for putting your hands on a woman, especially when that woman is someone I'm interested in.

I shove him off of me. First breaking his hold on me, and then again in the chest. I've never hit another person, not once in my life. But it feels good to push him this time. To stand up to him for once. To bash him for his poor behavior.

"Why the fuck would you think it's okay to hit her?" Sean and Damian straighten, their gazes finding us as I yell in Valen's face.

He only laughs, his appearance mimicking a Cheshire cat. The twins lean back in their matching stone thrones to watch the action play out with mischievous grins. They're even worse than he is.

"I didn't hit her," he snickers.

I take a step back, my chest rapidly pumping up and down. "She said—"

"I never said he hit me," Bri chimes in, making me spin to face her.

Have I just made a huge mistake?

I take two steps back, my hands running through my hair. The movement of my Adam's apple bobbing distracting me as I attempt to make sense of where I misinterpreted what she told me less than twenty minutes ago.

Her voice breaks me from my inner turmoil as she all but shouts, "This fucker had the balls to wrap his hand around my throat, then shove me to the ground!"

She takes a menacing step toward Valen. Only now am I noticing the discoloration on her neck. It's harder to see with her warm brown skin. But now that I have, there's no unseeing it. No mistaking the near-complete outline of his long fingers.

"Care to tell your *bestie* what you told me?" she scornfully mocks.

He sneers down at her face, his height forcing her to crane her neck back.

"Stay. The fuck. Away. From. Pierce." His finger pokes at the center of her forehead, punctuating each sentence as he forces her head further back. "Is your skull too thick to understand?"

I charge at him, spearing him to the ground. My fist colliding with his cheek with a sickening thud. A sinister laugh rolls through him as he does nothing to fight his way from beneath me. My considerably larger frame easily pinning Valen's to the floor. A first at having an upper hand in our friendship.

"I've never regretted being your friend," I yell. "Never not wanted to stand by your side until now. You don't speak to, look at, or touch my girlfriend. Understand?"

The room grows loud with everyone's gasps and then completely quiet while we all await Valen's response. Kaia is the only one wearing a smirk. She thrives on drama and the discomfort of others. Her eyes glisten while she waits for the bloodshed that she's sure will come.

I swallow, staring down at my best friend. Waiting.

I want to know if I just ended twenty-eight years of friendship for a woman who might not even want me. Even if she doesn't, I should have called Valen out for his behavior a long time ago. Only loyalty kept my mouth shut.

He raises his palms, his usual grin fading. There's no doubt he is still mocking us. Something in his stare confirming he doesn't take my threat seriously. Why would he? It's always been "Yeah. Okay, Pierce," with an eye roll. Why would my show of anger tonight make that any different?

"Fine. Guess if she's going to be around, we should teach her the rules."

Kaia shoots up from her seat. That glint is gone, replaced with the purest hatred I've ever seen. "Fuck. This."

I take that as an opportunity to flee, too. Grabbing Bri by the hand, we exit the same way we came, but now I'm leading her straight to my room. The best place for us to be alone right now, knowing Valen won't come around for hours.

Several students stop to talk to her as she jogs behind me through the halls. Her awkward waves and shouts of, "Talk to you later, bye!" are not enough to make me slow my pace. A pace I'm reluctant to break for fear that she might run away from me after my declaration if I let her go.

The moment my bedroom door slams behind us, I finally breathe. Bri wastes no time sitting on the edge of the bed. Her gaze focuses on me, and I know she's waiting for me to lose it, or confess, or I don't know what else. Her hands fold in her lap as she patiently gives me a minute to gather myself. On a deep breath, I sink onto the mattress next to her. Our bodies are situated close enough my knee knocks against hers as my legs fall open. My gaze casually scanning the room, hoping I hadn't left anything embarrassing lying around.

"I'm sorry—" my words cut short as her mouth slams into mine.

I'm thrown from my moment of astonishment as her lips move with a fierce hunger. Her fingers press into the nape of my neck as mine find their way into the large bun at the crown of her head. Our chests pressed together as we fight to get that much closer.

She inhales deeply, breathing me in. The tips of her fingers digging into my skin with a ferocity that will leave me with matching fingerprints for the ones that mar her throat. The same connection we found nights ago is still there. Just as suddenly as she came to me, she pulls away, inching just far enough that we no longer touch at all.

"I-uh-sorry," she stutters. "I was just surprised you defended me. I thought for sure I was nothing more than a hook-up to you. You know, that it was the residual effects of the Red Moon that night."

Her shrug does something to my heart. The heel of my hand wants to rub it away, but I don't. I keep them on the bed on either side of my legs. Usually, Bri seems so sure of herself. But mentioning post-ghoul lust, she fumbles and blanches. It's the most adorable thing I've ever seen.

I can't help but let out a laugh. These light wielders know nothing of our traditions. It's partially their fault for not caring to learn, and partially ours for keeping the sacred information to ourselves. Fragments of truth we hold to sustain just a fraction of power over our light counterparts. Control, I believe, has hindered us from better understanding and cooperation.

"The whole turned-on-out-of-control thing only applies during the Red Moon Festival, in the pits, with the ghouls. Within a few hours, you're back to normal. Sometimes the effects last longer, but that's usually those who have only done a few festivals."

Her eyes go wide. My body stiffening for several long seconds. Those deep gray and green beauties pull me into her. Our mouths meet again in a clash of teeth. This kiss, shorter than the last.

"I took you into that library because I wanted to be in there with you. Just like I want to be in here with you now." I link our fingers together, my forehead pressing into hers. "I didn't do what I wanted to that night, but I will now." My throat clears. "If you'll let me."

Heat blossoms behind her eyes. Her complexion betraying her blush rather than hiding it. A slight squeeze of her fingers against mine, the response I was hoping for.

It's as if time stops, the both of us breathing each other in before moving together. Our clothes haphazardly torn from our bodies as our tongues fight for dominance. Sharp inhales of breath mixed with her giggles and my groans. Each one makes my dick painfully harder, an ache that I can only relieve once I'm inside her.

A shiver runs down my spine the moment her bare palms meet my chest. My body refuses to participate in proper respiration as I sink into her touch. That night, I abstained from removing a single article of my clothing. It was all about her. The majority of my skin was a virgin to the feel of hers until now. A tingle of starlight runs just beneath the surface in response to her. A feeling I won't soon forget.

It's just the anticipation. It must be.

"Don't get cold feet on me now," she chuckles.

Yanking her to me, her core across my lap, with nothing more than her sheer panties and my boxers keeping us apart, I lower her to her back. My flat palm never leaves the center of her spine. Only the roll of her pelvis against mine forces me to switch to holding her at her hip. If I don't keep her still, I won't make it inside her before I come.

My essence courses through me, barreling into the wall of my skin, fighting to break free. The power I channeled earlier for classes is still alive inside me. Eager to mix with hers. But I hold it back. It's not common for lights and darks to come together, and frankly, I don't know what would happen if our essences decided to mingle.

My mouth lowers to her ear. The curve of my lip brushing over the shell before the tip of my tongue runs along the space where her jaw meets her neck.

"Never," my breath fanning over her skin, her body shivering in response.

That single word throws us back into action. She shoves my boxers down, leaving me naked before her. My throbbing erection bobs out in front of us before her fingers curl around it in a soft pump, eyes never leaving mine.

I've had sex with a handful of women. It's always been fun. I've fucked even more ghouls, and that requires no finesse. You get in, do what needs to be done, and get out.

I don't want to do that here.

Her fingers knead at my ass cheeks as I let my hips grind into her while I suck at her skin.

"Are you—"

"Yeah," she breathes. Where humans like to rely on birth control pills, implants, and devices or condoms, wielders usually just spell themselves to protect against pregnancy.

I slip two fingers under the band of her underwear that runs along her hip before I rip them from her body. The tearing of fabric turning her puffy lips into an exaggerated O.

A little more caveman than is typical, but my body refuses to break contact with her. The thought of me slowing for even a moment is one I can't allow. I fear if I do, the magic brewing between us might end.

I. Need. Her.

She's slick and hot between her legs. Every bit of her heavily coating my skin. I pant, wanting nothing more than to drive straight into her, but I have no idea what her sexual history has been. More importantly, I have no idea what type of sex she likes.

Fuck!

Will she want it rough? Does she want a slower pace or just a good lay?

I would never forgive myself if I didn't take care of her properly. If I didn't worship this woman, I can't imagine letting go of. There's that mischievous glint in her eye that's always there. Maybe she has kinks only someone like Valen or Kormoran could satisfy.

"You're thinking too much." Her hands find my cheeks, tilting my face so our eyes meet. "I want you inside me. Now." Her grin quirks high. "Please."

She's quick to grab hold of my length again. Her thick thighs are like a warm blanket around me.

Her free hand tightens on my back as she guides me inside her.

A ragged exhale loosed across her face as I sink into her for the first time. So tight it's hard to move. So wet and hot that it reminds me of an island paradise. Absolute bliss soaring through me as I dive deeper.

And damn, does she feel like heaven. If there was one, this would be it.

I've barely touched her, but I'm addicted to every part. Where most women sculpt their bodies to perfection, she has allowed hers to remain natural. No spells to hide the cellulite or magical tummy tucks to remove the paunch at the bottom of her belly.

I'd never admitted it before, but this is the type of woman I prefer. One that will fill my palms and curl into me with her soft body.

Her warmth holds me tight as I dip in and out of her. Her strong hips meeting me thrust for thrust. Short nails dig into my flesh as she goads me into going harder. Faster. Deeper.

Her moans and string of expletives drown out my grunts of pleasure.

My focus repeatedly drawn to the spot where we're joined. I watch my thick cock disappear into her, focusing on the flesh of her core as it gladly swallows me whole. Her walls squeezing me tighter with each retreat. Each pulse a tighter clamp to keep me in place.

"Bri, you're perfect."

"I know," she moans, suddenly throwing us into a sitting position.

She shoves me back, maneuvering me so I'm sitting on the side of the bed, her sinking directly onto my rock-hard dick, her back to my front. My hands want to be everywhere. Her soft stomach. Those luscious thighs spread atop mine. Her wet core spread wide for me. The curve of her ass covering my lap.

I will know every single piece of her, inside and out.

My thumb finds her clit, massaging tight circles. Her fingers snaking into the damp hair at the nape of my neck and holding tight. Soft, loose curls tickling my shoulder as her head flies back into the hard muscle and bone. The blink of pain is no comparison to the pleasure of her pussy squeezing around me. My release closing in. So close. Too close.

My name is a plea on her lips at the same moment my bedroom door swings open.

Motherfucker.

21

Bryony

"Get out," I groan, not pausing as my naked body bounces in Pierce's lap. His one hand is still working my clit, hard. The other grips my hip as if to keep me from flying away.

Most men I've been with don't know what to do when handling a woman my size. To a runway model, I'm as big as a house. Compared to the average size for a woman my age, I borderline on "normal." I have no shame that I haven't seen jeans sized smaller than a twelve since I was in high school.

Mom has done everything she could over the years to shrink me into the same size four she and my sister wear, but I've never been anything smaller than a ten and I like it that way. Along with being a Grisym, it's the one dead giveaway that I don't come from the same pairing as my siblings. Our genetic outputs simply do not match.

"You wasted no time," Damian scoffs as he leans against the doorframe. The toe of his sneaker digging into the floor as if he has all the time in the world, arms folded across his thick barreled chest. Either annoyance or humor shines behind his eyes.

Just the same, my orgasm builds deep in my belly. Pierce takes over, repeatedly slamming me down onto his shaft. My mouth falls wide open in a well-shaped O as my fingers dig into his thighs. The sweat lining my palms and his skin keeping my grip from staying put.

"At least close the damn door," Pierce grunts. Several more jerks before he drives into me one last time. His hot release fills my insides, invading me the same way his presence has already slithered its way under my skin.

All it takes is Damian biting his lip as he watches for me to fall over the edge.

I'm by no means an exhibitionist, but fuck.

Sex with Pierce was much better than I thought it would be, and Damian *is* hot. His large charcoal-gray eyes watching us come undone an expected turn-on. Yet, there's no lust behind them. Only that same amusement as if entertained by a child's antics.

He has the decency to turn his back to us as Pierce lifts me off his lap, disappearing into the adjoining bathroom the third years get. Quick to return just moments later with a damp towel in hand. Slow methodical strokes wipe me clean before we both dress. Soft kisses brushing across my cheek and neck several times in the five minutes it takes to slip back into our clothing.

"Is there a reason you couldn't have waited?" Pierce groans.

"Valen needs to see us." Damian uncrosses his arms, hands slipping into the pockets of his sweatshirt. "Now," he adds as his eyes trail down my body, a smirk pulling at the corner of his mouth.

"Not happening," I scoff.

"Not interested," he retorts.

Oddly enough, it doesn't sting like I thought it might. I've not done well taking any sort of rejection since my ex shattered my heart and stomped on it. I seem to be drawn to this group of dark wielders, so you would expect their rejections to burn, right?

At least that's how I convinced myself I would feel until now. It's clear I don't give a fuck about any of them except Pierce.

"He's really not," Pierce snorts from behind me, his front pressed into my back, placing a chaste kiss on my cheek. "Damian has been married since he was eighteen. Believe it or not, arranged marriages still happen and they work."

My eyes go wide, taking him in. I would have never suspected, but I'm not sure that makes me feel any better about him just watching Pierce and me have sex. Still, my eyes search for the band that should be around his ring finger, his hand freeing from his pocket as if he knows I need to see it. A thick black ring right there in confirmation.

"Tosch would like you," he chuckles, his hand sinking back into the hoodie pocket.

"I'm going to go." The strap of my bag dangles as I snatch it from the floor.

"No, you're not." Damian blocks the doorway. His legs remain wide, with those massive arms crossed over his chest. "You're with Pierce, so now you're with all of us."

"Yeah, well, we haven't had this whole *couples* conversation. So, no, I'm not."

I dip under his arm, shooting an apologetic look at Pierce. I hope he didn't take that the wrong way. It has nothing to do with him and everything to do with protecting me.

We've only been at school for three weeks. It's a little early to dive headfirst into devoted relationships. A fuck buddy, though, I can handle. But if Pierce keeps excelling at getting close to me, making my heart skip beats, I'm in danger of revealing parts of me he isn't supposed to know. The parts that will make him look at me differently. Maybe even turn his back on me.

As selfishly as I want to hang onto that doting glint in his eyes, I want someone who knows all of me. That loves me anyway and continues to look at me that way. Until then, it's only a partial truth. Whether it be intentional or not.

The halls are full of students as I make my way from the boys' wing to the opposite end of the Beauxgraton residence. I need to get to my room, take a shower, and wallow a bit.

Fortunately, Camilla is nowhere to be found as I dart into our room. She'll be able to sense that my emotions and thoughts are all over the place, pummeling me with questions. I'm quick to shower, relieved to find she still hasn't returned when I shuffle back from the common bathroom. The peace is a welcome reprieve as I lie on top of my comforter draped in nothing but my robe as my expensive hair oil revives my wind-blown strands under my microfiber hair towel.

Hours pass and I don't move. My skin is long since dry. Pierce's scent gone after scrubbing my body with the rose shower gel I've used since my teenage years. Not so much to get rid of him, but the feelings that he left behind. An attempt at erasing the way my body tingles just thinking of him. Or the warmth growing in my chest, encasing my heart as memories of things he's done or said flit through my mind. I can't afford to fall for anyone.

Not now.

Maybe not ever.

Camilla makes her grand entrance just as I'm securing the second French braid with a miniature rubber band. Her arms fly wildly as she recounts some story I missed. She never even makes eye contact or checks my side to know I'm there or listening. It's as if she simply knows.

It's not until she turns to face me, her version of a stern expression in place that I'm sure she does. The look she throws me a reminder of my nieces and nephews when they try to get the upper hand.

"Where were you missy?" Those same tiny fists push against her narrow hips. Her black school uniform dress washing out her pale features and hair. The girl looks like a damn ghost trying to give me the evil eye. My chest and stomach muscles clench as I fight to hide my laughter. The back of my hand discretely covering my mouth as I regain my composure.

"I, uh, went to the library."

Maybe if I stick to that part she'll let it go.

Lying back on my pillows, I release a yelp as her little bottom bounces onto my bed.

"The library doesn't make your face look lit up like a jack-o'-lantern candle on Halloween night."

I laugh at her phrasing. Especially knowing I was right about her from the beginning. Where the rest of us have no issues with crude language, Camilla weaves together weird sayings like this to convey what she's thinking. It's ridiculous mixed with her high-pitched accent. That twang is not getting any less pronounced the longer she's here.

With a sigh, I throw my arms over my face, blocking out the light. Blocking her out, too. Hopefully hiding what I don't want her to know.

"Missy, you will tell me all your dirty secrets or by the power in me I will force it out of you with that vile-tasting truth serum Whitney made us drink last week." I shoot her a wry look. My shoulders tense remembering that concoction. The iridescent copper fluid was as unappealing in scent as it was in taste. But damn could that girl kick up a serum.

I'm more terrified of that than Camilla doing me any real harm. My right ass cheek weighs more than she does.

"Well, you know how I kissed Pierce at the Red Moon Ball?" Not even sure why I posed that as a question. This woman knows my love life better than I do. There's no way she would have forgotten me giving her that shiny gold nugget.

She nods, inching closer. Her eyes are wide, lips tucked into her mouth as if trying to hide a smile. Giddy anticipation radiating off her in intense waves.

"Well, he found me in the library, and uh ... then we went back to his room."

"You two-bit floozy. You did the horizontal tango, didn't you?"

"The what? Really? What decade are you from?" Laughter bubbles freely from me. Camilla's personality is always pulling it loose. She's weird and quirky and everything I could need and want in a girlfriend. And I didn't even know it until now.

She waves off my insult, eyes focused on my face.

"Yes, we, uh, had sex."

"Oh, no." Her fingertips lightly touch her mouth. "Oh, no, no, no."

"What?" I question, worried maybe Pierce has a wife too, and I didn't know about it.

"Did he make you ..." she leans closer, wide eyes darting around the room as if expecting someone to jump out of hiding. Her final word barely above a whisper, "Scream?"

We fall into laughter together. My stomach muscles burn from the violence and duration of it. Tears free-falling down my cheeks.

"Not exactly. Damian barged in and, uh, interrupted."

"Dear gods. You *are* a two-bit floozy."

I swat at her arm ignoring the jab.

I'm not. Never have been. I've only ever slept with men I've been in a serious relationship with. Each broke my heart worse than the last.

One only wanted me to be connected to my parents. Another because I was a bet. A third because I would never praise and bow down to him the way he wanted a woman to, so he found someone who would. A woman who had been a friend of my family my entire life.

Another settled for a woman several years younger and thinner than me. My weight a never-ending issue for the year we lasted. The awful split with my ex nearly broke me. It was endless months of nurturing the wounds he left me with. Deep wounds that still burst open or seep from time to time. The memory that I didn't mean to him what he meant to me, the reason I don't believe the sex I just had with Pierce means much either.

"It wasn't like that. Their little group apparently had something urgent, and they had to run to Valen." My eyes roll as I pick at a small fray at the corner of my robe.

Camilla backs away from me. As if scared of my reaction. "What is your thang with him?" Her hands waving through the air as if conducting an orchestra.

I have many "things" with Valen.

Ones where I am attracted to him.

Ones where I'd imagined fucking that ghoul alongside him.

Others, where I wrap my fingers around his throat. Then I squeeze devilishly tight, his eyes bulging the way mine had.

More, where I envision him falling off a cliff or being hit by a bus or my essence tearing him to shreds.

Just normal thoughts.

"He can drop dead," I finally say shifting before scooting off the bed. "What movie are we watching tonight?"

She doesn't press any further.

A small mercy.

Camilla had asked for all my secrets, but like everyone else, she can only see what I allow her to.

It's safer for all of us that way.

22

BRYONY

IT'S BEEN A HELLISH week of classes. Only a month in and every professor has decided that they need to test us repeatedly. The practical exams made my palms clammy, and my heart rate so elevated I'm not sure how I haven't dropped dead yet.

"Preparation for the real world," they all said.

"Ensuring you don't embarrass us," others added.

I'm grateful it's Friday, but not for what the weekend brings.

My father and eldest brother, Harley, will be visiting. Important matters needing discussion with Headmistress Milgren, supposedly. In reality, I'm sure it will be more of her relaying a report on everything that has happened with me here thus far. That woman has been faithful to our family longer than I've been alive. No doubt she won't leave a single detail out. I'm fucked.

Harley will grill me on whether my being here has been of any use to Father's initiatives or the family. That look of disgust making me feel worthless the way it always has.

Part of me hates that my father asked me to befriend the other influential wielders attending here. Anything to try to gain additional information on what the intent is behind the school closures. The best and the brightest from wielding families around the world come here. The thought has always been they must have overheard something. That they must know something worthy of relaying back to Dad.

My dad isn't a selfish man, but I have no doubt this is not about protecting light wielders, but rather his position in the wielding hierarchy. I have no idea what he will do with the information if I do find any. Possibilities I try not to ponder because I'm not sure I want to know the answers.

It breaks my heart to think so negatively about my dad, but I can't help it. None of us are perfect. We all have something more important than anything else that we would burn the world and everyone in it to protect. For him, I have no doubt it's his position as director.

I had to make the precious hours before their arrival count. Their estimated grand entrance—which will only elevate my pariah status—should be just before dinner. Perfect timing for everyone in the entire school to be available to witness the Director of Education waltz in here with his prized son, a legend destined to follow in his footsteps of greatness someday.

Not only was I not looking forward to this at all, but I also wanted a few minutes of alone time with Pierce. Allowing myself to disappear into his warmth and kindness, just like I said I wouldn't. But also there's no way we're doing a meet-the-parents this weekend. Not a chance in hell!

Since the first day we had sex, it's become a daily routine. The two of us christening many of the hidden rooms here at Beauxgraton. A giggle escaping me every time he drags me into a new one. One of us reciting the history that comes along with our new locale in old, English accents as if that will bring the richness of what surrounds us to life. History, that is still mostly new to me. Fresh information I cling to as if releasing it will mean denying my dark side all over again.

Just as I didn't want to happen, I've allowed tiny pieces of myself to slip. I've allowed Pierce to sink under my skin. Fortunately, when we'd had the conversation about titles, he understood but assured me that it didn't mean he was giving up.

"If it's the last thing I do, you'll be mine, Bryony Avalon."

I believed him when he said it. My dreams were filled with those words, delivered in that sexy voice of his. Every part of me wishes that they could become my reality, but as long as our world remains the way it is, I have no chance at a happily ever after. No chance at a genuine relationship—ever.

It doesn't stop me from hoping there comes a day when I can give that part of myself to someone. Give all of me, without shame or fear. I hope for a day when those like me can once again live in peace—if they ever truly did.

A dumb grin spreads across my face as I close his door behind me, headed toward the main staircase. My fingers tug at my bottom lip, remembering the way it felt for Pierce's teeth to sink into it just as his dick entered me. Each time we're together is better than the last. The two of us learning just what makes the other scream loudest. The small shifts of motion that leave us writhing in pleasure. Riding the highs of our orgasms, wanting to never come down.

Pierce and I finished up with perfect timing. I'd been slipping into my army green bomber jacket just as Dad's text came through.

Dad: ***We just pulled onto the private drive.***
Dad: ***I can't wait to see you.***

I'd giggled through Pierce's kisses as he tried to keep me there longer while typing a message back to my dad. For once my smile was uninhibited with him. Still, I worked to stomp down the happiness he filled me with. I can't get attached.

My text back instructed them to meet me at the gate. Not sure why. It's not like meeting them at the threshold that would allow them to cross into this safe haven I've been living in would keep them from knowing I've felt a bit more myself here. Dad will know. He will see it in my eyes and hear it in my voice. He always seems to know when I'm more at ease.

I'd spent years asking my family to allow me to embrace my dark side—in private, even just a little. Each attempt shot down as forcefully as the last. Being here I don't always have to do that. I get to learn and participate in the things that comprise the other half of me. And it feels damn good. I won't apologize for it. I can only hope Dad will understand.

As I make my way to the front of the residence, a familiar voice stops me. "Uh, what are you doing in the men's wing?"

Graham appears right in front of me. The crooked boyish grin he often wears is nowhere in sight. Bright eyes sparkle against the chandeliers above. The green overshadowing the blue to complement the olive sweater he wears. Cashmere, no doubt.

"I was ... I was with Pierce."

"Oh, yeah. I heard about that. Greer is throwing a hissy fit about you dating his best friend."

I shove past Graham. This bullshit needs to stop. "Not his girlfriend."

"You're not?" his voice rises several octaves in question. His eyes going wide, then quickly closing before reopening in an effort to appear normal. But I'd seen the reaction. A response far too exaggerated to be nothing.

"No. Why do you care?"

"I-I don't care. I just don't think you should get wrapped up with guys like that." He takes a step toward me, a hand lightly placed on my shoulder. "You're better than the company he keeps." His hand drops, sinking into the pocket of his slacks as he clears his throat. His tone shifting from concern to something more authoritative. "You deserve better than that Bri. Better than someone like Pierson."

"Oh please. I don't need that kind of protective-friend talk from you."

"I'm serious, Bri." He grabs my arm spinning me back to face him. My body nearly tumbling down the stairs before he catches me around my waist. Our bodies press together. Much like the night of our kiss by the lake. The both of us awkwardly clearing our throats with averted gazes.

He releases me the moment he thinks I'm steady, his palms rubbing down the front of his designer pants. I don't know who told the man to dress up every second of every day, but it's unusual. We barely got him to leave his room in sweatpants just to come to mine for our movie nights.

There's something so uptight about how he presents himself through his wardrobe. So pretentious of a vibe that it makes me cringe, but if anyone can pull it off, it's Graham. And he does it well.

"What?" I bark, hands slapping my thighs. "What is so bad about Pierce?"

"It's all of them. I've ... heard things." He falls into step beside me. "They are working on something. Something dark."

Well, so am I, kinda.

I want to scream. Throw a fit at his insinuation that the dark is less desirable. Instead, I will myself to play it cool. "Well, they are dark wielders, so I think that's implied."

"That Sean guy killed two students last year. Is that who you want to be around?" His revelation makes me inwardly pause. My pulse kicking a little faster. I hadn't known that.

"Graham. Listen to me. I love our friendship. I appreciate what you're trying to do. But my relationship, or lack thereof, with Pierce has nothing to do with you. Butt out. Okay?"

He raises his hands, backing up the stairs, sadness filling his gaze. I want to feel bad for pushing him away, but I need everyone to stay out of my business, especially this weekend with my dad and brother here.

He'll be fine.

He just needs to learn some boundaries when it comes to me.

Yet, I can't stop myself from looking back just once as I make my way around the bend of the staircase. His form stock still as he watches me descend, hands in the pockets of his slacks again. The droop of his brow says everything he didn't verbalize. But now isn't the time to sort through our disagreement.

The main staircase, a crossing of four wider ones, with bends and several platforms, sits toward the front of the residence. Its positioning intended so it's always the center of what you see. The four branches line up neatly as you reach the foyer at the bottom. Looking up at the eclectic design there's a certain beauty to it. Yet, all the same, it is completely unnecessary, as all four individual sets take you to the same level—the fourth floor—spitting you out at four different spots along the terrace.

By the time I reach the first set of wrought iron gates, all the calm I'd felt is gone. With sweaty palms, I touch the invisible barrier. A tiny zing pricks me as the ward recognizes my essence's signature. Instantly, the twelve-foot gates swing open. Loud screeching creaks as the heavy metal rotates on its hinges. My shoulders scrunching around my ears at the unappealing sound.

The tension I'm holding only falls away as I catch the first glimpse of Dad's car. Spotless black paint shimmers against the rolling clouds above. I can only imagine Harley's mood will match the angry sky, but it does nothing to dull the excitement of hugging my dad. I can at least have that little moment before we're gawked at like rare pieces of art.

The car was necessary, as neither of them can teleport. A gift of mine Merrick once told me he envies. One I must have gotten from my mother since she's a transporter. Merrick insisted that since I am a mix, Mom's transportation gift morphed into what I can do.

Where I can teleport—take my body, and sometimes another, through space and time to a new location—my mother is a transporter. She can do the same, but not with her body. Only with objects. Most transporters can only move things through the current space they inhabit, but my mother is a powerful one. She can move an item through place and time with little thought behind it.

I step aside as the first set of gates swings open, the second still bobbing against the vicious wind we've had this week. Fall in the mountains quickly turns into winter. The transition so abrupt it's easy to be unprepared.

Dad immediately waves as he drives through. Harley not so much as bothering to glance my way. I try not to let it bother me, but it still stings. Every. Time.

We've never been close. He's one to play by the rules and I am against the most important one of our kind. Grisyms can't exist.

Yet, he's had to watch me grow up under the same roof for the past twenty-five years. Has had to keep his mouth shut, while likely all he wants to do is turn me in to the authorities. The Council sets our policies, but the Wielding Bureau enforces them—for light and dark wielders alike.

When we were younger, I would follow Harley around like a miniature shadow. I mimicked what he did and how he did it because all I wanted was for my brother to like me. To love me. Little did my fragile child's heart know, he never would. He never has. From the moment Mom held me in her arms and Dad smiled down at me, Harley hated me. For the rest of my family, it was easy for them to shower me with love and acceptance, despite knowing Roman wasn't my biological father.

It was my mother who held me one night, at twelve, and told me it was no use trying with Harley.

"Be yourself. You're not like him. You're special."

That was the moment I stopped idolizing him. He'd always been second to Grandma Avalon, but with her gone, he was the figure I always tried to emulate.

I walk along the car, as they pull off to the side. A barren dirt patch sits just under a copse of trees, their leaves hues of vibrant orange and apple yellow. There's nowhere to park cars here, so this is as good as it gets. The school prohibits students and teachers alike from having vehicles, and only a few select faculty members have their own off-campus. Even those are not permitted to be brought onto campus unless there is an emergency mandated by the headmistress, assistant headmaster, or Director of Education. Even the Council doesn't have permission to grant unauthorized vehicles on campus. It's odd, but a common rule across institutions.

With my father serving as the current director I wonder if he even needed to request permission at all. An answer I may never know because I simply refuse to ask.

Truthfully, cars are not necessary when everything we need either gets delivered via the internal spelled delivery system or we can create it ourselves.

"Hey, Dad." My arms wrap around his neck as he pulls me close. My brother stands off to the side, hands in the pockets of his ankle-length trench coat. The guy is so damn dramatic.

A ring glistens on his finger as he sniffs, running his hand across his pronounced nose. I knew he was engaged thanks to Merrick, but had no idea he'd gotten married. He didn't even tell me. Didn't even want me to know or be a part of it. Neither of my siblings nor Mom and Dad mentioned the wedding either.

The sting that lances my chest affects me more than I would like it to. I want to hate him and pound my fists into his flesh. Allow my essence to form the noose around his neck until he tells me why he hates me so much. But he doesn't have to. It's written in every look, every hug he's never given me.

I am a Grisym. I am against the rules.

I give him a nod as we make our way inside, Dad's arm loosely wrapped around my shoulders.

"Headmistress Milgren will be expecting us in her office. You can show me your room after," my dad chuckles. His strong arm pulling me to his side with a few quick tugs.

"Yeah, sure. There's not much to show, though." He playfully nudges me as if I'm being ridiculous. As if there's no way he wouldn't be proud to see where I've been living.

For a moment I freeze, trying to recall if I'd cleaned the space this morning. I was so focused on making sure I got in some extra alone time with Pierce that I hadn't even thought about it. If there's any scent of the sex we had before dawn still lingering, they'll know. Harley will be able to sniff it out like a bloodhound. Dad will ask questions.

It's a quiet climb of the stairs, my breaths heavy by the time we reach the top, where it veers off to the administrative wing. I swear walking these flights hasn't gotten any easier.

"This place hasn't changed," my brother sniffs again.

Throughout the years I wasn't the only one Dad took along with him on his school visits. Harley often went when I couldn't due to school constraints. Dad wanted to show him the ropes knowing more than likely Harley would follow in his footsteps someday.

"Do you have a cold?" I ask, wondering if it's pride that's keeping his nose held so high, or if he's sick and trying to contain a runny nose.

It's a common misconception that wielders don't get sick or fall prey to diseases; we do. Our bodies operate very similarly to humans. The shells of our bodies are just strong enough to hold normal levels of our essences or other stored power. The real winning feature of being a wielder is the extra twenty to thirty years we get to inhabit this earth, assuming our deaths are natural.

He doesn't answer as he sneers at me. His gaze swiping from my head to my toes, nostrils flaring as the corded muscles of his neck bulge. *This is going to be oh-so delightful.*

I ignore it. Ignore the pang that comes with my half-blood brother thinking I am less than.

We may not genetically share a father but we do share a mother. I wish that were enough for him. It always has been for Merrick and Sicily.

My father raps at the headmistress's door. Her hoarse voice ushering us in.

I'm the last to enter, closing the door behind me, only to turn around to a surprise.

What the hell is *he* doing here?

23

WYNSTON

THE HEADMISTRESS SURPRISED ME when she ordered me to her office this evening for a private meeting. It's not like I had anything better to do than read the new horror novel by my favorite author. But just the same, it's never a good feeling being summoned by her. Especially knowing Milgren must know about what I am. Something I thought nothing of before she all but confirmed it.

That voice poking at the back of my mind has convinced me that if one person knows, it's only a matter of time before others will, too. Before Milgren, my dad was the only person left in this world that could destroy me. The only one who would expose what I am, likely taking Bryony down with me. Janelle Milgren could be a second.

Most days, I can chase the worry away. If she knows but hasn't reported me to the Bureau, then it must not be something she cares much about. Wielders like her are fewer in this world, but they do exist. Those who protest the killing of innocent children. Grisym children.

Those who crucify those Grisym babies and their families have convinced themselves someone who might have more power than them is a threat. Their beliefs are concrete in the falsity that Grisyms could eradicate a whole portion of our species.

Milgren either fits somewhere in the pro-Grisym activist category or ... *No, don't go there, Knox.* But if she's known about Bryony her entire life, and protects her, what other explanation could there be? She's protected me too, hasn't she?

I can only assume this gathering has to do with our training sessions. Each update I've delivered has been through chance meetings or random passes through the halls. None of them planned or coordinated. That way, no one will suspect. There's no pattern to latch onto or predict. No reason to presume secrets exist between us. It's better that way. Safer.

In this world, there are very few who will protect what Bryony and I are. I don't know her family's reason for doing so or Milgren's, but I will accept it for now. And pray like hell to any god listening that there isn't betrayal at the other end of this protection. A dagger set to be driven straight into our backs should we be wrong about those we've chosen to give our trust to.

I hadn't expected her, Mr. Avalon, and her brother to waltz into the office. My spine immediately straightens the moment her dad extends a hand to me. My eyes search his face for any indicator that he might know about me, too. There's none. Relief loosing my breath and uncoiling the taut pull of muscles between my shoulder blades.

My next set of thoughts brings all that tension back in an instant. I wonder if he can tell how intimate our sessions have become. The various ways we've practiced touching each other's bare skin to elicit reactions from our essences. Where mine had held firm day one, it has slowly regressed, wanting more and more to mix with hers. Like calls to like, they say.

"Nice to see you, Director Avalon."

"Roman, please." He claps me on the back, a wide grin showcasing his not-so-straight teeth. Preoccupied with their appearance, most high-ranking light wielders will get as much spell work and plastic surgery done as any other celebrity. But Roman never bothered to fix the crooked row of his bottom teeth, or the top front left one that sits slightly askew.

I reach out to shake her brother's hand, but he simply glares at me. Disgust written in his features, as if I were something dirty he would never dare to touch.

"Right Bryony, if you'll please," Milgren waves her forward.

Bryony slowly steps toward her. Apprehension knits her brow. It's clear what they want to see. A demonstration of what it's like for Bryony and me to touch.

She stops right in front of me, my hands rising to the height of her shoulders.

Her's follow suit. Only a centimeter of space exists between our palms. Our gazes locked. An invisible force field of electricity prickling between us. A sensation that's always been there. One neither of us truly understands. The sparks ignite in my chest, only to shoot down to my groin. An aching throb I know will settle there for hours.

The more time I spend with her, the more it happens. It's as if our bodies call to one another. I've never asked if she's felt the same. Nor will I. The last thing I need is to be turned on by a student and the same for her toward me. It's bad enough our lives are in danger. Let's not add another offense to the docket.

One of the most followed rules at Beauxgraton is the fraternization of students with staff. It's a no. Not now or ever.

The second is relationships between staff members. They turn a blind eye if we're just messing around. But if it becomes more than that, one staffer will be gone come the next semester. Plain and simple. No questions asked. No time to fix the situation.

Many think the mandate is harsh and ridiculous. Why keep adults from forming whatever bonds they want? But the administration insists that pairing between professors will only make our dedication to serving our students a messy endeavor. It's forbidden. Period.

Bryony brings one hand forward, just the tips of our fingers touching as she swallows loudly. In an instant, her head falls back. Her essence shooting from her fingers and funneling out of her mouth in a quick torrent of onyx smoke. Mine is only seconds behind hers.

Our heads slowly shift back to neutral as the dark tendrils mix. As they freely become one. A state they've grown accustomed to.

Her eyes remain scrunched shut as if fighting that initial violent surge our essences create within our bodies when we first touch. It's gradually calmed down with our increased sessions, but not enough that it doesn't still knock the wind out of us at the onset. "Look at me," I whisper. Her eyes pop open in an instant. That unique green glinting in the light.

"Don't let go," she breathes.

The familiar vortex roars around us. Angrier than it's been in some time. More insistent on keeping close to our bodies. Its volume grows exponentially as we breathe each other in. Our feet involuntarily shuffle closer as the combination of us presses in. The tether that lives between us slackening with each gained inch.

Her arm quivers as she fights to bring her other palm to mine. Our skin slaps as she collapses into me, our fingers weaving together. Suddenly, our essences draw back. A calm swirl of onyx and midnight stars, the color slowly shifting from its darkest to a fair gray, covering the floor like a blanket of fog. Those same twinkling stars are brighter now. Each one easily seen.

"My word," Director Avalon breathes.

"Abomination," her brother growls. His palm slams against the bookcase at his back. But I don't look at him. Bryony is the only place my eyes want to focus.

"Miraculous," sighs Milgren.

Through each of their reactions, we never break eye contact. Our bodies have shifted closer. Chests brushing as we allow the darkest and lightest parts of us to envelop us again.

The heels of our right hands separate. Just a fraction and then more. Her doing or mine, I'm not sure. Our violent storm rolls back to life. So dense and so dark, there's no chance the other three can see through it to us. "What's happening?" Director Avalon barks.

We're closer still, our breath mingling. Our real breath. The briefest brush of our lips sends a wave of electricity through my body before she nods.

We leap back from one another. Both of us with palms wide open as we call our essences back to us. Fists curling tight straining against those parts of us wanting to break free until they've completely retreated within us. Back to the place where they live until called on.

There's an intense focus needed to ensure we are only taking in our own. Fear keeps us from allowing the other's essence within permanently. That's not a normal thing for wielders to do.

The room is silent, drug out for long moments. Bryony and I with our gazes locked, chests heaving from the energy it takes to call our essences back.

"Has it always been like this with you two?" Director Avalon asks as he takes a tentative step forward, fingers reaching for his daughter, before pulling back, tucking them under his chin.

I'd never truly looked at the two of them in comparison before, but it's so clear now as they stand side by side. Bryony is not this man's daughter.

I'd let what we've always been told cloud what couldn't be true. Roman Avalon is a light wielder, as is Geneva. Together, they couldn't have made Bryony. Where her features are similar enough to her mother's, several differ from the man she calls Father. The nose, for instance, is prominent on Roman and Harley's faces. The same large beak. But hers, the bridge curves, ending in a small bulb.

Those gorgeous eyes hold more of a slant, pinching ever so slightly at the corners.

The most telling is her hair. The only one with locks of luscious pecans, while the rest of her family has shades of sandy blonde and pale brown.

Bryony turns to face her dad with her shoulders hunched near her ears, head bowed just the slightest. "Yes, from the very first day of his class. The moment he touched me, I lost complete control." She takes a deep breath, looking back at Milgren. "Thanks to Janelle—" The use of her first name draws a gasp out of me. "She assigned Professor Knox to help me control it."

"And you Wynston? Has this happened with anyone else you've ever encountered?" Roman turns to me with a stern look.

"No, just your daughter." I shake my head. "And before you ask, no, I have never been in contact with another Grisym."

Her brother's face goes beet red. Not the red of embarrassment, but utter uncontrollable rage. His body physically vibrates with it. We've all heard of his policies against Grisyms. Furthermore, his agenda banning light and dark wielders from being together at all. Harley has never made it a secret. There's nothing he hates more than the light combined with the dark. I can only imagine the tantrum he must have thrown when light students joined dark institutions this fall.

"The both of you should be dead," Harley sniffles, his chin jutting forward. "Not perverting our world with your unknown wielding powers." The asshole may as well spit in our faces. "That was disgusting to watch," he continues as his grimace deepens.

Chancing a look at Bryony, her face is stoic. To someone who hasn't spent hours a day staring at her, they would think she is completely unaffected by Harley's callous comments, but her eyes give her away. A slight, glassy sheen is visible as she fights to hold back tears in response to her brother's cruel words.

"Enough!" Director Avalon barks. Her brother effectively shuts down every emotion on his face. "And who chaperones during these sessions?"

My brow scrunches low as I question if this man is a fool. Why would we allow anyone else to be in the room with us? It's bad enough that a handful of people know what we are. Powerful people. The kind that can ensure we disappear.

"It wouldn't be smart to allow anyone else on campus to know what we are."

"Well, someone does," Harley snaps, pulling a parchment letter from his inner pocket.

Bryony scans it before passing it to Milgren, who then passes it to me.

My heart stops.

Knox,

You shouldn't keep secrets from me. I would think we would think more of each other than that. She's cute, the student you're fucking. The same student who is just like you.

Part light.

Part dark.

A being that should be six feet under.

I'll keep your secret for now, but not for long.

The note is brief but to the point. No beating around exactly what it intended to do. Rattle us. Coerce us into making mistakes that could cost us both of our lives.

Fuck!

I am screwed. So is she.

24

VALEN

DAVID HAMILTON BEAUXGRATON SPARED no expense when he built this monstrosity of a home for his new wife and the future children they would have. Many know of his history. How he'd come from French immigrants who came to the United States looking for a better way.

His determination was deep-rooted in the many businesses and exotic ventures he partook in throughout his adult life. Though booming out the gate, they all failed in time. When the day came to sell the land, his grandnephew had one stipulation. The school was to retain the Beauxgraton name. A simple enough request to grant.

David was a man with as many secrets as those of us who live within its walls now and was likely riddled with paranoia. Every secret passage, moving wall, or obscured alcove meant for spying, was part of his original design. An advantage we continue to put to good use today.

Buckingham Proper was originally meant for entertainment. The room we now use as an auditorium, once a second grand ballroom. A series of forgotten rooms, similar to box seats in a stadium, line the top floor around the auditorium. Each one, hidden from the seats below by long, thick velvet curtains that span three stories, from ceiling to floor.

Each of those small rooms has a balcony that overlooks the Beauxgraton grounds from every angle; perfect for me. An ideal spot to lean against the expertly sculpted balustrades, still in their original condition, and watch Daddy and Brother Avalon drive onto our campus. A sleek set of wheels meant to show off their elevated position in the wielding community.

Fuck. Them.

My mood sours. My molars grinding knowing these pricks are the ones we put on pedestals, but never dark wielders like *my* dad. He's as good a man as any light wielder, maybe better. I let my emotions fester, let them rule me until I saw how her brother looked at her.

I'd thought I was cold to her. My every action meant to be a reminder that she shouldn't cross me. Despite Pierce threatening me at every turn, I've kept up my game with her. Kept her guessing. Continued giving her warnings so she won't forget I didn't want her around.

Honestly, the high of it has begun to fade. I've yet to get a real rise out of her. Without the fear overpowering her, it takes all the fun out of it. What good are my threats if she doesn't respond to them?

Pierce continues to bring her around when I'm sure to see them together. My jaw left in pain from constantly grinding my teeth. Her tiny smirk is a reminder that she knows exactly what they're doing. Her manipulation of the situation driving the urge to slit her throat from ear to ear with my favorite dagger.

I've known what she is since the second week of school. That tingling at the base of my spine that told me there was more to her shiny exterior was spot on. We all have secrets. We're wielders who still have to live amongst humans. Wielders who fight each other for positions of prominence in our communities. And sometimes we are born with gifts that could make us a target.

To my surprise, I got a two-for-one in also finding out Knox was a Grisym too. There was no other plausible explanation after peeping through the classroom door's window.

What are the chances that there are now two at this school? Who is hiding them?

It's a conspiracy happening right under our noses.

A complication to our plans? Maybe. Maybe not. Only time will tell.

I watched as her father embraced her. Held her tight like she was the most precious thing in the world. A lazy, but somehow sad, smile crested that mouth of hers as she held him back. His youngest, his little girl. Always.

Yet knowing she's a Grisym means she's not his daughter. He's raised another man's child. Protected it. Risked his life, reputation, and who knows what else to keep her secret. But why?

An obsession with finding the answer plows through my insides. I don't give a fuck if Grisyms are walking around, but not many feel the same way I do. So why would one of the most influential men in the wielding world protect an illegal wielder? Especially when Harley has made it very clear that he wants them eradicated. Permanently.

When Bryony was nothing more than a light wielder, it meant nothing to ensure her death. It was nothing more than a task to get her out of the way because it would remove her father from being able to carry out his duty. The display I'd just watched between the two of them proves that.

Although her death wasn't part of the plan, it would make ridding our schools of him that much easier. His depression over the loss of her would consume him to a point where he could no longer function. No longer able to carry out his duties, it would leave a gap in oversight when it comes to the fate of every wielding institution around the world.

There are two ways I could still play this. I could still murder her or ensure someone else does. An option that warms my insides and drags out a wolfish grin. Many would call me a hero for discovering a matured Grisym and disposing of it.

Or ... I could keep her alive. Keep her close. Learn more about her. Potentially use her as a bargaining chip or even better as an ally in our mission to bring about a new way of life.

My original plan to get close to her wanders back to the forefront of my thoughts. It's why I'd allowed Pierce's pathetic display when he called her his girlfriend. She's no more his than she is mine. For now, at least.

Only once she and her family entered the building did I make my way back down to the Vault. The dank scent of the cavern still serves as a comfort blanket that reminds me of home. Not that I had a bad home life. My parents were fine. They gave me what I needed. Treated my brother and me with the respect we deserved, but there was no heavy cloak of love over us.

Our house focused on duty. Taking the risks to win the long game. Understanding and creating a better version of this world for dark-wielders is what we fed on. It's who my brother and I have become.

Dustin, my elder brother, took that to mean political ambitions. He spent the last five years in a slow and steady climb through the staff that work under the Council. But I took a different route. A darker, but more direct one. One my parents may not approve of as law-abiding citizens, but they will thank me in the end. I'm sure of it.

Sean and Kormoran's deep voices reverberate off the Vault walls. The two of them are always in an argument over some stupid shit. Always at each other's throats. Yet it's necessary to keep them both around. Each of us has a vital role to play in the boss's grand plan. Even if the others are closer to being nothing more than flunkies than integral pieces of the puzzle to bring the final goal to fruition.

Everything I do, everyone I interact with, and every decision I make has a purpose. There's a design, intricate and beautiful.

I know my parts. They have theirs.

Only Pierce has no true role. His position as my best friend is the only thing that keeps him as welcome company for closed-door conversations. Truthfully, he doesn't have the stomach to do what needs to be done. He doesn't have it in him to lead the way toward the type of change that has resulted in only four light schools worldwide remaining open out of hundreds.

The rest of us do.

The dark magic that flows through our veins comes with a little more edge. A bit more bite and malicious intent.

His budding relationship with that hot piece of ass has given him purpose now. He can bring her closer. Potentially even coax her into sharing more of what she's hiding.

Suddenly I'm wondering if the power play I'd made to bring the Avalon men here was a good one.

Did I fuck myself over or do myself a better service by throwing blind panic into the situation?

Who doesn't love a little chaos?

Kormoran clasps hands with me, his monstrous palm slamming into my back. What he considers a soft touch nearly knocks the wind out of me with every tap. Sean does the same, immediately rattling off the correspondence we received from our contact on the outside. His rich brown complexion remains a unique contrast to his hazy, army-green eyes, always alight with glee when he has information to relay. After three years I should be used to it, but I'm not.

"Where have you been?" Sean questions.

Sean has one of those memories that can capture every detail. His essence allows him to extract those memories and store them away. Not to mention his ability to will someone to release theirs to him should he request it. A process where a wave of memory-filled essence exhaled, floats in front of the face of its wielder until spelled. Sean only has sixty seconds to snatch that memory, either for storage within himself or in one of his prized objects, innocuously displayed in his room.

For him to take in the memory, he pinches the tiny sliver of essence—always a vivid teal—between his fingers before letting it slither into the opening of his ear. His eyes roll back into his head as it flings backward while the memory lodges itself in his mind. Sometimes as long as ten minutes pass depending on the length of the memory. He'll stand there, his body rigid, palms stretched open at his sides. It's creepy as fuck to watch and happens the same way, whether it's his memory he's taking in again, or one stolen from another wielder.

I think of the gilded antique globe sitting on the nightstand. One of his most prized possessions. A beautiful antique that holds so much more than a map of the world.

Where most of us plan to leave school and immerse ourselves in the workforce, he'll take his inheritance and travel off the grid for as long as the money lasts. That globe he keeps close by his reminder of every place he wishes to see in this life.

"Handling business," I smirk.

Kormoran grunts in response, eyeing me as if I'm going to say more. "Did it work?" he finally grumbles.

I shrug. "They came, didn't they?"

"Is she really fucking Knox?" he asks, thumbs tapping across his phone screen. Likely setting up his hook-up of the night.

"Don't know. Don't care." Our vicious grins match. Sean leaving me with a knowing one.

Okay, a part of me does care. I can't have my friends and those who should have been my allies falling over that curvaceous woman who could ruin everything. It's bad enough that Pierce is so far up her ass it'll take a forklift to pull him out.

Kormoran fucks anything with a hole, so he needs to be kept away and Sean likes a challenge. And if I know anything, it's that there's nothing easy about Bryony Avalon.

The truth is, we need to know what Grisyms can do as mature wielders. The Council always ensures Grisym babies don't survive, so no one knows for sure.

Do they pick a side? Or do they have a side picked for them?

Are they a true mix of the gifts given from both sides?

I hadn't told anyone else in the group what I learned about Bryony and Knox. Only that I saw them in a compromising situation, and it would stir up trouble to bring it up.

It should. Milgren should be down his throat, should the Avalons reveal the contents of that note.

Suddenly, the truth hits me. It's her. Milgren's the one that's been hiding Knox. She must know about them both. No one else has the sway here on school grounds to ensure they remain a secret.

I'm mentally punching myself for not realizing it. An answer that would have been right there in front of my face if I had taken just a moment to see it. If only I looked beyond my plans and hatred of Bryony and what she stands for.

But I don't have time to wallow. I have more shit to stir up.

I don't stay long, the five of us reviewing our current recruit and active participant list. It's one of the updates I'm responsible for giving our liaison here on campus each week. Damian's ability to provide quick analysis keeps the process short as always. "We've gained seven this week," he reports scrolling through his tablet.

"Anyone worth highlighting?" I ask, my fingers running along my short beard.

"Not a single one," he snorts, the click of turning off the screen effectively ending the conversation.

Not even bothering to say goodbye to the guys and Kaia, who remained uncharacteristically silent, I jog back up the stairs to the main level of the residence. Only a few students linger as I make my way through the labyrinth of hallways, dinner still in full swing at the opposite end of the building.

It's easy enough to find Pierce. His long form stretches out in bed as I enter his room. The guy really should lock his door, or at least put the ward back in place. He's one of the few who found a way to remove the signature spell and just use a basic lock charm. A charm he rarely activates.

I think back to Damian's recount of barging in on Pierce and Bryony fucking. The recap left me readjusting myself in my jeans. A deep burn drilled down into the base of my stomach just thinking about her with someone else. She might be my favorite chess piece to manipulate, but I'm a bit annoyed everyone else is getting to taste and fuck her but me. It's nothing personal. I decided weeks ago Bryony is mine to do with as I please. Why wouldn't I want the perks before disposing of her?

"Let's go," I cluck my tongue at him.

"What's up?"

"Bryony's dad is here. Don't you want to meet him?" I keep my voice dispassionate. Calm. Inviting.

Pierce launches himself from the bed, spinning in circles. Looking for what? I don't know. He pats down his deep umber hair that's now sticking up in the back. The hem of his shirt tugged downward as if that will remove the wrinkles from it before following me out into the hall. Several deep breaths puff free at my back. Pathetic, but amusing.

There's no room for talking as we make our way down the flight of stairs to her floor and across the residence. He's too busy running his hands over his face, pinking his cheeks, or flexing his fingers repeatedly. His nerves getting the best of him.

Even as we stand perched against the unforgiving stone wall outside her room, his fidgeting continues. None of it doing a thing to calm him. His body whips straight to standing the moment she comes into view with her brother and father. Director Avalon's arm draped over her shoulder and hers around his waist as she looks up at him with laughter in her eyes.

"Oh!" Her steps falter as she spots us. "Hey guys," her voice is tentative. The words delivered unevenly. None of that usual Bryony confidence present.

"Hey." I turn on the charisma, throwing a wink in her direction.

Her brother glowers. Not at me, but at her. That dark glare of his is in complete contrast to the shimmering sapphire blue of his eyes. The coloring, a compliment to the short dirty blonde hair, perfectly gelled in place. His golden complexion giving him the appearance of having just returned from a tropical vacation.

"Who the hell are you?" Harley sneers.

"Valen Greer," Director Avalon smiles in greeting, sticking out a hand to shake mine. "How are your folks?"

"Still doing what they do best," I chuckle. He laughs at that. But not a genuine one. The type that's awkward when you're searching for a way to weasel out of a given situation.

"And you?" her brother asks as he points at Pierce.

"Oh, that's her boyfriend," I blurt out as if it's the most obvious answer in the world.

Bryony looks like she might faint. Eyes saucers in her head. The grip she'd had on her father tightens ever so slightly before dropping away.

Her brother might pop a few vessels or ten. Veins along his temple and neck bulge. Her father is stoic. Face completely blank.

He'd likely never truly wanted his daughter to date. It's not like children are ever in the cards for her. If she were to produce another Grisym, it would only continue this line of torment.

Pierce slowly extends his hand, Bryony jumping to his side, her arm going around his waist.

"Yes, Dad. Meet Pierson Flaggstaff."

They finally shake just before her brother stalks off. The clap of his designer dress shoes on the stairs beyond heard for long, awkward minutes.

The damage has been done.

25

Bryony

It takes an hour of scouring the school grounds before I finally find Harley standing out by the lake. His focus set on the horizon as if frozen in place. The spot he'd chosen is the same one I often find myself in at night. Part of me latches onto that sprinkle of hope that has remained all these years. Hope that maybe one day he'll accept me. Love me. See that we're not so different.

I do my best to shove it down. Fight to hide it within the depths of me, because I learned a long time ago hoping for anything with Harley equals nothing more than heartbreak and disappointment.

And yet it's strange that we find solace in the same place. Despite how much he strives to distance himself from anything related to me, this small thing still binds us.

Yet again, I had to convince Dad to let me do this on my own. He'd been hesitant, knowing the volatility that exists between Harley and me. The intensity of Harley's disgust toward me has only grown since I was fifteen. He moved from the silent treatment, and flat-out ignoring me, to yelling in my face that I was nothing more than a cursed spawn.

He'd broken a piece of me that day. Everyone else in the family could love me but him. That was when his relationship with Mom deteriorated, too. The names he would call her. Tossing her infidelity in her face at every turn. Not once did he *ever* curse Dad for allowing it, though.

No, Dad is forever his hero. He can do no wrong.

It leads me to believe that there is so much more to my creation than anyone has ever let on. Just like I have my secrets, they have theirs.

His body tenses as I stop beside him. Shrugging into the hoodie I grabbed before leaving my father and the guys in my room to chase after him, hands tucked into the sleeves under my arms, I let myself enjoy the serenity of the mountains beyond for just a moment. A place so peaceful I'm afraid that the tension between Harley and me will taint it. Everything about the way we interact is so poisonous.

"Harley—" I begin.

"Don't," he interrupts me, the letters crisply ended to ensure I don't pursue this further. But I need to. We need to at least be civil.

"No, Harley. I'm going to. I understand that you hate what I am. I've heard it from you so many times that sometimes I hate me, too."

My chin drops a fraction, a sniffle the precursor of my gaze finding his face again. For the first time, he's looking at me with something more than undying hatred.

"I get it," I continue, hands dropping to my sides.

"No. You don't. You think you understand the position you've put us all in, but you don't. The lengths that Mom and Dad went to—"

His words stop abruptly as he runs a hand over his face. His focus returns to the still lake in front of us. The silence between us seemingly echoing in the wind.

"Despite how you feel about it, Harley, I didn't put us in this position. Mom and Dad did. They decided to keep me a secret. They chose to keep me alive. Not me. Hate me all you want, but maybe drive a bit of it their way, too." The words flew out of me, no longer tethered to the anchor I'd kept them tied to for the past decade. Harley is always so intent on blaming me, not once do I think he considered that I didn't choose this. I love my family, but I would never continue to endanger them if they *all* wanted me gone.

"You're an adult. You should have left. You should allow us to live without the weight of you hanging over our heads."

True. I could have, but that wouldn't change that they'd raised me, hid me. "And what would that have changed when the Council found out? Think about it, Harley."

"Stop saying my name!" he growls. The veins pop at his temple and throat.

"Or what?" I didn't come out here to fight with him, but that's all Harley ever wants to do. Hateful words are the only way to hold even a morsel of my brother's attention. I can't bite my tongue even as he sneers at me. "Exactly. Nothing." The bite to my words surprises even me.

His glare becomes murderous. "I, at least, wouldn't have to look at your face and see him."

Him.

My biological father.

Every fiber of my being itches to ask the question. I need to know who this man is that fathered me. But just to spite me, Harley will stare me down while I suffer before he ever tells me his name.

I hate that a single tear slips down my cheek. I hate that I am giving him any more of my love and emotions after all this time. He's right, I could have taken off in the middle of the night, but what good would that have done? The moment someone found out what I was, they would still come after my family. It's not like my face and name are a secret to anyone. The wielding community knows me the same way they know our nation's president's children. There would be no hiding.

I should just walk away. I should finally bolt shut the door on Harley and me. But I can't. That pinprick of hope just continues to test the waters.

We're silent for a long while, gazes focused on the scenery in the distance.

"Why did you react so poorly to me having a boyfriend?"

It was the simplest question to ask even if it's not the one I truly want the answer to. I want to know what he was going to say about Mom and Dad's sacrifices.

"Because you shouldn't be alive. You shouldn't have the option of bringing more life into this world. We won't even touch on the disgrace of you claiming that piece of shit dark wielder."

His harsh words have been spoken so many times I'm usually desensitized to them, but fury boils inside me now. The burn of overwhelming sadness forcefully shoved back down. My insecurities and desire to be loved by my brother forgotten as my chin lifts a fraction higher.

"Having a boyfriend doesn't equal having a baby. And I *do* belong here. *Alive.* Mom and Dad believe I do. So why can't you?" My eyes stay glued to the side of his face. Drilling holes into his temple, hoping that maybe some sense will find him.

"Boyfriend. Ha," he huffs in my face. "That why you're fucking your professor, too?"

I shove at his chest, so angry and full of raw emotion that I can't think of what else to do. Instinct takes over. The inner turmoil billows over the edge, and my essence is now fighting to break free. The struggle to hold it back nearly lost over and over again. Harley only stands there as I shove at his chest two more times. His frame is so solid, he doesn't even move.

"Believe me or don't. I am not sleeping with Professor Knox. He's helping me. He's the only one who has in a very long time."

His eyes narrow on me. "Well then, stay with him instead of coming back to our house. You're not an Avalon, so you don't get to live like one," spittle flies in my face as he spews that last bit of venom before pivoting on his heel and storming away.

That same stomp carries him back over the grass to the rear entrance of the Beauxgraton residence. I'm quick to turn my back on him, choking on a sob I don't want to let free. I don't watch him go. I can't. All I can do is let the cold encase me as my heart shatters once more.

I finally let my essence free. Allow it to consume me. Its natural state free to stream from my fingertips. A wall of black surrounds me. So tall it seems as though it meets the night sky. The opaque hues blend. My stars mimic the ones above. I'd never appreciated the beauty of what I can produce. Not until now.

The freedom of allowing myself to be what I am opens my eyes to the true beauty of my essence. A vibrancy I'm not sure I've ever seen it hold as I twist tendrils through my fingers. Darkness coats the world around me. The tiny sparkling flecks that exist in my essence are the only light left for me to see. *This is who I am.*

A weight lifts off my shoulders as I let more and more of me pour out into the world. The speed with which it moves is aggressively fast. I have no idea how far it stretches. No clue who might be able to see what I have produced. What I am.

I'm lost to it until arms grab me from behind. Instinct pulling my essence back into me as my body lurches forward against the strong arms holding me in place.

"Out here all alone. And causing such a display." I don't have to see his face to know that a wicked grin pulls at the corners of his petite mouth.

Valen's voice is deep and low in my ear. His arms holding me firm while I try to catch my breath.

"Get off me," I squawk as I struggle to get out of his hold.

"Not until your body calms down."

I don't have the energy to fight him *and* fight that part of me trying to break free again. My essence has felt what it's like to be truly free. To be unquestionably embraced by me, and now it wants back out.

I'm not sure how much time passes before he releases me.

"What, no pointed barbs? No knives flying at my head?" My voice is low as I right my sweatshirt, trying to ignore the butterflies tumbling through my stomach at having Valen protectively hold me so close, for so long.

He cocks a smirk as I scuttle away from him. "Not tonight, my Little Forbidden Fruit. I need to make sure your stupidity doesn't have someone else coming to kill you first." He moves in closer, his face only an inch from mine as it tilts to one side, and then the other, as if observing an unexamined object. "I've already called dibs."

A bolt of electricity shoots down my spine and into my lower belly with his words. I don't wait for another promise of death. Turning on my heels I make my way back to the main building. Back to my room. Back to the safety of my warded door and warm comforter.

I know I'll find my dad there. I know he won't leave until he's sure Harley hasn't damaged me more than he has in the past twenty-five years. I can only hope Camilla won't be there to witness it, too.

My mind drifts off to nothing as I weave through the hallways to my room. Those that wave my way only get a quick shake of my hand, but no real acknowledgment. I'm not in the mood to be the friendly woman my dad asked me to be. The cheery one I've always pretended to be.

I pause at the door, raucous laughter assaulting me.

It swings open to reveal my dad seated in Camilla's chair. Camilla, Whitney, and this other girl, Taryn, are all seated in a neat row on my bed. Whitney braiding Taryn's long black hair into small box braids as her cackling laughter vibrates through the room.

The boys—Graham, Pierce, and Collin—are all lined up the same on Camilla's bed.

Taryn and Graham's faces are bright red, tears streaming down their cheeks from nonstop laughter.

"Bri. Hi!" Dad waves as I enter. "Did you find Harley?"

"I did. Not sure where he went." My shrug hopefully is enough for my dad to think I'm okay. To not pry and ask questions like he usually does.

The mood in the room immediately sombers and I feel like an ass for being the one to ruin the buzz that circulated only a few moments ago.

"So, who's going to tell me what's so funny?"

26

Graham

None of us expected Mr. Avalon to stay until the wee hours. Nor his return Saturday morning to take us all off campus for breakfast. It was as much fun as it was awkward. Namely thanks to Bri's brother, Harley, choosing to attend.

He stayed as far away from her as possible. Ignored her, even while remaining cordial with the rest of us, especially us light-wielders. He'd asked questions about our studies and goals. While he didn't give Collin, Pierson, and Bri that level of interest, he at least listened to what Collin and Pierson had to say.

When our group arrived the diner staff was clearly surprised. I guess a place like that caters to regulars not big parties of young adults who aren't from around here. Several waitresses pushed a few tables together for us grunting under the effort of moving the four person-squares that likely haven't shifted in decades.

Fortunately, there were enough of us present for multiple conversations to happen at once. Numerous plates of greasy fried foods littered every table surface as we talked and sometimes laughed. Whitney and Collin picked off each other's dishes the entire time, a bad habit the two have developed. Except usually it's all of our plates, not each other's.

While everyone else seemed distracted enough by food and conversation, I was drawn to the disastrous interaction between Bri and Harley. A tension so thick, machetes may not be able to cut through it. Her body so stiff every time he outwardly waved her off or sneered at her. But only once did she allow her eyes to glass over. That one tiny moment of losing the fight of pretending she isn't hurt by how her brother treats her.

No one said anything about Harley's blatant dismissal of his sister. How, if he did look at her, it was with scorn. The scowl that pulled at his features when she hugged and kissed their father goodbye nearly sent me running for the hills. None of us were brave enough to say a word until I was alone with her in the library yesterday. Her happy place. Surrounded by books, knowledge, and the scent of aging pages. "A ticket to exploring the whole world through ink," she'd once said.

Yet when I asked her if she was okay after Harley treated her so poorly, she brushed it off as nothing. Claimed every family has that one sibling that acts like an asshole.

For someone else who doesn't know her, it might be believable. An acceptable answer for the person who has never seen her when the clouds of doubt and pain funnel into her vision. For someone who didn't see the curve of her spine despite her chin held high when he spoke to everyone but her through a three-hour long breakfast.

Despite her telling me not to, I showed up at her door bright and early this morning. Her hand thumps into her chest as she nearly tumbles into me leaning against the wall just outside her door. Her panting breaths and wild eyes drawing a chuckle out of me.

Partially, I wanted to make sure she was okay. My other curiosity revolved around these early morning sessions with Professor Knox. I won't ask because Bri is not the type to tell, but if I'm already there when the curtain closes, I might sneak a peek.

"You nearly gave me a heart attack. What are you doing here?" she sucks in several deep breaths before dropping her hand.

"I thought I would walk with you to Professor Knox's office. It's practically still the middle of the night."

"Uh, thanks, but I'm good."

She struts past me, her long legs filling out the commissioned dress slacks we're all supposed to wear. I don't. They don't compare to my designer ones. The fabric bunches weirdly at my crotch and waist, turning my appearance less than perfect, the way I prefer it.

I stand there, watching her go, picking up on the cues she doesn't want me to follow. Bri is a morning person so when she cuts you short, you know she means business.

There's nothing suspicious about her hurrying off down the hall until she looks back. A narrowing of her gaze as she searches the platform and hallways behind her. The set of her brow and mouth only relaxing when she sees no one around.

That look in her eye is the only motivation I need to follow.

I wait several more minutes for her to disappear down the first flight of stairs, doing my best to stick to the shadows. The quality of my expensive shoes allows me to creep down the steps behind her in silence. The unease growing in my gut at invading my friend's privacy quickly stomped down. I tell myself I just need to know she's okay. That this isn't wrong.

I've never been great at lying to myself.

As she reaches the floor below, I know she should be heading off to the right. That's the quickest way to the administrative wing, where the staff offices are, but she doesn't. She continues to fly down the stairs, so quickly, you'd think someone was chasing her.

She takes one last look behind her before exiting the main doors. My body is just small enough to fit into the nook at the edge of the foyer. I hold my breath as I wait a solid five minutes before I head to the doors myself. The groan of the hinges likely noticed if she's still close by.

Jogging down the main pathway, I don't see her until the gates come into clear view. My jaw drops, my heart racing as I watch her take Professor Knox's hand just beyond the second gate and disappear into thin air. A ripple through the space they'd been in is the only proof that they were there.

They just teleported.

An exceedingly rare gift. It's difficult to do with one body, let alone two. Forget that I've only heard of a handful of wielders proficient enough to carry out the act. One wrong move leaves the body mutilated. There's no way of knowing which of them has the ability with their hands bound. The churning in my gut tells me it's her. One of the many pieces of herself she refuses to share with anyone, even me.

Why the hell would they be leaving campus together at five in the morning?

It makes sense they had to move beyond the far gate to teleport. They wouldn't be able to do so on the campus grounds. The school has wards that block that type of dangerous gift from being used by anyone other than a few faculty members. That can only mean they're going somewhere in private. A place to be alone where students like me can't watch them through tiny glass windows.

Something akin to heartbreak or betrayal settles in my chest. Everything I thought I knew about Bri continues to warp. That's two big secrets Bri is keeping from me. How many more might there be?

I can't say how long I've been standing here on the front steps waiting, actively convincing myself she might just reappear. Imagining I simply missed them disappearing behind a tree or something. Any minute she'll pop up behind me with some snarky comment about not giving her privacy before giggling loudly.

But I know I didn't imagine it. I couldn't have.

They were there in the middle of the paved road and then gone.

Shit. Bri, what are you doing?

Better question, why do I care so damn much?

Because she's my friend. Because I want her to be safe. Because whatever trouble she is going to bring her way by breaking school rules, I don't need bleeding over onto me. The opportunity to be the top-ranked student here at Beauxgraton remains open for me—without any help. I don't want to jeopardize that.

The chill of the outdoors fully settles into my bones before I finally decide to head back inside. Bri isn't coming back, at least, not anytime soon.

I'm the first one to enter the dining hall. The closed doors force me to pry the solid panels of thick, carved wood apart, disrupting the most breathtaking designs. It would be nice to be as proficient as others at summoning doors opened and closed, but alas that skill remains a challenge for me. It doesn't matter whether I've channeled strong power or not. The normal assault of rich aromas is faint as they part. Today's breakfast must still be in the process of being prepared behind the wall that houses a kitchen the size of a football field.

Pulling a textbook from my bag, I do my best to distract myself. To pretend like I didn't just see my friend poof off campus with a professor.

Even the flat surface of the benches digging into my ass doesn't distract me from the images of Bri's hand in Professor Knox's. A sense of peace in the connection as if they've done it a million times. No amount of rummaging through my mind can help me settle on an explanation as to why they would be together, leaving campus hand-in-hand. At least not an explanation I am willing to let myself believe. I'm missing something, but I have no idea what.

It's another forty-five minutes before anyone else starts filtering into the hall. The scent of pancakes and bacon finally drawing me away from the text I wasn't actually reading. Not a single word was retained or understood as my mind wandered to that single image repeatedly.

Our normal set of table mates starts funneling in. Camilla, then Whitney. Then Drew, Frankie, Taryn, and Collin. One by one they surround me with trays, while I never even get up to make my own. My focus is anywhere but on the friends surrounding me and the delicious scents wafting up my nose.

That same book remains open in front of me. The words taunt me as if they know what I witnessed mere hours ago.

I'm still lost in my haze when Bri drops down next to me, her hair slightly disheveled. Her fingers are warm as they wrap over the curve at the top of my shoulder. The same wide smile and bright eyes as always as she hugs me from the side. Not a single indication she's just been outside.

"Want me to grab you anything?" she asks. Her demeanor is as if she hadn't seen me this morning. The upbeat lilt of her words drawing out Camilla's groan. She may be the perkiest person I've ever met, but not before eleven.

Bri pecks me on the cheek—something she often does since we started studying together daily—before making her way to the line. An action she'd dismissed when I asked her why. Her response full of that cool nonchalance she shields herself in like armor, "*Sorry, I'm not sorry for loving my friends.*"

I'm pretty sure it has to do with my curiosity about her. Almost as if she can sense I'm going to ask questions she doesn't want to answer. It's an easy way to throw me off my center so I don't voice what's on my mind.

She returns with that same glimmer in her eyes. Fingers curled around the type of wooden trays used for breakfast in bed. It's an interesting choice by the administration, but the least of my concerns this morning. There are several plates piled high. The scent of bacon and pancakes and sugary syrup leaving me salivating.

"You gotta eat, Graham," she chides as she slips a strip of bacon past her lips.

Her attention immediately turns to the group when I don't respond. All of them carry on as if nothing is wrong. For them, nothing is. They didn't see her. They didn't witness what I did. Their closest friend isn't sitting next to them, pretending as if nothing happened.

Leaning in close, I whisper into her ear, "Where did you go?"

She looks at me quizzically. "Knox's office. You know I have to meet with him before class nearly every day. Stupid mandate from my dad." She rolls her eyes, clearly for my benefit. Her show is a good one for anyone but me.

"Right, but where did you guys go?"

She drops the fork full of eggs onto her plate. A rough wipe of her napkin across her mouth as she sighs heavily. Her voice even as she answers. "His office. Like always."

I do my best to say nothing more, to let her lie to me, but I can't hold my tongue. "Why are you lying to me?"

She sighs loudly, again, grabbing another piece of bacon. "Graham, if you are my friend—at all—you will drop it and not bring it up again."

So, with a grunt, I shove away from the table and leave.

She might be okay with lying to my face, but I don't have to sit here and take it.

27

BRYONY

TODAY STARTED GREAT.

Knox and I have been sneaking off each morning to practice in a cabin that is part of the Beauxgraton family property. An additional perk when the Council purchased the land to open the school here. However, unlike the residence and accompanying buildings, it sits halfway down the mountain, miles off campus. A well-hidden, mostly unknown, one-room structure for when the faculty requires covert meetings.

Our sessions qualify.

In only a week, we've made significant improvement. Our control and manipulation of our own and each other's essences comes more naturally. The display we'd given for my dad, Harley, and Headmistress Milgren was a simple opening act compared to how we can respond to one another now.

Nevertheless, our touches are getting more intimate with time. It's never beyond the exposed skin of our necks, faces, arms, and hands, though. The most we've bound ourselves together so far is by linking our fingers the way couples do, until today.

This morning was the first time Knox suggested we embrace. A hug is such a simple, yet complex gesture. One that can be as platonic as it can be foreplay.

I'd hesitated knowing there was a deeper connection between us that we don't understand yet. We knew, without even touching, the hug would be the farthest thing from platonic, but it didn't stop me from wrapping my arms around his middle. My body pulled flush against his as his arms wrapped around my shoulders. I'd relaxed into him, turning my face so my forehead brushed his throat and cheek sat high on his pec. The dig of his cleft chin into the crown of my head a welcome pressure I somehow craved without knowing it.

At first, we'd been completely still. Our bodies were slow to respond. Our magic a gradual churn before it began to leak free.

To our surprise, our essences streamed from us in soft tendrils. Floating happily as a pewter hue, my stars still intermingled throughout. For the first time, our essences didn't rush from us in a violent storm. The ethereal flow as if they were content that we'd finally come together—physically.

The longer we held each other, my palms flat on his back our bodies pressed against one another, the more we filled the surrounding space.

Our essences seemed at peace as our bodies heated with proximity. My ear to his chest, the rapid beat of his heart thrummed through me, pacing with mine. My flesh called to him as his erection swelled between us. Even then, he never pulled away. Instead, pleaded that I stay put so we could continue our test. But it wasn't only his plea. Our essences begged for it too. Begged us with such an urgency I swore they had voices of their own in my head.

I obeyed. Willingly. Happily.

I couldn't have moved away even if I wanted to.

My body seemed to agree, my insides heating to unimaginable heights. Nervous butterflies in my belly shifting to the light fluttering ones that form when your crush finally talks to you. An ache built between my legs as I breathed Knox in. My libido simply isn't immune to his handsome face and the hard lines of his body against mine. Or the bulge in his pants that throbbed against my belly.

I inhaled his fresh scent and wondered what this would be like flesh to flesh. What it would be like for more than his palms on the curve of my neck to touch me? A chance to explore the hard planes of muscle hidden beneath those button-ups and sweaters. Fantasies of him seemingly stirring my essence to a more playful thrum through my insides.

I wondered what it would be like to have sex with him instead of Pierce, or maybe in addition to. The thought stunned me, stiffening my body against Knox's torso. Our mixed magic aggravated by my sudden loss of calm. His arms held me unimaginably closer, whispered words into my hair drawing out deep breaths that took me back to our tranquil state.

Only after we broke apart did we have a conversation. One where Knox suggested taking me out to test me siphoning from a ghoul at the next Red Moon. The ominous cloud now hanging over me, realizing it's only a few months away. The prospect is as exhilarating as it is terrifying. He may have been okay siphoning from a ghoul, but who is to say I will be?

He'd revealed his plan for us to get out there before everyone else. An attempt at keeping us hidden, so hopefully no one would see me with him. He'd already gotten permission from Milgren and Schouten, so no one can question that. The problem will be explaining why an innate light wielder is out in a ghoul pit in the first place if they do spot me.

A reenactment of this morning has played through my mind on repeat. Every word, breath, and touch is still alive within me. Vibrating with life as we made our way back to campus this morning. My teeth sink into my bottom lip as I let the memories of Knox's body distract me. That endless loop better and better each time it replays. New details further flushing out the movie that has quickly become my favorite.

My mood instantly shifts as I make my way through the twists and turns of Beauxgraton's halls. The artwork and tapestries may be the same, but the lengths and corners leading to new hallways seem to change daily. As if the house has a mind of its own, continuing to morph and change as it chooses. I'm pretty sure there's an urban legend or a movie about a house that does that. That must be where the idea came from. But my brain tricks me into believing the truth in such a preposterous thought. The possibility of that reality sending a shiver down my spine.

Only this time, the maze that is this school doesn't distract me from Graham's prying this morning. The look in his eye and the persistence of his questioning unnerved me. It hadn't stopped at breakfast. Those same words repeated to me through each of the five classes we've had together today. His jaw working each time I told him to drop it.

Paranoia grips at my insides. Maybe he saw us. Was he the cough we'd heard outside the door that day in Knox's office? Has he seen our true nature?

I struggle to convince myself that I am just paranoid. He can't know anything more than I'm meeting with Knox each morning. I tell myself, he couldn't have seen us. Lie to myself that he's just curious, but knows nothing.

At the end of the day, it doesn't matter. He just needs to stay out of this.

Begrudgingly, my thoughts flit to the next trying event of the day. Pollin was supposed to administer one of her brutal tests. Lucky me she changed it at the last minute due to a few other first-years stealing the answers. It became a practical instead of a written exam.

I'd fumbled through, both my body and brain so drained from my session with Knox that I couldn't focus my essence. Couldn't quite make it do what I wanted. It's always like this after the more intense sessions. As if I left so much of me behind with him, there's not enough to power me through anything else. As if without him my essence refuses to comply.

The day tumbled further into the pits of hell when Valen announced I'd allowed Damian to watch Pierce and me fucking during lunch. That was an absolute blast. So much worse than his death threats and thrown knives. The tiny pieces of myself I chose to keep private were laid bare for everyone else and there was nothing I could do about it.

The students already looked at me differently—my father's appearance here last weekend did not help with that—but now they see me as a slut too. I'm no stranger to those forming the wrong opinions about me. It's part of being a figure in the public eye, but this just hit differently. This felt so much more personal than a stupid journalist making shit up.

But it wasn't enough for Valen to air my sex life to the entire school. He only sweetened his proclamation by stating he was next.

Motherfucking asshole!

Rage boiled beneath my skin. My essence, *poke, poke, poking* at my skin. Wanting to break loose and strangle the life from that skinny son-of-a-bitch and his taunts. Sensations I've never experienced before roared through me. My vision sharpened into pinpoint focus on Valen's smug face. Heart racing at a pace that would make a regular human's heart fail.

I wanted to kill him with my bare hands. A realization that frightened me. I am not a violent person. I never have been. Thoughts like that do not live rent-free in my head.

Only Pierce draping an arm around my shoulders and leading me to one of the lounge areas brought me back down. The dark clouds outside the bay window so similar to the ones that seem to loom over me. We'd stayed there in my brooding silence until we had no choice but to venture to our respective classes. Just the same, his presence there meant everything to me in those moments.

My last class of the day ended with a slip of parchment from Headmistress Milgren. A summons to her office, yet again. The cherry on top of my shit-filled cake.

The thick paper crumbles in my fist as I march down the corridor to her office. The sweat coating my palm increasing its pliability the longer I hold on to it. It's not Milgren I'm pissed at, yet I know the moment she voices something not remotely in line with my thoughts, I will take it out on her.

Janelle Milgren has known me my entire life. Years under her belt of witnessing the rush of anger I sometimes can't hold in. She'll let me release every bit of my frustration as she sits there, patiently waiting for me to calm down again. Frustration she's watched me allow to get the best of me when my magic didn't behave properly, or when I missed my grandmother so much I couldn't stand it.

I take one last deep breath, prepared to knock when she calls out to me through her door. The same summons she's always had for me when I enter the room. That voice I've known all my life, gruff as if I'm infringing on her day, and it's more than she is willing to tolerate.

"You wanted to see me?"

She peers up, removing her reading glasses. The tortoise shell design in stark contrast to her pale skin and snow-white hair. Her eyes close briefly before blinking open to reveal the unique deep rust irises I've always known.

"Yes, I want to get your honest opinion on your sessions with Wynston." Her use of his name has me double-taking as I focus on the purse of her tiny mouth painted in nude lipstick and the crow's feet at the corners of her wide eyes.

"Headmistress—"

"No." She raises her hand. "Behind closed doors, we can be familiar. You can act as we always would."

Letting those emotions flood me once more, I race around the desk, throwing my arms around her middle. The same way I have since I was a young girl. Hers holding me close the way she always has. Her perfume is one of the most familiar scents I know. A mix of peppermint and soft florals. Janelle is the one part of being here that still feels like home.

Janelle and my grandmother were the best of friends. Our relationship came to life before I could even identify who she was. There have been countless nights where she's been over for dinners and parties. More after Grandma Avalon passed where she tucked me into bed or held me and told me the wild stories of them growing up.

To this day, I don't know how they met. I've never asked, and I've never cared. All I know is these two women paved a path for light and dark to be more than acquaintances. To be more than cordial or associates. One where they were friends. A chosen family that sometimes meant more than their own because blood never forced them into it.

She wipes a tear from my face, gesturing for me to sit in the seat across from hers. Straightening my spine, a shuddering breath releases from me before I tell her how today felt.

"My dear, you know I need to ask you if you have been ..." she clears her throat, not wanting to ask her actual question. "Intimate," she finishes.

"Janelle, gods. No!" My voice rises several octaves as I sink further into my seat as if that will somehow reverse the previous volume and pitch. "It's not ... Well, it feels ..."

"Dear, please understand you two are an opportunity for us to truly understand what it means for two Grisyms to explore each other. We wouldn't fault you for where that exploration might lead."

"Janelle, he's—"

"I know. I am only saying we have an opportunity to learn here. That is all your parents ever wanted. All your grandmother wanted." She pats my hand, which somehow found its way between hers. "Think about it."

With a nod, I sneak back around the desk to give her one more hug.

"Remember, my dear," she starts. Her thin fingers stroke the hair at the back of my head. "You are different. You are allowed to embrace that here. Whatever that may mean."

There are so many hidden nuances in her words. Roads I want to explore and ones I am terrified of acknowledging because I can't truly know what they might mean. Knox is one of the scariest by far.

Neither she nor my father ever said others couldn't know about our relationship, but something tells me no one should know besides Knox. The comfort I can find behind closed doors with Janelle is something I need to protect in this world.

She is silent as I exit her office.

Head down, I'm quick to turn down the corridor, Knox colliding with me just several feet outside the room.

"Come with me," he whispers, pulling me along by the forearm. *What now?*

The hallways are clear as we weave through the administrative wing. His sure steps leading us through a secret passage the same as Pierce has done so many times.

We nearly tumble down a tunnel, the toe of my perforated brogue retro lace-up Oxfords catching a loose stone. The scent of old water and age surrounds us. My sleeve stuffed under my nose to keep from breathing it in.

He doesn't release me until we come to a door. Its surface solid steel, with bolts lining the edge. He wrenches it open revealing a narrow spiral staircase, the rungs the same brushed metal surface. Slick spots slow my pace as I cling to Knox's hand and the railing. Gasps escaping me with each tug forward.

Step by step, we climb. Creaking metal and my ragged breaths are the only sounds to keep us company. A wooden door coming into view as we crest the stairs at floor four. He opens the door slowly. Holding me behind him, his head shifts left and then right before tugging me through the doorway with a grunt.

As we enter, I'm struck by the modern flare found in this part of Beauxgraton. I know we're still on the campus but I'm honestly not sure which building this is. The same gray is everywhere, but it's painted drywall instead of stone. The decor is a mix of abstract prints and paintings that are a direct contrast to the tapestries and portraits of the main residence.

I'm distracted enough that I trip again as he shoves me through a door I hadn't noticed we'd reached.

A living and dining area glares back at me. The interior outfitted in the same modern but minimalistic style found in the hallway.

His apartment.

I am in Wynston Knox's apartment.

"Why are we here?"

"Because I just got this." He bends, snatching a piece of parchment from the coal-black rectangular coffee table.

I take it, holding the folded sheet between shaking fingers.

With the day I've had, no part of me wants to open it. So, I just stare. Hoping if I do so long enough, it, too, will disappear.

28

Bryony

I've been staring at the aged parchment in my hands for far too long. A million combinations of words roar through my mind. The potential of what they must say draws sweat to my pits and lower back. Knox fears little other than being discovered. What could this tiny sliver of paper possibly say that made him risk sneaking me into the professors' quarters?

Students are strictly forbidden from being here. Like, expulsion-if-you're-caught type of forbidden. Rule number five of the doctrine we're all forced to sign before stepping on campus comes to mind.

Mandate Five: No student, of any tier or age, is permitted entry to the Beechum sleeping quarters. No loitering, sleeping, or any other activities are permitted by a student within Beechum walls. Any student caught within the building, for any reason, will face immediate expulsion from The Beauxgraton School of Wielding. In addition, that student will be blocked from admittance to any other institution for a year following the infraction.

I am all for exploring this Grisym thing but not at the expense of being here. The risk of being locked in his apartment with him puts the possibility of me making my dad and family proud at risk. Yet, I don't walk away. I physically can't seem to make my feet move toward Knox's apartment door.

Drifting further into the apartment, I slowly take in Knox's space, avoiding whatever piece of torment waits in my hand. A way of distracting me from the whirlwind of emotions and thoughts riling my insides.

The longer I stay, the more bile creeps up my throat. The list of people I'm set to let down by breaking rules with Knox compiles in my head.

Dad. Mom. Merrick. Grandma Avalon. Janelle. Myself. All the light wielders that depend on me to be a resource and example they can use by attending this school. A responsibility bestowed upon me just by having the last name Avalon.

Janelle's protection wasn't the only reason I came to this school. I came here to do more than hide, and it's time I carried myself as such.

"I can't be here." I shove the note back into Knox's chest. His fingers curl around my wrist, holding me in place.

"Bryony, listen. Just focus." His voice is low. Stern. Desperate.

I snatch my hand away from him; the paper crinkles as I rip it open. One final deep breath fills my lungs before I peer down at words that I know in my heart will change everything.

My eyes bulge as I let out a choked cry.

Bryony,

I was asked to stay away from you. I was told to never make contact. I've respected that wish. But the stakes are too high now. Your safety is in question, and I refuse to let another day go by without offering my help.

Enclosed you'll find a map and a photo of me. You may not have known it, but you do know my face. You have always known your birth father's face.

The night of the next Red Moon Festival, you and Wynston will find me. I've entrusted this letter to him because it is safer.

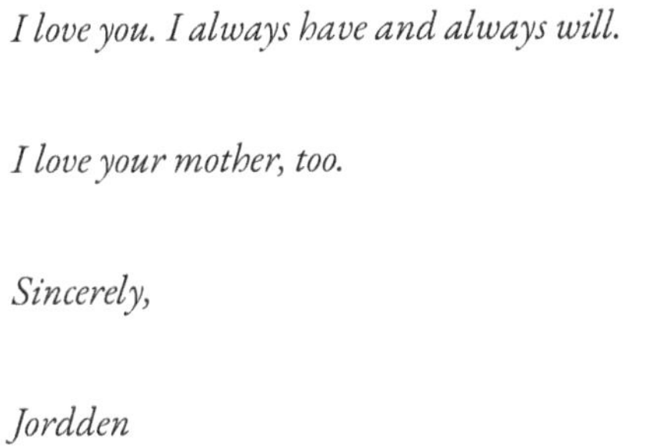

I love you. I always have and always will.

I love your mother, too.

Sincerely,

Jordden

Tears flood my eyes as I read the letter for a second time. The words blur together behind my tears as I fight to keep my composure.

"Did you know?" The words release in a breath.

"No." The answer is simple, yet truthful.

"How can this be true?" I've always known there was a dark wielder out there somewhere that was my father. But not this man. Him, of all people.

"Bryony, I honestly don't know. We can ask Milgren if that would make you feel better." His words come out more patronizing than I think he meant them to sound. But I let it go.

The photo glares back at me. The eyes, deep-set, so close in coloration to mine. The nose, slightly upturned, is also a match. His hair is darker than mine but holds a gorgeous wide curl that I wish I could pull off. His features are a perfect complement to the olive undertones of his skin. *My father.*

In so many ways, he is the opposite of my mother. Of my dad, too.

The genes he passed on to me are the reason I look so vividly different from the rest of my family. I'd only caught minimal looks from my mother. But it's my father, Jordden Guthrie, the dark wielder who leads the New Order, that I truly resemble.

There's no need to confirm it. It's there in the picture for me to see. For anyone that took just a few seconds longer to look, to see.

Without even asking, I sink onto the couch. My elbows dig into the meat above my knees as I continue to stare at the picture of my father. Convinced if I study it long enough, I may know the truth about him. Time soaring by as I uselessly wish for answers that the small picture of him cannot give me.

I stare, hoping something in this picture will tell me he's not a terrorist to light-wielders. That he isn't planning world domination. His focus has always been on bringing dark wielders to the light, so to speak. The stereotypes casting all of us from the dark as nothing but simple, evil creatures, a mindset he's always wished to erase, by any means necessary.

"My father is a murderer. He's literally the most wanted wielder in the world." The words sound ridiculous and empty on my tongue. Like a message meant for someone else's fantasy life, not mine.

Knox sits next to me, an arm automatically cupping around my shoulders. "I'm sorry. We can figure this out."

I so badly want to believe him. A pit deep inside me knows learning who my father is has only made my situation worse. Myself and Knox are now in greater danger than before.

"Yeah, *we.*" The sarcasm is thick in my tone as I take a big sniff. *His* father isn't the man the light-wielding community would rather see dead.

His fingers find my chin, turning my head to face him. Our eyes search one another. The connection is immediate. Our essences swirl just beneath the surface as if they understand the decision that's already been made between the two of us. As if our insides knew we'd move as one. That our mouths would meet in a clash of flesh and teeth. As if they knew we would hold this moment. Hold on to each other because, as far as we know, there are no others like us. Who else is there to understand what we live with each day?

But more than that, the tension that's been brewing between us for weeks is now so intense it's impossible to ignore. We both know the way our bodies react to one another is nowhere near appropriate. How they call out to one another, but there's no stopping it.

I inhale him as our mouths slant in unison. The brush of his chest over the fabric of my button-up is just enough friction to pebble my nipples inside my bra.

"We shouldn't," I whisper.

"I know." His mouth finds mine again. My fingers sinking into the newly trimmed hair at the nape of his neck. Soft strands tickling my oversensitive skin.

"Janelle—" My words stopped as if stolen from my very lips.

"I know," he breathes again, the tip of his tongue brushing against the seam of my mouth, taunting me to open for him.

I lose the battle of pretending like this isn't what I want. Like I don't feel this predestined connection growing between us every day. The fight to keep our sessions appropriate is harder and harder with each passing moment.

"We shouldn't." The words are less firm this time as his body climbs over mine, my back pressing into the cushions of his couch. I say them, but my fingers cling to his shirt. My pelvis rolling up into him, negating my weak declaration.

"Is it because of Pierson Flaggstaff?" The words are broken up as he trails wet kisses over my jaw to the bit of exposed skin at the hollow of my throat.

"He's not ..." A long sigh releases from me as his hand molds around my breast. A squeeze just firm enough that my body arches into him. His length is already solid between us. "... my boyfriend."

"Didn't think so," Knox snorts as his hands yank my shirt from the waistband of my pants, exposing my soft belly to his touch. His lips brush over my skin before licking inside my navel. My hips flexing up into him once more.

He looks back at me, his eyes darkening to a near black as his pupils seem to disappear.

His mouth is back on mine as his fingers undo the button on my pants. The zipper swiftly slides down behind it. A brush of cool air following to accompany his roaming fingers.

"Bri." He never calls me that. "Do you want to stop?"

I shake my head, pulling his face back to mine. My essence is finally free to leak out of me as one long finger finds its way into my damp panties. Just a slight brush against my slit is enough for my essence to vortex through the room. The gusts are so violent a lamp flings itself to the floor. Papers fly up to float down like oversized snowflakes.

Finally, removing my fingers from his hair, we fight together to remove his shirt. His essence seeping from his mouth, angling straight into mine. My inhale of those onyx tendrils so deep it's as if my body prefers him to air.

He dances inside me. The part of him that lives within his shell, mingling with my magic. Embedding itself to become part of me. Infusing into my DNA. Pieces of him that will forever live within me.

His entire hand finds its way into my panties, one, then two fingers slipping inside me, while his thumb presses against my throbbing clit. His movement is rough and possessive. The curl of each digit is like a brand declaring ownership of my flesh.

It feels as though he does. As if he always has. I'm not sure we'll ever understand just how connected we are.

"Will you come for me?"

"Mmm-hmm," I nod, licking my lips. At his quickening pace, my mouth drops open.

"This is only the beginning, Bri. Are you ready?"

I wish I had coherent words or thoughts to adequately describe all the ways I would like to answer that question. To explain every way I have imagined Knox having his way with me. Claiming me.

In truth, no. I am not ready. Not for what's coming. Not for the danger that comes with Knox and me being what we are and doing what we're doing. There's too much at risk—as always—but I couldn't stop if I wanted to. My essence controls my thoughts and actions now. Erasing the fear and stress that took over before Knox invaded my body. It's haze, allowing me to stay in this moment with him.

The moment my orgasm hits, I lose control of my essence. A blast of darkness covers every inch of the space. Enveloping us as he captures my mouth with an insatiable hunger that leaves me groaning.

The only thing left in my mind is the echoing call of our essences as they demand the removal of all barriers between us. My hands fumble to remove his dress pants as quickly as possible. His boxer briefs shoved down with them. He does the same for me, holding my lower half off the couch with one arm as he shucks my pants free. Suddenly, he tears my shirt, buttons scattering across the floor as he unclasps the front hook on my bra.

The moment our skin touches, with his length cradled against my throbbing core, the world stops. A single inhale forces my eyes shut.

The exhale to follow flings them open.

"Fuck. Bri. Your ... eyes!"

29

WYNSTON

I'VE NEVER SEEN SOMEONE'S eyes change the way hers did.

Truthfully, it terrifies me. My fight-or-flight reaction tells me to run. To get as far away from her as fast as possible. But the essence that lives inside of us, a combination of our light and dark features, won't let me. Not now that our bodies have touched. Now that my essence knows the inside of her, there will never be a way to erase our connection. No possibility of ever tearing us apart.

I can't say for certain how I know that to be true, but I do. Every fiber of my being sings that single truth as an angelic chorus.

It's a connection I'm not sure either of us will even understand. I assume it's just that we are both Grisyms. That the differences within us call to each other and it would be the same for me with any other Grisym.

I wish I could better understand this special bond between us. One that seems as though it could last forever. Bryony is not like other wielders. She's not like me, and it goes deeper than just being a different combination of light and dark. There's something older within her. Something ancient, anchoring me to her.

I find the strength to look her in the eyes again. At first, they are nearly all black. A tiny pinpoint of white barely noticeable at the center of where her pupil should have been; until it grew. I tried to tell myself it was a figment of my imagination until I could deny it no longer. Until there was more white than black. An iridescent bright frost overshadowing the ebony rim that continues to shrink. Only a sliver of glossy black lining the shape of each eye in the end.

"Yours too." Her voice is soft as her fingers graze my jaw with wonder.

Where I'd surely looked at her in fear, she stares up at me with awe. Her hand traces higher up my cheek, through the stubble I'd let grow the past two days. Rough under her fingertips.

"Breathtaking," she murmurs before pulling my face back to hers.

There's a niggle at the back of my skull. Something that says if we go there, if I have sex with this woman, there will be no pathway to turn back. There will be no route to redemption or recovery.

Sleeping with Bryony will be claiming her as mine.

A right I don't have.

Yet that prickle isn't enough to keep me from shifting my hips against her. Her slick flesh coats me, lubing me up so I can slip inside where my fingers just were. A warm wet cavern I've been craving since I had her pinned to that tree only a month ago. A lifetime ago, it seems.

It's been so long since I've been with anyone but Fiona, the anticipation of knowing someone new nearly has me shoving into her. But I don't. Feeling the flow of our essences mixing inside me has my body tingling. As if every nerve ending is sparking to life at once. It's a foreign sensation. One I lean into. One I crave more of.

"Are we going to do this or what?" Impatience coats each of her words.

I wasn't sure I could. Wasn't sure I wanted to give in until my eyes pulsed in time with hers. A single beat of movement. The color shift is just as startling as seeing her eyes do exactly what I think I felt mine do. The whitened area shrinks only to expand once again. I felt them match hers and knew it was as if our essences were taunting us, daring us to take the plunge into forbidden territory. To further merge ourselves as one.

"I'm not a gentleman."

Her smirk has me double-taking as if my mind imagined it, but it did not. "I'm a sturdy woman. I can take it."

Her hand snakes between us, manicured fingertips running down my sculpted abdominals before she wraps her fist around me. A shift of her shoulders lining me up perfectly with her entrance. Even poised outside ready to enter, her walls pulse in time to the throb of my rigid length. It begs for me to sink into her depths. To allow her to give me as much pleasure as I hope to give her.

"Your turn." Another taunt. Another flash of that mischievous grin.

I push forward. The head of my dick shoving past the ring of muscle as I work to sheath myself in her. She's unimaginably tight. My eyes roll back into my head as I fight to gain ground. To envelop myself in her heat. To merge us in the best and worst possible ways.

The roll of her full hips sends shockwaves through me. Her flesh filling my palm as I grab hold of her thigh, hiking her leg that much higher. The outward rotation of her knee giving me that much more access. More room to drive deeper into her uninhibited.

My body does as it pleases. Pumping into her with as much ferocity as we can muster as a team. My growls accompany her hisses and snarls. A vicious combination that only drives more blood into my cock.

As one, our essences stream from our mouths, cycloning around us. Violent at first. A churning wave meant to swallow us whole. The same as her cunt around my aching dick. The shift to that soft billowing fog, so smooth, but so sudden, that I nearly miss it. The same pewter cloud that surrounded us that day we held each other drifts through the apartment. So peaceful that I never want it to dissipate.

The combination of us two is a specific hue no one else will ever be able to create. The swirling tendrils sparkling in the dim lighting of my apartment as she moans beneath me. Her body begging for more.

In one swift motion, I'm leaning back onto my heels, arms wrapped tight around her torso, pulling her body up along with mine. Her walls squeeze me tighter in punishment for the quick change in position. Her head falling back with a laugh, long hair pooling on the sofa beneath us before she rises to capture my mouth once more.

Our tongues dance, matching the pace of her bouncing atop my lap. Fingers digging into the rear of my neck, holding herself up. The pliant curve of her ass molds to my hands as I squeeze. Her giggle only enticing me to knead harder.

I've never liked to be held, even as a child. It's an odd thing for me to think about. I preferred my own space. But Bryony makes me believe I will fall apart, losing every piece of myself, should she let go.

"Are you going to be a good little student and come for me again?"

She grins. The tip of her tongue searing my skin as it drags up the side of my throat.

"Are you going to be a good little Grisym and fill my pussy?"

A growl leaves me. The vibration of my chest against hers sending a shock straight down to my dick. Fiona doesn't do dirty talk. Only Bryony has ever challenged me. Every taunt brings out a side of me I haven't known since my younger years. One that aims to dominate. To claim what I'm considering mine to take. Rightfully or not.

My fingers knot in the long strands of her hair, exposing the column of her throat. My lips latching on as I suck at her pristine fawn-complected skin, soft and supple, glowing in the fog of our essences.

A part of me wants to mark her. To let others know she is not free for their taking. But is she mine to claim? *No*. Does that stop me from sucking harder? Also, no.

"Bri, I'm going to need you to come with me. Right now."

"Not yet."

"Now!" I bark. Her walls tighten. My jerking motions aiding in filling her with hot jets of my cum. Our combined releases seeping out of her core as my dick continues to twitch inside her.

"I don't like to be rushed," she breathes. Her damp forehead resting atop my shoulder. Her complexion is a match for the endless freckles that cover my bare torso, shoulders, and back. Just another way that parts of us are the same.

"Well, I don't come before my woman, so deal with it."

She doesn't lift her head, but I feel her smile. I did that. We did that.

Our essences still calmly float around the room. A thin fog reminding us just how much control we can have when we keep those parts of us happy. I can feel it within me. A contentedness that will remain should more of this happen.

"I should go." She begins to unwind herself from me. The slurp of my dick slipping free is a reminder of what we just did. Of a line, we just crossed that we can never go back from.

The beautiful gray clouds that just enveloped us turn dark. Blazing with speed, knocking over knick-knacks on my shelf. Her palm opens, and with its closure, both essences return. Her head twisting to the side as they fight her.

It was only a few days ago that we learned they would willingly go to either of us with the right intent behind it. Since then, we have continued to test the theory. This moment is a clear representation of how well it now works.

"It's likely better if you stay for a while. Our building will be busy until about two. It'll be too difficult to sneak you out."

"Two? As in the morning?" Her eyes go wide as she swipes her cheeky panties and bra from the floor, disappearing into the bathroom a few feet away.

She emerges only a few minutes later, both items secured in place. Two tiny bits of fabric I want to rip from her body. My intent: to leave her as bare as I remain.

"You guys really party all night and then teach the next day?" she huffs, her hands going to her hips. The curves of her body tempting me to pull her back onto my lap and fuck her again.

I painfully clear my throat. "Uh, yeah. We're not as boring as we seem."

"Well, I'll be damned. So, what are we going to do for another six hours?" she snorts.

Her brow quirks. And I wonder if she's thinking the same thing I am. More fucking on every surface of this apartment, preferably.

"I could actually use a nap," I say with a long yawn. I am tired, but I figure it's an easy way to get out of deeper conversations and control myself. Maybe what just happened was just a one-time thing because emotions were high.

There were topics avoided by the sex we'd just had. It's unclear if it was intentional on her part or not, but I can't find it in me to care. I've had a taste of something I badly wanted. And I want more.

"Yeah. Good idea." She quickly pivots back toward the small hallway that houses the bedroom and bathroom doors. Her barely covered ass the best view as I watch her go. My mental plea for my dick to stop hardening a lost cause as I slip my boxer briefs back on with a long sigh.

It only takes me a second to follow her. I shouldn't be surprised to find her already curled up against *my* pillow on *my* side.

"Wrong side."

"Don't care," she sighs.

I climb in behind her. Keeping distance between us until she yanks at my arm, draping it over her stomach.

"I'm a cuddler."

Right. Of course she is.

I do my best to relax with her. To pretend as if having sex with that woman, one time, didn't fuck up my entire world. Doing my best to pretend like I don't want to again, tomorrow, next week, or years from now.

"Are you going to say anything to Pierson?"

She rolls to face me, hands tucked under her cheek. "No." A simple answer. No further explanation will follow, so I press.

"Why?"

Tendrils of magic curl in my chest, hoping her answer is because she prefers me. Experience reminds me I won't get quite that lucky.

"Because this is our business, not his."

We go silent again; her body snuggling in close to my chest as she breathes softly. The softness of her curves is a perfect counterpart to the hardness of the lines of my body. A cut frame I work hard to maintain as I age.

"Do you know my father?" she asks. Her voice is raspier after staying quiet for so long. And I press my eyes shut to drown in the sound of it.

When I open them again, I do the only thing I can do. I lie.

"No."

30

PIERSON

FALL HAS COME AND gone. A sharp transition overnight from crisp autumn air to a frigid sting with any time spent outdoors. The length of each day shortens as the midnight sky brackets the beginning and end of our days. Personally, it's my favorite time of year.

I've always been a fan of the change to the colder seasons. The old stripped so the new can be reborn in the spring. Bri has done that to me. Stripped away the exterior I strut around with as Valen's best friend only to reveal the bare bones of me beneath. A woman like that isn't one you let go of. You hold on tight.

I spend my nights lying between the cool sheets, arm stretching out to the side, pretending it's Bri there next to me. Wishing it was her warming me instead of fleece pajama pants and the pseudo-fire I like to create using elemental spells. Damian always barging in spewing jokes about how he's surprised I haven't burned the place down with it yet.

There are nights when she does fill that space. Her body curled into my side as she clings to me. A thick thigh draped over one of mine, while her fingers dig into my side. Her grip so firm I can almost imagine she needs me as much as I do her. Those are the nights I sleep best, my greatest obsession wrapped in my arms, only to spiral when she disappears for several nights without joining me again.

The woman consumes my every thought. A single glimpse of her sends my heart racing. I do my best to convince myself that I cannot monopolize all her time, yet I put myself in her path every chance I get. Abandoning the crew for meals to wedge myself between her and Graham. Intruding on their study sessions or her and Camilla's movie nights. Infringing on the alone time she likes to take by the lake outside.

She never forces me away, but sometimes I feel her deflate at my presence. That trapped-animal-look in her eyes as if she's trying to get out of a cage. Only that sheen of her gaze can force me to retreat. To allow her to be Bri without me.

With every passing day, Bri becomes my every breath.

In just two short months, I can't see anyone else. Don't want anyone else. Refuse to have anyone else. She is mine. My fall for her has been so far and fast, with no net to catch me. Should she walk away, only death waits at the end.

Valen has always given me shit for being like this. The hopeless romantic who thinks true love is lurking around every corner. I've avoided having the talk with him. He'll rant about how delusional I am to believe there's no doubt in my mind there's a genuine connection between Bri and me and that we are something more than just a short-term relationship. He doesn't have to tell me what he thinks about me. It's there in every look and smirk. I've become another lost puppy for a woman who sees me as nothing more than a good time or a passing boyfriend. That's what Valen has always thought of me.

They leave me. They always do. Sometimes they find someone a little rougher around the edges. A Valen. Other times they've found a Damian—the man that they shouldn't have fallen in love with, but do. Or they find a Kormoran or Sean—men who have no ties and more kinks than sex clubs.

Most just walk away because I'm too nice. Too attentive. Too sweet and caring all the time.

As Valen puts it, I am in danger of smothering them to death with as little as a single thought.

But Bri is different. She was made for me, and me for her. They'll see.

Unfortunately, my past girlfriends aren't the only ones who've walked away. My parents did too, when I embraced a different side of wielding.

Dark wielders carry a reputation for pure evil. Our gifts are meant to take where light wielders give. Yet, I love my parents as much as I always have. They're not bad people per se. I just didn't turn out as they would have preferred.

The age-old dynamic of good and evil, adopted by either side at the beginning of time, still holds strong between the two sides for many wielders. Though that ancient way of thinking has somewhat faded with time, we play into the stereotypes. Many became what someone else told us we were. What we should be.

I chose to learn to be different. To be like the light wielders and use my gifts to give.

My parents didn't care for my decision. They packed every single one of my belongings into boxes while I was away from home on a trip with Valen at twenty years old. Their way of saying I was no longer welcome under their roof.

For humans, it's not common to stay with your parents past schooling years, but for wielders, we often do until we either marry or our magic matures. At age twenty, I was still enrolled in a human college with no intention of moving out soon.

It was a dark time in my life. One where I struggled to find my true place in the world. Valen was the one who was there for me, finding us a house to live in and sticking by my side until we came here at twenty-five. Many will never see that side of him. They will never know how kind and generous he can be to those he cares about. A ruthless protector for those he deems to be worth his time.

When I first submitted my requests for attendance to wielding schools, I'd applied to all light schools, with Beauxgraton as the only dark institution. My position here as a legacy was sure to make me an easy acceptance should the light schools not take me, which they didn't. No one wanted a dark wielder—even one who wanted to be different—attending their schools.

My thoughts continue to alternate between Bri and how I got here. I release a sigh, recalling how she has twined with me to build a future neither of us can see just yet. Flipping to my back, the mattress silent beneath me as I stare up at the ceiling with a dumb grin on my face, I imagine all the possibilities for Bri and me down the road. Exhaustion from a day of practicals draws me deeper into the pillows, still dressed in uniform and too lazy to strip out of more than just my shoes for the day. But it doesn't matter. Nothing ever does when Bri consumes my thoughts.

The slate gray slacks hike up my calves as I roll to the side at the creak of my bedroom door opening. Valen waltzing in as if the room is his and not mine. Typical for him.

"Alone again tonight?" His ability to pick at my wounds grates on my nerves. I tolerate it most of the time because he is my oldest friend. But the more time I spend with Bri, the more I want to retaliate for his barbed jabs.

"What's up?" Choosing to evade the topic altogether, I launch myself from the bed. Stretching the taut muscles of my back from the side, a pronounced groan eases free. Today's classes somehow made me feel a hundred years old.

"Come out with Kor and me. There's a ghoul sighting near town. I could use a power boost."

"Hell no. Do you remember what happened the last time we tried to chase a rogue ghoul?"

His laughter tells me he does. How we all almost ended up dinner for the damn thing because it was so out of its mind, enraged by the spells the hunters had hit it with. It's amazing what you can pack into a three-inch-long dart.

"Come on, man. You used to be fun."

My tether snaps. I can no longer hold back the things I should have said a decade ago.

"No, Valen. Your version of fun has never been mine. No matter how much you try to force it, I'm not like you." My body quickly slumps back down to the mattress, a heavy sigh escaping.

Amused laughter bursts from him. Hot breath coats my skin as his fist digs into the navy blue comforter on my bed. His body curves over mine, veins popping on his forearm that's covered in tattoos depicting death. The most prominent is a half-faced Nigeros that seems to glare at you.

I'm quick to shove at his chest. His feet stumbling a few paces back.

"You're funny. Okay, if you're sure you want to pass," he snickers.

With a sigh, I'm up off the bed, tossing my uniform jacket to the chair. A hoodie torn free of a hanger in the closet, my arms shoved through the sleeves with a huff. With a shake of my head, I shove my feet into the first pair of sneakers I see. Regret already brews in my gut. It always does when Valen or Kormoran come up with stupid ideas like this.

Here we go again.

"That's what I thought." He throws me a smirk as we leave my room. The swagger of his stride, firmly back in place, knowing once again he got his way. "Maybe you can stop thinking about *that girl* for five minutes now," he snorts.

I choose to bite my tongue. No good will come of me arguing or defending Bri.

It's hours of slinking through the nearest town; the quaint city of Northam. Nothing but small shops and diners and bakeries. A custom clothing shop with awnings showcasing family names and a jeweler, each storefront now barren as the shops are closed for the night. The many comforts that humans—and wielders alike—are so attached to.

It's not until we've nearly given up heading back along the pedestrian-free sidewalks we hear a scream. The pitch creates a cringe-worthy screech, long and never-ending.

The three of us bolt down the street without a thought. Kormoran and Valen with wild grins on their faces. I'm just praying to whatever gods still exist that we don't find more trouble than we can handle. Praying that none of us end up injured or dead tonight.

They both zip around the building at the end of the street. The tall lights above are just enough to give a clear path of sight as the soles of our shoes slap against the cement.

I slide to a halt as we take in one of the largest ghouls we've ever seen, its rust-colored skin complemented by the street lamps. A Cupprein, maybe. A breed that needs to fuck multiple wielders on the same night or it will rage out of control. I'm not entirely certain. Without Valen there to correct me, I often confuse them. My focus is only on the breeds that work for me.

A young woman lies tucked into the fetal position behind her car as it sniffs at the air. Those white eyes do nothing to give it any sort of actual vision. Yet, they operate as well as any other sense would on an animal. A tool for finding their partner, or prey.

Its glowing white spheres cut into the surrounding darkness. The massive head swiveling left, then right, looking for its target. Those sensors seemingly flicker as they decide which essences they want to siphon magic to. The ones that are a compliment to it. Wielders who can handle the magic they offer.

But this one is searching for her. Ghouls respond poorly to humans. We have no idea why humans send them into a rage, but this terrified woman still being here is only making the situation worse.

While the two of them sneak behind the beast, I go for the girl. Helping her up by pulling under her arms.

"You need to go. Now!" I whisper-yell, my gaze darting back over my shoulder, hoping the ghoul isn't focused on us.

She only whimpers as I grab her shoulders, my face even with hers. "Listen to me. Get in your car and get out of here!"

The panic in my voice must be enough for her to move this time. Her body shaking violently as she climbs behind the wheel. A quiver so forceful, I wonder if she'll end up just crashing before she clears the small lot.

I turn back to Kormoran. His enormous frame is already naked from the waist down, fucking the ghoul ruthlessly. His body is alive with power as he thrusts into the beast over and over. He's already lost to the power. There will be no pulling him away until he chooses to.

"Val, get in here," Kormoran grunts.

Valen has always liked to watch as much as he likes to take. His cock juts free from between the zipper of his jeans as he strokes. I never noticed how disturbing it is that my friends don't mind watching each other fuck. Or is it hot? I'm not sure I can tell the difference anymore. Especially after I'd let Damian watch me with Bri.

The roar of an engine rumbles down the road, something heavy-duty like artillery as Valen switches with Kormoran. His small, toned ass cheeks flexing with effort as Kormoran roots for him.

As much as I would rather watch anything else, I can't tear my eyes away from the scene in front of me. These are the people that I spend my time with. The ones I've allowed to partially mold me over the years. I'm so lost in thought I nearly miss the high-pitched whistle of a dart flying past my face. So close, the breeze created by its glide seems to tousle the hairs of my eyebrows.

"Move. Move. Move. Move," a gruff voice barks as five men come sprinting past me. More darts fly. Valen refuses to move out of the way or pull his cock from the ghoul. Power seeping into him, so quickly he can't let go, his essence curling around him as if in protection.

"Guys, let's go!" I shout.

The ghoul hunters don't even look at us. Two of them yank Valen away. He fights them, only concerned with siphoning more power, but doesn't get a chance to get close again.

Another car draws to a stop just as the ghoul topples over. The thunderous vibration of the ground leaving me reaching out to the sides for balance. A light snore rumbling through the horde of hunters. Its white eyes are still wide. I know it's not dead. It's simply knocked out from the seven tranquilizers sticking out from its body.

"How did I know I would find you here?" A familiar voice. I turn once more, his face coming into view.

"Professor?"

Shit.

31

Bryony

Time seems to pass faster since I came to Beauxgraton. The days blend into weeks. Each filled with the men dominating my life and new friends. Private sessions with Knox. Pierce's obsession. Late-night study sessions with Graham. Movie nights with the most genuine group of friends I've ever had.

Both fathers have me on edge. The one I've always known dwindles in his communication. The texts come less frequently. His calls are shorter and always focused on the progress I've had with Knox. Outside of that, his only other focus seems to be on any unsightly events that have happened during classes of which it seems each week is littered with at least a few.

I tell myself it's just that Roman Avalon is a busy man. He always has been. His plate is even more full as he tries to find the answers to the light-wielding school closures while also fighting through the issues many dark-wielding schools are having from the mixing students.

Surprisingly, things have been pretty smooth sailing between the light and dark students here at Beauxgraton. Only a few fights broke out in the first few weeks. Likely a side effect of the type of students that tend to gravitate here. Not to mention, the place is big enough that—outside of classes and the dining hall—if you choose not to interact with one another, then you don't have to.

It doesn't help that when I do call Dad his first question has become, "*Did you find something?*" There's none of the previous warmth he'd always given me. Only glimpses of it seep through when I give him tiny bits of information. When I've called him out on it, he always sighs and says, "*Bryony, sweetheart, you know I love you. We just have work to do.*"

I'm convinced that the disappointment I hear in his voice is now echoed in the faces of my peers.

Many of my classmates look at me differently now. Every slip-up either pushes them away or draws them closer to me. Those that dare to linger are either my actual friends or gawkers, curious about why I tend to lose my shit at the worst times.

I do my best to brush it all off. To ignore the stares, whispers, and snickers. There was always a possibility this would happen, regardless of where I went. No matter what, I'm too well-known to escape the scrutiny. Too many know my face to hide all of myself from them.

Yet, I am fighting too. Every day. Protecting myself and Knox from the curious eyes. Protecting me from Graham's questioning and Valen's knowing hints. I've tried to convince myself for weeks I was mistaken about him knowing about me, but I know I'm not. The question is, what to do about it?

Daddy number two—the stranger we all know through news articles—occupies more of my thoughts than any of the other bullshit. His ruthless history ricochets through my mind. I can't logically figure out how a woman like my mother ever loved a man like him. No matter how many scenarios I put together in my head, I can never seem to find a plausible one for how they met and fell in love.

The winter Red Moon is only a week away. Seven days until I meet him. Our meeting is my chance to understand who I am and where I came from. The darkest parts of me want to unveil the half of me I've always kept hidden. The half of me that feels more natural than the light side I've always lived as.

There's an edge to me. One so sharp that I'm cutting those around me. Camilla notices. With her sweet innocence, she thinks she can work the explanation out of me. That if she stares at me long enough, with those big blue eyes, I'll reveal everything swarming my mind.

But I won't.

I can't.

It wouldn't bode well to release the secret of my biological father any more than it would to reveal that I am a Grisym.

Both will leave me crucified. Destined to be put to death and everyone I care about sentenced to go along with me.

Yet she tries to coax me into calm. Time in the sauna. Or a walk through the herb gardens I'd nearly forgotten existed. The indoor greenhouse akin to a sacred space where we harvest plants for the countless spells we use and many of the remedies that the medical staff swear by. I was still in my early teen years the last time I was here and got to walk past those indoor gardens. It's been amazing to see the area has tripled in size since then.

I admit the gardens help the most. The richness of the greens and vibrant colors overshadow the dark and mangled vines that cover the grounds. They all remind me of ghoul skin. Each plant is beautiful and helpful in its way. I wish I'd learned more about herb lore growing up. I could better manipulate spells with the use of them. But that is a class I'll have to wait to take third year—should I make it that far.

Until I have better control and predictability of my magic, I'm stuck with spells I already know. Ones created by someone else. Spells that are tested and proven trustworthy. Fear keeps me from even thinking of creating my own. If I can't do the ones that countless other wielders can, then what would make me believe I could concoct my own and execute them without issue?

Vivid visions of those plants fill my mind as the frigid cold of five a.m. envelops me. A cold so intense, it would be enough to wake the dead. Gusts of wind whip at my exposed skin like pointed chunks of ice striking. I tied my hair tight atop my head and yet, those baby hairs—and the bangs I insisted on cutting two years ago—still work their way free of my hair tie, slicing through the air.

The hinges of the front gates I wait next to, creak loudly with each gust of wind. The noise making me flinch each time.

My breath forms clouds in front of my face. A chatter finding its way to my teeth as I wait for Knox. He's never late, often beating me out here. With shaking fingers, I draw my phone from my pocket again. Fifteen minutes late without a word is very unlike him.

Panic slithers its way into my chest. A burn and a weight that no amount of rubbing with the heel of my hand will erase. I can only hope he had some sort of staff thing to do. Yet that devilish voice whispers in my ear that he's been caught and it's only a matter of time before I am, too.

"He's not coming," Graham mumbles from behind me.

His hands have disappeared, deep into the pockets of his wool coat, shoulders braced against his ears. The tip of his nose, bright red against the cold, as violent shivers work their way through his body.

"Who?"

I know there's no point in playing dumb. Graham has hinted—not so subtly—time and time again that he follows us in the mornings. Watching in hopes of discovering what Knox and I get up to. Curious where we go for hours. His questioning always circles back to why it's the two of us leaving alone.

I won't tell him.

Sure, our sessions started as mandated necessities to ensure we were doing what needed to be done so I could control my essence around him, but since we've had sex, that hasn't stopped either. Each session is destined to end with mutual orgasms. Not to mention the few other times we've snuck off to rooms no longer used to ease our essences into submission. They've had a taste and expect to be fed regularly.

I've been no better with Pierce. His body is the one warming me at night. The man I walk the halls with, hand in hand. The epitome of the perfect mixed couple for everyone else to emulate. At least that's what they see. What we let them see. I'm no more in a relationship with Pierce than I am with Knox.

Knox knows about Pierce and me. Never brings it up. Never questions. Not since our first time. The few times Knox has spotted us together around campus, I've felt our mixed essences stir to life. Internal revolts, attempting to force us together. It's exhausting.

The same isn't true in the reverse. Pierce is sweet, kind, and caring. His every moment seemingly revolves around me and my happiness. His style is sometimes suffocating, yet I can't bring myself to tell him to back off. No one—not even my mother—has doted on me the way he has, and I'm not ready to give that up. Unwilling to go back to a world where I have to live without someone's world rising and setting with me. I understand how selfish that is, but we all desire to be wanted and cared for whether we're brave enough to admit it or not.

Pierce would never understand how I could have feelings for him yet continuously sleep with another man. Let alone a professor with whom I share a deadly secret. No. Pierce finding out about us would break his heart, and I can't do that to him.

If there comes a time when I have to choose ... Well, I will think about it then.

"Come inside, Bri. It's not right that he's kept you waiting." Graham's plea abruptly pulls me out of my spiraling thoughts.

"No one kept me waiting." My chin is high as I wrap my arms around myself. A violent shiver works through me, forcing my eyes closed for several long seconds.

"Bri, cut the shit. I've watched you for months, running off with Professor Knox at the ass crack of dawn. Don't try to play me for a fool."

I take a step closer. My mouth pressed into a grim, straight line as I speak through chattering teeth, "And I told you not to. I'm not asking this time."

"Now you're telling me what to do?"

"In this case, yes. Take it or leave it."

He takes several steps back. Then several more, as hurt shines brightly across his features. His sandy hair and greenish blue eyes are so resilient against the dark surrounding us. An expression filled with agony, as if I'd stolen life from him or physically brutalized him.

I guess in a way I did.

"I thought you trusted me," he whispers before turning his back on me. Head bowed low, shoulders hunched around his ears, he stalks back toward the residence. His mumbled words, lost in the wind.

"I do ..." But I speak so softly that my words are also carried away on the billowing winds.

It's another twenty minutes of standing in the frigid cold before Knox shows up with apologies on his lips. My eyes remain glued to the front doors of the residence where Graham disappeared refusing to look back. That's the part that hurt the most. The man, who is becoming the best friend I've ever had, didn't even bother to look back.

"We had an impromptu faculty meeting. There have been more ghoul sightings." He cups his hands around his mouth, breathing into them before rubbing them together.

My grandmother's words ring back to me. All the warnings and predictions she'd made when I was a child replay in my head now. The ones everyone wrote off as her being nothing more than a crazy old woman.

She wasn't.

Things have been happening just as she said they would. Ghouls are breaking free more frequently without the gateway of the Red Moon. An increased number of hunters and spelled darts needed to take them down. Not to mention the ten deaths of hunters in the past month alone. Bodies sprawled all around the world. Their families left devastated in the end.

She predicted that there would come a time when the Hell Gates that we'd once bound the ghouls behind would crack. The fissures just big enough that those who were looking for them could find them, use them, and exploit them. She knew that ghouls with rebellious magic would thrive.

Grandma Avalon was right.

I can only hope the rogue ghouls were all she was right about.

We move beyond the gates of the school in silence. His fingers slipping through mine as I whisper the enchantment that allows me to teleport. Our bodies shred into tiny particles, moved from one place to the next in less than a minute. The first skill I mastered when I matured into my magic at an early age.

A single thought is all I need to place us in the nondescript woods. Just in case we're ever followed, I never put us right at the cabin. I always leave about a half-mile of distance in different directions between us and it.

The crunch of dried leaves vibrates off the naked tree trunks as our bodies materialize into place. It's been some time since these trees were full of lush greenery. Heavy winds, coupled with the rapid drop in temperature, shook them free by the end of September. The knobbed branches, now stripped naked. "Have there been more sightings in Northam?" I ask.

"Not that I've heard, but several other towns close by. Too close for Milgren's liking."

"What is the Council doing about it? I haven't heard anything from my dad or any of my classmates."

There's no one out here but us. No need to lower our voices or avoid the large piles of crisp foliage beneath our boots. I huddle close to his side, his arm strapped around my shoulder.

"The initial thought was locking down the school tighter. Right now, students have free rein to leave campus for a few hours, without special permission. But likely over the winter, Milgren is going to significantly reduce that luxury."

"That won't affect ... us. Right?"

I think I am just asking about our sessions. About the progress we've made with what we've been able to do with our combined essences. Creation and destruction produced in equal waves. It's as exhilarating as it is terrifying to witness.

"No. Our permissions won't change."

"But ...?"

"But we may have to get more creative with you sneaking in and out of my apartment. Further, lockdown won't just apply to students. It'll be us too. If you get caught at Beechum, there's nothing we'll be able to do to explain it away. Milgren will have to act. I'll be terminated, and you'll get expelled."

I don't even want to think about my family's reaction. Namely Harley. They may suspect what's going on with Knox and me, but they'll never forgive me if we're caught.

"Right ..." I draw out the word so long it begins to sound as if I'm carrying a tune. That reminder of the many things the two of us have to lose is always there at the forefront.

I trudge forward, my footfalls heavy as the tiny cabin comes into view.

"Look Bryony, I don't know what this connection means between us. Frankly, I don't care. I've had you and you're mine now. We'll figure the rest of this shit out."

His mouth finds mine, hand gripping tight around my jacketed biceps. I breathe him in always in search of the fresh ocean scent he carries. It's been years since I've been near a beach. But a single whiff of Knox ignites a longing to let the waves crash against my shins. To feel my toes in the sand during a violent storm.

Suddenly, my love of storms is that much clearer. Maybe that is why my essence prefers to act like one.

He breaks the kiss, taking my hand in his as we enter the cabin for what seems like the hundredth time. A space that has become as familiar as my family home or my bedroom at Beauxgraton.

With a snap of his fingers, the fire sparks to life. Rich flames flicker high, heating the tiny room. The place is so small. Only a bathroom at the rear and the doorway into the kitchen alleyway mark spaces off from the rest of the living area.

From day one, there hasn't been much furniture here. A pull-out couch, an old television with an ass that rivals the size of mine, and bare planks of wood for walls. A coffee table crafted of the same cedar as the walls sits a foot from the edge of the sofa, but nothing else.

Old, mismatched china stocks the shelves of the kitchen, almost as if multiple people left pieces of their lives here. The hinges creaking so loudly as they're opened that I often catch myself wincing. There wasn't even a shower curtain on the tub-shower combo in the bathroom. Yet there were hand towels on the rack and a bar of soap sitting along the rim of the sink. The aged porcelain filled with cracks, but clean.

It's always been basic, but cozy. A place I've appreciated sneaking off to with Knox. Not just because of our sessions or my newfound hobby of forbidden sex with him, but because I've always been a woman who enjoyed the simple things in life. Sure the luxury that comes with my family name can be fun, but it's never truly been what I longed for.

In that way, I am unlike my whole family. The large mega-mansion we've lived in my entire life, fancy cars and clothes, they're nothing more than materialistic things I've never valued the way they do. Give me footy pajamas and a comfy couch with a book any day.

In truth, I always felt as if I was putting on a front. Pretending to be a Bryony that has never actually existed. I smiled when I was supposed to. Fawned over the things they found value in, but it was never really me.

Then I came to Beauxgraton, and the glamour began to melt away. This cabin stripped whatever veneer I still carried away, leaving me truly bare for the first time.

Here I can just be Bri.

Knox is the first person with the privilege of seeing me completely naked.

And I love it.

32

Bryony

"What should we work on today?"

Knox's voice washes over me. The heat from his body at my back forcing the roll of my neck. My shuddered deep breath nothing more than a failed attempt to calm down. Anything to staunch the wants of my essence until I decide to release it.

An arm loops around me, his large hand gripping the canister he always uses for coffee. A pop of the top releases that dark aroma. Some special something he gets from Brazil. I don't care where it's from; it's intoxicating.

If nothing else, he always ensures we have coffee, water, and snacks. The man knows the way to this girl's heart. I never even had to tell him.

"Actually, can we just ... not practice today? I have so much on my mind. And I am so nervous about meeting Jordden. I just want to let it all run through my head. Ya know? Everything I know. Everything I don't know." I fall onto the couch, fingers pulling my two French braids in front of my body. The ends tapping the middle of my torso before settling in place.

"Okay, so let's talk through it."

I shoot him a small smile. A thank you, of sorts.

Knox is a conundrum I hadn't expected. So many things wrapped in a single package. The fear is always there. A sliver of it that likely only I can pick up on thanks to living with that same dark cloud hovering over me since birth. Then there's his ability to logically work through any situation, putting each piece of the puzzle on the table in front of him, and then analyzing and assessing his next step with ease.

Throw that in with the man who takes what he wants in the bedroom, who is also just as much of a softy as he can be a brooding asshole, and you've got five different men in one. Somehow, all of him is a compliment to me.

"First, I need to ask you a question. Not that I am doubting your previous answer, but I feel like there's more you're not telling me." My voice is low as I angle my body toward him. My eyes focus on my thighs before I dare to look up into the dark pine that reminds me of the trees surrounding my favorite lakefront spot.

He's silent as he stares into the distance, focused on nothing in particular. A tiny, dark wave escapes his pointer finger as he rests his hand on my knee.

"You said you don't know my father, but do you know his son?" My choice of wording is intentional. It's been a lot to imagine the man who helped create me, coupled with knowing I have another elder brother out there. One who may treat me as well as Merrick—that's the hope, at least—or the opposite and loathe me the way Harley does. One option is exciting, the other heartbreaking. All of this is becoming too much, and Knox is the only person I can turn to without hesitation.

His face is too stoic. His pause, too long. There's no doubt in my mind he's about to lie to me again. I can't say for sure that he did about not knowing Jordden, but my gut told me he did, willingly omitting information that could help me. Help *us*.

"Yes," he finally breathes, turning away from me, all contact broken. My essence rolls beneath the surface, angry that he would pull away. My body trembling as I fight to keep the mixture of us that now lives within me locked away.

I shove every dark tendril back down. Secure the padlock that keeps it in its chamber until I give the command for it to unlock again. I've begun to tame it with my thoughts. Only once I've gotten answers will I allow it to break free.

"How?" I do my best to compose myself waiting for a response I may not want to hear.

"He's a few years older than me. Our paths crossed during our schooling years. Back when it was normal to do internships at other schools. I'd been in London at the Integretew School of Wielding studying essence manipulation."

He must have studied under Professor Perrue. A brilliant woman in her own right. I've only met her once. Her retirement from instructing young wielders long since passed. Where light and dark professors generally stick to their respective schools, Professor

Perrue chose differently. A pioneer of a woman electing to teach at a dark school as a light wielder. Historically, foreign institutions are a lot more willing to mix and match wielders than the schools here in the States.

From what Dad taught me, almost every school around the world was fighting for her. She chose Integretew because it was one of the few schools that promoted these internships where others could come to study any subject, regardless of whether they were born of the light or the dark. An institution that still prides itself on inclusivity and teaching wielders to just be wielders. Not to think of themselves as from the light or the dark. To just be great. Learn from the best and become the best.

"He's an interesting guy, you could say." The muscles of his biceps bulge as he runs his fingers through the hair at the rear of his skull. His focus anywhere but my face.

"Explain," I gently command, my voice even, despite the climbing curiosity soaring through me.

"Well. He, uh, enjoyed using his gifts."

I freeze. A chill shoots through me, my internal body temperature plummeting to subzero. I'd heard the stories of what Vincent Guthrie could do. Most dark wielders view his gift as neither a give nor a take—or maybe it's both. His specialty is necromancy. A version where, not only can he raise the dead for prolonged periods, but he can also read their thoughts as if they were his own. Their memories are movie reels for him to watch. Copies made, or originals stolen, before he returns them to their resting places.

From the rumors I've heard, there are several old supporters of Jordden's that Vincent has raised. Their bodies have yet to be returned to their resting sites.

Unlike humans, wielders do not bury their dead six feet under. We're kept in tombs, similar to ancient cultures. We often inscribe our vaults and the surfaces of our caskets with scriptures and spells to ensure our essences don't leak free while we roam the afterlife. They contain us in death, while our bodies remain displayed in the Cavea de Mors. Its structure nestled in the heart of London's underground, where humans will never find it. A labyrinth of a world full of history dating back to the fifteen hundreds.

With Jordden having his status of notoriety, the world is also privy to the things Vincent does. There's nowhere he can turn without his life appearing as an open book for all of us to see. Roaming amongst our dead in search of whatever information he pilfers from them. It makes sense that he would make a home there.

"Of course he does. He is the son of the most wanted dark wielder in the world. I can only imagine he raises them to get information for my ..."

I've only been able to think of that man as my father in my head. Weeks of having time to get used to the idea of coming face to face with the one I share DNA with. But I've only ever called him Jordden out loud. Outwardly acknowledging who he is creates nothing more than another heavy burden for me to carry.

"I honestly can't tell you. I didn't spend much time with him. To be honest, he's creepy as hell. You've seen his face." A shudder works its way through Knox's upper body.

I have. The whole world has.

The short dark hair, almost black. That one dark brown eye, a shade matching that of caked mud dredged from a river, the other, a crystal gray so pale it might as well be ghoul-white. The pupil of that watery eye gives the only added dimension. He is not someone I would want to see in a dark alley, yet he is my blood. My brother.

But so are Harley and Merrick. My sister Sicily, my blood too. Yet I am an outsider beside them. The only half while they are all whole.

I'd always wondered how he ended up with mismatched eyes. It's even rarer than being a Grisym. Features of both.

"Do you think he's like us?" I ask. My voice is high as the thought wanders free.

"A Grisym?"

I nod.

"No, he can't be. But then again, he does have the gift of raising the dead and that one eye ..." His words trail off. His head shakes as if trying to convince himself there's no way. "No. He is proud of being a dark wielder. Boastful even, of being one of the few unique dark wielders. The guy nearly shouts it from the rooftops with just his stare."

I wait in silence for Knox to continue. Only speaking when I'm sure he won't. "But we've spent our whole lives telling people we're one thing."

His mouth opens and then closes as if pondering my words. As if considering the potential truth in them for the first time. His silence stretches so long that I begin to question the validity of my statement. "You're right. He is what he is."

My head falls to Knox's shoulder. One strong arm snaking around my waist, pulling me closer. An endless yawn escapes me, eyes fluttering shut before I can stop them. My mind blank for the first time in weeks.

I wake to heated hands on my flesh and a head between my legs.

"Shhh ... You kept grinding against me." He places a wet kiss to my inner thigh, briefly squeezing my flesh with both hands. "So I figured I would give you what you want."

As consciousness slowly dawns on me, I realize that I'm naked and stretched out across the pull-out mattress, no longer a couch. I'm not sure who stripped me, but I don't give a shit. Not as his tongue swirls through my folds and then pierces me right where I need him. The violence of an orgasm already nearing its peak before I've even fully woken.

"You shouldn't strip a woman in her sleep and then eat her kitty cat when she's not even awake to enjoy it."

His eyes find mine. Hooded and filled with lust. A quirk of a grin plays at the corner of his mouth. I'm always happy to challenge him, but only occasionally let filth pass my lips. The dynamic of him being the dirty old bastard of a professor teaching his student is a joke we frequent in our sexual encounters.

"Sweetheart, you tore your *own* clothes off. Not me." He blows over my sensitive flesh, making my hips squirm in his grasp. "And you may not have verbally asked me to lick up and down this sweet cunt, but your essence did. So, lie back and take it."

I do as he says, rolling my pelvis up to his face. The stubble of his cheeks is abrasive against my flushed skin. Knotting my fingers in his hair, the strands just long enough to wrap around each digit, he's held in place. My body ready to let its release free when a bang sounds against the cabin wall.

Then another.

"I know you're in there."

That voice.

His voice.

Shit.

33

VALEN

IT WAS EASY ENOUGH to figure out where Bryony and Knox snuck off to. This cabin is no secret amongst the students. Many of the faculty members have made their way out here for various reasons this year already. Covert meetings—both approved and grounds for removal—at all hours of the day. Those idiots talk louder about the shit they should keep quiet than you'd think.

I hadn't even been thinking about Bryony and her pouty mouth and infuriating retorts until I caught her *bestie* Graham storming through the halls, mumbling to himself about her bending over backward for Knox. The guy might as well have shouted it for anyone to hear. Such a compromising position he has put her in. One I used to my advantage.

He really should have been paying attention to his surroundings. More careful of the words he spoke under his breath to himself. Been more careful of the secrets he gave away.

To my benefit, he's presented me with a great opportunity to hold not only Bryony under my thumb, but Knox, too. One professor here to watch my back and protect me from any punishment is great, but two is better.

Bryony and Knox hadn't noticed me standing on the porch that wraps around the front half of the cabin, staring in through the window just before they fell asleep. His fingers stroked the exposed skin at her throat, before she started removing her clothing some time later, eyes closed as if still sleeping. But she couldn't have been. Not with the way she moved. Not with how her essence billowed through the tight space.

I was convinced they weren't anything more than a rumor I cooked up. Until I saw them there this morning. Her full figure curled into his side as if that's something they always do. The same way I've seen her and Pierce sleep when I've snuck into his room to watch. She and Knox were nothing more than chaos I'd created until I watched the way she responded to his touch. His head buried deep in that pussy that I'm still pissed Pierce has tasted.

She stretched her body out on the old mattress as if in presentation. Soft flesh and supple curves that I would willingly run my hands over if I wasn't constantly debating murdering her instead. My eyes roamed over her body open and exposed for Knox. A sight I've enjoyed countless times now thanks to Pierce never locking his door. Irritation bubbled through me once again watching another man that isn't me getting to touch her.

My dick grew hard while I observed her essence seep from her parted lips, coaxing him forward. I'm not sure if that's a Grisym thing or if it has something to do with them both being innate wielders. It was a first for me to see. Curiosity over what it must be like to share an essence with someone left me adjusting myself repeatedly.

A black tendril formed from her, appearing almost like a finger as it settled beneath Knox's chin, guiding him to the spot between her full thighs. Only to swirl past his ear as if whispering to him. His hesitation was only apparent for a moment before his face buried into her glistening cunt.

Dick hard in my pants, I watched. Mesmerized by what they could produce as one. Her deep moan reminded me of the damage I was there to do. Eager to hear screams of terror versus pleasure.

That's when I threw the first rock.

The crack of its hard edges against the aged wood was not nearly satisfying enough when they didn't start yelling from inside. The fucker didn't even raise his head from her swollen flesh.

So, I threw another. That one pulled her out of the trance.

"I know you're in there." My voice a humorous taunt.

I wonder if they will come out. There's no doubt my voice is the one that already haunts her dreams. It must be, after all the death threats I've showered her in. Never skipping an opportunity to throw my spelled daggers in her direction. But she's said nothing. Done nothing. Maybe she fears what I say I'll do. Maybe she doesn't give a shit.

I don't know for sure until the door creaks open, her legs bare, toes wiggling against the chilled wood. His shirt serves as her cover-up as she glares at me.

"Not even going to try to hide it, huh?"

"What's the point? Your sick ass was likely already watching through the windows."

Lucky guess. She hadn't seen me. Her focus never once drifted in my direction as I watched Knox eat her pussy like a greedy dog.

"Going to invite me in?"

The old steps creak beneath my combat boots. I'd voiced it as a question, but I hadn't truly meant it as one. I was coming in regardless. It's the only way to truly unnerve the two of them.

She steps aside, an exasperated sigh leaving her. Knox is at her back, moving with her as if they're connected by invisible strings. Their tether is that much more obvious in the small, enclosed space. Unbreakable, even.

A connection no one would understand. It's unclear what might exist between two Grisyms. Their lives are supposed to end after only a few short breaths. The majority never mature to experience being in the presence of anyone other than their birth mother and their reaper.

The oldest one I've heard of was five. The Council hounds snatching and then slaughtering her in front of her opposing parents. They made an example of her. Every one of our news outlets broadcasted her mutilated body for everyone to see. That young couple locked away for daring to go against the law, creating and then harboring that little girl.

I was ten when that happened. Each bit of imagery is a vivid memory. I'd fought myself then. Tried to convince my mind that I should be sad the little girl was dead. That it was wrong of the media to broadcast her broken body for all to see, but I felt nothing but relief. I understood then that Grisyms weren't supposed to exist. They were a gross corruption of our wielding gifts. They were a threat to light and dark alike. Their existence was sure to further upset the unbalanced scale between the two sides.

The power they possess is beyond what even innate light wielders have. Their gifts are so much more than altered versions of what we should be. Unpredictable. An unknown we will never understand in our lifetime. As I've aged, I've released some of that mindset. Grisyms are no threat to me as long as they don't stand in the way of my goals.

There are too few records of Grisyms. The truth lost to history. Light and dark alike feared what they could do. How they could manipulate each side's powers of give and take to make them their own.

As fascinating as they may be to study, I can't have her and Knox potentially ruining everything. It's the dark side's time to move to the forefront.

"What do you want Valen?" Knox's mouth pulls into a tight straight line, the bow of his upper lip nearly disappearing.

"I want to know how we got two Grisyms at our school and why someone is protecting you both?"

They both suck in a gasp of air. Chests frozen, puffed out as if exhaling is an option long forgotten. They have matching eyes. Wide, but oddly rimmed. Knox's pinky wrapping around hers, as a tiny tendril of dark essence leaks out the tips. Its swirling loops twirling tightly around where they remain joined.

"Who told you?" Bryony finally snaps.

Her free fingers tap at the bare skin of her thigh. My eyes trailing from her bare feet, nails painted black to match her fingers, roving up her well-sculpted calves to the shapely thighs, slightly dimpled, but seemingly still toned.

I can't deny I want to fuck the woman. Her full frame is the opposite of the waifs I've always avoided. Skin and bones bring me no comfort when I want something to squeeze or hold.

Stepping toward her, I grip her chin. The tendrils of dark smoke coming from her and Knox immediately blast out in a thick fog, swirling around the room. The few pieces of decor tossed to the floor scattering to odd corners.

"I would suggest you stop touching her," Knox growls.

I narrow my eyes at him through the swirl of black-speckled crystals, gleaming like tiny stars. I thought I'd caught glimpses of something glittering in her essence many times, but convinced myself it was nothing more than my imagination. Now that I see it clearly, her differences were always right there for all of us to see. We were just too dumb to pay attention.

I only keep hold for another moment before shoving her face away from me. Immediately, their essences calm, the color shifting from the drapes of night to a soft gray. A calm and serene haze floating over the floor, our feet obscured from view as it simmers just above our ankles.

Still, only their pinkies stay joined.

"To answer your question … No one told me." My smirk erases the glare in Bryony's eyes. Replaces it with something like fear for the first time since she's met me. "But you just did."

She's silent for longer than expected as she rearranges her features into that stoic expression I know well.

"And what will it take to keep your mouth shut?" Knox steps forward, breaking their connection. Their essences roar into a vortex around them, Bryony's outstretched hands just outside its soft edges. Palms facing me, both arms quivering for a few seconds before her fingers curl into tight shaking fists. Every tendril of their magic is suddenly gone. Sucked beneath the surface of her skin in seconds.

I have never seen anything like it. Never witnessed essences merge so easily, commanded by another. It was as if his essence belonged to her in a way only her own essence should. Each swirl of dark smoke was more than willing to call her body home.

This is exactly why they're not supposed to exist. They're unpredictable. There's too much unknown to count on or trust them.

"Not much," I shrug. Knox shifts closer still until Bryony holds him back with a palm to his chest.

"I've had enough of your shit. What is your deal with me? You clearly followed me here. You knew something was different about me. So. What. The fuck." Her finger jabs at my chest. "Do. You. Want?"

Her sneer is mean enough to scare almost anyone away. Anyone but me. A man drawn to the dark and dangerous. One that laughs in the face of a woman who most certainly has a murderous impulse as intense as mine.

I am that man. A man curious about what secrets she keeps between her ears and tucked between her legs.

Stepping closer, my mouth near her ear, no longer able to contain the wolfish grin, I whisper, "You."

34

GRAHAM

I'VE SPENT THE ENTIRE day worried about Bri. She never showed up to any of our classes. That seat to my left, repeatedly empty. High-level panic courses through me. A rage of waves crashing relentlessly. Maybe something happened. Maybe whatever she and Professor Knox got into went wrong.

Pierson was the one person I thought for sure would know where she was. The only thing more tied to her side than her shadow. His obsession with her is definitely on the brink of unhealthy.

Valen denied seeing her, either. Before he abruptly ended our call, the clip of his tone was one of irritation that I would even bother asking him about Bri.

His hatred of her is so profound. I have fantasies of shoving him off the mountain cliff the way he's threatened her. Only his stolen glares betray him, implying maybe her death isn't all he desires from her.

When I couldn't find Professor Knox either, I went to Headmistress Milgren. Her cool demeanor was dismissive as I brought up my concerns. The woman didn't even bother looking up from the collection of aged parchment she wrote on as I pleaded with her to do something.

"You're overreacting, Mr. Mayer," she hummed. "I would suggest you return to whatever you had planned for your evening."

Yet I didn't leave. Instead, I pled more. Harder. Longer. More ferociously. Reminded her a student like Bri doesn't miss class. Repeated that the last time I saw her, it was nearly five thirty in the morning and she was standing out in the cold waiting for Professor Knox. His name spewed with all the skepticism I hold for him.

Milgren denied that to be the truth. Stated he was off campus for a few days. Adamant that, though he is serving as her advisor, they would not be traveling off-site together. And especially not alone.

I'd been stunned into silence at her blatant lie. Advisor? Professors don't act as advisors—a practice used in human schools and colleges. Wielders need more than one person to guide them through their early years of magic. Various gifts and talents are needed to mold us into productive contributors to our world once we complete our studies.

Maybe status as Roman Avalon's daughter gives her perks the rest of us aren't privileged enough to receive, but why Professor Knox? Out of all the accomplished men and women here, why pick one of the youngest and least experienced? The students and staff alike are more likely to discuss his looks than his magical proficiency. It doesn't add up.

I had to shake my head at that last thought. The words recited in my head with vehemence, my inner voice laced with something like jealousy. A reaction that makes no sense to me. Bri has become my closest friend. That's all.

Bri has yet to show any specific gift the way many of us have. That fact alone might explain her need for someone like Knox to guide her. His ability to manipulate foreign essences is unmatched here at Beauxgraton. A necessary ability for someone who lives in the spotlight, but also doesn't have talents of her own.

This thought only heightened my fear. My words spilled out of me as I then used the last bit of sway I had revealing Valen's behavior to the headmistress. The knife throwing and the bruises he's left on her arms and neck. Milgren did her best to pretend as if it was nothing. As if she didn't care. But for the briefest of seconds I saw the spark of concern in her eyes. Those lithe aged fingers curled tight around her fountain pen.

I've wondered for some time if she knew Bri before coming here—in a personal way. She's been in the woman's office far too many times since we got here for it just to be school-related or ensuring she is having a pleasurable experience to appease her father.

I'd tried to convince Milgren that, if Professor Knox wasn't here, then Valen must have done something to Bri. Taken her somewhere or done something awful to her.

Still, she did nothing more than shoo me away.

For hours now, I've sat in Bri's room waiting for her to return. Camilla endlessly paces, alternating between gnawing at her bottom lip and chewing her already short nails to the quick. She's constantly tugging at that white-blonde hair as if that would make her roommate and self-proclaimed best friend walk through the door.

Pierson's fingers move non-stop over the screen of his phone. It didn't surprise me when he came to the room after I'd texted again, asking if he'd seen Bri. He hasn't looked away from his phone for a second. Who knows how many messages he's sent to her, his friends, and Valen, especially when I mentioned what a dick he'd been to me on the phone earlier. No one has seen either of them.

Valen supposedly disappeared before anyone even woke up this morning. The only communication we've had with him is through texts and my single phone call. Pierson claims that it's nothing to question. He sometimes has *things* to take care of. I pressed my mouth shut, wanting to ask about these mysterious things, but knowing it would only come out as an accusation.

The bells toll midnight. The last ones of the evening until seven tomorrow morning.

"Where is she?" Camilla whimpers. The poor girl is doing everything not to fall apart. Her thin arms wrap around herself as if trying to keep from shattering. A small quiver making her appear so fragile.

" I wish I knew," my voice a trembling whisper.

Worry seeps into the fine lines around her mouth and the droop of her eyes. I've never met someone who cares the way Camilla does. She always greets others with kindness—unless they piss her off—and makes sure her friends are taken care of. The shyness she originally started school with has slowly melted away with her blossoming friendship with Bri.

She was like us. The side character that never quite belonged. Our group of friends changed that for her. Our dynamic has been the driving force encouraging her to come into herself and be no one but herself. Now that little pixie of a woman shines as bright as that near-white hair of hers.

My eyes just start to drift closed as the door slams open. Valen trails ahead of Bri with Professor Knox bringing up the rear.

"The next time I catch you both off campus after hours, you're going to get a lot more than the talk and escort we had tonight. Am. I. Clear?" Knox's voice booms through the space. His face contorts with more fury than is likely warranted in this situation.

My eyes dart between the three of them. Strong words, but the body language is all wrong. I'm quick to glance them over, head to toe. Trying to pinpoint just what is so off.

Bri wears the same clothes from this morning. But I'm most surprised to see Professor Knox. Here. In her room. He's not supposed to be on campus, which means he's either back and caught the two of them out, or he was never gone in the first place and Milgren lied.

Camilla launches herself at Bri. Her arms lock around Bri's middle as she makes weird humming sounds. "Missy, if you ever pull a stunt like that again, I will skin your backside myself and feed it to whatever fish live out there in that lake."

Bri's laughter fills the room. Its timbre and joy cut through the tension.

The moment Camilla releases her, Pierson has her wrapped in a tight hug. His hand cupping her cheek, mouth pressed to hers.

I only watch them for a moment. Something twitching in my chest at the display. It's just weird watching my friend make out with her "not boyfriend," that's all. The story I will keep telling myself to ignore whatever it is strumming the threads of my heart.

My focus shifts to Professor Knox. His fists ball at his sides, jaw working fiercely as the muscles tick in time to the pulse bounding at his throat. A thick vein bulges alongside his temple as he fights for self-control, his eyes homed in on the connection between Bri and Pierson's mouths.

I don't understand what's happening here. This dynamic that's floating between us all is odd. Off. And, certainly, I wouldn't say I like it.

Pierson finally steps back, draping his arm around Bri's shoulder while her head rests in the crook of his collarbone. At some point, someone closed the door, but Knox and Valen are still planted in place.

"Uh, Bri. Can I talk to you alone for a sec?"

Her jaw pops with an extended yawn, but she nods, placing one more quick peck on Pierson's mouth, his body falling back onto her bed the moment she pulls away. Valen gets nothing more than a pointed look from Bri. One filled with vitriol and hate. But she stops at Knox's side. Her hand lightly grazes his forearm, just above where his bare skin sits.

"Thank you," she all but whispers to him.

Then she takes my arm and follows me out into the hallway.

I wait until we've reached an alcove at the far end of the hall, ignoring Professor Knox's retreating form as he jogs down the stairs. A pang similar to jealousy rings through me for the second time today as I watch him look back at us one more time. Bri's back is to him, so she misses the odd emotion in his eyes.

"Where were you all day?"

"Valen was helping me practice some of my wielding." She relays the answer so nonchalantly that it seems exaggerated, even as she tries to pass it off as if it's the truth. But I see through the lie.

"No," I say. "When I saw you this morning you were waiting for Professor Knox."

"No. You think I am sneaking off with Knox, but I was waiting on Valen."

My brow furrows, trying to decipher if it could be the truth. My mind searches for what she and Valen could be working on together that was more important than attending classes.

"You were gone all day, Bri."

"Hey," she coos, stepping closer to me. Her hand cups my cheek. Instinctually, I lean into her touch. I hadn't even realized how much I wanted it until I felt the warmth of her palm. A reassurance I needed to confirm she's safe.

It's not that she doesn't touch me often. She does. Hugs. Random grabbing of my arm. Occasionally, she takes my hand as our group walks together like some sort of weird cult. There are the many pecks on the cheek. Then there was the night she kissed me. Right after we met. I'd felt something then. Who wouldn't, with a girl like Bri? But we're friends. Even if I'm holding an internal competition against her to be the best student here.

But in this moment, my body betrays me, seeking out her comfort despite her leaving us drained of our sensibilities for the day. I want to yell at her. To hold her. To lock her in her room, so she can't give us a heart attack again. But none of those things are my job. None of those things are what I should do. Only what I want to do.

"I know you were worried, but I'm fine." She grabs my face with both hands forcing me to stare down at her. "I'm fine." She smiles wide—a glistening bright light between us.

"Okay. Yeah. I just ..."

"It's all good, okay," she laughs. Taking my hand now, she leads us back to her door. "Go to bed. I'll see you at breakfast." Two small pats on my cheek bring a flush up my neck following the innocent gesture.

Just before she places her hand on the door, a chant on her lips to let her through, she turns back to me one last time. A soft peck placed over the spot she'd just tapped me. So close to the corner of my mouth, the slightest turn of my head would bring our lips together.

She opens the door to Pierson and Valen sprawled out on her bed. "You guys coming?" I call.

"No, we're good," Valen smirks. A quick swipe of his fingers shutting the door in my face.

A groan sounds from him behind the closed door. Camilla's high-pitched laughter following. Bri likely punched him.

That's enough to send me to bed with a smile.

That's my girl.

35

BRYONY

IT'S BEEN SEVERAL DAYS since our fiasco at the cabin. It hasn't stopped Knox and me from traveling there each morning. Our sessions, a little shorter each day, skipping to him burying himself inside me. The both of us commanding our essences to obey various orders before, during, and after. Those moments with him are when I feel most like Bri.

Valen hasn't shown up unannounced again, but he seems to be everywhere at school. I turn around, and there he is. His trim frame lurking like a predator. One of his enchanted daggers always flipping between his long thin fingers. The upturn at the corner of his mouth slipping into place the moment we make eye contact.

I fucking hate him and wish he would disappear.

Today, of all days, I'm antsier than ever. My leg won't stop twitching. My pits are a nonstop pool of cold sweat. The bite of my teeth into my bottom lip verge on drawing blood. The plump flesh will be nothing more than a pulverized mess before lunch rolls around.

It's not the exam I am nervous about. I'm decent at spellcasting, most days. I expect this showcase of our skills should be easy enough, seeing how we randomly pull from the spells we've already been working on in class all semester. Theoretically, there aren't any I haven't done.

Rather, it's the note from my father burning a hole in my pocket that keeps me teetering on the edge of a breakdown. I'd convinced Knox to let me hold on to it. Naturally, he'd fought against it, fucked me over it, and then eventually gave up. Sure, it would be safer in his hands, locked away in the teacher dormitories, but a part of me needed to keep this tiny piece of parchment close. As if letting it go would make it less true.

Or that feeling the texture of the note between my fingers might convince me that anyone other than Roman Avalon could ever fill my father's role. *My Dad.*

I've never needed to know where I came from. Never truly cared who my father was in the sense of wanting him to be part of my life. The only information I wanted to know was his name. All I ever needed to know was that bit of information tacked to the dark wielder that created me alongside my mom. There was nothing else of importance. For me, no one could replace the man who raised me as his own and had shown me nothing but unconditional love and respect my entire life.

Now another dark secret looms over me.

It's not enough to be the daughter of the Director of Education.

It's not enough to be an illegally born wielder.

I have to be the daughter of the most hated dark wielder on earth, too. The most ruthless wielder who has done the most unspeakable things in the name of the change he wants to see in our world. The New Order standing behind him, doing his bidding. Those followers live their full lives in plain sight, refusing to stay hidden in the shadows.

Not much is known regarding how the New Order internally operates, but we all know what they stand for. They want the downfall of our current structure. No more council. No bureau. Positions of prestige dissolved to bring about greater equality between wielders. Simple.

The issue is there is no definitive proof that Jordden and the New Order have done the despicable things linked to them. Murder. Theft. Attacks. Kidnappings. You name it the New Order has been accused of it. But without proof, the Council and the Bureau have no choice but to let them remain free, living their lives uninhibited. A group that remains untouchable.

My eyes dart from corner to corner as if there's a member of the New Order next to me now. I wonder who I've encountered that follows Jordden. Who has been watching me for him? The notion is ridiculous. He could have found me at any time in my life. He isn't watching for me. He was ordered to stay away, and per his letter, he has done just that.

That note seems to twitch in my pocket as if telling me to reverse that thought. The man who wrote it says he loves me. Should I be so quick to dismiss what he might do to know his daughter's life?

Add in having a half-brother that would make Valen piss his pants with what he can do with his powers, and I've hit the complicated life lotto.

If people had a reason to hate me before, now they have many more to hunt me down. There is a renewed urgency to keep my secrets concealed lest someone outside my trusted circle find out and remove me from this world. Or worse, use me as leverage against either of my fathers.

Maybe most wouldn't. Without the letter in my pocket, no one would know my father cares about my well-being at all. That he even knows who I am or that he wants to see me. They wouldn't even know I'm his.

"Ms. Avalon," Professor Caulder calls.

It takes me a moment to realize I've been called to the front of the room. My hands tremble at my sides, knowing I am seconds away from having to display my skills. A silent prayer sent to any of the gods willing to help me keep my essence within my control today whispered on my lips. I can't afford any more mishaps that would bring my dad and Harley here.

Graham quickly shoves at my arm when I still don't move. A look of concern drawing his features into a scrunched appearance.

Jumping from my seat, I tug at the bottom of my uniform jacket. The heather-gray a reminder of the mixture that now lives within Knox and me.

My hand refuses to steady as I reach into the cauldron to pull out the spell I'll have to cast. Seeing as our professor's last name is Caulder, he thinks it amusing to cover every surface with the curved pots. All shapes and colors, heights and depths. Today's made of metal so thick that it chipped the stone floors when a boy from our class accidentally knocked it over the first week.

A sliver of paper flutters into my palm as I open it within the mouth of the cauldron. My fingers quickly coil around it before I yank my hand free. The tremble more forceful for several brief moments.

The torn piece of parchment falls open in my palm as I extend my fingers straight. Uneven edges glow a vibrant orange as if they're alight with flame. Yet, it doesn't burn.

The edges don't blacken, as they would if the paper was actually on fire leaving nothing but ash piled against my skin.

Mens Imperium. Mind Control.

It's one of the more difficult spells to cast. Only made easier if the recipient is of a weak mind. Better if yours is unbelievably strong.

This was the spell the entire class struggled with. Graham performed it just a bit better than I did, a tidbit that still brings about the grinding of my molars. That day, I'd tried my best, instead of making intentional mistakes. A tactic I'd been using when necessary that made me appear more level with my peers. But not that day, and still, he outdid me.

I take a deep, filling breath, pinching the tiny piece of paper to show it to Professor Caulder.

"Very well, then."

He signals one of the assistants forward. A girl with short dark hair, angled in a severe bob that only sharpens the deadly lines of her jaw. Her harsh features a disturbing contrast to her large doe eyes.

Stepping forward several paces, I face her. I take more calming breaths, clearing my mind so that I may invade hers. A stillness washes over me as I imagine nothing but my essence filling me. No bones or muscles, tissue or fat. Just that swirl of my mixed magic, looking to make a connection with the mind of the woman in front of me.

She stands there, stone still, as I stare into the pits of her forest-green eyes. The pupils dilate unnaturally as she winces. The first prick of me invading her consciousness. My lips repeatedly tap as I mumble those two words over and over and over. So quiet, no one will hear.

Mens Imperium. Mens Imperium.

My essence finally breaks through, finding hers holding the shield against me. Grabbing hold of it, I pull with enough force to shatter the wall she'd built to keep me out. She shudders. Her body convulsing forward as my head tilts to the side.

I can't see the change in my eyes but I feel it. The white beginning to take over the way it does when I have sex with Knox. For a moment, I fight it. Will them to return to normal, to not give me away, but my true Grisym nature has grown strong. We released it and now it refuses to hide in the corner as I've made it do my whole life.

With an intentional blink, I let it free.

I can't look away, my eyes held open by some invisible force.

Only a single whispered word enters my mind before it's tossed into hers.

Kneel.

Her knees hit the stone floor with a sickening crack. Her face contorting into one of agony, mouth twisted up in pain, her eyes shut tight. A quake of her body as she fights me. Her chest heaves with deep strained pulls and pushes. Ragged breaths bursting through her parted lips as tears stream down her face.

"Please," she begs.

But I am lost in the connection I've made. I'm barely aware that my head cocks to the side once more. Eyes unseeing as the girl begs in front of me. I see nothing but sense everything. Her fear. Her essence cowering inside her, ducking away from mine. Something about my combination is a terror it refuses to stand against.

The whispers from around the room go ignored. They know nothing. They *are* nothing.

All that exists is this. My powers have the chance to show what I might truly be capable of. That I am not one to trifle with.

Another command soars to the front of my consciousness.

Stop breathing.

Immediately, her lips seal. The plea for release, still etched on her face. Her nostrils sucking in, attempting to find precious air. The cotton of her shirt soaks through with her tears. Tension holds her body taut as she fights for one precious breath. Fingers extending straight, but unable to leave her sides. The chords of her neck so pronounced they form their own mountain ranges along her skin.

My intent is for her to stay just as she is while she suffocates.

"Bryony! Stop!"

I hear the command, but my essence won't let go. It's caught hold of her mind and it wants to keep it. It will bend her to my will. Make her bow to my whims and thrash beneath my commands.

Dark thoughts flow through me. Ones that should make me recoil in disgust. But there's a smaller part of me, now at the forefront, rubbing its palms together, happy to embrace the nature so many believe every dark wielder possesses.

A slow grin spreads on my face. My cheeks lift with it. A soreness creeping in as I hold it there.

"Bri." Firm hands shake me. Still, I can't break the connection. I don't want to.

I want this power. This control. I need this darkness to consume me. To wreck everything in my path because that is what I was meant to do.

Who I am meant to be.

"Bri!" a voice roars in my face. Someone shakes me harder. My eyes finally blink. I feel them retreating to their normal state. A split second of blurred vision before they focus.

Graham's face comes into view in front of me. Every other student in the room including Professor Caulder, stares at me in fear as he cradles the apprentice on the floor.

"Call for help," he bellows. Several of my classmates run from the room at once. Careless shoves to throw each other out of the way as if I'm a bomb set to explode.

"Bri. What did you do?" Graham whispers.

All I can see is the girl on the floor. Professor Caulder urgently chanting a spell over her. Her knees bleed from their impact with the stone. The deepest shade of blue shadowing her lips, eyes open and unseeing. Glazed with imminent death.

Panic unfurls in my gut. Nausea takes over as I hunch forward, a hand cupping over my mouth muffling my sob.

For several long moments, I can't move. My gaze trains on the woman, unable to look away from the horrible thing I'd just done until my breakfast rushes up my throat. My face barely hovers over the trash bin as I vomit uncontrollably. The tears burning my eyes, punishment for what I've done.

36

Bryony

It's a horrific day when you ruin the exam for the class. Add in nearly killing—or maybe succeeding at murder—an apprentice. Terrifying everyone. Getting called into the headmistress's office to be reprimanded by that fearsome woman and your parents, who arrived only moments ago. *Best. Day. Ever.*

Another piece of me fractured with each phone call I ignored from Dad. I promised I wouldn't disappoint him and look at what I've done. No part of me is looking forward to seeing those emotions splashed across his face.

Professor Caulder, Knox, Mom, Dad, Assistant Headmaster Schouten, and Headmistress Milgren are all seated around the elongated conference table as I enter the room marked "Staff Only." All eyes are on me as I slip into one of the open chairs, each with their fingers laced in front of them. I refuse to look at my dad. A poor attempt at delaying the inevitable.

Caulder's eyes repeatedly shift in my direction. His shoulders held high around his ears, as if terrified I might suddenly lash out. The moment I'm seated, he rises, relocating to a chair as far away from mine as the table will allow. His seat slightly pushed back from the edge, body erect as if he will need to run.

Was I truly that frightening?

I laugh to myself. Yes, I was. I'm just trying to make myself feel better by pretending I didn't just become a ruthless villain who cannot pull my gifts back.

Schouten sits with the same posture, directly across from me. My parents flank me on either side, as if in protection. Mom reaches for my hand, only for me to pull away. I'm scared to have anyone touch me. What I've done with only a single set of mumbled words is too fresh for me to allow physical comfort from anyone right now.

"Today's display was unacceptable," Headmistress Milgren tuts.

Knox stiffens next to her. They both know this goes beyond being naturally gifted at spellcasting. This has something to do with my Grisym mix. A part of me I was supposed to be learning to control.

My parents know it, too. I can feel it in the heat that radiates off my mother. And the panic that seems to pump my father's beating heart. Each *lub dub* thunderous against the quiet of the room.

"Headmistress—"

"Silence," she barks. "I am disappointed in you, Ms. Avalon. You have been a star student thus far, so to ignore your limits and push this spell further than it needed to go only tells me you have no regard for the responsibility that accompanies being as talented as you are."

I can't believe she's saying this to me. As if I intentionally went too far. As if I tried to purposely wield that spell with such ferocity that the poor woman nearly lost her life.

Part of me knows I let my control slip; and then encouraged it to go further. That tiny seed of guilt takes root, sprouting within me. I could have tried harder to pull back, but I didn't. So caught up in the high of just being exactly who I am that I'd forgotten the consequences. Forgotten what we all have to lose if I am exposed. There are dire consequences if the things I do can't be undone.

The truth is, my ability to wield has only grown stronger. The things I am asked to do come so easily that I barely have to think. I can only assume it's because of my training with Knox. Something about the two of us internalizing each other has changed my magic. The very core of who I am, altered.

I want to plead my case, reveal every dark secret to those in this room.

But those who don't know the truth will not understand.

"Furthermore, Ms. Avalon, because of your unnecessary display, you are now on lockdown until further notice, as you clearly cannot be trusted." My head drops, chin digging into my chest. It's not that I feel sorry for myself, but that I've become the exact thing I promised I wouldn't. A disappointment. Milgren's continued speech draws my attention back to her. "You are not permitted to attend the Red Moon Ball this Saturday evening, either. If I hear even a whisper about you attempting to take part in the festivities, you are done here at Beauxgraton."

My chin falls to my chest again. I don't care about the ball. It's just a chance for us to dance, laugh, and drink. To celebrate a tradition that's as old as time. I can do that alone in my room. I care that I've fucked up so badly I'm jeopardizing my family's name. Our reputation. My place here amongst my peers.

"Lockdown" was the worst part of every word that came out of her mouth. The opportunity to meet my father for the first time yanked from me because of my stupidity. Because I liked how it felt to let the entirety of what I am to the surface.

Losing the freedom of disappearing off campus with Knox has me spiraling. The progress we've made is sure to be stunted. He's brought me this far. But beyond that, I just like being with him. I long for those moments when I don't have to be anyone but Bri Avalon, a Grisym. I have to hide from everyone else, but never him. A truth for him, too.

"Raulf. Mighel. You both can go. I have a bit more to say to this young lady and her family. Wynston, as her advisor, you will stay."

Professor Caulder follows Schouten from the room. The shuffle of their feet so quick they nearly trip over one another. So eager to get away from me, their "goodbye" to my parents is carelessly tossed over their shoulders without a single glance back.

We wait in silence for five, ten, fifteen minutes. Long enough that those two are long gone.

"Roman, if you will."

My father stands, hands running back and forth in front of the surface of the door. His tendrils of essence are a blinding white as he barriers the room, the shade of his essence something I've always coveted. No one may enter or exit without him removing it. No one will hear us beyond these walls.

My father is generally even-keeled. He works through situations with a calm that most never find; even in their sleep. Today will not be that type of day. His light features seem to darken as he turns back to face us. The chords of his neck threaded tight.

"Bryony, explain to me what the hell happened?"

His normally perfectly coifed hair stands on end. The pale honey-brown strands sticking up at odd angles. As I look at my father now, it amazes me how anyone believed

I was his daughter. There is nothing about us that resembles one another. At least I share my mother's complexion. My siblings are several shades lighter than me, but that's not uncommon with mixed-race children.

"Dad, I—"

He leans down in my face, my body arching back into my mother's. Knox shoots from his seat, palms slamming into the table as he stares at my father. I can't tell if it's his essence I feel stirring in me or my own. Either way, it's pissed at the imminent threat my magic has deemed my dad to be. The fight to hold it within leaving me trembling.

I can't explain Knox's reaction. I've seen him like this before. Standing up for me out of turn when others might notice the reaction to be over the top. The clearing of his throat preceded by his pointed exit or attention drawn elsewhere.

"You sit the hell down." My father points at him, yet Dad's eyes never leave my face.

Knox only makes his way around the table. Eye contact never breaking from the breath of space between my father and me. This three-way stare-down driving my bounding pulse. The beat paced so high that I swear I'm having a panic attack.

Only when Knox is inches from him, their heights comparable, eyes nearly level, does Knox speak. "You wanted to find out what happens when Grisyms interact. You *all* pushed us together. Forced us to mix and now you have the audacity to come in here in an uproar when the results aren't what you wanted or expected. You are at fault as much as everyone out there that wants us dead." Each "you" is another point of his finger toward the occupants of the room. His outrage barely contained as his nostrils flare impossibly wide.

"Are you saying?" my mother breathes, one hand on her chest and the other cradling me.

"Yes. I am. Bryony has my essence, too. When she cast that spell, I felt it."

My gaze drifts to his, mouth wide open at his admission.

"I could fight it. She could not. I am more advanced than her, and those gifts are not something she is always going to be prepared to handle."

My mother's chin drops the same as mine did. Her hands cover her face as she weeps.

In her world of artifacts, she is the queen. Her steps never falter. She never shows her emotions unless she chooses to expose herself. So seeing her breakdown now tears my insides to shreds.

Not once have I ever considered the reality of her position as the mother of a Grisym in this way.

She's never given me a reason to, with her overwhelming positivity and steadfast way she carries herself; why would I? But I see it now. Flashes of fear behind her lush brown eyes as she studies my face.

"We have to tell him," she cries. Her plea seems to suck all the air from the room.

"Knox, sit down." My father's voice returns to the cool breeze it usually carries as he gestures to one of the open chairs. No surprise, Knox chooses the seat my dad previously occupied, his body unabashedly close to mine.

His fingers knot through mine as he pulls me to his side. My mother's eyes darting between us. I try to give her a look that says "Don't ask," but I don't have to. As Knox's skin hits mine, our essences flow out of us. Black, shifting to that sparkling pewter. A shield enveloping us like a suit of armor, keeping us from everyone else in the room. There's a virulence to it as it swirls around us that usually doesn't accompany this coloring.

But I feel it. It's desire to protect. To defend.

My mother's jaw falls open at the sight. Everything that needed to be said was made clear in that single moment. "Oh, my gods." My mother's hand slowly curls over her mouth as she gasps.

"As I was going to say ..." my father begins as he sags down to the table. "It wasn't just the mix of you two that likely made Bryony lose control. She matured at fifteen. Her power has had a decade to mature and become what it is. It also means she is more gifted than she has any right to be."

Knox twists me in his arms so he can look into my eyes. "Were you going to tell me?"

"No." My eyes search his for forgiveness. "I couldn't tell anyone."

A heavy silence falls over the room. No one knows what to say or how to move the conversation forward. Too much has been revealed in the past few moments. More than anyone has ever known about me outside of my family.

"Do you know why she matured a decade early?" Knox asks, pulling me closer to his side.

My mother sobs again. Even I have never asked this question. She sniffles several times before looking up.

I've never seen my mother look so lost as her eyes find my face, the answer to Knox's question nothing more than choked words on her lips. "Your father made it so."

37

Wynston

I'm frozen in place. Thoughts swarm my mind as I search the faces around the room. Who knew? Who is just as shocked as I am?

Only one knew that truth.

Bryony's mother.

Her father barely restrains himself. A vicious storm of anger roaring beneath the surface. The tense shifts of his head and roll of his neck are all that's needed to know how hard he is fighting to maintain composure. An endless struggle to only show the exemplary man we are used to seeing. That's all someone like him can ever afford to be.

"You—" he starts, smoothing his hair back. "You—" he tries again.

"Roman, please," Geneva whimpers. Tissues appear out of thin air. The little white sheets dabbed at bloodshot whiskey eyes. The tears that still ease down her cheeks, carrying her makeup with them. The destruction of her perfect exterior ignored by her husband.

"Let's all just take a moment," Milgren's pragmatic tone cuts through the tension. Her palms pat the air as if they will erase the violent swarm of unhinged emotion surrounding us. Nothing can erase Geneva's admission about the circumstances that surrounded her daughter's power maturing early.

I knew Bri was more than she let on. I always thought it was her keeping a piece of herself from me—by choice rather than obligation. It never occurred to me it wasn't something she could give.

Who knows what Jordden did to her to make her mature so early? I wasn't even aware something like that was possible. No text or manuscript I can recall ever stated that someone could force a wielder into early maturity.

There are only a handful of instances throughout history detailing natural cases. But not by a decade. Weeks or months or even a year. All periods well within the finish line of what's considered a wielder's childhood years.

From the look on everyone's faces, except Geneva, none of us knew such a thing was possible. More than likely, Roman and Milgren just assumed it was some weird occurrence because of Bri being a Grisym.

"Mrs. Avalon," I start.

"That's not my name. Since we're sharing all of our secrets now." She sniffs, lowering her tissue-filled hands to her lap. "My last name is Guthrie. It always has been."

The room goes silent again. Bri wrenches her hand from mine, resulting in a black tornado as I fight to reunite our palms. A calmer version once again settles into place the moment I squeeze my fingers against hers. My heart rate relieved to slow once more.

"Mom," Bri breathes, launching herself at her mother.

For a hug? To strangle her? I'm not sure. Another raging storm fills the room. Frames knocked from the walls, and chairs toppled. Roman yells and swears as he's assaulted with the mixture of us. A storm I can't stop on my own. Not when it's like this. Full of rage and pain.

Again, I fight to pull Bri back to me. My arms finally find their way around her middle, the immediate calm landing me on my ass and her in my lap. I bury my chin in her neck. Placing as much of my skin as I can against hers. Our essences eventually settle into that mystical fog at our feet.

Deep breaths fill our lungs as our racing hearts sync. My palm and her mouth open simultaneously, summoning our essences back to us. Our mixture captured effortlessly and equally.

Each pair of eyes watches, amazed at what they've seen. For us, this is normal. It is who we are. Who we've become.

"Your father ... Your real father is Jordden Guthrie."

"I know." Her parents stare at her, dumbfounded, but her mother continues.

"Your father knew you and your brother were special. Strong bloodlines like ours combined could do great things. Your brother Vincent matured early on his own. At seventeen. Your father thought maybe he could force the change in you, and he did."

"Are you telling us there is another Grisym out there? That Vincent is a Grisym?" I ask.

Geneva smiles sadly, her hands knotting in her lap. The strong woman the world normally sees is washed away by the defeated one in front of us now.

This woman is conflicted. She's heartbroken. She's as "human" as the rest of us.

"Me and Roman were always a cover-up. He needed a wife to gain prestige. I was for—" she stops abruptly, a loud swallow bobbing her throat before she continues, "—needed to hide my love for your father, and Vincent, at the time. So, Vincent is your true, full brother. Harley, Sicily, and Merrick are your half-siblings."

"Mom." The single word Bri seems able to produce since her mother revealed a truth she has kept hidden for too long.

Geneva's posture is just a little taller as she continues to speak. The weight she has carried all on her own seemingly lighter. "I'm so sorry I kept this from you, baby. You, too, Roman. I should have been honest with you. But those things are not important anymore."

"I beg to differ," Milgren quips from her seat, pointed nails gripping her chin.

Something shifts in Geneva's demeanor. Her small-framed back straightening. The tears instantly dry. A switch flipped before our eyes.

As a whole, we wait in silence, unsure who is going to speak next. If there are new revelations set to release or if this meeting has come to an end. I'm hoping for the end. This has been more stress than my old body can take today. A drain on my energy that might take weeks to recover from.

"Now," Geneva begins, her mouth set in a grim line. The unforgiving expression on her face is so much like Bri's when she's upset her essence isn't cooperating. "Will someone please tell me why my daughter is sleeping with a professor?"

"Mom!" Her gulp is audible. The press of her fingers into mine bordering on pain.

"Don't, Bryony." A finger points at her daughter before her focus returns to Milgren then shoots to Roman. "I approved of them doing this little experiment. I said they could put you two together. Find out what might happen. You only knew your brother for a few short weeks before mingling my two lives together was too much of a danger. But I do not approve of my daughter being pedaled around like some common whore."

"Mom!" Bri shouts. "Will you listen for one minute?"

"No, I will not. I've had enough of allowing others to use you, my dear. We're leaving. Clearly, this was all a mistake."

My mind spins. The woman in front of us is a completely different Geneva than the one I've ever known or the heartbroken woman I just witnessed. A pissed-off mother hen who isn't going to leave without her chick at her side.

My essence bursts from beneath my skin, zipping forward, knocking Bri's mother from her chair. The dark tendrils pin her down at the wrists and ankles as she wrestles to get free. I hadn't even had a moment to react to its rise. Hadn't been able to comprehend what was happening to keep it from attacking.

We've known our essences like to protect us from anyone that it deems a threat to us, but this is different. The urgency with which it flew free was not something I could have stopped even if I wanted to. No amount of control or preparation would have been enough to make that so.

Bri leans forward, palms open, calling my essence back to her. Calm finds me once more, as my nose presses to the side of her face. A deep inhale inflating my lungs as I breathe her in.

"No, Mom. I'm not going. Yes, this ... experiment got a bit out of hand, but there's something deep with Knox." Geneva scoffs, her hand flapping through the air. "It's not just about sex and he didn't take advantage."

Her mother sighs as she straightens her skirt rising from the floor. "I taught you better than this."

"No, Mom, you didn't. You taught me to hide. To allow myself to be used. Knox is the first person who hasn't used me for his own gain."

Her mother gawks at us both. Her mouth switching from that straight line to a deep frown. One that reveals the sadness behind her eyes. Each regret etched into the fine lines of her face.

"I only wanted to keep you safe."

"Well, you can't. Not here. Not anywhere." As if attempting to be the most defiant child known to man, she kisses me. Deeply. Unquestionably. Our essences swirl back to life. I don't have to open my eyes to know both mine and Bri's shifted to those white orbs. A side effect of our intimate moments together.

The kiss breaks. Our foreheads pressed together. My chest heaving against her arm. Only gasps fill the quiet of the room as we both peel our eyelids open.

"Since we're being so honest, Mom. You should know my father is coming here. I will get to meet Jordden on Friday night." As if it's the last blow she can stomach, Bri shouts her words so loudly the ward Roman built shivers.

He doesn't have to be asked to take it down. He simply does. Geneva retreating in a flash with him on her heels. Her final words thrown over her shoulder before disappearing around the doorframe, "I don't understand what you've become." Then she's gone.

We're silent for a time before Milgren clears her throat.

"So what do we do now?" Bri asks.

"You two carry on as you have been. Be discreet. No one else can know what was revealed in this room."

My conscience tells me I should warn her about Valen.

My self-preservation says to keep my mouth shut.

So I do, leading Bri from the office, her fingers linked with mine.

The thought "It's us against the world," playing on repeat in my mind.

Just *us*.

38

Bryony

My hands tremble as Knox leads me through the dark. The events from earlier this week have kept my anxiety sky-high. Neither of my parents bothered to reach out and check on me since that afternoon. Only Merrick video-called me when he found out about the whole fiasco. His reassurances that everything would calm down were likely not what he believed. Nonetheless, I appreciated his efforts.

Knox leads me through an area of the woods I've never visited on my nightly walks. The pathway different from the one I took with Valen and his friends months ago. Unfamiliarity keeps me focused on my steps instead of the shit show that is now my family and my life. The weight I've grown so used to carrying ten times heavier than it's ever been.

My gaze drifts over my surroundings, Knox giving my hand a reassuring squeeze as if knowing that's what I needed. Here in this portion of campus, the trees grow closer together in a dense block that sometimes obstructs our view. The bark flakes under my fingertips; darkened and aged. An unnatural silence exists here that I assume belongs to a secondary ward. One that keeps those who shouldn't wander into this space from doing so. The thought gives me pause. The only people allowed on the campus are those with authorization to be here.

Despite my obsession with it, I can't bear looking up at the bloodied moon. Its glow peeks through those treetops, just the same as it did before. That glow that I've always loved cresting over my skin, leaving me curling in on myself. Anything to escape what tonight might mean for me. Anything to erase the uncomfortable sensation of the muscles clenching in my stomach.

Knox promised I would be fine. He has been fucking ghouls since he matured. According to him, it helps to tame his dark energies, while suppressing the light. Something he believes might help me with the effects of maturing far too early and having to manage the bonded essence between us two. It's a lot for a girl to tackle all at once.

So far, the night is tranquil. As the trees subtly thin, they reveal the open area of the ghoul pit beyond. The only sound in the air is the harsh puffs of breath coming from the ghouls, growing louder as we near them.

The moon seems to glow brighter as we approach, illuminating us. Knox assured me no one else would be out here this early. This is his normal, designated time slot for coming out to siphon. A time Milgren protects for him. A gift she granted him, and he hadn't even realized why.

The wind kicks up around us. The long strands of my hair whipping out in front of me as I wrap my arms around myself. Did it suddenly get colder, or am I just that nervous?

"Are you scared?" he asks.

His fingers squeeze mine as he links them together. A new normal for us as we walk side by side when we're alone. The soft connection puts our essences at ease as if they can't stand to be apart. When we're near, and don't touch, they roar beneath the surface, itching to break free and create those familiar violent storms. It makes class with him horribly difficult. A constant concentration on keeping our innards controlled so as not to reveal our connection or what we are to the entire class.

It's bad enough that Valen knows. Even worse, he hasn't mentioned *what* he knows at all. Not in passing or as a taunt. Not a single word. A personalized weapon poised for whenever he may choose to use it.

"No, I'm not." It's a short answer, but also an entirely honest one.

Nervous. Excited. Filled with unwavering anticipation. But not scared.

I'd already been near the ghouls with Valen three months ago. It seems like a lifetime, thinking about it now. The ghoul he'd been railing had let me touch it. Had sighed, its eyes rolling back into its head—I imagine—as my fingertips grazed the leathery flesh of its thigh.

A zap of energy went through me at that first touch. A feeling like home, of kinship, settling my beating heart. A sharpened understanding between me and the beast.

"Good," he breathes with a nod. "It will sense any fear you might have. Even if you don't feel truly confident, you have to be when you choose your ghoul, so it chooses you back."

"I want to find the black one." He stops, lifting his hands to my upper arms, his fingers curling around my biceps, halting me too. "The Nigeros," I add.

"They're rare. It's very unlikely it will be here again."

"Just the same, I'd like to check. I felt something when I touched it."

Knox only nods back to me. His fingers weave back through mine as we hit the edge of the clearing. I hadn't expected to find the ghouls crowded atop one another. Their grown cocks bulging as they drive into each other. I mean, I'd heard orgies were a thing amongst them, seeing as how they can be whatever sex they choose at any given moment, but to see it is something else.

The dried flesh rubs together as their grunts and roars of pleasure seep out into the night. The rippling musculature of their bodies causes the muscles of my core to tighten in a carnal response. A throb so intense vibrating through me that squeezing my thighs together only intensifies it.

My eyes are wide as I take in the sight before me. Desire building in my lower belly, drawing out my need to claim a ghoul. An animalistic fuck to fill me with more power than I'll ever use.

"They'll separate once the wielders begin to show. This is their normal state, though," Knox whispers to me.

We're slow to move through the groups of ghouls as they rut, tangled together. Some of them latch onto us with their eyes. Skin of rust, greens, and even a dark royal blue. But the black one is nowhere to be found.

An internal cord repeatedly tugs at me as we circle back hugging the edge of the pit. I intently scan the grounds in search of which ghoul is calling to me. Several of them clear a path for that same dark blue ghoul I'd noticed earlier as it struts toward me. With each deliberate step the ghoul takes, the ground trembles as if in fear. There are a few blue-skinned ghoul variations, so it's difficult for me to tell which this is. My eyes strain to place the breed as it continues forward, its knees consistently bent. The creature's gangly, but muscled arms of gnarled flesh undulate against the moonlight as if performing its version of a seductive dance.

"You," it snaps. The tips of those razor-sharp teeth clicking together as it calls to me.

My gulp so loud it echoes in my ears. Knox gently shoves me forward. The creature's dick growing out of its pelvis the closer it gets to me. One clawed hand reaching out toward me, palm open, as it waits for me to place mine within it.

I reach forward as a small quiver finally takes over. The flesh is hot and rough against mine as it yanks me forward, falling to its back, taking me with it. A grunt of air is forced from my lungs on impact as we land. In an instant, Knox is there, gripping me from behind with strong hands curled around my waist as if to steady me.

I brace my hands against the solid abdominal muscles of the ghoul as I force myself to sit up, shaking my hair out behind me. There's no need for instruction. I know what I'm here to do. I'm no virgin after all. Assuming what I already witnessed is any indication having sex with a ghoul is no different from a man. Both are dangerous. Both can tear you apart from the inside put in a single night. I purposely wore a sweater dress, all the easier to allow a ghoul to slide home.

The events of tonight were at the forefront of my thoughts all week—alongside the anxiety of meeting Jordden. The two destroying any sense of peace I'd hoped to have.

Slipping my panties aside, I don't hesitate as I slide onto the girth of the giant beneath me. No need to test how wet I am. The heat of my arousal blossomed the moment I started watching all the ghouls fuck each other, wishing to be the center of it all. Wanting to be there in the middle, while they all took their turns delivering undeniable pleasure.

There's no way to describe the sensation of its bare skin inside me. Its cock fills me beyond what I believe I should be able to tolerate. But in the same breath, it feels made just for me.

The ghoul's roar vibrates through my chest as my ass taps its thighs, the clench of muscles pronounced beneath my fingertips and in my core. Clawed hands grip my bare thighs, the deathly tips pressing hard enough I should be worried they'll break the skin.

Sex with a man who has a big dick can be uncomfortable, exhilarating, delicious. So many things, but the size of them doesn't change. They are what they are. Not the case for ghouls. It's impossible to put into words the sensation created as its cock buzzes while it adjusts to my insides. A shifting of length and girth to fill me. Its purpose is only to fill every spare crevice inside me. Custom made just for me.

Then we move. The both of us. Its coarse, leathery flesh massages my insides. The uneven ridges of its skin creating sensations I've never felt with a man before, forcing me to drop my head back in a wide arc. Sensations I'll never feel with anything or anyone but the creature beneath me.

Suddenly, hot breath spreads across my neck as lips suck at my skin. Large palms cupping my breasts through the thick fabric of my dress, kneading in time with the roll of my hips.

"That's it, baby. Ride him. Open up. Allow all that he has to offer to enter you."

Knox's words come out low and hoarse. His desire evident in every syllable. Clear in the way his hands confidently slide under the dress bunched around my hips. Possessive in the way he snakes them around the swell of my lower belly, then shifts my bra up and out of the way.

I don't question why Knox now refers to the ghoul as a *he* instead of the *it* they've always been. There's no room to care as ecstasy unfurls through my body. A sudden stream of my essence floats past my lips surrounding the three of us.

"Off," I pant. "Take it off."

Knox tears the sweater from my body. My nipples pebbling against the frigid air. Goosebumps break out over my skin, immediately soothed by Knox's warm palms. His mouth trailing wet heat across my skin as his tongue traces parts of my body. A single thumb suddenly pressed against my swollen clit, pulling a groan of pleasure from me that drifts out into the night.

The ghoul's claws dig into my soft flesh. The pump of its hips up into my groin only serves to further ground me in the moment as snarls cut through the sounds of gratification filling the pit.

Fuck, this feels too good to give up.

I need more.

A new sensation fills me as the ghoul finally begins to relinquish its dark magic to me. My body siphons it in long drags, like a parched man who's found water in a desert. Thick waves of foreign power filling the open spaces within me, shoving mine and Knox's essences aside to make room for itself.

"Mine," the beast grunts. Knox growls in return as the tendrils of his essence wrap around my throat, pulling my back to his bare chest.

The two fight for dominance over me through their fog of lust and magic. I'm too far gone to care which wins. As long as they don't stop. They can never stop.

"Turn," Knox orders.

The ghoul assists me, dislodging my aching pussy from its cock before roughly shifting me so my front faces Knox. My back arches hands braced on the ghoul's chest as I spread my legs wide. Knox's eyes glazing over as he takes in my glistening flesh on display for him. His finger swiftly runs through my soaked folds before he uses my arousal to lube his dick. Only to dip his fingers back into me several more times before both palms run down my thighs. A yelp escapes me as he roughly shoves my body back against the ghoul, all of me exposed to Knox. A single thumb sliding through my arousal one last time, only to press into the puckered hole of my ass.

Sweet mother of…

"Relax, baby," he coos. Fuck, this is too much. Too good. Way too much. I've had my share of sexual encounters, but anal has always been off the table. That tiny hole was a virgin to intrusion until seconds ago.

My chest heaves as I lie on the stomach of the ghoul, rough skin scratching at the bare skin of my back. Legs held open by its claws as Knox does as he pleases. My eyes press closed the moment his mouth clamps around my clit. His tongue piercing me for mere seconds before he forces me up. His muscles bulge as he lifts, then impales my ass on the ghoul's waiting dick. A howl bellows from both me and the beast at the intrusion.

Those same claws dig back into my flesh, more forceful than before as it moves at a rapid pace. Thrusts so forceful, I know I'll wear more than just bruises tomorrow. But nothing compares to the power that fills me. The feel of its massive cock plowing into me from behind toeing the line between pleasure and pain. A warm trickle of blood streaming down the side of my hip as a claw finally pierces the skin.

It's a fight to catch my breath when Knox shoves into me, too. My hands pushing off the taut abdomen of the ghoul behind me to clutch onto the curled hair at the nape of Knox's neck. Mouth dropping open, my essence streams free again, caught only as Knox takes my mouth with his.

My gods, I am so full.

Our essences duel for dominance as more and more of the ghoul's dark secrets fill me. My orgasm building with such violent ferocity I'm not sure I will live out the remainder of this moment.

"Mine," the ghoul snarls as he jerks me up and down his textured length. My screams fill the air. Other ghouls now stopping to watch our threesome from only a few feet away.

A tendril of Knox's essence coils around my throat, ever so slightly tightening as my release finds me just in time to notice his cock twitch. Hot jets of cum filling me to the brim. The jerky movements of his hips bringing a lazy grin to my face.

The ghoul only pumps harder. Thrusts deeper. Pain sears my sides as it creates more puncture wounds with the tips of its claws.

"More!" it roars. The harsh tone making me flinch.

For the last time, I'm switched again. The ghoul fills my pussy. Tighter than before. Its cock enlarges by the second, infiltrating me. Stretching me. My body continuously impaled on the hard rod inside me.

"More," I breathe. An echo of the creature beneath me.

Its magic pours into me. Endless streams of ancient power I shouldn't have, but I will now crave like air.

I feel the change without seeing it now. My eyes shift from their normal state to that eerie white that matches the ghoul in front of me. Its sockets widening as if it can see the change. As if shocked I am a match.

"Mine," it growls one last time before it blasts me with enough dark power that I come, seeing stars, body collapsing onto its stomach as nothing but pitch-black darkness surrounds me.

39

Bryony

I'm not sure how long I've been out when my eyelids finally peel open. It could have been minutes or hours. Just long enough that Knox has redressed me. The ghoul who'd filled me with more than my shell of a body should be able to handle is gone.

Only quick blitzes of crimson come in and out of focus. My fight to keep my eyes open a lost battle.

A groan leaves me as I fight to sit up. My entire body aches as if hit by a bus. The three different essences swirling through me poking and prodding at each other. Warring for space. My mind is too fuzzy and unfocused to truly pinpoint which is which or who is winning. I only know my insides are a war zone. Multiple essences all fighting for their place on the throne.

"Knox."

"You're good." He swipes my hair back from my face. A touch filled with so much tenderness that I melt into him.

I nod, my eyes drooping. Sleep threatens to pull me back into the dark. But I keep fighting it.

"Need to see Dad."

"Not tonight, baby. You'll see him tomorrow."

With a sleepy nod, I burrow into his chest. My eyes closing once more. The uneven movement of his gait, confirmation of our forward movement.

It's the last thing I remember before I wake again, my comforter drawn up around me. Knox is nowhere to be found, but a dark figure lurks in the corner. The dim light from the hutch on my desk casting their form in shadow.

"Cammie," I croak, my throat hoarse and dry as if I'd been screaming for hours.

I had. Hadn't I?

Images of Knox and that ghoul filling me filter back to the forefront of my mind.

Fuck, that was amazing.

That power soared through me while they both dominated me. Owned me and did as they wanted to. It was the freest I've ever felt.

My body itches to go back out there, but I know I can't.

Not now. Not when others could potentially see me.

I find my phone on the nightstand, the bright light from the screen burning my eyes. Nearly midnight. The final bells of the evening set to chime in a few short minutes. With a trembling hand, I turn the bright beam of my flashlight in the direction of the figure sitting in silence. A loud gasp breaking free as his face comes into view.

Valen.

His legs are wide as he leans back in my desk chair. Far enough away that he might not be able to make out the scrutiny in my stare. Or the pulse of my anger knowing he somehow broke into my room while I was passed out. So much for those signature spells to keep everyone out but those it's crafted for.

"She's awake," he says. I can't see the smirk on his face but I hear it. Right there, in that smug tone that he enjoys taking so much.

"Get out," I grouse. I attempt to clear my throat, but it does nothing to alleviate the scratchiness of it.

Where is my water bottle?

He stands from the chair, stalking toward me, my body curling up under the comforter. I'm still soaked from the sex I'd had hours ago. The cool slickness uncomfortable against my warming skin as I slightly shift away from his approaching form. I'm not scared of Valen, but something about what I did tonight makes me feel vulnerable as if I have something to protect. Another secret I'm meant to hide.

Whatever power the ghoul gave me courses through me. Tightening my insides. Taking up every ounce of space as it pushes aside my innate magic. Its composition attempts to change my very essence. The essence that is now very much a combination of Knox and me. If I carry all three, what does that make me?

He leans close, his head cocked to the side, fists digging into the mattress. I refuse to cower away from him. To show him the fear that he thinks he can pull out of me. He's been threatening me for months. Part of me believes if he truly wanted me dead, he'd have made it so already. Jammed one of his precious daggers straight into my chest, then walked away, cackling with diabolical laughter. So, I stay where I am. His breath fanning out over my face.

His lips brush mine as he speaks. "Someone still has their secret on display."

I realize he can only mean my eyes. They haven't changed back. The white still overtaking my sockets. Shoving him aside, I jump from bed, launching myself toward the small bathroom at the edge of my room.

The bright lights burn my eyes as I flick them on, taking in my reflection in the mirror. A shudder runs through me at the sight of my ragged appearance. Skin flushed and the plum coloring of bruises already forming. Dirt speckling my dress in odd places.

My hair, a straight ponytail when I'd left with Knox, is now disheveled. Sections of hair bubbling out in random places while the hair tie remains in place. My edges curl in thick rings around my temples from the sweat we'd worked up despite the cold. My lips are puffier than normal, still swollen from Knox's kisses before he led me out to the pit. The cover of the tunnels gave us just a few hidden moments alone.

But Valen is right. My eyes are stark white. The normal black rim is nowhere to be seen. I've never questioned whether I could see when the change happened. I've always been able to. However, seeing them for the first time like this, I wonder how I can now. If the woman I am seeing in the mirror is still me, or maybe just a different version of me.

My fingers slowly rise to the dark circles beneath my eyes, pausing just before touching my skin. My hands drop back to my sides as if too timid to go near the unnatural glowing frost staring back at me.

Valen slips into the bathroom behind me. His body pressing in close. The tiny room, equipped with a sink, shelving unit, and toilet, is not spacious enough for two people to occupy it at once. I ignore the heat of him at my back, my focus still on those glowing white orbs. Too distracted to notice the knife he brings to my throat.

"I should slit your fucking throat. You and Knox aren't supposed to exist. You're nothing more than a warped version of a wielder. Wrong in every way possible," he spits.

He presses the knife deeper, the blade drawing blood. A second set of wounds in so many hours. My new essence leaks free, wrapping around the hilt and his fisted hand.

"Is that what you really want to do, Valen?"

Desire creeps into me as the new essence touches him. Darkness I didn't have in me before eager to continue this night of debauchery. No matter if the man behind me wants me dead. The ghoul magic inside me wants me to fuck him.

I want to fuck him.

Shifting in his grasp, I turn to face him. The knife never leaves my skin. Only pressing hard enough to skim across the surface before digging in at the side of my throat. Right along my jugular. That pulsing vein taunting the sharp metal resting there.

"Well. What are you waiting for?" My voice is sultry and low. Those white eyes of mine see more than my normal ones do. The pulsing of his vein at his throat. How the moisture from his tongue, which just swiped across his lips, seeps in. The hitch in the pump of his chest as my fingers find his belt buckle. "Is this what you really want, Valen?"

Knox warned against the residual lust that comes with fucking a ghoul. Made me promise to keep to myself for a few days. My body is likely to demand things I may regret later. His warning comes to me in hushed tones, shoved away by the ghoul's dark essence.

Valen's mouth crashes into mine, the knife digging deeper into my flesh. The warm trickle of blood rolls down my skin, soaking into the neckline of my dress. A red so rich it matches the brilliant moon shining bright in the sky through the window.

His other hand tangles in my hair. My ponytail wrapped around his fist as he holds me in place before he nips and pulls at my bottom lip, drawing moans from me. My hips roll against his. Demanding more. Demanding everything.

There's nothing soft about this kiss. Not like when Pierce kisses me. The opposite in every way.

My fingers fumble through the motions. My greedy pussy aching for another dick to push inside. To take up the space the ghoul and Knox had filled so perfectly. Waves of dark magic vibrate through me as I fumble to undo his button and zipper. Each one sending my body lurching forward into his, a dark chuckle on his lips.

"Eager, are we?"

There is no room for hesitation as I shove his pants and boxer briefs down his legs, his hard dick standing proudly between us.

Pulling my mouth from his, we pant, staring intently at one another. Wrapping my fingers around his length, I yank him toward me. His wince a delightful sight. My head flies back in laughter. That blade cutting into my skin, a delicious bite to push me over the edge.

The tip of my tongue drags up the side of his throat before taking the lobe of his ear in my mouth. "Is. This. What. You. Want?" A tiny suck of his skin between my lips with each word.

He takes a ragged, deep breath, stepping back from me. The knife finally pulls away from my skin as something like disappointment bows my mouth into a pout.

"I *want* you dead," he snarls.

"But..." My hips swivel as I corner him against the wall. Anything to staunch the ache. To alleviate my need to fuck the traitorous bastard in front of me. The ghoul magic within the only energy driving my actions.

"I *need* to fuck you." He slides up to me, teeth clamping on the flesh that spans the space between my neck and shoulder.

A laugh bubbles out of me. My control snapping back into place as if all I needed was for him to admit the truth of his desire for me to be satisfied.

I disappear through the doorway back into my room, a towel pressed to the two spots where he's drawn blood. I swear I'm going to look like a rabid dog mauled me for a week.

That same dark swirl dances around my ankles. A tickle against my bare skin.

Valen follows too. An angry drag of his pants back up his hairy thighs.

"What the fuck was that, Bryony?"

"What? You think you can come in here and hold a knife to my throat, threaten my fucking life every day, and think I'm just going to lie here and let you fuck me? You're either just as insane as I always thought, or just fucking delusional." My finger digs into the side of his temple, pushing hard.

His grip on my wrist is painful as he grabs me. "No." He slides up close to me again. The opposite hand fisting around my ponytail so fast I can't react. The mixed essence of me and Knox shoots free to tangle around his throat. A warning should he make another move. "My little taste of forbidden fruit I expect you to participate."

My tether of control I'd just found, wobbles. There's a gush of sweet arousal between my thighs as I think of what it might be like to fuck Valen, too. His vicious nature is sure to tear me apart, only for him to walk away while I work to stitch myself back together.

This place is changing me. My true nature is changing me. But there is some truth in what the Red Moon does to us dark-wielders. Our inhibitions lowered. Our desires drawn to the forefront and our libidos on overdrive.

I'm the one to kiss him this time. My mouth molds to his as my fingers sink into those dark, luscious locks. His bun full of curls, which I've always wanted to run my fingers through, now fills my palms. They're just as soft as I imagined. Smells just as good as I'd dreamed.

"You have thirty seconds to get inside me or this isn't happening."

He smirks as he lets his pants fall back to his ankles. He hadn't even buttoned and zipped them again. Only covered himself.

It's only when he has me propped against the edge of the bed, legs wide as he trails kisses down my throat, that I realize my panties are gone.

The brush of cool air over my sensitive flesh is enough to make me moan loudly.

His head snakes beneath the hem of my dress. Lips tasting me. Long lavish strokes swallowing my arousal. A tug of his teeth at my sensitive bud sets my hips to grinding into his face. The short facial hair scratching against the already scraped-up skin between my legs. His tongue sinks inside my throbbing core when a knock comes at the door.

Fuck my life.

Why is someone always trying to interrupt me when I'm getting some?

40

VALEN

I'M QUICK TO ROCK off my knees to standing. A swipe of my hand, throwing the door wide not caring who's there. Not caring who sees me fuck this gorgeous sexpot of a woman into stupidity.

She doesn't seem to care either. Her legs spread wider, waiting for me to return. Her fingers lazily playing with herself as slick arousal shines in the dim lighting.

I shouldn't have come here after I watched her fuck that ghoul and Knox. Both filling her at once. It drove me crazy because all I could think about was shoving Knox aside so I could be the one to plunge inside that sweet cunt. To be the one who sank into her with wild abandon before pumping her full of my cum.

A grin curves my lips. I'm damn glad I followed her. That pussy is sweeter than I would have imagined. A decadent cake destined for me to devour until her nectar coats my tongue.

That first taste was reminiscent of the forbidden fruit I've named her after. That's what she is, isn't she? Something that none of us are supposed to have. A treat that tastes so good but will ruin all of wielding-kind if we let it.

I'm still a fucking mess from watching her and then quickly finding my own ghoul to fuck until my dick went limp. Still, that lust rages through me. I couldn't get her out of my head. I figured I would find her here after Knox carried her away. His pansy ass, too scared to stay with her. Too stupid to ensure she's protected after her first time. Not worried enough that a man like me might find her, eager to get a taste of that greedy cunt too.

I sat here and waited. Watched as she breathed so soundlessly. Her first fuck with a ghoul put her out cold for hours. It happens to a lot of us. Maybe it was worse for her because she's only half dark wielder. The light half of her must not be helping in processing the change. I honestly have no idea how it works for Grisyms.

A question I could ask Knox, but that would mean being cordial with him. For all I care the fucker can drop dead. There's no way I'm showing him an ounce of anything but disdain. Not after having tasted her. I know I'll want her again and he will only stand in the way.

Just the same, I'd waited for her to wake with a feeling akin to hope in my chest. Hope that she would still be crazy on the high of her fuck and want more. That my dick would suffice to satisfy the urges now coursing through her.

I hadn't meant to pull the knife on her, but old habits die hard. My mind still grappling with whether to keep her alive or kill her. She could benefit me on one end. On the other, she needs to be kept away from my mission here. Kept away from the man I serve.

I'm not even paying attention to who walked in behind me. My hand roughly shoving her dress higher, mouth going back to work on that sweet, sweet cunt. I might already be addicted.

Bryony's fingers tear at my hair, crotch rocking into my face. My hair tie tugged free from her frantic movements.

I don't pay attention to her words. Or the sound of the male voice in the room with me.

Only the slam of my skull on the nightstand as I'm thrown aside brings me back to the present. I'm immediately jumping to my feet, knife in hand, to face my assailant. To murder whoever is dumb enough to think they can attack me.

"What the fuck are you doing?" Pierce screams in my face.

"What you weren't here to do," my snarl forces him back a step. The throb at my temple intensifies before the murmured spell casts the pain away.

He looks at Bryony with panicked eyes. Her face flushed from the pleasure I'd already given her. She says nothing as she watches us stare each other down. Those same fingers playing with her swollen clit, so relaxed, as if watching a movie with popcorn in hand. Her chest pumps up and down as she brings the orgasm that was meant for me to the surface. Loud groans further hardening my dick.

"Why do you always have to fuck everything up, Valen?" he sneers. His teeth bared in my direction. Yet he keeps his distance. Hesitant to assault me again.

It's not often I get this kind of emotion from Pierce. He's often laid back and calm, but since meeting her, a whole new side of him has emerged and I must admit I like it. I like his challenge and the way he stares at me with anger. At least then, he's not just some pussy taking whatever people give him.

I smirk, shuffling past him, dropping back to my knees in front of her. "We share everything else. Why not her?"

Pierce takes several steps back as if slapped.

"Bri?" he breathes.

"Ahh, you don't mind, do you, Bryony? Three is better than two, isn't it?"

I know Pierce is losing his shit as my hands cup the back of her thighs, tongue darting out to lick down her slit, lapping up her juices. My face angled so that I can focus a glare on Pierce's face. He's clearly pissed at me, but I wonder if any of that will be directed at Bri for not saying no. Her lack of response loudly speaks volumes. He may be all those things, but he's turned on, too. The noticeable bulge in his jeans is all the confirmation I need.

We've never actually shared a woman. Never even been with the same woman, period. But tonight I don't give a fuck. I want to fuck this feisty woman in front of me, and, unless she kills me herself, I'm damn sure going to.

I'm taking the night off from trying to murder her so I can indulge in what's sure to be the sweetest pussy I've had. Her voluptuous body will give me so many places to hold and knead at her soft flesh as I pound into her.

"Either join in or sit down," I smirk at Pierce. Her hand extends with my comment, beckoning him forward.

I don't wait for a response from him, eyes closing as I enjoy her. My tongue caressing her walls as she writhes beneath my touch.

The smack of their lips announces his obedience to her plea. The groan of the mattress giving away his eagerness to be with her, too, as he joins us. As he touches her. Kisses her. Shares the one thing he's ever had that I didn't with me.

"Mmm. Baby, you taste so good. This mix. I like it." The words spoken just low enough, that neither of them likely heard them.

Pierce shifts next to her on the bed. "We'll talk about it later," she breathes pulling him back to her. His shirt falls to the floor beside me. The thick sweater dress follows shortly after.

Her moans fill the room as Pierce's hands roam her body and I push her toward her next release. The pulse of her walls against the intrusion of my tongue, a giveaway. Her body teeters on the edge. I've already watched the first two, but this one is mine.

"Come on my tongue, just like you did on their dicks."

She groans loudly, her chest heaving as her walls tighten. Her release coats my tongue. Thick arousal for me to swallow down in earnest.

"Well done," I praise, patting her thigh as I stand over her. I shove her thighs wider before I croon, "Are you going to let me in?"

Her mouth pulls away from Pierce's, eyes glazed, but no longer the milky white of earlier. Once again, their normal hue of grays and greens. Being with me returned her to the Bri she normally is. I'm not sure if that's a good or a bad thing.

A careless grunt of satisfaction vibrates through my chest as I climb onto the bed, too.

"Shut up and—" her words cut short as I shove into her. Her body lurches forward at my rude intrusion. Frankly, I thought it would be fine since she's warmed up, but my gods, she is the fucking tightest thing I've ever stuck my dick into. I swear there's not enough room for me to move inside her.

The shift of my hips is not nearly enough force to get me in. Several long strokes allowing me deeper each time. The squeeze forces me to grit my teeth as I work my way in, those walls still pulsing around me. And yet, I never make it all the way home. An issue I force out of my mind.

"Pierce, how the fuck do you handle this?"

"Tight, isn't she?" he chuckles.

My gaze shifts to him as he toys with her nipples. His confidence is not something I am used to. Pierce doesn't talk like that. Doesn't objectify women. But those three words were like they'd been stolen from my mouth.

She yanks him forward, his boxers pulled down around his thighs. Her fist working him as he groans and leans into her touch. My gaze persistently glued to where she touches him.

"Come closer," she whimpers. She lets loose a sharp hiss as my angle shifts us.

I've seen Pierce naked nearly as much as I've seen my own dick. It's part of who we are as dark-wielders. Ghoul pits aren't a place for modesty. I've never looked at him with anything more than anatomical indifference until now, as I watch her fingers curl around him and pump. His head thrown back, Adam's apple bobbing as he chokes on his groans. I'm fascinated. Not by him, but what she can do to him with a simple touch.

My focus only returns to where we're joined as she takes him into her mouth. Those full lips pressed against his solid shaft before she twirls her tongue around the tip, sucking down the pre-cum that seeped free. A hiss snakes past his teeth as she takes him deep again, only to pull back with a graze of her own.

Fuck, this is so much hotter than I ever expected it to be. Being with her is so much better than I envisioned. The three of us in this bed, together, is its own fucking magic.

It changes nothing between us. She is the enemy. Her kind is the enemy. Her family members are the ones standing in the way of what I am here to do. Of what he has recruited me to do.

I can fuck her tonight and hate her tomorrow.

My hips pound into her. Her pelvis flexing, meeting me thrust for thrust. I'm too restless to mix it up or make it fun. I just have to have her. Watch my dick disappear into her brown flesh over and over, drawing me deeper with every thrust. It's everything I never knew I needed. The dark hair at my pelvis offsetting the paleness of my skin against hers, complementary. A series of contrasts that are simply pure beauty to me tonight.

My balls draw up. Dick hardening further. A violent release ready to shoot free. My head clearing her entrance just in time for jets of me to coat her perfectly rounded bare tits. Those dark nipples drenched in exactly what she did to me. The same milky white as her eyes before Pierce interrupted us.

"Now clean it up," I grunt.

She doesn't hesitate, abandoning Pierce's dick to swipe her fingers through the mess I left on her. Each finger disappearing between those lips, one at a time, as she sucks them clean.

It's just tonight, Valen. Just this one time.

I fasten my pants and leave before she's wiped up every drop of me. Neither Pierce nor Bryony says a word to me as I go.

Just. This. Once.

41

PIERSON

HOURS PASS AS BRI lies curled up against my chest. A silence stretches between us that weighs on me, but it doesn't seem to bother her. Or maybe it does. Maybe the shit that just went down with Valen has her twisted in knots that I can't see because all I can focus on is her naked curves pressed against my lean muscle. The small puffs of her breath against my chest warming me.

Too many thoughts flutter through my mind. Too many questions.

She'd clearly been into what was happening between her and Valen. And it's not like she can blame the effects of being with a ghoul on them. She's a light wielder. They don't fuck ghouls. They don't feel those same burning desires with that glowing red sphere in the sky.

There was a comfort there between them. Almost as if they shared a secret which makes no sense. Valen has made it clear Bri is someone he would prefer to erase from the face of the earth than fuck the way he just did.

But there was no missing the way his face lit up as he licked and then fucked her. He wanted it just as much as she did.

Her arm tucked around my middle is the only thing relieving me of the thought of her leaving me for him. I don't know what that was, but she's still here with me. She never called after him or watched him leave with longing eyes. The moment he climbed off the bed, she had me back in her mouth, finishing me off in minutes before pulling me down to lie next to her. The same way we have been for hours now.

I'm doing my best to stay away from his comment about three being better than two. It can only mean one thing. And it's something I would prefer not to admit to myself. I don't want to think about the many reasons Bri won't agree to be my girlfriend, no matter how close we've become or how frequently everyone else calls us out for our couple shit.

She keeps that barrier between us.

"We're friends who fuck," I remember her saying. *"Keep it that simple. It's better for all of us."*

Now I wonder, as she snuggles in closer, a soft purr vibrating against my chest if she meant that *us*. If there were others she was with? Maybe this wasn't the first time she was with Valen. Maybe she's been with that best friend of hers, Graham. I know she kissed him the first week of school. Valen made sure to broadcast that shit.

Or maybe the rumors Valen kick-started about her and Professor Knox hold some merit.

That theory is the first I brush off. No way either of them would jeopardize their positions here. Not for sex. Not to mention she's in the public eye because of her family name. The attention something like that would bring wouldn't bode well.

"Mmm, I love how warm you are," she groans into me. Her arm tightens around my torso. There's no helping the way my body moves impossibly closer to her. Breathing her in.

My girl.

"Are you okay?" The words are so quiet I'm not sure she heard them until she answers.

"Yeah. Why?" There's no inflection in her tone. Nothing to give away one way or another what she might be thinking.

"I mean that whole thing that just happened with Valen. That wasn't—" A long sigh escapes me. "That hasn't happened before, right?" I choke on the words. Each one comes out flustered and mumbled. Her body jerks upward, palm flat on my chest as she stares into my eyes through the dim light of her room. The gray overpowering the green.

"No. Never." She pauses. Her frown deepens as she continues to look into my eyes. The corners of them dip low as if already asking for forgiveness.

"But ..." Maybe if I say the word for her. Start the statement for her. Whatever it is she needs to admit to me will come out easier. Maybe she'll know that it won't change the way I feel about her.

"But I have been with someone else." She casts her glance downward before looking at me again. "Repeatedly."

My eyes close. A burn fills my chest as I wrap her hand in mine, still pressed to the bare skin of my chest. It hurts. Like those daggers Valen loves so much, burrowing into my flesh. Digging through the sinew and bone. Tearing my insides to shreds.

I think I always knew. I just never wanted to admit it until I heard it from her. Decided it was easier to pretend to be blind to it.

"Hey." She turns my face back to her with a hand on my cheek. "It doesn't change anything for us."

"Doesn't it?" My tone is harsher than I intend it, yet she doesn't recoil from me. "I will always be the guy who wants you more than you want me. Who needs you like I need to breathe, but I'll never be that for you."

"Pierce, that's not true. It's, well. It's complicated," she sighs falling back into her pillows. Her naked breasts jiggling as she does.

I want nothing more than to touch her now. Make her forget that she's been going behind my back with someone else. Is it really behind my back, though? When she never committed to me in the first place? The semantics don't matter. My heart still breaks, as if she betrayed a sacred bond we never agreed to.

"It's fine. Do what you want, Bryony."

I shift my body from underneath hers. Scooting down the bed. I'm not mad. Or maybe I am. I'm not sure. I'm just ...

I'm losing my fucking mind over this woman I met only a few months ago. A woman who has undone my entire world. And all she can say is, "It's complicated."

Back to her, hands in my hair, I ask the question I don't want the answer to, "Is it Graham?"

Her warmth envelops me from behind. An arm slinking over one shoulder, the other under my arm, and across the front of my torso. Her nipples are hard against my back, but her body is so soft. A cocoon I wish I could stay buried in all the time.

"No." There's no further explanation, but I hear the genuine tone of her voice. She means it. She's telling me the truth.

"Will you tell me who he is?"

"Baby, it's not important. Nothing changes for us. I am still with you. I promise."

As sweet as Bri can be, she comes with hard edges. A shield she keeps up so only those she chooses can see the real her, the absence of which is not lost on me. Right now, there's a softness I've never seen. A vulnerability that makes me shift in her arms, my mouth finding hers. Our joined bodies fall back onto the mattress.

My hands are slow to explore her. Touch her curves. Every ripple. Every smooth rise of muscle.

"Will you tell me if things change? If I need to back away?" Not that I believe I ever could. Not now. Only in another life might I be able to free myself of her.

Her hand is on my cheek again. Her thumb rubs a soothing arc that has me leaning into her touch.

"You don't need to go anywhere. But yes, if that time were to ever come, I will tell you."

It's enough for me. Enough for me to forget the weirdness of this night and the chunk of my heart she ripped out. Just enough for me to be in this moment with her.

Our mutually held breaths release as I slide into her. Languid thrusts, slowly bringing us back to our peaks as she sighs in my ear.

This will do for now.

I snuck out of Bri's room at the crack of dawn.

Camilla returned at some point while we were sleeping. The tiny mound of her body a bulge under her comforter this morning. For such a tiny thing, that girl snores like a freight train. I have no idea how Bri sleeps through that every night.

I feel like an ass for sneaking out and not saying anything, but I need to find Valen. Need to ask him what the fuck last night was about. I believe her when she says it's never happened before, but I don't put it past him to have orchestrated this whole thing. Made it so she would want to sleep with him so he could rub in my face just how poorly I'd chosen with her. How I should be on his side in terms of trying to get rid of her. How she is a threat to everything we are trying to do.

A plan I only know a part of, but I'm Valen's boy, so I will always have his back. Or at least that's how I used to feel. Somehow, I convinced myself a long time ago that I owed him my blind loyalty.

Likely, he's already been up for at least an hour by the time I reach his room. My knock is soft, but that first tap is enough for him to summon his door open.

He's still in bed, clad in nothing but his boxer briefs, fingers laced behind his head against the headboard as I enter. There's no need to turn on the lights as I settle into the armchair in the corner. A black leather number he insisted on us hoisting up here last year. The things we do for our friends.

"Go ahead. Ask," he tuts.

"Why not just tell me? You know that's why I'm here," I retort with a huff.

He smirks as he sits up in bed. The feathered muscles of his torso twitching with the movement. His veins are darker, a soft shade of black, under his fair skin. They always are after he's had a ghoul feast. It's a side effect for those of us who are pigmentally challenged. If we siphon magic dark enough to hold within our veins, it will show through our pale skin. A delayed response that's visible, but usually fades within a few days.

"Fine. I followed her to her room last night. Watched her sleep. One thing led to another. I was still high on ghoul magic, and she was willing."

He makes it sound so factual. As if it's not a big deal. Like he didn't follow *my girl* to her room and sleep with her.

"Why her, Val?"

"Look, Pierce. It didn't mean anything. Red Moon lust and shit. She was there. I wanted to know her secrets."

I'm suddenly perked up shoulders rolled back as I stare at him. I know I should wait for her to tell me what those secrets are, but I'm eager to know what he knows. What she doesn't feel comfortable telling me.

"What secrets?"

His stupid smirk leaves me wanting to knock it off his chiseled face. Those sculpted cheeks of his always slightly sucked in. His facial hair always perfectly cropped, a match for the blue-black of the bun he wears at the back of his head. Even a blind man could see Valen has the bad boy look so many women crave.

A loud laugh extends my way. "I figured she would tell you. Guess not."

"Val." My head drops, elbows resting on my thighs.

"Damn, you do have it bad. She's been fucking Knox and was out there fucking a ghoul with him, so I followed them back."

At least I'd sort of guessed right. But that also means the rumors Valen was throwing around aren't rumors. It makes sense why she wouldn't tell me. Something like that would ruin both of their lives and reputations. The type of information you'd never share.

The admission should make me back away. Drive me into a hole of depression, but I need her. I want her like I've never wanted anything in this world. She is mine. She has to be mine. Knox is just a phase. One that will end when we leave this place. He's just temporary.

Just the same, I can't fathom what makes him worth the risk. Why am I not enough?

"Why would they do that? It's so reckless."

They're both done here if the wrong person finds out.

"Shit, man. You've got to stop acting like her pussy is gold," he sighs, scratching his scalp. "If you promise not to freak out, I'll tell you what you really want to know."

I do my best to keep my composure. To not appear like a dog eager for the tasty treat dangled in front of my face. Yet, I know my eyes are the size of saucers. Saliva likely dripping down my thin lip as my mouth hangs open.

He eyes me with pity. It's not the first time, nor am I convinced it will be the last. "It's pretty pathetic. I mean damn, Pierce, she's fucking other men and you're determined to chase her."

There it is. The opening Valen has been waiting for. A perfect time to remind me that the softness that lives inside me is my worst quality. That the way I feel about this woman is a liability.

"I know," I mumble as my gaze drops to the floor, shoulders sagging forward. "I know, but ..." I can't bear to look back up at him until he speaks again.

"Let's see if you still want her after this. Your girl is a Grisym, and so is Knox."

How did I miss this?

Fuck. Me.

42

Bryony

I'VE BEEN PACING MY room for hours. The crimson gown I was supposed to wear tonight draped across my bed. The sheer lace bodice with demi cups is likely a bit too sexy to wear to a ball. But fuck it. I love my body and I have no shame in flaunting it—within reason.

The translucent fabric and flowing chiffon skirt stare back at me as if taunting me to go against Janelle's orders. The delicate design of the lace too beautiful to go to waste.

With a sigh, I drop onto the mattress, landing beside the gown. The two of us, side by side. My eyes press shut as I remember that there are more important things to do tonight than wearing a jaw-dropping dress.

I'd convinced myself that Janelle's banning me from the ball was a front for Caulder and Schouten. A way for her to show me no favoritism in front of others, only to then turn around and say, "Just kidding." But she'd been serious about every bit of reprimand she'd given me. Our shared history did nothing to win me any favor with her.

Her warning text arrived early this morning. The buzz of plastic vibrating against the nightstand waking me from a deep sleep.

Janelle Milgren: ***If you so much as even think about testing me Bryony, I will wring your neck myself.***

Janelle Milgren: ***I love you, but my punishments hold.***

Several minutes passed before her final text came through.

Janelle Milgren: ***Good luck with Jordden tonight.***

I hadn't known she knew that I was still going to sneak out to see him. The wards, I was told, that were supposed to be in place to keep wielders like him out, were non-existent. But the rumor is enough to be a deterrent.

Janelle might support who I am. She may even be willing to hide me so nothing bad happens to me, but she has never been a fan of Jordden Guthrie. That much was clear as I grew up. Her endless rants over that man and all the harm he was causing to the peace that took hundreds of years to achieve between the light and dark wielders left an impression on my young mind. I always felt as if there was something more, something deeper to explain why she was so against him, but I never asked. Never had a reason to, because, for me, Jordden was nothing more than the man standing opposite of the Council. Opposite of my father—the one I've always known.

That was all I needed to know.

And now I stand on the precipice of meeting the man responsible for half of my DNA, and I hate myself for never asking. For never pursuing the details of what others said about him, whether those statements were true or not. So that, tonight, when I sneak through the walls of this institution in search of him on the grounds, I can ask those questions. I can find out those truths for myself.

I've asked myself a million times if the truth would change what I want from him. Would it make me want to know him any less? To understand him any less? The answer is always a resounding no.

Everyone actively kept me from knowing my true self for twenty-five years, and now that I'm allowed to know the real me, I can't put her back in a box. I don't want to.

I refuse to go back to living half a life again.

I am not saying I want a relationship with him. I honestly don't know if I do or not. I might want to know him, but more so, I just want to understand more of what I am.

I understand the light sides. The pieces of my mother that I inherited, but what did I glean from him? When my dad and Janelle trained me all those years after I matured, did they even try to tap into what came from him?

I honestly don't know what his gifts are. Hell, I have no idea what mine are. Unless you count my essence going haywire in the presence of another Grisym or deciding to attempt murder in class. He's notorious for his stand against the world order not what gifts he was born with. I do know he's innate, like Mom and I are. Like Knox is. And Milgren.

Vincent's abilities are much more well-known. His necromancy is the talk amongst many in various circles. But now, knowing he is my full-blood brother, I understand the peculiarity of his gift.

The light gives.

The dark takes.

He can do both with his necromancy gifts. The life he can give for whatever duration he chooses, and the memories and words that he takes, whether that deceased wielder wants to give up those secrets or not. They are no use against him.

His face flashes through my mind now. That dark hair that hangs just above his shoulders. The same burnt pecan as mine. Whereas I got the browner complexion from my mother, he hosts a paler olive hue from our father. That one dark eye, almost black, and the other a crystalized gray. A gray I am now noticing is quite similar to the shade of mine as it blends into the green.

Where my particular shade of green came from is beyond me. Neither my mother nor my father holds that unique tinge of sage.

Pulling my phone from the nightstand, I bring up a photo of Jordden. The one I've been staring at non-stop since Knox handed me my father's note. A recent moment captured in time where he's staring off into the distance with a focus so intense it's unnerving. His face is in profile as it often is in any photo I've found online. It's as if he purposely keeps the entirety of his face hidden in shadow.

To stare at Vincent's face is terrifying so I've only done so sparingly. A hardness there that seems present in every photo and video captured of him. I should have asked Knox more about him, but now I'm glad I didn't. He may have suspected I knew more than I do.

Vincent has twelve years on me. I was too young to remember him. And I can only assume I never saw him again. But I hope someday he can tell me of our brief time together.

Come to think of it, I don't remember any of my childhood before the age of five. I want to know more about those years. Whether it's because I was too young or because someone stole those memories from me; it makes no difference.

I can only assume once Mom stopped mixing her two lives there was no further contact, but something tells me that's not true. An inkling deep in my gut urges me to believe there were more moments than just a few short weeks.

The short time frame ensured Roman was the only father I'd ever know. My half-siblings the only ones I would ever have a relationship with. Vincent and Jordden destined to be men I would never know or have in my life.

"Good lord, will you please sit down? You're makin' me more nervous than a mouse caught in a trap," Camilla groans.

My bottom lip tucks under my teeth. The flesh pulled into my mouth, hand cupped around my chin as I pace endlessly. I hadn't even realized I had stood again. My mind is everywhere but on the actual present.

"I'm sorry. Just a lot on my mind." But my feet won't stop. They won't still as the jumble of thoughts flutter through my head. One after the other, presenting me with more and more questions I don't know the answers to.

Tack on the text from Pierce this afternoon and I am practically reeling.

Pierson Flaggstaff: ***We need to talk. I know what you've been hiding.***

I can't even think about that right now. Nor do I want to think about how he likely found out.

Valen.

That piece of shit. He'd likely been waiting all this time to rub it in Pierce's face. To remind him how wrong we are for each other. How wrong *I am* for him. It might be the truth but it doesn't make me any less angry at the wedge Valen is working so hard to shove between us.

Pierce is good. He doesn't have secrets. He deserves someone who will always be able to give all of them to him. Who won't always be looking over their shoulder waiting for the inevitable hammer to come down on their head.

That's my life.

I will always be hunted.

By law, death is the only fate that Knox and I should ever expect.

"Do you want to talk about it?" Camilla groans.

There is nothing the girl hates more than not being privy to my inner thoughts.

"Huh?" My response is distracted. I'd heard her, but my thoughts are loud.

"Ya know, tell me all the juicy stuff that's keeping you wound tighter than my intestines after chili nights."

I throw her a deadpan glare, fighting so hard not to laugh. Only Camilla could say something so off-kilter that all I want to do is laugh until I have stitches in my side. Not to mention her unfortunate reactions to the chili from the dining hall she continues to indulge in, even though it does not agree with her.

Her odd sense of humor is just what I need to get out of my head for a few minutes. Tossing a pillow at her, I let loose a genuine laugh. The tension I'd been carrying loosens a fraction. Her face catching the pillow before she shoves it into her lap with a grunt.

"I'm good. I promise."

"Are you really not allowed to shake it with us tonight?" she whines. The higher pitch makes me wince. Most times, I can ignore it after months of listening to her specific timbre, but tonight, it grates on my nerves. Or rather, grates on my already frazzled nerves. Not in the way it used to with annoyance, but this time setting me further on edge.

It bugs me that I can't pretend as if it doesn't drive me crazy tonight. In truth, her friendship has become a comfort I need. Camilla is one of the most genuine people in my corner. It seems like maybe I've never had that. Not until her and Graham and Pierce. Beauxgraton gave me that.

Maybe I still can't say that because she still doesn't know the truth about me. And if I can help it, she never will. It's a piece of me I need to keep hidden from as many people as possible. Not only does it protect me, but them too. Death is just as much their fate, just for knowing me, if decreed so by the Bureau.

"Come on, let's get you dressed. Graham, Whit, and Collin will be here any minute." I throw her a smile I hope is convincing. I don't need her or any of them thinking about me tonight. I need them to focus on having fun. So distracted by the music and the booze and the wave of their bodies together and the laughter they create that none of them think of me. That they won't feel the need to check on me.

It was a hint Graham had already put out there. Our miniature argument over him hanging out with me for the night, or me at least allowing him to check on me, has come up repeatedly this week. I can't have that.

All they'll find is an empty room, and I can't afford for them to search for me themselves, or worse, bring it to the administrators. Janelle might be letting this slide, but Caulder and Schouten heard what she said.

It doesn't take long for us to get Camilla into her dress. Her long hair artfully knotted atop her head in a combination of beach waves and braids. Every bit a princess in her long gown with the two-foot train. All she needs is a sword in hand and she'd be a royal warrior from a fantasy novel.

"Are you planning on spending tonight with Mailee?" A flush covers her pale skin, turning her a harsh pink. Only a few shades lighter than her red-painted lips. The smokey rust and gray combination brushed over her eyelids more daring than she would ever wear without my prompting. The demure southern belle she'd arrived as is slowly merging into the woman before me. One with a little more bite than others would think.

"I, uh ..." she chokes on her words. "Well if she wants to ..."

I chuckle, adding a bit more rose blush to her cheeks.

I wish she had more confidence in herself. She's gorgeous and she should embrace it.

"You know, looking like that, you'll definitely catch some extra attention. If Mailee doesn't care to notice, countless others will." I throw her a wink. The soft pink that had crested her cheeks now matching her fire-engine red gown.

Her small hands fan at her face, tiny puffs of breath meant to calm her. Any mention of the fourth year does that to her. But maybe tonight she'll have a boost of confidence. The two of them seem to get along well enough. Their weekly coffee chats have turned into an almost daily event these days. Mailee's arm is often hooked through Camilla's when I've seen them walking through the halls. A picture of fun and affection.

A knock sounds at the door just as we break from a crushing hug. Our group filing in only to strut out. Camilla blows me a kiss just as she turns through the doorway. I do hope she has the best time. It's well deserved after dealing with my anxiety-driven antics for hours.

Graham is the last to leave. His hand paused on the handle as his sad eyes gaze back at me.

"Go," I laugh, shooing him away.

Go and please don't look back.

I have a family reunion to get to.

43

BRYONY

THE FOG IS THICK as I jump from the ledge at the rear of the main building. The same exit we snuck out of the first night that Valen and Pierce took me to the ghoul pit. A night that seems eons ago, but only yesterday, all at once. That turning point looming over us as if teasing me with reminders of where it all began.

A chill hits me, the wind whipping at my ponytail. My hair's natural combination of waves and curls is on display tonight. I made no effort to straighten the strands to perfection. Tonight I wanted to be as close to my authentic self as possible. For my father to see just me the first time I lock eyes with him as an adult. I want him to see Bryony. No, I want him to see Bri.

I pull the map from the back pocket of my black skinny jeans, a gift from Damian, of all people. Artistic tears along my thighs and knees expose my bare skin to the cold of December in the mountains. Not the smartest outfit choice, but they made me feel bold. A little boost of bravery as I trek through the woods alone to meet a stranger.

The parchment waves in the gusts of wind. The corners fluttering as I do my best to get my bearings. Only the three buildings and the lake are truly identifiable on the map. A memory of Damian's deep baritone reminds me the map is hand-drawn so I need to pay attention to the details he chose to include. Out of all of Pierce's friends, he is the only one who takes the time to say more than a single word to me. He even told me a bit about his wife, Tosch, at dinner this past week.

It takes a few minutes, but I think I know which direction to head in. His personalized depiction of the campus tucked back in my pocket before I pull my wool coat tighter around me. My essence leaks from my fingers in black waves, shifting to a shimmering dove gray with just enough shine to illuminate my steps with the assistance of the vibrant moon above.

It shouldn't be possible, but the glow of the moon seems brighter tonight. As if proud I am set to reunite with the other half of me. I can imagine the roar of the ghouls held behind that silencing barrier in the distance. Students can only siphon the first night of the Red Moon, but I would assume staff can come out here as long as the ghouls remain.

Gazing up, my eyes burn under the glow of the moon. The leaves crunching beneath my flat boots, loud in my ears. My breath billows out in front of my face. Cheeks so chilled, they almost feel frozen.

It's not long before I've wandered through the trees in the pattern that should lead me to a small clearing. An odd curve created by how the trunks crowd together. Thick, angry roots burst through the near-frozen earth. A formation that I can only assume is man-made. The narrow path clear as if leading me to my destination. The location situated on the opposite side of the campus from where the ghoul pit sits.

On the map, it just looks like a small patch of land uninhabited by trees. In reality, it's a perfect oval space. Stones sit lined around a fire pit. Someone constructed the area as if its sole purpose was to tell spooky fireside stories. If only the reason I'm here held the same innocence.

"Bryony," a gruff voice sounds from behind me.

I spin far too quickly. My foot catching a rock as I stumble around with a yelp. Firm hands gripping me beneath my arms to correct me.

My mouth opens and closes. Instead of words, only odd squeaks escape me. I've thought about this moment a million times.

What I would call him?

What I would ask?

But nothing comes out. I can only study the handsome face in front of me analyzing every similarity I've already memorized from his photo.

The swirl of rich hickory brown hair swept straight back, sides cut close to his scalp. Eyes of lead, speckled with a lighter shade. The blanket of night and the treetops keep me from making out the exact color. Not a single picture I've studied gives a clear depiction of the color that breaks up that harsh gray. Only the base shade reveals the key to where Vincent and I got our irises from.

His nose also matches mine, nostrils flaring as he waits for me to say something. His features remain stoic, except for a single muscle ticking in his cheek as if unsure what my next reaction might be.

Yet his face is different than the tabloids and internet photos. Those pictures missed the scar on his right temple. And the bits of gray sprinkled along the edges of his hairline. The deep line through his forehead from years of frowning. They missed the man behind the deeds. They missed how his mouth sits crooked when relaxed. One corner just slightly off-center from a neutral position. They ignored the road map of his life, all visible through his imperfections.

This is the man my mother is in love with. Has always been in love with. Her true husband—whether that only be in thought, or legally, I'm unsure. My father. My blood.

"I—" The words still won't come as I step back from him. "You—"

"Hi, sweetheart." The term of endearment sounds odd in his voice, with his features. The darkness that clouds his eyes tells me he shouldn't say such sweet things. That he shouldn't want to address me that way.

"Mr. Guthrie." That corner of his mouth that sits askew drops. His brow furrowing low. Those dark irises giving the illusion of a tornado accompanying a violent storm.

"You can call me Jordden if you prefer."

I nod, unsure what to say. My feet guide me backward until I hit one of the boulders, my ass colliding with the stone.

Tendrils of essence swirl faster around my feet as if trying to reach for him. A reach for the known. Whips of smoke strike against his legs before curling around them with ease.

"Right. Well, I would like to spend some time with you, but for now, we need to talk." His voice is deep. A command to it that makes me want to flinch away. Yet, I believe I have nothing to fear from him.

"So, talk." I raise my chin, pursing my lips. Putting on a front as if I am in a better position than I am.

"I would appreciate it if you wouldn't treat me like this." He clears his throat as he calls my essence up to his fingers. The stars dance through them the way they do for me.

"Like what?" I ask, my brow quirked.

"As if I am a stranger."

Is he serious? He is a stranger. I may have spent part of my younger years with him, but he must know I don't remember him. I don't know anything beyond what the media says about him.

"To me, you are. For me, I only found out you were my father a week ago. I don't recall knowing you. I don't know you at all."

"That will be fixed. For now, we have more important things to worry about."

"Such as?" I don't mean to cock an attitude and I can tell by the flex of his jaw that he is working hard to maintain his composure. According to what I've heard, he has quite an explosive temper. Must be where I got mine from.

"You were sent here for a purpose. What have you found?"

"Other than the world hates what I am, nothing. No one talks about the school closures or what might be happening with the Council. At least nothing but idle gossip. Nothing useful." The words tumble from my mouth as if there's no consequence to voicing them. My brain slow to process that he shouldn't know that information. "How do you know why my dad sent me here?"

The audible grind of his teeth fills the night before he asks, "Have you tried to get answers?" A complete skirt around my last question.

"Excuse you? You don't get to show up here, out of the blue, asking me if I am taking what I was asked to do seriously." The words suddenly tumble from me. I glare at him as I respond, ticking my answers off on my fingers as I go. "Yes, I've tried to get answers. Yes, Janelle Milgren is still in my back pocket. No, the majority of the professors have nothing to say. Nor do my fellow students who have associations with those on the Council. I've got nothing."

"I feared this would happen. I warned Roman and your mother not to send you here. That it wasn't safe to send you here."

"Why not? Janelle has done nothing but keep me safe. And Wynston Knox, too."

"Ahh yes, that Knox boy. He's proven to be an asset, being here with you." He paces slowly, fingers running over the close-cropped beard covering the point of his chin.

"Look ..." My hands rise in front of me as I get back to my feet. "I have no idea what you're getting at or what is going on. I was sent here for information. Dad wanted to find out what sorts of things are going on in the underbelly of this place. It's only been three months. I think you can give me a break."

"We don't get breaks," he growls, stepping closer to me. His height towers over me, casting a dark shadow in the faint glow of the moon.

It should be fading by now. The color softening. It's redder still.

Something isn't right.

"Tell me what you want."

"I want to know my daughter. I want her to trust me. More importantly, I need you aligned with someone that I know is a supporter of mine. One that would do anything my people ask of him."

"Here?" I question, confused by his response. Something approximating hope blossoming in my chest.

Some of the notions I had about my father are true. Or so they seem. He does care for me. Likely has had others around all my life looking out for me. It also puts me at ease that, all this time, he has been working alongside my dad and my mother. But hurts just the same that I've never been allowed to know him.

And now ... Now I don't know if I want to.

"Yes. Do you know Valen Greer?"

My breath hitches in my throat. My heart racing as my essence forms a wall shaped like a U behind me. A protective barrier without keeping my father out. *Interesting.*

If he had said any other name, I might have been excited.

Fuck my life.

44

Bryony

Now is not the time to blow up. Not the time to have a breakdown or show fear. Not the time to question anything, yet I am questioning everything.

If my father had been watching me from afar, he would know Valen is the absolute worst person to have aligned with me. He would know about the threats and the bruises. The rumors he's spread and the number of secrets of mine he has learned and then used against me.

He would know Valen is the best way to keep me from listening to a thing he says.

My heart sinks. Every bit of hope that had bloomed only moments ago wilts away because this man won't care if Valen Greer is the answer.

"Well?" he prompts. "Do you know him?"

"You could say that." My teeth grind, arms crossing my chest. Memories of his body moving inside mine less than twenty-four hours ago flash through my mind. His heated skin sticking to mine. The taste of his mouth and the pressure of his tongue entering me.

Just allowing the thoughts in leaves my already sore vagina throbbing. Eager for more. But it won't happen. Not with Valen. It was a one-time slip in judgment, blamed on the post-ghoul lust.

Instead, I latch on to the ring of his fingers that remained a faded purple and blue around my tawny throat for weeks. His first warning to keep me away from Pierce. Only turtlenecks and popped collars could hide it. I gently bring my fingers to the curve of my ear, now missing a chunk of flesh thanks to one of his daggers. I'd had to let Graham spell the damn thing to stop bleeding because I refused to go to the infirmary to explain it.

"Start talking." He grabs my biceps. Just hard enough that I'm forced toward him, but not to the point of pain. Something closer to desperation shines behind his eyes.

"He's been trying to kill me since I got here."

"Impossible."

"Excuse me, but it's not. Let me paint a picture for you, *Dad.*" His title spoken like a curse. Yet his eyes widen at its use as if he can't believe that small three-letter word left my lips. A sense of relief, almost, that I would use the term of endearment on him.

"He's choked me. Throws daggers at me almost every day. See these cuts on my neck. Yeah, the guy you're asking me to trust gave those to me last night."

My blood boils. Angry at Valen for being such a dick. Angrier at myself for allowing him to have any part of me last night. Angrier still at this man who wants to be my father after twenty-five years and he didn't even know.

He backs away. Hands running over the short sides of his perfectly styled hair. Two fingers running from the top of his goatee to the bearded portion before his fingers rove over it in thought.

He closes his eyes, palms extended out. His essence, even darker than mine, void of those sparkling stars, drains from his fingers. A slithering, dark entity that roams over the ground. Two streams, about two feet long, stalking off into the trees.

He remains in that same position for longer than I would think possible. Unmoving. Even his chest seems still. Only those narrow nostrils flare with every few inhales. His palms remain extended open, not a single twitch of his fingers.

"Jord—" I begin, but I'm cut off by a single finger raised to halt my words.

Nothing more for me to do than sit. The hard stone a block of ice against my backside.

It's at least ten minutes before those tendrils reappear. Slipping back into his fingertips where they'd first escaped. His eyes open once they've returned. The color is gone. The entire socket black. His long lashes bracketing the pits that stare back at me.

"Do your eyes change?" he asks. His long frame takes a seat directly next to me. So close, our thighs touch.

I want nothing more than to pull away. In the same breath, wanting nothing more than to stay close. To embrace the man I wish I'd had the opportunity to know my entire life. The back and forth of my emotions are on the verge of giving me whiplash.

A gust of heavy wind sweeps by us. A shiver running through me. The woman who wants to know her father is comforted as his arm drapes across my shoulder, pulling me into his side.

I sit in silence thrown off by the question. Unsure how to answer.

"Yeah, they do. White with a narrow black rim," Valen's voice comes through the trees. His panting breaths announcing him before his body comes into view.

His tux jacket rests open, his tie undone and hanging around his neck. The shirt and pants perfectly sculpted to his lithe frame. A body I had on top of me not long ago.

"Jordden." He kneels at my father's feet. A plume of dry dirt wafting around him as his knees land. The impeccably clean tux, now filthy.

Jordden signals for him to stand with the twitch of two fingers. The hard angles of his face darken. Become sharper. Deadly as he stands to stare Valen down.

"You summoned me."

"I did." Jordden's eyes are still those pits of black, but Valen doesn't flinch away from them the way I did. "My daughter has told me some very interesting things."

"Your what?" Valen stutters, spinning to face me. His mouth falls open, eyes bulging as I wave at him with a taunting grin. I don't wish harm on many, but maybe I'll get lucky, and my father will pulverize him into dust. Not sure if that's possible, but it sounds cool in my head.

"Do you not serve me?"

"Yes, I do, but—"

"Shut the fuck up until I tell you to speak." Finally, the black fades. The gray then sage flecks shifting back into place. *Sage.* The same as mine. Had there been any doubt this man was my father before, somehow, I have none now. "Did I not tell you what you needed to do?"

"You did," Valen pants.

"Then why the fuck are you threatening my daughter?" He stares intently at Valen as if he can see straight into him. "I can smell her on you. Did I tell you to fuck my daughter?" An urge to sniff under my pits has me twitching. Do I still smell like Valen? I've had two showers today. How is that even possible?

"No, sir. I didn't know."

"You didn't know or you didn't care to notice?" Valen shifts from foot to foot. Eyes darting back and forth between Jordden and me. The recognition settles into his stare within seconds.

"Jordden, you asked me to remove any barriers to your plans. Anyone who would stand in the way of what needed to be done to bring the light to heel. I've been doing that. At a great cost to me and my friends." Valen's lip curls with a snarl.

"I don't give a shit about the sacrifices of you and your friends," he roars. A chunk of hair falling forward into his eyes. The end bobbing, then tangling in those long lashes that I envy. "You're disappointing. You don't deserve to wear my name."

Valen kneels again, his chin tucked into his chest. The muscles of his back quiver. For a split second, I almost feel something like sympathy for him, but quickly shove it away. He doesn't deserve anything but my cold shoulder.

The bastard deserves to get his ass handed to him.

"Get up!" He's slow to rise. "You will continue your assignment, but if I hear even the slightest mention of you so much as looking at my daughter wrong, you will not like having your gifts turned on you. I will make you remember every person you've fated to lie there while their bodies ate themselves. You'll live that same fate. And then, because I like entertainment, Vincent will come to raise you from the dead. How fun it will be to watch you live that cycle over and over. Am I clear?"

"Yes, sir."

"Get the fuck out of my sight. I will see you and that bunch of heathens tomorrow night. You will bring Bryony with you."

Valen dips his head, and then he's gone. His form disappearing so quickly into the dark cover of the trees I can almost imagine he hadn't just been standing here cowering before my father.

"You didn't have to do that," I whisper.

"Oh, but I did. Valen works for me. He will respect my blood."

I don't know what to say as I sit back on the same stone. Exhaustion pulls at me. My limbs are suddenly heavy. Too much excitement in the past days for me to handle.

"What is his assignment?" I ask.

Jordden tucks his hands behind his back, staring down at me. The hardness he's adopted in his features for Valen, still firmly in place.

"Have your *parents* told you nothing?" He winces at the word, then tries to cover it with a long press of his eyelids.

"I would like for you to tell me."

"You were sent here to find out why the light-wielding schools were closing. Were you not? Sent here to see if anyone knew why they were?"

I've already picked up on how Jordden prefers to speak. Unsure if those were actual questions for me to answer, or rhetorical ones he knows the answer to, I search for an appropriate response as silence stretches between us.

"And why are they?"

"Because a new age is coming, my dear." His thumb swipes my cheek as he cups my chin in the most fatherly way, pulling me to my feet. Our height difference requires me to look up at him. A slow blink as I stare up into a face I can see my resemblance in.

"What does that mean?"

"It is time for Grisyms to rise, don't you think?"

"I—"

There's no processing of his words. An ideal that's not once crossed my mind. The wielding world condemns us to death at birth. So why would I ever have considered a version where they didn't? Where we didn't have to hide or pretend to be anything other than what we truly were.

It's not a future I've ever believed the wielding community willing or capable of.

"Soon, my dear, you will no longer live in the shadows. You will no longer live in fear. You, my child, will stand tall next to your brother and you will bring with you a new regime of acceptance and infinite power."

There are no words as Jordden pulls me into a hug, holding me tight, my arms remaining limp at my sides.

For once, I have nothing to say.

45

Bryony

Seeing my father rattled me. Having his face so close to mine, his breath brushing across my cheeks was too much to process. Those eyes so similar to mine staring back at me with love I didn't think my biological father had for me. An easy conclusion since I never knew him or even who he was before that letter.

My flesh and blood, right there.

He promised he would return soon. Allow us the time to get to know one another as we are now. At the beginning of the night, I can't say I wanted that. I can't say I wanted anything other than the questions zooming through my head answered—every detail my parents didn't want to tell me through the years laid bare at my feet.

I wanted to know why he never came back for me. Why he never fought to know his daughter all these years, especially once I turned eighteen? Sure in wielding years, twenty-five is the equivalent of eighteen for humans, but it counts, right?

But now?

Now I want more than their secrets. I want his laughter and his love. I want hugs and all the daddy-daughter days we never had.

Well, I think I want that. The hug he left me with brought those wants and needs to the surface. I may not know the man but my essence does. The very core of my being recognized him. Could never forget or replace him. Maybe I just want the chance to choose that connection for myself.

I think I want to know my birth father and what he stands for. To understand the New Order's mission from his perspective and what the school closures truly have to do with it. More than that to understand where I fit into all this. That feeling of being nothing but a pawn washes over me anew.

I think ...

I've been sitting out here alone for hours by the lake. My knees tucked in close to my chest, rocking my ass into the cold dirt. There's no focus on anything in particular, head cocked to the side as the breeze whistles around me.

The moment I woke this morning, just before noon, I came straight here. The sun was already lower in the sky. I can't remember the last time I slept so much. Slept so deeply that I missed repeated calls from Pierce and Graham, and Camilla's one-woman dance party. My body nuzzled comfortably under the warm blankets as that new ghoul power aimlessly flowed through me.

The only soul I've bothered to talk to today was Knox. Concern drenched every strained word. The number of times he asked me how I felt, in various worded combinations made me want to scream. It was exhausting. As if using different phrasing would prompt my answers to become the ones he was expecting.

As refreshed as I felt when I did wake, my mind has been a mix of troubled and blurry thoughts. So, I came here, hopeful I could cast them out into the mountains. A silent wish for clarity to replace what has been plaguing me for weeks now. Hopes that I might know what direction to go. An easy decision made on whose side I was to take.

Or maybe make sense of the fact that my tormentor, the man I willingly fucked two nights ago, is one of my father's trusted supporters. Or how about the fact that whatever is going on with the schools and the Council has to do with me and my brother, Vincent. Jordden hadn't explicitly said it, but I sensed we are at the center of it. Whether that's because we're his children or Grisyms remains unclear.

Jordden's words were carefully structured to convey what he meant but still kept parts to himself.

"It is time for the Grisyms to rise, don't you think?"

He spoke as if there were more of us. As if Vincent, Knox, and I aren't the only ones out there.

If there are, I want to know them, too. We should test what Knox and I have uncovered with others.

That single statement opened up a world of possibility beyond the walls of Beauxgraton. The mountain range beyond, draped in a soft orange glow, gives me pause as I consider the infinite possibilities. The endless expanse of space between myself and where other Grisyms might be just waiting to be traversed.

Have they lived life hiding and in fear, like Knox and me? Or is there somewhere out there in the world where we can be ourselves, safely, without death or retribution? If such a place exists, that's where I want to be once I graduate.

Fuck what my parents have planned for me. I've tasted that sweet freedom of releasing what has always lived inside and there's no going back.

I hope there are others. More where we can explore the theories of what Grisyms can do together. Knox and I might not even be an accurate representation of the possibilities. After all, we both seem to hold a mixture of abilities from our parents. I can only assume that's true for all of us, but honestly, we have no way of knowing for sure.

As Grisyms, none of us are pure. Essences and power don't work that way once mixed. Per the few texts that speak of Grisyms, then looking at Knox, Vincent, and me as examples, we become an entirely new force. Only a little of each side, and a heaping portion of the unknown.

The wind kicks up, tossing my curling edges across my face, obscuring my vision for a fleeting moment. As I squint into the distance I'm convinced I saw a figure across the lake, looming just behind the treeline. The moment the wind calms, my hair strands settling against my back, the lurking figure is no longer there.

I likely imagined it.

Get it together, Bri.

Maybe the surreal reality of meeting my father has my imagination in overdrive. It seems even more unlikely that he's somehow not the demon the world has painted him. How can I not stand behind someone who wants those like me to have full lives? A man who refuses to leave us cowering in the shadows.

It seems only fair. Only fitting.

We are wielders, too. If others only took the time to understand us, to know that we are not the harmful beings they believe us to be, life would be so different. Then maybe I could have a chance at a normal life, too. We all can.

Maybe we can save the lives of babies all over the world. Beyond that, maybe, we can save what little slice of humanity we still hold on to as well.

Wishful thinking, Bri. You're not equipped to go out there and change the world after five minutes of knowing the truth about your lineage.

A loud sigh escapes me as I lean back on my hands. The final rays of sunshine warm my cheeks. The glow should be fading into darker pinks and purples, but it isn't.

The peaches merge into pinks. The pink to a glowing red.

My eyes widen as the Red Moon rises in the sky, the sun still coasting out of sight before disappearing beyond the horizon. Their paths crossing for mere seconds, darkening to the color of wine before the sun finally falls, destined to rise in another part of the world.

I rub my eyes. This time, I'm convinced I *am* hallucinating. Never in the history books have I read of a Red Moon lasting longer than its coveted forty-eight hours.

What will it mean for us all to have the moon continue to shine? Will new barriers be erected for the ghouls that will gain an extra night on the mortal plains? From what I understand, the glow of the moon unlocks the ward magic that keeps the ghouls in their dwellings underground. If it is out so are they—theoretically.

Those wards should have sealed back into place the moment the last sliver of the moon disappeared this morning. A new morning, the beginning of the next ninety days, ghoul and Red Moon free. So, either the gates never locked, or they are open once again.

I should make my way back to the residence. I should tell someone. Janelle, or Knox. Should I call my dad? But I'm frozen, glued to my spot. My gaze unforgivingly latched onto the glowing red orb in the sky as it halts high above me. The soft blue of the sky, now nothing more than midnight darkness. The stars that usually shine, hidden as if in fear.

Something stirs within me. Like tiny spider legs walking through my body. The sensation is odd but not unpleasant. It seems to grow in intensity the longer I stare at the moon as if the sight alone is riling it up. I wonder if this is the ghoul's power within me. The dark, ancient power that refuses to stop roaring with life.

I've felt foreign power before. Old, new, different. The types are so varied, it's impossible to recall them all. But nothing feels like the magic from the ghoul flowing through my veins. The veins on the underside of my forearms tinted in a blue so dark they match the ghoul's skin. I hadn't noticed it that night, but I did yesterday morning as the warm spray from my shower washed over my skin. A feeling like rich aged leather and fine cigars filling my insides as if it belongs there.

Jordden assured me it was nothing to worry about. Promised it would fade in a few days as I began to use my essence again and cast spells in class. Even the simple ones of opening my bedroom door would slowly deplete my magic stores from the ghoul. Each use easing me closer to my normal baseline.

He told me since this was my first time siphoning, I was likely to blast through that new power quicker than a typical wielder would. Either because my body is eager to rid itself of the foreign, or it's already so addicted to the tempting lure that it won't be able to stop tapping into it.

I have nothing to compare this to. I wish I had asked questions instead of fucking Valen, avoiding Pierce's questions, and losing any semblance of thought when meeting my father.

I allow a tendril to release from my fingertip. The dark swirl shimmers the way it always does but is less transparent than usual. There's a depth to it now as I twirl it around my fingers. As if these smokey tendrils are thicker. Rubbing my fingers together, I feel it. Drawing them apart, I expect there to be a residue, but there isn't any.

Suddenly a wave rolls through me, jerking my body forward as I gasp for air.

What the fuck was that?

I stumble to my feet. Nausea crashing through me as I angle back toward the residence. Another wave hits me throwing me face down. My body convulsing as I flip to my back. Dark waves of essence stream out of me, blasting in all directions. Every bit of light from the moon blocked from view as the wisps encircle me.

Help.

A single-worded plea in my head as tears stream down my cheeks.

Pain radiates through my entire body. Muscles clamping tight in protest. Heavy jabs assault me, like daggers mutilating my insides. The mixed essence of Knox and me, panicking. Attempting to push against whatever is causing my body to come undone.

Help me.

I wish I knew what was happening. How to help myself or control whatever this is. But I'm helpless as I writhe on the ground. The wall of thick fog blankets me from anyone who might be outside. But who would be out after sundown? It's far too cold and, more than likely, everyone is recovering from their hangovers or studying for whatever tests are coming their way tomorrow.

Fear squeezes my chest. Maybe this is the end. Maybe I took too much. None of us know if I have a body to handle this.

Knox is the only example I know, but the combination of what he is doesn't make him a match to me.

Shadows darken my vision. My head swimming as I lie there waiting for whatever this is to stop. For the pain to subside. For the torsion of my arched back to relax.

Prayers sent to gods I don't believe in for someone to find me. Save me.

There's nothing but the darkness of my essence. Not even my stars remain. There's just black.

My imagination concocts voices in the distance. An attempt at deceiving me into believing help is coming.

My eyes close, consciousness leaving me.

My body caught in the in-between.

Movement.

Maybe.

Black, indefinitely.

I'm ...

46

PIERSON

I DIDN'T KNOW WHAT to make of Knox storming into Valen's room. His fingers dug into Valen's arm as he dragged him to his feet and straight out the door. His features scrunched in disgust or anger. I couldn't tell and didn't have time to ask.

Knox didn't even bother closing the door behind him as he sped down the hall. The thud of his and Valen's boots against the carpet vibrating through the empty hall.

Not once did Valen pull away or fight him off, simply smirked as he let Knox pull him along while I followed.

I didn't expect to find Bri writhing on the ground by the lake, alone, with swirling droves of essence black as the night billowing around her. The tendrils formed thick whips slashing at me and Valen as we drew closer. Only Knox was able to reach out to it. To touch it with his own and gain passage to her.

No matter how many times he shook her or called her name, she never responded. Not with words or anything intelligible. Just mumbled sounds as he scooped her up and carried her to her room. The hallways, thankfully, were relatively empty. The few students we passed ran in the opposite direction the moment Val snarled in their direction.

The veins at Knox's throat bulged as he fought to hold their essences at bay. A light haze of dark clouds shadowed his hands but didn't allow it to break free once more. His and Bri's secret kept locked away.

Valen and I followed in silence. Seeing her like this confirmed everything he'd told me. My insides went cold at seeing how out of control her magic had become. Is this what she keeps under wraps all the time? Or is this a result of her being with that ghoul?

Blue species tend to carry very volatile energy. Not to mention, she's innate. She doesn't need to siphon power. Doesn't matter if she's a light or dark wielder. Her body comes with its own stores that can replenish themselves with time.

Our bodies can only hold so much. One of the most important warnings for younger wielders clearly states: never take more than one ghoul in a given night. Never take more than your body can hold. The majority of us stick to a single partner until we're well into our forties. You need years of honing power and training your body to accommodate more of what they give you. The preparation of your body is needed to keep you from the brink of death.

It's the primary reason extrinsics and charters are required to take classes on ghoul history, anatomy, and classification. It's imperative to understand what we take and from whom the power comes. Incompatible magic is akin to mixing two averse chemicals in a lab. The reaction of their properties could be nothing or an uncontrollable explosion.

Our bodies can retaliate. The structures we were born into, unable to hold us together. Our minds lose touch with reality and our bodies fight off the foreign magic like an infection. Very few ever recover from improper siphoning. Their bodies typically fail them in a relatively short time. It's typically only a matter of time before death follows.

The ones who do survive, are never the same in the end. Their abilities just a bit off from what they should be. Siphoning is usually a problem. Spellcasting is often limited to the most rudimentary of charms that even those who haven't matured can perform with relative ease.

Only as I watched Knox cradle Bri to his chest, his body quivering from the exertion of carrying her and fighting to hold their essences within him, did I begin to understand a fraction of what every day holds for them. The unknown. Unbeatable control. Fear.

Knox left hours ago. Valen and I stayed, unwilling to leave her side. She never actually wakes, only continues to mumble as she tosses and turns.

Knox did something to keep her from being swallowed whole by her raging powers. Long moments of his mouth hovering over hers while dark tendrils of fog passed between their lips. His mumbled words were soft even in the quiet.

"Have you ever seen something like that?" I ask Valen, tired of the prolonged silence.

"No."

I've never been scared of another wielder. Never feared what they could do to me because I knew I could do worse. I do my best to ignore how my gifts prefer to be used. The malicious intent they would prefer to take.

I've always been a natural spellcaster. Even in my younger years, before my power matured, I could create unique and complicated spells experienced wielders couldn't duplicate.

"Stop worrying," Valen scoffs, pulling me out of my thoughts for a moment before I dive back into them.

I prefer spells that don't impact free will. Yet my specialty is snatching away another's choice with a single thought. Just a hint of intrusion, and I can force someone to do anything I please. Howl like a monkey. Strip down naked. Impale themselves on a sharp object. There are no limits for someone like me.

Some spellcasters need relics, while others focus concentration on the spell they are trying to invoke. Many more can speak it with intent. Their creations brought to life moments later.

Then there are those like me. I barely have to form the thought of the spell I want to conjure for it to come to fruition. Just a tiny, fleeting thought and the spell rushes its target. Should I add even the tiniest bit of focus, the strength of those spells exponentially increases. A grip so strong that I often have to use counter-spells instead of just undoing or releasing the one I'd chosen.

What makes that worse is my essence prefers spells like binding, mind control, body control, and self-harm. I realize it's part of being a dark wielder. We are the takers. But that does nothing to stop me from wishing I was different. That, as a subtype within our kind, *we* aren't different. Disappointment knowing only forceful work against our nature can tamper it.

My brother has always called me a chump for being so soft. For aligning more with the light-wielding way of things. Shame flashed in his black eyes at my dismissal of all that I'm capable of. Gifts he wishes he could have.

We're only two years apart, but we couldn't be more distant if we tried. He chose to attend school in Prague, where they revel in the most vicious of magic. Like me, he channels best from the earth. The force with which he can pull from it puts my abilities to shame. Think dark wizard and you've got Levi's entire vibe captured.

I may be a powerful caster under any circumstance, but earth magic elevates my abilities beyond imagination. The unfortunate part is that not all chunks of earth are equal in their release of borrowed magic. It's why I always participate in the Red Moon. It's the next best thing for me. Magical artifacts almost always send a spell slightly askew for me.

I stopped using them years ago. Only dire need or a class provides a good enough reason to so much as look at one.

The power I siphon must be stored in more modern-made vessels if I'm to use it properly. It's a trick I learned shortly after becoming a student here. Foreign power must settle within me for a few days before channeling to my vessels, and then utilizing it for a specific spell. It's limiting but keeps me in check.

A knock comes at the door. Valen and I exchanging a look. His wrist signals for me to open it as he returns his gaze to Bri's scrunched features.

I'm slow to shuffle to the door, hand extended with a nervous quiver. Tense about what type of shit might come our way. Had someone seen her? Or us?

Graham and all his luxuriousness wait on the other side. Pressed jeans and a button-down styled with expensive footwear. Shoes shined to perfection. I've never understood why he insists on parading around like a model, but it is what it is. He's Bri's friend and I honestly don't mind him all that much.

Collin had been the one to bring us together surprisingly. The three of us joined some of the other guys on the lawn for a game of touch football a few weeks into the school year. Honestly, I was surprised such a pretty boy would get dirty in the mud. He didn't know the game but had enough natural athletic ability to keep up. There was a newfound respect for him as he brought our team the victory touchdown, tackling the ball from another light wielder new to Beauxgraton.

Valen, on the other hand, would likely slit his throat just as quickly as he would Bri's. Just his association with her is enough to condemn him in Val's world.

"How is she?"

"Ah, Camilla found you," I mutter cupping the back of my head.

"Yeah, she did." He shoves past me, his mouth set into a straight line. His eyes are glassy as if he'd been holding back tears.

"Man, you don't need to be here." I follow after him, closing the door quietly.

He's already settled on the edge of the bed, brushing her waving hair back from her temples. The unruly pieces bouncing right back to where they were only moments before. Even her hair emulates her stubbornness.

She mumbles in response, shifting before settling deeper into her pillows.

His touch is tender. One that conveys more than friendship to me. Bri's words ring through my head. Promises that what she and Graham have is nothing more than a close friendship. Weeks ago, I would have fought to not believe her. Now, I do. Bri was meant for me so I know she's telling the truth about this despite his obvious affection. Technically, she'd told me the truth about Knox too, just not his identity.

"If you wake her, I will *fucking* gut you," Valen snarls. The silver dagger his father gave him twirling between his fingertips with ease. For what he can do to someone's body with his gifts alone, it's interesting that he would rather stab someone than leave them there to rot inside their skin. His violent tendencies need that physical release, according to him.

I'm not sure what that says about him. Or me, for that matter. I accepted what and who he was a long time ago and, at some point, it stopped bothering me. It just became a simple fact.

"Fuck you, Valen. She doesn't even like you. Why are you here?" Graham snips.

The anger that coats his words surprises me.

Graham is the nice guy.

Graham is the calm one.

The funny one that keeps her laughing.

Her academic rival, even though they choose to help each other rather than fight.

The man who makes sure the girls in their group lock their rooms up before he returns to his own at night.

That's not who is sitting next to my girl right now, petting her with so much sweetness it gives me a toothache.

"She already did."

Graham's eyes go wide before they narrow on Valen. My heart is racing. Disbelief but not shock that he would throw their one-night stand in someone else's face. I was able to overlook it when it was me. Pointed in my direction, I thought it was personal. Against Graham, I don't know what it means.

Graham is her friend. Valen, her enemy.

"You're a liar. Get out of here." Graham jerks his head toward the door, shifting that much closer to Bri. His body curving over hers in protection.

"I am, huh? Pierce, you were there. You watched me slip into that sweet pussy for the first time."

Graham stalls for two point four seconds before he launches himself at Valen. The both of them tumble to the floor. Instinct pulls me out of Camilla's desk chair in seconds. A shoulder catching my ankle, tripping me into the bed with Bri.

They grunt as they roll across the floor. Valen purposely keeping his dagger hand to the side. Graham throwing punches I wouldn't think him capable of. There's a spray of blood across the light-colored comforter as Val's lip busts open, his cackling laughter only driving Graham's anger higher.

I finally pull Graham off, holding him back by his arms. The well-put-together, gentle soul I've always known him to be comes undone as his essence slithers free, shoving me into the dresser across the room.

The three of us stand there panting. One eye focused on the other. Each of us waiting for the other to strike again.

"You need to go," I breathe.

His essence still dances in front of me as I point at the door. His hands brush down the front of his torso, smoothing his shirt before tucking it back into his jeans. The clack of his shoes on the floor finally settling my racing heart.

I've barely locked the door behind him when a tortured groan sounds behind me. A blast of essence shoots from Bri's fingertips and mouth in an instant, her body jerking awake with a whimper that shatters my heart.

Bri wakes with that same outpour of her essence just as I reach for her. The swirl of dark waves around her like a veil, protecting her or blocking us.

This is so much more than I can handle.

47

GRAHAM

I TOUCH MY THUMB to the corner of my mouth. Bright red blood stains the pad. A hiss through my teeth as I gently graze the same spot for a second time. The action repeated several more times as I stare at the ebony door in front of me, attempting to will the slab of wood to reopen. Hoping for Bri to let me back in.

Instead, all I get is uneven shuffling and her deep groans growing louder by the second. Not groans of pleasure but endless pain. I clench my fists, my short nails digging into my palms. Fury rages through me. Pierson might be her wannabe boyfriend, but he had no right to kick me out of that room.

I should be in there. With my friend. Taking care of her. Protecting her from Valen, the vile being that he is.

It takes everything in me not to try to knock the door down. To demand they let me in. A single fist rises several times before I finally let it fall to my side in defeat. My forehead meets the cool surface with a plea, praying to conjure a spell that will break through the ward and allow me entrance, without one of them having to open the door from the inside. No, the only way I'm getting back in that room tonight is if Bri demands it.

Instead, I go find Collin and Frankie. My two closest friends besides Bri.

My head pounds as I stomp down the hall, jumping down one of those short staircases before hooking a sharp left. I touch my thumb to my mouth again, a longer hiss rolling through my teeth. My cheek throbs. For only using one hand, Valen kind of kicked my ass.

Maybe I deserved it. Maybe he did.

He's been nothing but a dick to Bri. So, the fact that he would make up lies about her sleeping with him doesn't surprise me, but still pisses me off just the same.

Fucking, liar.

Those two words repeat in my head until a thought hits me. The admission was there, in those denim-blue eyes.

Pierson never denied it.

He didn't even try to say it was false.

Bri and Valen.

Bri and Pierson.

Bri and Knox—although I don't have confirmation of that one. Yet.

I do my best to shake away the fact that three other men are occupying my friend's attention. Tell myself it's not jealousy but protectiveness. That she could have chosen better. Chosen a man like her—a light wielder. Not a professor and a duo of delinquent dark wielders.

Pierson is a good guy. I will give him that. His undivided attention has always stayed on Bri. He's never done wrong by her. Never made her feel anything but wanted, seen, and special, but that doesn't change who he associates with. You are the company you keep.

Valen is a fucking monster. And Knox—Knox is a motherfucking predator for going after her. If that's even what's happening.

It could be. I saw her with him early in the morning. I've watched her wait for him in the freezing cold. Bri can tell me she's been meeting Valen all she wants, but I'm not blind. Knox has been the man occupying her mornings. Their age difference is continuously at the forefront of my thoughts. His authority would be something Bri couldn't go against. I can't help but wonder if he is threatening her into silence.

Knox should know better. A man in his late thirties shouldn't want her. Dark thoughts of what he must be holding over her supply my reasoning for their "relationship." It's the only plausible explanation. Or maybe it's the only one I am willing to accept.

My thoughts finally relinquish their hold on me. The moment stolen, as Knox himself darts past me up the main stairwell. His long strides take the stairs two at a time. Panting breaths reverberating through the open space as sweat streams down his temples and throat.

There's no reason for him to be headed toward the east wing on a Sunday night. No reason except ...

Not allowing him to get away, I run after him. My feet ache in my dress shoes. All this physical exertion lately is more than my non-active muscles can take. I swear if I don't get murdered by Valen tonight, I'll start working out next week.

Knox just slipped through her door, the momentum of him slamming it open only to bounce off the wall behind it quickly shutting it. Just enough time for me to shove my foot against the frame, keeping it ajar. My great toe painfully shoved against the inside of my shoe as I grunt loudly. My whine exaggerated as it starts to throb.

The moment I step inside, a violent swirl of black fills the room, knocking my back into the door. A bolt of pain shooting through my shoulder blades and ass from colliding with it.

Tsunamis and hurricanes are less violent than the storm brewing around my best friend. Black winds whip at the three other men in the room. Her mouth wide open as her essence free-flows from her in an opaque torrent.

"Get the fuck out of here, you idiot," Valen growls.

He and Pierson hold down Bri's limbs, her body thrashing against them. Sweat beads along her exposed skin. A dark flush altering her complexion, her veins seemingly darkening before my eyes. The nightshirt she wears bunches up around her waist, exposing her stomach. But they ignore it, fighting to hold her down.

Those mixed eyes of hers remain closed, lids forcefully pressed shut. Her lashes flutter against her cheekbones. Yet, her face is completely calm while her body fights. Had I only seen her face, I would think she was in a deep sleep. The dream world keeping her safe from all of this.

I wish it were a dream. That what I'm seeing is nothing more than a practical joke. Or a figment of my imagination, because for me to be witnessing my best friend expelling an essence as dark as the midnight sky means she is not what she says she is.

Bri is supposed to be a light wielder.

Her essence shouldn't blend in with the three dark men around her. It shouldn't look like the night sky spewing past her parted lips.

"W-W-What's wr-wrong with her?" My voice is not my own. Fear leaks into every syllable. Disbelief brings out a stutter I've never had.

"Shut it, Mayer," Valen barks. I'm shocked into silence. I never even knew he knew my first name, let alone my last. So, to hear it come from his mouth has me falling to my ass on Camilla's bed. The soft mattress, thankfully, void of the energetic female.

Her new "girlfriend" keeps her occupied more and more these days. Enough so the two are always seen as a duo except in class.

I watch quietly as Professor Knox climbs onto the bed, his legs straddling her middle. Fists digging into the mattress on either side of her head, he slowly leans forward, as if not wanting to startle her. His mouth gradually widens, that perfectly chiseled jaw stretching more than should be natural. A long exhale of his essence flows directly into her mouth. Its dark curls weaving with hers instantly. The color shifts so quickly that I wonder if I imagined it. A faint purplish-gray, calm at the connection between their mouths.

Then he inhales, taking it all into himself. Every drop of their essences sails into that hole and down his throat. A bob of his Adam's apple with every swallow.

"What the fuck?" I blurt, nearly knocking myself off the bed.

What the fuck did I just see?

Her eyes flutter open seconds later, first finding Pierson and Valen holding her down, then shifting her focus to Knox's face. There's no panic in her eyes, but something else I can't identify.

Tears slide down her cheeks. Smooth streams of clear liquid soaking into her pillow. Her small nod is his invitation to lean in and kiss her.

One that is passionate. A bond between them I cannot even fathom. The kiss of two people who know one another intimately.

It's short-lived. Her eyes close briefly before she whispers, "I think I'm good guys."

They release her. Her body slow to sit up, Knox helping her with a palm to her lower back and hip. A tiny tendril of essence slips free of her mouth immediately going from black to that same color I'd seen moments ago, before retreating back inside.

She finally turns to me and this time I fall from my spot. My body crumpling to the floor as I scoot away from her. Terror stretches my features, muscles taut as I tell myself I am imagining things for the umpteenth time tonight.

"What the hell are you?"

"Graham, please." She moves to stand. Her balance wobbly as Knox helps hold her up. A hand at her waist and another under her arm. "I got it," she groans.

She takes a few tentative steps toward me. I scramble with my arms and legs, attempting to scoot back. Inch by inch, putting distance between the two of us. As much as the room will allow. My skull hitting the edge of the desk with a sickening thud.

She winces but keeps coming closer. Hands raised in a gesture of peace.

I can't take my focus off her eyes. Glowing white. No irises. No pupil. The eyes of ghouls.

"Bryony, don't come near me," I wail. Panting breaths drive my heartbeat to a wild staccato. My eyes darting every direction searching for a way out.

She pauses at my use of her name. Neither of us can likely remember the last time I said it instead of calling her Bri.

"Graham, let me explain."

I don't have words. My friend is something else and never said a thing to me. My heart hurts as I absorb the myriad of things she's kept from me. Every secret and lie bears down on us with the force of a boulder. Crushing us so thoroughly that we'll never be the same.

"What. Are. You?"

She looks at me with sad, pale eyes and whispers, "Grisym."

48

BRYONY

IT'S IMPOSSIBLE TO SAY how my entire world got flipped upside down. How I went from a kind-of-normal woman to the one standing here, staring down at my best friend as he stares back in horror. Every detail is a reminder of how the world sees a Grisym. They turn their backs on us the moment they find out we are "other."

I'd always hoped Graham would be different if he ever found out. That he could be like my family or Janelle. Hope is a cruel thing to hang on to. A stupid notion, best kept close to the chest because, inevitably, it will be nothing more than a letdown.

"Graham, I'm sorry."

His eyes won't leave my face. His complexion so pale that my comforter of frosty blue holds more color. I want to look everywhere but at him right now. Anything to avoid the fear in his eyes.

The blackout curtains Camilla insisted we get, even though they don't match anything in the room.

The pile of clothes at the end of my bed. Countless outfits discarded as I tried to find the perfect one to meet Jordden.

The mattress releases a slight groan as Valen and Pierce shift on the bed behind me. Both are as quiet as Graham. The cadence of Knox, Pierce, and Valen's breath at my back soothes me. All three men allowing me to navigate this situation on my own.

Graham's chest seems frozen. No breath passing between his lips to empty then refill his lungs. His silence stretches so long it further frays my nerves.

His knees tuck in closer to his chest, eyes wide as saucers as I take a single step closer. His body instinctually attempting to scoot further back, head smacking into the edge of the desk for a second time. His designer jeans—ones that likely cost more than all the furniture combined in this room—bunch, a single calf exposed as they hitch high.

"Look, we don't have time for this, Bri." Valen's exasperation is clear in his voice.

I'm quick to spin at his use of my nickname. Not once has he ever called me anything other than Bryony and Forbidden Fruit. He rolls his eyes as I gawk at him as if he knows exactly what I'm thinking.

"We're already late," Valen snaps, his steps already carrying him toward the door.

It's as if the contents of my brain emptied. My father's threats to Valen less than twenty-four hours ago filtering back into my consciousness. The meeting he'd ordered Valen to bring me to, forgotten until now. A special guest to whatever their rendezvous is meant to be.

"Graham, you're coming." My words voiced as a split-second decision.

"Hell no! I am not going anywhere with you. You're dangerous. You're—" He swallows loudly. "You're—" The hitch of his breath is loud in my ears.

Rejection shreds my heart to ribbons. I always knew this was a possibility, but facing losing the man who has become my best friend, buckles my knees. My male double in so many ways.

"You know I'm not. I'm still your friend. I'm still the same woman you've always been friends with. Now you just know my secret," I shrug, hoping the soft tone will get him back on my side. Hoping the plea coating my words will get him on his feet.

I can't afford for anyone else to know about me or my father, but his reaction is so exaggerated that I refuse to let him out of my sight. Maybe he'll sit in his room in silence and say nothing out of fear or loyalty. He could also run to spread the word out of fear or self-preservation. Until we can have a reasonable conversation, I'm stuck to him like glue.

"Let's go," Valen growls. "If he says a word, he'll be dead tomorrow."

Graham's panting breaths grow louder. Faster. His head colliding with the edge of the desk for a third time. How the boy doesn't have a concussion at this point is beyond me. His howling cry rings out through the room, making me want to check him for one, either that or an open wound.

"Pardon me, but where the hell do you guys think you're taking her?" Knox snarls.

"Wynston, this has nothing to do with you," Pierce warns. A tone much harsher than I've ever heard from him. His glare darker. More aggressive.

Okay, this pissing contest isn't going to work for me either.

"Look, we need to go meet with—" I pause not wanting to reveal another secret just yet to Graham. "We just need to go. You all have big dicks, now get your shit."

Valen slashes his signature smirk, another knife teetering between his fingers.

"Graham, get up," I command. "Knox you're coming, too. I swear you four can be such a pain in my ass." I'm not missing a chance to talk to Jordden about what happened here.

Pierce pulls Graham to his feet. The two of them first to follow me from the room, with Knox bringing up the rear.

It's easier than it should be to sneak through the halls to the hidden passages within the residence. My four decent-sized men flanking me like the directions of a compass. Pierce due North. Graham, West. Knox, East, and Valen to the South.

My father is already in the Vault, perched on a stone bench when we enter. Kaia and Kormoran snarling as I lead the way down the stone steps. If they weren't fans of me before, they're about to hate me that much more. The looks on their faces revealing they still believe me to be nothing more than a light wielder.

Well, children, you're in for a surprise.

Sean pretty much ignores that we've entered. He and Damian huddled together, looking at something on Damian's phone. His gaze only flickering up to meet mine for a few seconds before returning to his phone. Flames from a sconce glint off the smooth surface of the ring I'd failed to notice when first we met. That tiny circle of metal somehow reassuring me I'm safe with him.

"You're late," Jordden sneers.

"Uh ...Jordden, I had some issues. They were helping me." My hand waves at the four men standing at my back as if that will explain it all. Every terrifying moment of my body reacting poorly to the ghoul magic and potentially losing my best friend.

I can hear Graham shuffling behind me. This is so much, so fast, for him. The poor guy is likely ready to shit his pants. Or report me to the Wielding Bureau.

"What sort of issues?" Jordden holds me by the biceps, his elbows bent, bringing me closer. The sharp point of his nose too close to my face.

"I don't know what the fuck is going on here, but why the hell are you here? And while you're at it, take your hands off her." Knox's heat brushes at my back. My thighs press together as the Red Moon lust still consumes me. He may have been fine with me meeting my father, but made it crystal clear he doesn't support the things he's done or what he stands for.

Brutality.

Death.

Destruction.

Oh, Knox. Noble to a fault sometimes.

"Mr. Knox, I would suggest you shut your mouth and not instruct me on what I shall or shan't do when it comes to *my* daughter."

Graham bolts. Kormoran catching him with an extended arm to the chest. His back colliding with the stone floor as he flies backward. Graham's body immediately curls in on itself as the pain rolls through him. This time only groans accompany his form balled up at our feet.

"Graham. Please, just sit," I plead as I help him up. His weight sinks into me as he welcomes my touch. A deep inhale as his nose sinks into my bush of curls.

His arm tightens around my middle. So tight you'd think I'm the only one who could help. The only one he can trust.

He sits on the stone, furthest from Kormoran. Eyes darting between Kaia, my father, Kormoran, and Valen. Those four comprising the group he's most terrified of.

"Bryony, you and I will have a chat after this gathering ..." Jordden softly smiles at me despite the distaste in his tone. "But for now, we have business to tend to."

I nod, squeezing in next to Graham. If anyone is going to be able to keep him in his seat it's me. He presses into my side. His back curved oddly, likely from the impact of his fall.

Tension radiates through the room. So many secrets and half-truths were exposed with a single sentence. If any of the others doubted what I was before they don't now.

Jordden Guthrie wields from the dark.

Geneva Avalon—Guthrie—from the light.

"Achterberg was secured today," Jordden announces.

The name sounds so familiar. Long minutes of searching my memory for how I know it scrunching my nose. A flash of a memory suddenly hitting me.

Denmark.

The light-wielding school is hidden in one of the many historical castles in the heart of the country. Former home to the royal family, converted to the school's new campus in the early eighteen hundreds when its student base became too large for the original structure that housed the institution.

Only faint memories of the interior find me now. The regalness of the walls and decor kept as close to their original state as the school could accommodate. My chance of returning there, now gone.

Kaia smiles wide as if this is a victory.

"Why are you doing this?" I ask. I am genuinely confused about how closing the light schools is a good thing.

"The next waves of Grisyms will take up residence in the palace at the start of the next semester," Jordden continues as if my question never met his ears. "The students who started the year there will be transferred to dark schools of their choice. This is just the beginning my child."

"Wave? As in, how many Grisyms?" Knox interjects.

"Only a few hundred are in that territory." My father doesn't even feign looking Knox in the eye to deliver the answer.

"Jordden, are you telling me you are responsible for the closure of every light school to harbor Grisyms?" disbelief coating my words. Knox takes several steps in Jordden's direction as the words funnel from my mouth. A threat evident in the puff of his chest and tightening of his fists at his sides.

"And do what with them, exactly? Teach them? Help them hide some more?" With each word Knox's voice rises, his tone becoming more accusatory. Skepticism setting his brow low.

Gray eyes find mine before my father speaks. "I would prefer if you would call me by something other than my first name." His implication is clear as he ignores more of Knox's questions. He wants me to call him "Dad." To embrace what he is to me, but I'm not sure I'm ready for that. I might be coming to terms with wanting to know the man, but embracing what he never got to be for me is a bit much.

I've known Roman as my dad my whole life. A man I knew was only my father in practice and word. It didn't matter that I didn't know the other man responsible for the other half of me. He was nothing but a set of genes coupled with my mother's to make me. A truth that coincided with what I am. With who I am.

"But to answer your interjection, Mr. Knox, yes. The world hates me for the atrocities they've seen me commit. For the ideals I stand for. I do what I do because it is the only way to bring about change. It is the way Grisyms will rise. Those like you and my daughter here. Like her brother. Those like my mother. "

My breath halts as he mentions his mother. What he must have passed down to me by being the product of a Grisym himself.

"Damian, Sean, Pierson, you will travel to Denmark on your winter break. I trust you three to ensure things run smoothly."

"With all due respect," Sean raises a hand, "We have no experience with Grisyms. Why would you send us?"

"Are you not loyal to me?"

They all nod.

"Show me then."

One by one, they remove articles of clothing. Damian, Pierson, and Valen tug at their shirts.

The intricate designs of Valen's tattoos are mesmerizing. As he turns, I catch the name prominently etched in blocked letters between his shoulder blades. *Jordden.*

The hieroglyphics that run down Pierce's side are a beautiful design of symbols I've traced countless times. This moment revealing I'd been tracing my father's name all this time.

Down Damian's spine, in an intricate cursive. *Jordden.*

Kaia reveals the letters looping around her ankle.

Sean, on the inside of his bicep.

Kormoran's, an intricate design of letters interconnecting over his chest over a well-sculpted pec. The collar of his shirt released the moment Jordden nods his direction.

Each one of them bears my father's name on their skin.

How many more wear a tattoo of this man's name?

The dedication that must come with a permanent reminder like that is unfathomable. A loyalty that must run thicker than blood.

"Why do they all have those?" I gasp.

"You'll understand in time. Those loyal to me will always bear my name. Without it, you cannot be bound to the strength I offer."

My brow furrows not quite understanding what he is saying. "So, you are bound to each other?"

He runs his fingers across my cheek and under my chin. "No, my dear. Each one is infused with a piece of my essence. A tiny sliver that binds them to me until death tears them away. It is a one-way transaction. Think of it as ..." his voice drifts off as he hums low, "...a blood oath to me."

I think I'm going to be sick.

49

WYNSTON

MY BRAIN CELLS REFUSE to fully process our current situation sitting here in the former catacombs of the residence surrounded by truths and omissions. It was easy enough to pretend Jordden wasn't her real father until I saw her stand beside him. Until this weekend I'd put him out of my mind altogether.

For whatever reason my consciousness doesn't want to accept that Bri is the daughter of Jordden Guthrie.

The Jordden Guthrie that slaughters any wielder—light or dark—that stands in his way.

The Jordden Guthrie that has made it publicly known he will not rest until he overthrows what the Council has built. The destruction of centuries of tradition locked into place.

The Jordden Guthrie who recruits wielders to his ranks. Giving them jobs and assignments that often leave them dead as they work to hone their gifts.

The Jordden Guthrie that can mind speak with wielders and ghouls alike.

This horrible man is her father. Their king.

What he is doing to protect and bring Grisyms out of hiding does not erase the awful things he's done. Yet I can't find it in me to hate him.

My spine remains straight as he makes eye contact with me whenever he mentions Bri's name. He does the same with Graham, Valen, and Pierson as if he knows we all have a unique connection to her. As if he is warning us that his daughter is his most prized possession.

My essence itches to touch her. A constant drum beating at the barrier of my skin to get to her, but she chose to sit next to Graham, her fingers woven with his. His body, a mix of rigidity and an odd slouch. He might be terrified of her, but she's also the only one he's going to find any comfort from here.

Where Valen and Pierson might get the opportunity to see her interact with Graham, I've maybe only seen them in passing once. Despite tonight's shock, I can tell his love for her hasn't dimmed. Only pieces of what he can't understand or accept about her loop through those rays of connection. He'll need time, not distance.

I had no business falling for a student, and maybe if she weren't like me, I wouldn't have. But seeing her with them—with anyone else—riles up my insides. My essence swirls with possessiveness, beating at the underside of my skin. A threat to anyone who thinks they can claim what it already has with each hammering fist.

I try to ignore the sight of her head now resting on Graham's shoulder. Shove down the power inside me that's fighting to break free. Restraining it with gritted teeth as I try to listen to what Jordden is telling us.

The plans he's been working on for decades are revealed in this private cavern. Plans that likely originated in his teenage years, when he watched his mother dragged from their home only to be burned alive in front of him. He'd hid when they came for her. The way she told him to if anyone ever showed up. But that image never left him, and he doesn't want that for his children.

The public doesn't know this story, otherwise Jordden would have been put to death a long time ago. The child of a Grisym is still considered a Grisym. But hearing the facts now, they frame the narrative, painting the picture of how he became the villain we know him to be today. But standing just to the side of where his daughter sits, that's not at all what I see. I see a man torn apart by unspeakable violence. A man forced to realize if things didn't change, that's all life would ever be.

Still, I doubt him.

Still, I can't turn my back on him.

An internal battle rages inside me.

He may say he only wants a better future. He may claim his only true crime was falling in love with a light wielder. There's some truth there, but not entirely.

"Bryony will be guarded by Valen," Jordden's voice lowers as he shoots Valen a pointed look.

"Hell no." I don't mean for the words to shoot out of me. Or maybe I did. "He's a sadistic prick that's literally been trying to kill her since day one."

"Wynston, sit down." A roll of Jordden's eyes, as if I am a complete waste of his breath and time. "I am aware of Valen's missteps, and we've spoken about them." The connotation is clear: should Valen step out of line and hurt his daughter, he'll no longer grace this earth.

"I'm still saying no. Bri sticks with me."

He snorts. His body shifts to face only her. "Bryony, you choose."

"Uh ..." Her eyes dart between Valen and me. Then to her dad. Then Graham. Then Pierson, his eyes lighting up. "Well, I would prefer not to be guarded at all. I can take care of myself. However, when my magic goes crazy, I need Knox around."

Triumph has me nearly grinning. Why I needed her to pick me is something I won't bother analyzing right now. Thoughts that I won't let settle into the heart of me for the fear of what is yet to come.

"Done. Wynston you will ensure my daughter stays safe until I can extract her from this institution."

"Uh, Jordden, I am finishing the program."

"A discussion for later," he dismisses her, continuing with his next bit of business.

I'm unable to process any further instruction from him as I sit with my elbows digging into my thighs. There's always been a lot at stake for us, and now they are higher. Sky high. One of us is destined to end up dead at the end of all of this bullshit.

I only regain focus when Jordden dismisses the room. Bri's arm slipping around my waist, with a light squeeze.

One by one, they file up the steps. Kaia and Kormoran are the first to bolt from the room as if their asses are on fire. Damian escorts Graham. Sean's thumbs type out a message on his phone. Not a single look back when Valen claps a hand on his shoulder. Pierson comes up last. His hand cupping her face as he passionately kisses her. A stake to his claim for me and her father to see.

Once the room empties, the groan of the stone wall above shifting back into place, Jordden turns to us.

"Sit. The both of you," Jordden sighs, his fingers rubbing his eyes.

Long legs extend in front of him before leaning in, knees close to his chest thanks to the squat stone he chose to perch himself on. Long fingers steeple in front of his mouth. Several deep breaths fill the silence before he chooses to speak.

"Wynston, you are a smart man. Are you not?"

"Yes." There's no doubt that I am. I wouldn't be here teaching at this school if I wasn't. Yet, I know that's not what he truly means.

"Then you need to understand that I want nothing more than for you and Bryony to continue to explore your connection. For you to protect each other. There are too many here that know who you are."

Not once has Jordden ever referred to us as a *what*. Only *who*. As if we're not godforsaken creatures that aren't supposed to exist.

"But you must also understand the more people see you together, the more they will suspect. I've already heard the rumblings that some speculate on your sexual relationship." Bri shifts on the stone next to me. Her thigh, formerly pressed against mine, pulls away as if that will hide our relationship. Soreness creeps into my jaw as it works overtime in response to her pulling away.

"Jordden, that was Valen." Bri rolls her eyes. Jordden's shoulders curl forward in the slightest with her using his first name again. I'd noticed his every cringing moment when she addressed him as such. As if he expects her to call him something different after only knowing the man for twenty-four hours.

I can't wrap my head around just how much has happened in a single day. Our worlds have tilted on their axis, with more weight dumped onto our shoulders. More weight than we may be able to handle.

"I don't care who started spreading those ideas. They are true, are they not?" His points are so often punctuated with questions. As if it's not enough for him to speak the truth. He needs to hear you say it too.

"Um ..." Bri starts.

"It's true. It started as just an exploration of how our essences responded to each other's touch. As simple as only our palms, but it escalated from there."

"Describe it for me." He shifts his focus solely to me. A silent command for me to lay our relationship bare to him.

So, I do. I tell him about the very first day I'd touched her. How she'd lost control during her demonstration. The weird after-effects of me touching her. It was almost as if she lingered within me for days after those short moments.

When I tell him of the visit from Roman and Harley, it's a tug at his patience. "And how did Harley behave?" he asks. There's an edge to his voice. A fight for composure.

"He acted the way he always has towards me," she sniffs. Sadness coats her words. My fingers slide through hers, a light squeeze from her before she tells him more. "Harley has hated me from birth. He treats me like shit."

Jordden only nods. "Continue Mr. Knox." Jordden may have failed to respond to Bri's admission, but I have no doubt he tucked that info away for later.

Jordden's anger at how Harley has treated my woman quirks the corner of my mouth. There's no doubt in my mind if Jordden gets Roman alone, he'll be proving a point the hard way.

The words flow freer from me now. My confidence in this man having Bri's best interest in mind allows me to spill it all. Allows me to give him a little more of my trust, despite it being clear he doesn't trust me.

His eyes narrow and twitch as I recall how we'd eventually gotten our essences to call to each other. Then trained them to not automatically respond violently if there was an anchored touch. A tiny grin pulls at the corner of his mouth when I divulge how protective our combined essences can be of us.

He listens intently, with no further interruptions. Only adding in his chorus of noises at certain points. He seems fascinated by the color of essence we can create together. A glint of curiosity shining brightly in those gray eyes.

"What a unique combination," he croons. Bri once again squirms next to me. "I've yet to see what you've described."

Bryony's fingers clutch briefly against mine. A steady pressure follows, freeing our essences from our fingertips in a calm swirl. Tips of the twisting smoke poke at Jordden's legs, accepting his presence and then shifting to the color that's purely us. The tiny stars of hers flashing a soft orange in the glow of the firelight.

I've noticed those stars often change colors in different situations. My curiosity begs me to figure out why, but I'm not sure there's a person out there that would know.

"Fascinating," he breathes.

He simply watches the combination of us float through the space for long quiet moments. Watches us inhale some of the mixture equally. When he finally speaks again it takes me a moment to focus, the stirring of our joined essences bringing my desire for Bri to the surface. *Not. The. Time.*

"I do not mind that you have been with my daughter, Wynston. I know you to be a good man." Bri tenses next to me, our calm fog starting to tumble faster. I open my spare palm, snatching it back. Trapping all of us back inside me. Jordden's eyes go wide as he watches. "But let me be clear, she better be your *only* priority. Am I understood?"

"Yes," I breathe and I mean it. Bri has been my priority since the first session.

She is more than an assignment or obligation, but rather, a responsibility I want to hold on to.

Whether I wanted us to be what we've become or not, the inevitable came. And now I'm not sure there's a way to safely separate us.

Whether we planned it or not, we belong to each other.

"Now, my dear, I think it's best that you avoid threesomes with ghouls and this one here."

An uncontrollable cough barrels out of me and a laugh from her.

"Noted," she snorts. Jordden's glare focuses on me as those gray eyes darken.

I swear if another parent of Bri brings up my sex life with her, I'm throwing myself off the mountainside. The moment Jordden nods in dismissal I'm up out of my seat tugging Bri behind me.

Darting for the stairs, I can't get away fast enough.

50

Bryony

Two weeks of silence pass. No more school closures. No whisperings of how the world has turned upside down. Nothing from my parents or Jordden.

I've suddenly gained more "friends" than I had in the past few months. Students flock to me with questions about the state of the world. It's like they can see all my secrets hidden under my clothes. A perfect explanation to why they crowd around me with news articles and things they've seen on media sites like I will have all the answers.

Their questions are the ones I started this year asking them.

"Bri, do you have any update on the light schools?"

"Bryony, have you heard? They've all been warded?"

"Ohmigod! Bryony, did you hear about all the arrests for trespassing at the former light schools?"

"Bri, does your father have a plan for re-opening them?"

They are endless and stupid. Months ago, I would have had no answers for them. Now I feign a smile, pretending I'm as clueless. Just as clueless as they all were to me when I arrived.

The most notable new "friendship"—if you can call it that—is Damian. His random appearances to walk with me around the residence when the guys aren't around have become frequent enough it's not unusual to suddenly find him beside me anymore. Those short periods filled with meaningless conversation or sometimes silence.

I can't figure out why he goes out of his way to accompany me now. The rest of Valen and Pierce's friends either ignore me or sneer in disgust. It's odd, but not unwelcome. Damian's unbothered demeanor is often the distraction I need from my intrusive thoughts.

Knox and I have continued our sessions as if nothing has changed. Sometimes, Valen shows up unannounced, and sometimes, he stays so far away from me that I can almost imagine he doesn't exist at all.

Though the verbal death threats have stopped he doesn't hesitate to twirl those daggers of his close to my face, or intentionally shove past me on the stairs, just enough of my balance maintained to keep from tumbling headfirst. I've said nothing to Jordden about it. Valen might be an ass. A very hot ass, but I'm not in the mood for the shit I might endure if Valen knew I tattled on him.

Not to mention, I have no doubt my father will kill him. I've seen the dark gleam in his eye. The determination for me to be kept safe is at the forefront of his mind. It is beyond me why he is suddenly so adamant about it, while simultaneously pushing toward a time when I'll be able to be in the limelight. He's had my whole life to protect me, and from what I know, he hasn't. Or maybe he has. Those intricate details remain hidden in shadow for now.

The past three months of revelations are nothing more than jumbled moments in my head. A complete upheaval of the life I thought I was supposed to be living.

The looming cloud of end-of-term exams coming up helps to keep me distracted. Studying and test spells occupy my thoughts and time. A barrier to my obsessive thoughts over what's to come and everything I have to lose.

Janelle has excused me from my spellcasting final. Our professor doesn't want a repeat of what I'd already done. Frankly, since that day, Professor Caulder barred me from casting any spells in the class, aside from the ones I put on myself. Stupid stuff, like the ability to change my appearance or barricading my mind against another student. The professor keeps far away from me the moment I enter the room and only seems to release a held breath as I am about to leave.

Several of my other professors have taken a similar stance. Physically putting distance between me and them. Each refuses to give me hands-on teaching. I don't blame them. I understand. Nothing about my magic seems to be predictable in the class setting the longer I've been here. The ease with which things go sideways happens more often the more I bind myself to Knox.

I don't blame any of them, though. I blame this world for shunning us. If we'd had the same opportunities as any other wielder, maybe my experience here would be different. Maybe they wouldn't gawk at me with fear because of my magic or my last name.

I hate it. I hate that what I am is hindering me from what I want to become. It's not fair that a single incident is keeping me from hands-on learning in class. From improving my skills like every other student here. I appreciate that Knox is doing everything he can to help, but he has his own students to tend to. Despite Jordden forcing him to make me his sole priority, I won't do that to him. I won't expect him to cast aside everything he has worked so hard for just to babysit me.

Pierce is the only friend who has volunteered to work with me. My ego was only able to tolerate a single night of studying with him, though. His pitying gaze was too much to stomach day after day.

Studying with someone else only made me miss Graham more. Sure, we'd all spent late nights sequestered in one of our rooms or the library, but it hasn't been the same without him always being my go-to. The one that challenged me and made me better.

Graham will barely look at me. I catch him in my room often hanging out with our group of friends. None of them understands why my appearance now makes him run. They're questioning about the distance between Graham and me so uncomfortable nausea floods my insides. Camilla did everything she could to get the answers out of me, but I denied them. I can't stand putting another person I care about into the crosshairs of this mess.

I can't afford for someone else to know what I am. I can't afford to endanger my friends or possibly expose my father or Knox. But mostly, I can't bear having another person I care about look at me differently. With fear or hatred or pity. I need what few relationships I have left to remain untainted.

Knox is the only one who knows every truth but still looks at me the same as he always has. With understanding, worry, and awe. Like I am a precious gem for him to hold on to, and then examine until he understands where its beauty originates from. That thought brings a sad smile to my face as I stop in front of Graham's door. A final deep breath before my knuckles rap against his door.

My palms are sweaty as I wait for him to answer. Anxiously rubbing them down my thighs is no help at all. We haven't talked or hung out since that night. I miss my friend. I miss *us*.

"I'm busy," he greets me. A coldness to his tone he's never used with me before. The drop of my stomach almost making me turn away.

"Graham, come on." It hurts that he's treating me this way, but I'm also pissed.

I am the same person I've always been. The same woman he has spent countless nights laughing with. The same one who battles him to shout the answers first on study nights. The same one that kissed him months ago.

"Bryony, I have stuff to do." His eyes dart to the side. The interior of his room is perfectly quiet. He wasn't watching a movie—he never pauses them. He wasn't studying. The blast of ambient music would have hit me by now. He's completely dressed in gray checkered pants and a crisp button-down so he wasn't napping.

Graham forgets I know him. I know his habits. Every little nuance that could only fit him. Who he is, both in private and in front of other people.

Pushing against the door, I let myself in, automatically dropping onto his bed. His roommate's made with hotel precision, revealing Graham to have been here alone.

I pat the bed next to me. "Let's talk."

He's reluctant but eventually sits down beside me. His thigh rests only a finger-width from mine. A little figment of hope flickering in my chest that he chose to sit so close to me. That maybe my best friend might be able to stand to be close to me again.

"First, I need you to understand that it wasn't that I wanted to keep things from you. It's that it was safer. For you and for me. You have to understand what I am is a death sentence." My swallow is loud against the silence. The beat of my pounding heart thunderous in my ears. "For me," I hastily add.

Tentatively, I place my palm on the center of his thigh. His gaze drifts to where I am touching him, expression unreadable. I go to move it away. Ready to be free of his warmth and blank stare, but his hand holds mine in place. A steady weight grounding me and encouraging me to go on. "For you, or anyone else who knows, you're in danger now."

"I just thought we were close enough that you would know you could trust me with anything. I've never had a friend like you. Never shared so much of myself with someone else, so to find out Valen, Pierson, and Professor Knox all knew, and you didn't even bother to tell me. It gutted me."

"And …" The single word is an encouragement for him to say the rest he's choking back. The knob of his Adam's apple bobs as he forces repeated swallows.

"And frankly, I'm terrified of you now. In class, when it just seemed like your power was off or like you were having trouble controlling it with new or certain assignments, I thought nothing of it. Finding out you're a Grisym—" He pauses, his fingers curling around mine. "And not just any Grisym … An innate Grisym, born to obscenely powerful parents, one of which is the dark wielder the world fears most. It's a lot to take in." I want to correct him. Remind him my father is not just a dark wielder, but a Grisym too. But I keep quiet.

He wraps his fingers tighter around mine, turning my hand so the palm faces up. His gaze trailing along the light brown crisscrossing lines before he continues. "Bri, I am still terrified of you. Of what you can do. And now I'm wrapped up in whatever this is you have going with your father and Valen's friends."

I understand everything he's saying. And if I were in his position, I would run for the hills, too. I would do everything I could to save myself from whatever bullshit comes with knowing someone like me. And yet, it would break my heart for Graham to walk away. For him to turn his back on me as if we hadn't become what we are.

My head falls to his shoulder, my arm snaking across his midsection. "Graham, I'm sorry. And I'm selfish. But you don't get to pull away from me."

He holds me in return, yanking me close to his side. "I'm trying not to, Bri. I just need some time. Okay?"

My head nods against his shoulder. The curls I've recently come to embrace sneak free of their bun. I don't know how much time passes before he finally lets me go. His body separating from mine, taking all his warmth with him.

"I guess I should go." I smooth my hands down the front of my jeans, moving to stand. Not wanting to give him the space that he asked for. But I can do that much, at least. It will give me time to determine what I can do so he won't fear me. To help him see I'm the same Bri I have always been.

I've nearly made it to the door when he pulls me back. Long fingers wrapping around my exposed wrist. Pulling me to him, my body collides with his, my palms flat against his chest. His head bobs close only to pull away, lips parted as he holds me in place. "I—" His words fail him.

I don't know what he meant to say, and I won't bully it out of him. So I nod, as if I understand, pivoting away, once more. A feeble attempt at trying to give him space. But he keeps me there, his face lowering close to mine. His exhale releases as if expelling all his pain just moments before his mouth meets mine.

Our first kiss wasn't organic. But this one is. An act as old as time.

This time there's a familiarity and a passion behind it. Something I've not gotten with Pierce or Knox. A puzzle piece I never realized I was missing.

His lips break free of mine as a moan fills the silence. The peel of flesh parting, prolonging the moments of us touching. My lashes flutter against my now-flushed cheeks as I look up at him. The rosy hue of his face darkening by the second.

"Just give me some time," he says again. Then, he lets me go. My feet miraculously carry me directly to the door. Back colliding with the wall just outside of it, fingers pressing to my lips.

Each of my men's names flit through my mind.

Pierce.

Knox.

Valen.

Graham.

Bri, what the hell are you doing?

51

VALEN

HISTORY IS MY LEAST favorite subject. It was in human-based schools and it is here. The only exception is this class. *Historical Significance and Classification of Ghouls.*

It's one of the few classes I sit a little straighter for. Two hours of my undivided attention. That saying, "knowledge is power" is what makes this particular arrangement of material so enticing. So necessary.

There's an art to siphoning ghoul magic. Compatibility and pacing are both necessary for optimal results. The more suited the ghoul is to your particular gifts, the more power your body can hold without having to transfer to artifacts.

At the end of the day, ghoul power is still a foreign essence in our wielder forms. It's not meant to be there, despite extrinsics and charters needing it to use the gifts we were born with. It's a concept that humans who know about us don't understand. Despite not being born with a personal well of power that replenishes its stores, we are still wielders. We are still "other" in comparison to humans.

From day one, I took advantage of learning all about ghouls, determining what power was out there for me to take. My body doesn't do particularly well holding onto channeled magic. If I don't offload almost all of it within twenty-four hours, I fall into a bit of a catatonic state until it burns itself off. That's how I knew what was happening to Bryony. I've gone through similar moments more times than I care to admit.

We were all young and dumb at some point. I might still be. Back when I first matured, I never wanted to relinquish any of the power I'd funneled into myself. I convinced myself that I could be invincible if I held it in. Wrong! For years, I suffered. Hoping my body would acclimate to what I wanted it to be. It never did, hence my extensive dagger collection.

All it took was a little extra spellwork from Pierce, and they became my signature. Two years worth of honing my abilities and learning the proper amounts of essence to hold within. All while also accepting siphoning versus channeling would always be better for me. Then Jordden found me. He made me into a machine.

Once I'd garnered what I needed to know for myself, I began to pay attention to those around me. Which ghouls were best suited for my crew? Which ones were the most violent with their release of power? Of those demon-like creatures, which could be our downfall.

The first two years of this class were critical for establishing my foundation. The key to honing ghoul magic into a weapon. This year, I've added current events to the relevance of my studies. The repeated sightings of ghouls breaking through the barriers are an intense topic of conversation. They should not be able to get past the Hell Gates that hold them underground without the Red Moon, yet more and more are.

It's never the same ghouls caught each time. No rhyme or reason to which breeds find their way here as rouges. Each sighting only raises more alarms. Panic is settling in and taking over our ways of life. Theorized speculation growing centered around possible evolution taking place within the ghouls themselves.

My father, Lionel Greer, is part of the Ghoul Conservation Program, or GCP. The name makes it sound like we're trying to save the earth or some shit. But, rather, it's a special task force that's dispatched for rogue ghoul sightings, or even during the Red Moon weekends, for those who break free of the pits. Instead of hunting them down the way the light-wielding trackers do, they investigate. Determine how the breach happened. Analyze bloodlines and where the escapees are coming from.

From the perspective of most light-wielders, my dad and his team are the bad guys. Saving and then harboring fugitives, when those ghouls would otherwise meet a grisly end. Letting any of those beasts continue to live increases the risk of that same ghoul going rogue once more—or so they believe. No amount of rationale or research will convince the Council otherwise. The GCP has produced countless data stating otherwise, but they refuse to listen.

It's one of the many areas that the board of men and women on the Council fails us. They fail to understand the true nature of ghouls. Fail to realize there are reasons behind all that happens in our world, and that ghouls are worth exploring. Fail to care about what dark wielders might hold sacred.

Sure, there are a couple of rough ones out there, but most of them were aggravated by either humans or wielders. Ghouls are generally nonviolent with the proper wielder. Only the release of their magic can, at times, be hard to take or tame.

Only a few are truly dangerous. But light wielders show up with their spelled guns and potion-filled darts, starting a war the moment their feet touch the ground. Then they wonder why these ghouls rage against them. Why they tear at their throats and leave their bodies in pulpy messes.

My dad is the one who taught me about the true nature of ghouls. Just like innate wielders must allow their essences loose, so must ghouls. Anybody that holds magic is nothing more than a vessel. A vessel with finite space. As your essence or magic stores drain, they will refill. Yet, for those who harness a higher volume of power, those who are more gifted, it's not as simple as hitting the fill line and stopping. It continues to build and build.

Something like eighty-seven percent of the rogue ghouls have had so much built up in their systems that they had no choice but to find a release. The clock ticks until the magic consumes them. Ghouls only release one way. Once a quarter, at the rise of the Red Moon, they fuck us, giving over what their bodies have accumulated for three months.

It's been studied for years. Most wonder why this siphoning can only occur through such an erotic act. The only conclusion is that the intimacy of touch and the connection of sex allow us to open ourselves to each other. Sounds like some stupid romantic bullshit to me, but no one has found a better answer yet.

Without those two nights, the power of the ghouls can eat them from the inside out, much like my own powers. Stealing your energy and nutrients to continue to feed it.

The GCP believes they are simply looking for that release. Ghouls can't fuck each other to get it. They need wielders. It's the only way for their power stores to be siphoned off. What they don't understand is why so many are reaching limits so much quicker than they used to. What has changed in the past decade to make it so that these ghouls can't last until a Red Moon?

My dad has kept me up to date on each ghoul sighting. The coloring. Type. Magic levels. Location. Temperament. I keep it all in a notebook that stays tucked in the inner pocket of my leather jacket. My gaze roves over the most recent sighting a few nights ago. Another extremely close to where we are. Each of the neighboring towns has had at least one rogue visit since the start of the school year. It's too many, too close.

I'm distracted by the correlations between green and blue ghouls and their temperaments. Their aggression is the most exaggerated out of those captured thus far. The reds with the highest internal levels of magic. Nearly double what the thresholds should be.

I'm so lost in my scribbles and notes along the margin I miss Assistant Headmaster Schouten shuffling in through the classroom door. He's a meek man. One that, on appearance, you would never consider a threat. Straight tufts of thinning gray hair scattered around the rim of his head, leaving a large bald spot in the center. The guy is only fifty. He'd be better off just shaving it all.

Yet he is one of the most profound telekinetic dark wielders in the country. A snap of his fingers is enough to turn the entire campus to rubble. If the stories are true, he had a very hard time controlling his emotions when he was younger—before he matured—which resulted in the three different homes his parents had to purchase for them to live in while he was still under twenty-five.

His mature powers somehow leveled him out. The transition time where the shell of our bodies reconfigures itself to possess the strength needed to control our natural abilities. If you ask me, his talents are wasted as an assistant headmaster. I've tried to convince Jordden countless times to recruit him, but I'm always brushed aside.

"*That's not something you need to worry about, Mr. Greer.*"

"Class, everyone is to return to their rooms," Professor Gorman Artock wails. The pitch of his voice screeches high, as if still in puberty. His ultra-thin body, coupled with his stature that barely reaches five feet, struggles to broadcast his voice through the massive lecture hall. "Classes are canceled for the remainder of the day." The words come out cracked as he finishes his statement.

A roar of whispered cheers and confusion fills the room. Each voice is low, but together they shake the very walls. Slapping my notebook closed, I wait for nearly everyone to funnel out before stopping in front of Artock's metal desk. The only one like it in the whole school.

"What's going on?"

"Oh, Mr. Greer." He flinches away from me, his voice several octaves higher. His features scrunch, as if in fear of me hitting him. Hell, I might stab the bastard if he doesn't tell me what the hell is going on. "Y—Y—You—" His stutter irritates me more than the fact that we're stuck in our rooms for the remainder of the night. My ass crashes into the side of the desk as I cross my arms, his body involuntarily jumping back to avoid contact with me.

"Don't make me ask again."

Just like Bryony has pull around here that she never uses, so do I. Many know of or suspect my ties to Jordden Guthrie, and they don't fuck with that. They don't fuck with me. Nor do they want to end up on his bad side. Catch Jordden on a bad day and he'll kill first, think about it later—or not. Zero regrets to go along with his later assessment.

"Last. Chance." I flip around so my hands brace against the surface of the desk. The cool metal against my heating skin only controls my frustration by a fraction. Artock slips backward, leaning oddly in the chair before tipping the whole thing over and rolling across the elevated stage floor.

"Please, Mr. Greer." I hold back a laugh. One of unhinged hilarity witnessing a grown man so terrified of a student. Petrified to the point of cowering in the corner and pleading for who knows what. Death. Mercy. Space. Understanding.

I crouch down next to his head, elbows resting atop my spread thighs. Head cocked to the side I wait for my answer. My eyes stay locked on his face, unblinking.

"An ... A—" He swallows loudly. "An Azukeen o-on grounds," he croaks.

Fuck.

I immediately stand gathering my stuff from the floor beside the desk.

If one of those is loose on campus, there's sure to be a death or two. Yet, Bryony fucked one and still lives. The damn thing laid on its back for her.

The memory is enough to bring a salacious grin to my lips.

This will be fun.

52

BRYONY

"WHAT IN THE BLAZES is happenin'?" Camilla blurts buzzing into our room only seconds after me.

I've barely kicked off the first shoe, and she's got her arms flying in every direction. Her version of an uproar in response to her day of classes being disrupted. And now lockdown will keep her from spending time with Mailee.

I feel for her. I had planned to meet up with Knox tonight since we couldn't this morning. He had to prepare for another practical exam with one of the other professors, so we couldn't chance not making it back on time.

"Just sneak out. I'm sure whatever is going on will have all the teachers occupied elsewhere."

"Bryony Avalon, I am no rebel," she says in mock offense as she giggles, falling back onto her bed. "For real, you think I won't get caught?"

"Not if you're quiet," I shrug. A word I would never associate with Camilla.

"What do you think is goin' on? It's a little frightenin' that they decided to lock us all up. Just a bunch of little tigers locked in our cages," she sighs with a shudder.

"No idea, but I intend to watch a lot of TV, and maybe pass out early." The new agenda without the possibility of seeing Knox. My essence roils with disappointment. It's been two days since we last had sex and our essences are raging.

"No handsome fellas on the agenda tonight, then?"

I quickly look back at her, the gleam in her eye suggestive.

"Don't look at me like that," she chides. "You've got all three of those scrumptious men in your back pocket. Take your pick."

I know she means Valen, Graham, and Pierce. There's no way she could know about Knox. We've been careful—as much as we could. She knows he's my advisor and his gifts complement my magic, so when my essence has gone haywire, he's the one to call, but she can't possibly think there's more to it than that.

Too many people already know too many of my secrets. Knox is one bigger than just a teacher sleeping with his student. I've accepted I may not be able to protect what I am anymore, but I will protect what he is, for him.

"Nope, me time tonight. My poor vagina could use it."

Camilla launches herself off her bed and onto mine. Her tiny body strewn across my lap. "I thought Valen was only a one-time thing."

"He was," I nod.

"So, then you've done the nasty with Graham too?" *Nasty. Whispered*, as if someone is around to hear her say such a vulgar word.

I should have known this line of questioning would come with an answer like that, but of course, I can never keep my mouth shut.

"No, uh, just a lot of time with Pierce."

"I knew that boy wasn't as nice as he seems. He's a real beast in the sheets, isn't he?"

I burst out laughing. Camilla's phrases give me stitches most days. A brand of humor she likely doesn't realize makes her authentically great. The best part is, she isn't trying to be funny, she's just being her.

I'm glad she's buying my story. That it's just been me and Pierce. Although these days I would say I have more sex with Knox than with him. Sometimes, it feels like if we don't daily, our essences will rebel. The mixtures react within us at the most inopportune times. Fighting and clawing at the underside of our skin to get to each other.

It's weird but exhilarating, too. I never thought I would be able to find that kind of connection, that need, with someone, until him.

"Okay, off." I shove at her. Our laughter fills the room. "I'm going to get some reading done before my movie marathon."

She slips free of the bed, a knock sounding just as her feet hit the floor. She tugs the door open, barely looking at who's on the other side. No doubt she expected Pierce only to reveal Valen.

My mood instantly sours. My night instantly fucked in more ways than one now.

"Get your coat," he nods in my direction, actively ignoring Camilla's sneer and crossed arms.

"Nope, I'm already comfy."

"Bryony, I've already had one person test my patience today. Don't be the second."

"Fuck off, Valen."

"Get your shit!" he yells as he stomps toward me.

I'm stewing in anger as I nuzzle down further into my mattress, crossing my legs for comfort and opening my textbook just to spite him.

He yanks at my legs until my feet hit the floor. Then wrenches me by the arms to stand directly in front of him. My book crashes to the floor, pages bending as it lands. A twirl of his fingers raises it to rest back on the comforter. Closed, as if never violated.

"You're such a dick," I groan.

His body slides up to mine. Fingers barely touching beneath my chin, lifting my gaze to meet his. Warm breath glides over my parted lips. My insides tingling remembering how rough things kicked off last time.

"And you loved this dick," he smirks.

I want nothing more than to shove his smug ass down a flight of stairs and hope one of his daggers, or all of them, puncture every vital organ on the way down. Then I'd like nothing more than to twist each one several times, just for good measure.

Choosing a different method, I press in closer to him, my arms loosely hanging around his neck. My mouth is so close, my lips will brush his as I speak. His breath hitches the slightest, hands coming to my waist. His fingers pulsing at my sides, pressing into my soft flesh.

"I loved it as much as I loved your dagger at my throat." My lips brush his as my sultry grin morphs into a disgusted snarl.

"That can be arranged again."

His body is impossibly closer. Our shared breath ignites the flames between my thighs. The tiny shift of my hips only worsens the ache. My core tightening in response. Every muscle clenching unmercifully in anticipation of what my cunt thinks it's going to get. Begging for a repeat of our one night together.

Fuck no!

Wrong!

"Just say the words, Forbidden Fruit," he taunts.

"Fuck right off, Valen."

The bite to my words lessens only a fraction. No doubt he noticed it because why wouldn't he? It only gives him more ammo to hold over me. To taunt my traitorous body with. Who would have known the whole dark villain vibe would do it for me?

He leans in a fraction closer. "If Pierce isn't getting you off right, I'll show him how it's done."

With a defiant huff, I snatch my wool pea coat from the end of the bed. It takes me a moment to remember Camilla has been standing there staring at us the whole time. Valen now propped along the edge of my bed, legs straight and crossed at the ankles. His arms folded at his chest stretching the unforgiving leather of his jacket. The same one he wears almost every day.

Not like I want to tear it from his body with my teeth or anything. Nope, not at all.

"My word. I have no idea what all that was." Camilla's arms wave wildly through the air. Her little body twisting, long hair flying with her exaggerated movements. "But it was *so* hot." Her "so" drawn out long enough, I began to think it would become a song. She fans herself, and I roll my eyes in response as I shove Valen through the door. "Be safe!" she yells behind us.

I have the distinct feeling she is not referring to a dangerous magical quest.

There will be no sex with Valen. Never again.

He's silent as he guides us through the halls and down the main staircase. I've gotten so used to moving through walls and hidden passages it seems odd to defy the rules so callously and just walk straight out the front door, but we do. Frigid air smacks against my cheeks, my quickly numbing fingers tugging my coat closer around me.

Valen only eyes me oddly, as if he doesn't experience the cold the same way I do. Maybe he doesn't. Wielders come with a wide array of variations in gifts and quirks. I honestly have no idea what Valen's are. I never tried to make a point of getting to know him and I'm not starting now. Dude can freeze to death for all I care.

Yet I'm curious where we are going when we're supposed to be on lockdown. "So, what super-secret mission are we headed on?" My tone is thick with sarcasm as I nudge his shoulder with mine.

I've yet to be anything close to playful with Valen, but something tells me it might yield different results tonight. Maybe keep him from shoving me off the mountain in such cold temperatures. Nothing more than a body left mangled on the jagged rocks just in time for the snow we're set to get tomorrow.

"To see an Azukeen."

"Are you insane?" I blurt, abruptly halting at his proclamation. After what happened with the last blue ghoul I'd fucked I'm not sure I want to go near another. After that night I never even considered what that midnight hue of its skin represented. I just knew I couldn't tell the exact breed for sure.

My adrenaline was too high. My thoughts, too scattered. There's just too much knowledge I'm lacking.

I'd fucked an Azukeen and lived to tell about it.

Dad is going to be so pissed.

My face falls into my hands only to look back up, realizing I'm not sure which "Dad" I was mentally referring to.

"There's one loose on campus. It seemed ... " His eyes roam from my face down my body and back up again. "Taken with you, so why not see if the theory holds?"

"Valen, you've lost your mind."

Real panic starts to build in my chest. Hell, I knew he hated me enough to try to murder me on several occasions but to bring me face to face with a rogue Azukeen is something entirely different. "I can't afford for my essence to go ape shit again. You want to go after a rogue ghoul?" My hands up as I take a step away from him. "Do it without me."

My voice is strong, sure, and even as I stare him down. Challenging him to go against me on his dangerous idea.

If my dad wasn't pissed enough at me already, he'll be the one murdering me for this indiscretion. This time, I know I mean Roman. The only man I've ever called Dad.

He's in my space again. The warmth of his body pressing against mine frozen fingers digging into the cut of my jaw as he yanks my face up toward him. There's nothing tender about his hold. Dark fury in his stare. Those ebony eyes boring into mine.

"Bryony, you're going to come with me to find this Azukeen. You're going to make it compliant. And then, as long as you behave like the good girl your daddy expects you to be, I will reward you."

I fight to contort my features into those of disgust. To will away the tingling below. Yet there's no stopping my hips from rolling against him. His dick rock hard in his jeans. A small choked sound escapes me as his mouth grazes along the rear edge of my jaw. "Are you going to be a good girl, Forbidden Fruit?" The low vibration of his words makes me groan aloud.

I hate myself in this moment. I hate my body and I hate Valen-Fucking-Greer.

"You get me killed and I swear I will haunt you every day for the rest of your life," I grunt, stomping away just slow enough that he catches my cheek with a peck.

This is a terrible idea.

53

Graham

Lockdown was not the plan for the evening. Rather, I thought it might be good for me to spend some alone time with Bri. Allow her to show me the truth about her if she wants to.

But no such luck. Most of us first years are not brave enough to hang out with each other without knowing what the threat at hand is.

So, while everyone stays stuck in their rooms, they don't notice me as I sneak into the history section of the archives. Fingers grazing over endless tomes about wielding history. The hordes of texts relaxing me for the first time since I found out about Bri. Aged leather spines, both soft and uneven, cool under my touch.

You'll find nothing on the human side of history here. The majority of us learn that information when we attend human schools growing up. Part of the façade we keep in place, so those who don't know about wielders suspect nothing. The humans who are aware of what we are each have their stance on how they interact with or cope with the idea of our kind. Whether they accept us or not, our history is not important to them.

Those who view us as earthly devils are the reason we work so hard to blend in seamlessly with the human world. We look the same. Our bodies mostly function the same. It's just easier that way.

Many of us grew up with human friends and did normal human things. We celebrated holidays and attended the same functions. Physically there is nothing to tell us apart. Nothing that you can point to on my body that screams wielder.

Only another wielder can sense it. The magic that lives in us. The core of what we are curling closer or rearing away is dependent on what your essence can sense.

All wielders are born with an essence. It's only innates that can wield it without acquiring foreign power from other sources to fuel it. In that way, charters are more similar to extrinsics. A group of us that just didn't quite get there in terms of evolution or development or whatever makes us wielders. Some go as far as calling us defective innates.

You would think our community would have laws that protect us from others and ourselves. But they don't. Namely, it's only Grisym law that is upheld and executed.

My eyes trail over a text that aligns with my thoughts *Wielding Law of Today: Why We Must Protect The Bloodline*s. The title insinuates more modern thought processes, so it's not unreasonable to think this book might be a more recent addition to the collection. But cracking it open, the spine creaks loudly as a plume of dust wafts in my face from inside the pages. A text that is three hundred years old. So dated, I can't believe we still hold to whatever is written on these pages.

The Council behaves as if we're a species soon to go extinct. In reality, we span just over a third of the world's population. More than half are those with some level of magical blood in our veins, even if we cannot use it. But we cling to old notions like a protective blanket. Continue to remind our kind it only takes a drop of wielder blood to produce a wielding child, but not a strong one. Promoting that fear of creating offspring likely to be a low affinity-wielding extrinsic. The lowest of the low.

My parents' bloodlines are what made me a charter, both were born charters themselves. My father, the product of a human and innate wielder, while my mother has parents that are half-human.

It baffles me that our laws don't keep us from procreating with humans, but it's forbidden for a light and dark wielder to produce a child. The outcome—we're told—is so catastrophic we cannot allow them to live. Yet, I've been in a room with Bri and Knox countless times, and only on a few occasions have I ever feared for my well-being.

Only now do I realize it's the same fear I would hold for any newly matured wielder that lacks control of their gifts. A wielder who can't tame what they hold can be deadly. A potential way to ruin lives in the blink of an eye.

While I scan the titles on the dusty shelves, I think of all the moments I've spent with Bri since I learned of her secret. Pulling large books from the shelf, I stack them on my forearm. Their weight straining my muscles as I attempt to balance them atop the sleeve of my designer shirt.

My mother begged me not to bring all my nice clothing to this place, but really, what else was I supposed to bring? Did she think I would become like the other guys my age and dress in nothing but jeans and hoodies or henleys? *No*. It's never been my style.

My father taught me to dress to impress if you're going to step out of the house. Let people always see you at your best. It will make them believe in you. Make them buy into your confidence—even if you lack it. Force them to drown in the words that exit your mouth. They will place you on a pedestal and give you a price tag they can't possibly determine.

It's always worked.

Our Forbidden Past jumps out at me. The book, much thinner than many of the others I'm still balancing. Grabbing it between pinched fingers, I head for the sitting area I most prefer in the furthest dark corner of the library. It's where Bri and I often study. The gloom of the old tomes and the slight scent of musk discourage most from our desired seats.

Just as I suspected, it's abandoned now. The black leather chairs are well-worn, but still in one piece. Not a tear or scratch. Just the natural crack of the fibers that come with time.

I start with the last book I pulled from the shelf. Another small puff of dust hits me as I crack open the cover. The creak of the spine is loud from years of neglect. A book long since forgotten or even ignored. If there's one thing our kind is good at, it's framing the narrative for what we should and shouldn't stand behind, without needing the support of research or literature or even those who might be experts in the area.

The first few pages yield no new information. Turning to the fifth page reveals a letter snugly tucked into the crease. The paper is newer, its age likely much more recent than the publication date printed at the front of this text. Observing the paper now, it's easy to see the difference in texture with its browning edges from years of being tucked away between the parchment pages.

Carefully, I open the precisely folded sheet. Its thickness diminished with time. So soft to the touch that I worry I'll tear it.

Dearest,

I pray that you are well. I pray that you know peace in this time of hardship and confusion. I pray that you will understand I did what was needed to ensure the continuation of my kind. One day I hope to look upon your face and know you have forgiven me.

It was never my intent to deceive you. I was always truthful as to who I am. The man who has always loved you. The man who will follow you to the ends of the earth when you are once again ready to look upon my face.

I have taken our son. He is safe. You will be safe. No one shall know of the joy we made together. If only you were here to see his bright eyes and warm smile. He will be proof that bringing together the light and the dark is good. He is good. He is ours, even if you do not want to claim him.

I only write this letter, so you know we are safe. Should you ever want to see us again, you can find us where the Red Moon meets the gate. The line of green will lead you to the tunnel of truth.

Please, my love. Find it in you to love us the way you did before you knew. Before the darkness that runs through my veins and now our son's turned you against us.

With all my heart,

Gavin Milgren Von Tavern

I read through the letter several more times, latching onto the name signed at the bottom. It's no coincidence Headmistress Milgren's name matches this man's. I have never heard of him. Never has our history named him as a man of importance. Yet his letter lays tucked into this vital text.

Tucking the letter back into the book, and hoisting the rest of my stack under my arm, I sneak through the large silver and black library doors. Technically, I don't have the clearance to remove historical texts from the archives, but hopefully, no one will notice since everyone should be in their rooms.

I'm quick to stalk through the halls, mumbling to myself. "Gavin Milgren Von Tavern. Who are you? Why are you important?"

Bri, please be in your room. Please. Please. Please.

The sequence repeats as a low whisper on my lips the closer I get to her room. The urgency behind each syllable increasing with each step.

Giggles come from behind some of the doors in the female wing as I stalk down Bri's hallway. Somehow I know she'll be on board with helping me solve whatever it is I think I've found.

I knock softly. No sounds greet me on the other side. My second *tap, tap*, louder. More insistent.

Still, nothing.

Fighting to get my phone from my pocket, I thumb a quick text to Bri.

Me: *Hey open up.*

I watch for those dancing circles for way too long. She always answers me right away. Especially since I found out about her, as if she doesn't immediately get back to me, I'll drift away from her forever. It could also be a fear that I'll share her secrets.

I hope she knows I'll always be here. Even when I'm scared of her. Even when I don't understand her. Even when I've started—

No.

I shake the thought from my head. It's not going to happen. I need to forget about that even being a possibility.

I only wait for five more minutes before I head back to my room. I crack my laptop open the moment my ass falls into my desk chair.

The search for Gavin Milgren Von Tavern brings up more than I would have expected.

Wealthy land developer from the 1920s. The epitome of an entrepreneur in his day and age. His parents were immigrants and dark-wielders. He was a prominent manipulator of emotions, which is what made him so great at securing the business deals he wanted.

For the many who loved him, that many more hated the man and all that he stood for.

His disappearance in the late twenties still circulates in discussions on conspiracy theory blogs. The most popular revolving around changing his identity or faking his death.

Going deeper, I find a birth certificate for Conrad Milgren Von Tavern. *Gavin had a son*. One with eyes a faint crystal blue, eyes of a light wielder. His untimely death in 1967 took his family's legacy with him. A tragic fire in the dead of night left him, his wife, and his daughter dead.

Sources say the home burned so thoroughly they couldn't truly determine if the bodies were present.

I run the math in my head. Run it again. And again. Then stare at Conrad's face.

How his nose bridges and his eyes are small with a downturn at the corners. The purse of his mouth. Minor things. Possibly coincidental things, but still matches for Headmistress Janelle Milgren.

Fuck me.

Her father was a Grisym.

So is she.

54

Bryony

After an hour of searching for this damned creature, I'm nearly an icicle. Valen refuses to give up. Constantly mumbling to himself, likely cursing the world for his grand, master plan disintegrating into stupidity and frostbite.

I'm done. The tolerance I'd allowed my libido to dictate for me has long since diminished.

Our stomping steps crunch against the hardened ground when it seems to shake beneath me. A quiver I couldn't have possibly felt. Then another. And Another.

I'm frozen in place as my eyes search the woods. The earth continues to rumble beneath our feet. The trees that still hold their evergreen leaves shudder in time with each quake.

Nothing is slinking between the trees. No sign of the mountains crumbling in the open area at the far edge of the range. One of my favorite places to come watch the sun as it sets and rises. A place where I can remember how small and insignificant so many things are in this vast world.

A loud snort has me turning quickly. My boot catching on a tuft of grass as I stumble backward. My fingers scrape at the solid earth as my feet struggle to find purchase beneath me. Valen is at my side, a hand wrapped around my elbow, steadying me just before I tumble to my ass. Our heavy breaths white clouds in front of our faces.

It's as if it appeared out of nowhere. Ten feet of midnight blue leathery skin shoves the tree branches out of its way as it stalks toward us. Those glowing white orbs seemingly focus right on me. They have no vision, but it feels as if they can see me cowering away.

I want to scream. Shout for help, but nothing comes out. No words. No sounds. Just heavy breathing as I stare at the creature approaching.

Valen shoves me toward it. My heels digging into the frozen earth in protest. Anything to keep me from approaching the beast that made my body rebel. "Command it," he orders.

"Are you crazy?" I'm well past panic. I am literally to the point where I will likely hyperventilate. Death by self-asphyxiation rather than commanding a fucking ghoul.

What would even make him think I could do such a thing?

The cold that had me numb to the bone only moments ago seems to switch to a scorch so high I'm damn near ready to tear the clothes from my body. My pulse races. Blood vessels throbbing at my throat and wrists in response to my elevated blood pressure.

Fuck.

I have no idea what to do as I turn and curl into Valen's chest. My hands fisted around his t-shirt.

Slowly, he pulls me back from him. His grip on my arms is strong, as he whispers, "Trust me." Those dark pupilless pools clear as he orders me once more. "Command it."

I'm not sure what shifts in me. Why my essence responds, snaking from my fingertips. Slithering toward the approaching ghoul Valen guides me to face it once more. Squaring my body to the Azukeen whose magic I can still feel rolling through me, his clawed feet are only a few steps from us now. Those long legs stretching before him.

My essence spreads across the ground. Black with stars, shifting to the same color as the skin of the ghoul. I've never made that color before. I didn't call for it. Didn't think it up. It simply came to be. An exact match for the Azukeen that now stands stock still before me. It stares with those blank white spheres. It's breathing even. Only a slight sway to its naked form as if it's fallen asleep on its feet.

Stepping forward, willing my breaths to slow, I reach out my hand. Tendrils of midnight wrap around the forearm of the beast. A shiver running through me as its body shakes with a slight tremble. Yet it no longer moves toward me. Large feet anchored to the ground where it stopped. No other reaction noted as my essence continues to swirl around its limbs. Whatever trance it's in now remains so solid that I am unsure if it will even hear me.

"Kneel." My voice is soft but strong.

The ground thunders as it drops to its knees. Those white eyes stare straight into me. The dick it didn't have moments ago growing. The length and girth rival its previous form from our last encounter.

A loud swallow lodges the saliva in my throat. Valen's hands still rest on my arms, holding me in place as if I'll run should he release me. My libido reminds me I haven't had sex in two days. Lust and want thrum through my veins. My essence continuing to knot through the ghoul's claws as it strokes itself.

Oh, the shameless sex addict I've become. I can't help myself as my eyes fall on that huge cock. The pulsing rod I'll more than likely impale myself on again if Valen—and my greedy core—get their way.

My body warms as the ghoul presents itself to me. Offers what I so badly want to take. The feelings I'd felt that night rush back in full force. The act had been something out of this world. The aftermath, horrendous.

But maybe this time will be different. My body will understand. It will recognize what was once foreign as familiar.

I take another step forward. "Do you know who I am? What I am?"

Most ghouls cannot speak coherent words, but I recall that the one I'd been with could. Only a single word leaked from him, but it was clear.

"Bryony, mine," it growls. The words are garbled, but there's no mistaking them.

"Why?" I ask. Another step, just close enough that I can brush the skin of its forearm if I reach for it.

"Bryony, rule." It puffs air into my face, my hair blowing back, floating above my shoulders like a cape. "Bryony, mine."

It shifts to its back. The same way it had at the Red Moon Festival. Its solid length jutting into the air in presentation. Those unseeing eyes focused on where I stand.

"No."

It roars. A piercing sound that shakes the trees.

Valen was on to something.

A conversation we will have to have later. How he could have known this would happen unnerves me. Yet, he has been under my father's wing for years. There's probably so much he knows that I cannot even fathom.

"You will return to your home. Do you understand me?"

It nods. But its body trembles with anger. With being ordered to go against what it had wanted to do. Its emotions felt within me as if they were my own.

"Bryony, with me," it bellows. A strangled noise shattering the silence. One that makes me flinch away from the high pitch.

"No. Go home."

It stands yanking me forward. Its claws curve around my waist, my back arching, putting distance between our bodies. "Bryony, with me." The words are clearer this time. Its dagger-like teeth bared. Where the canines protrude, yellowed with time.

"Bri, just fuck the thing so we can go," Valen groans.

It grunts as I stare back at Valen. A roar cast in his direction at his audacity to interrupt.

Maybe I should. Cast terror aside and believe that my essence and my body will be able to handle what the Azukeen siphons into me tonight.

"Put me down." It does so quickly, lying on its back. A large solid dick still waiting for me. Waiting for me to claim it. To take all the dark magic it has to offer.

My insides sing for it. Its remaining essence riling up the combination of mine and Knox's.

I ignore the cold and the clench of my pussy as I strip out of my jeans and sneakers. Panties pulled aside, I slip down onto its cock. Its hips immediately hammer into me. Shots of its power filling me, stretching me. There's no fullness like this. No sensation that could compare to the ecstasy of fucking a ghoul. Or maybe just this ghoul. I have no way of knowing if it will be different with another.

It pounds into me, eventually sitting up keeping me straddled across its lap as I ride it with reckless abandon. My head dips back, the column of my neck exposed where my coat splits. Wet warmth hits my exposed skin. My eyes peeling open to watch its tongue flick over the divot at the base of my throat. The end forking to wrap around it. Two strips of textured pink flesh gripping tight.

"Mine," it growls again. That single word distorted, but so clear I wonder if I heard it in my mind.

"Yes." A breathy moan as my orgasm tears through me. Its roar rattles my ear drums.

More and more and more power funnels into me. My essence beginning to rebel. I feel it. Mine and Knox's putting up a barrier to what the Azukeen freely gives. Attempting to give me the willpower to stop taking uncontrollably.

"Enough," I croak. It continues to pop its hips into me, a claw tearing through the fabric of my coat. "Enough!" My barking command halts the ghoul mid-thrust.

Immediately I'm dropped to the ground, the frigid earth seeming to burn my naked ass cheeks. The Azukeen kneels before me, eyes downcast, and waits.

"Go home."

It snarls but stands. "More. Come." With a final swipe of that forked tongue across its non-existent lips, it swivels away from me. Then it runs back into the trees where it came from.

I barely register that I am still on the cold ground, nearly naked, when Valen lifts me under the arms, pulling me to my feet. His shoulder is my tool for balance as I shimmy back into my jeans and shoes. Grateful for his silence until I'm dressed again. I let the feel of the ghoul's essence travel through me. Fill me and find its home within.

"Happy your point has been proven?" I sneer, turning to head back toward the residence. Back toward warmth, a shower, and my bed.

My body is bursting with the Azukeen's magic. A reminder I need to tell Knox so he can be on standby, just in case. Possibly even sneak me into his apartment, so we can have more privacy.

"Not even close, Forbidden Fruit." I glare back at him. A different expression than I've seen from him before. One I can't quite identify.

"Why are you looking at me like that?"

He comes closer, one of those daggers appearing, the tip tracing the veins on the side of my neck. "Because I want nothing more than to fuck you right now."

Well, shit.

55

WYNSTON

EXHAUSTION PULLS AT MY limbs as I shuffle into my apartment. They never found the Azukeen on campus, but several swore they heard it. The hunters searched for hours, as did some of the staff better equipped to handle a rogue ghoul. Still, no such luck. The search was surrendered hours ago. Instead, the gathering transformed into a staff meeting led by ghoul hunters lecturing us on what to do should we inadvertently find that Azukeen.

Almost three hours gathered in the auditorium while those light-wielding hunters lectured us on school safety before any of us were allowed to leave. Ghoul hunters preaching to dark wielders on the steps to handling our traditions, not only pissed us off but was a complete waste of our time. The same cautions and facts reiterated that we already know.

The whole fiasco spawned from Director Yaven from the Wielding Bureau choosing to make an appearance. His presence "warranted" in response to the ever-increasing number of rogue sightings near us. Especially since we are the only wielding school left in the state.

The Council will also come in this weekend. Edina Libras, a ward specialist, traveling with them by request. Not only to investigate the walls created eons ago, but also to build us new and better ones. A barrier with protection from outsiders such as rogue ghouls or anyone without a Beauxgraton-registered signature essence.

I collapse onto the bed, not even bothering to remove the corduroy pants or the button-down with a matching sweater over the top. My shoes are the only things that make it off.

By choice, I kept my phone on silent most of the afternoon. The lockdown announcement put us all in a defensive mode and I had no desire to be bombarded with countless notifications. Some of us handle the stress fine. Hoarding the students away, ensuring things get locked up properly, scouring the halls for anyone we see not obeying orders. Usually, the elder professors prefer that task. As if their graying hair and age will make adults younger than them obey more readily.

Frankly, as long as they weren't outdoors, I have no problem with them lingering in the hallways. Let them spend time with their friends. It's not like an Azukeen is going to break into the school buildings. It was roaming outside. Searching for something. Or maybe just lost beyond the gates that keep it trapped in the beyond.

For me, there was only so much trouble the students could get into when the protection wards were up. Their signature blocks most of the magic and spellcasting students might choose to do, as well as protecting the building from an entry that wasn't of a compatible signature.

It blows my mind that such advanced wards can't keep any and everyone out. That we must have a wielder as world-renowned as Edina come to reinforce or completely build new ones. More so, it's unnerving. I've always felt protected here. Safe. Hidden.

Then Bryony arrived, and my entire world began to crumble. Tiny bits, piece by piece, falling apart.

Months ago, I would have traded anything to go back to a time before I knew about her and her me. Now, I don't see how I survived with such detached loneliness. Never having someone around who understood and cared for me just as I am.

It seemed simple enough to watch these young adults slipping into their friend's rooms or sneaking away to fuck like rabbits with nothing to occupy their time for the rest of the day. Why should they know isolation and loneliness the way I always have?

Milgren hinted that we may be operating much the same for the remainder of the week. Just enough time for all of us to go a bit stir-crazy. But all I heard was less opportunity alone with Bryony. My person. My companion. My match.

It made me itch for Bryony. Something shifting within me leaving me uneasy. My essence stirring. At one point, it punched at my skin as if trying to break free. As if trying to get to her. I told myself that it's been a few days since we've practiced, since we've allowed our essences to further co-mingle, learning each other. Those tendrils swirling together as a delicate bond akin to making love.

My phone screen lights up with countless notifications. The calls and texts from Bryony are the ones that catch my eye.

Bryony: ***I may have done something stupid***
Bryony: ***Yup, definitely stupid***
Bryony: ***I'll need you on standby***
Bryony: ***Valen has your number in case he needs to call you***

I have no reason to be jealous. But I do have plenty of reasons to fear what Valen may have gotten her caught up in. It amazes me how reckless he is given his talents. He's an insanely smart guy, but you would never know it by the swagger he insists on walking around with, using intimidation instead of camaraderie to get his way. He may cow to Jordden, but I am in no way disillusioned to believe that he truly fears him enough not to endanger her.

He won't harm her with his own hand, but someone else doing so will probably light up his face with a grin.

Fighting the exhaustion, I throw my legs over the side of the bed, slipping on my boots instead of the loafers I've been wearing all day. I shrug into my coat as I slam my apartment door behind me, shoulder colliding with the person I hadn't seen. *Fiona*.

"Hey," she waves. "I was just coming to see you since we'll more than likely be cooped up for days."

"I, uh, have somewhere to be."

Her pout is exaggerated. Nothing like the natural one Bryony always has. Lips so soft I can't help but want to be pressed against them. To feel them moving in sync with mine as I drive into her sweet depths.

Fuck!

I need to get it together.

This is not good.

Stalking past Fiona, she grabs the sleeve of my jacket. Her features scrunched, making her look like a disgruntled pixie. "You've been avoiding me. I thought we had a good thing going here."

For a while we did. A place where we could escape into each other. Take care of our needs without any commitments. Until recently. I knew the moment I kicked things up with Fiona again at the beginning of this year, it would mean more to her than to me. That her attachment would be to more than just my dick.

In all honesty, since the moment my mouth brushed Bryony's the day her father and brother were here, I haven't so much as even thought about another woman. I'll keep lying to myself and say that's just because we've been busy protecting what we are and leave it at that.

I won't even entertain the idea that something beyond the "experiments" we've conducted does or could exist. It can't ... can it?

"Are you seeing someone else?" she whispers. Her eyes are wide, as if I'd just spoken my thoughts aloud and confirmed it for her.

"Yes. I am."

There's truth in that answer. More truth than I would like to admit to. Or maybe more truth than actually exists.

Am I technically dating Bryony Avalon—or Guthrie—depending on which side of the fence you want to stand on. *No.*

Am I fucking her almost daily? *Yes.*

Do I feel more connected to her than I have anyone in my life? Also, *yes.*

"Do I know her?" Sad eyes search mine. Fiona's final attempt at hanging onto the tiny string between us that's quickly tearing. Frayed edges billowing in the wind, soon to be lost to the skies.

"No. Look, Fiona, I really have to go. I promise we can talk later."

She finally releases my sleeve, accepting that I am walking away from her. That I won't be back in her bed or she in mine. There's not a single emotion that flows through me as I jog down the hall, taking the stairs two at a time. I won't miss Fiona. I never felt anything real for her in the first place. There's nothing for me to reminisce about.

I don't bother taking cover or trying to hide the fact that I am making my way straight for the female wing of the residence. Bounding up the main staircase and jogging down the carpeted halls. I ignore each one of my colleagues calling my name as I head straight to Bryony's door, my palm slamming hard against it in three thunderous cracks.

There's no answer. My essence reaches out touching the center, then quickly retracting as if to tell me she's not there. That it can't reach her. I felt it too. Only a trace of her, but not the actual Bryony behind the panel of wood keeping me out of her room.

Something tells me to close my eyes. Allow myself to sense her. To feel her flow through my insides. To fill me the way she always does when I'm inside her. My essence blossoms within as if telling me to follow it. To allow the combination of us to guide me, and I will find her. Its tiny slithering form weaving down the hallways, through passages and walls straight to the Vault.

I've only made it halfway down the stairs when the rustling of clothing hits me. Heavy breathing and her chuckle intermingled.

Valen slips back into his shirt as I clear the last step into the chamber. Bryony laid out on her back on the long stone that serves as a bench. Her cheeks are flushed. Lips swollen the way they are after I've been with her. A sated grin pulling at the corners of her mouth.

"Bri?"

She bolts upright, her eyes not quite right. "You got my messages."

"Uh, yeah? What's going on?"

"We found the Azukeen," Valen snorts, slipping onto the stone behind her, legs spread on either side of hers. His front solidly pressed into her back.

My teeth grind, jaw working at how he's propped up behind her. How his hands graze her thighs, and she says nothing. Her post-ghoul high has a tight hold on her. The scent of her arousal swarming my nostrils.

"Bri?" I hold out my hand hoping she'll come to me, but Valen snakes an arm around her waist holding her in place. That wicked grin only he can wear spreads as he rests his chin on her shoulder.

"It listened to me, Knox," she purrs. Her head lolls back onto Valen's shoulder, eyes drooping.

The shuffle of fast-moving feet grows behind me. My body shifting out of the way just in time for Pierson and Graham to come barreling into the space.

"Oh goody, all of my men are here." She yawns loudly, jaw popping. Her eyes close but she holds her head straight as if still staring at us.

"Bri, I've been looking for you." Graham comes forward. A number of books coiled under his arm. Streaks of dust dirty the stark white it once was. His hand stretches for her, just as mine did. A sudden urge to knock his hand aside making me shove mine into the pockets of my coat.

"Bri, what's going on?" Pierson steps forward now. His gaze darts between Bri and Valen. Then the purpling bruise already forming around her throat. Switching to Valen's hand, stroking her pussy through her jeans as she moans.

"Who wants to fuck?" she yawns.

It takes everything in me not to let my hand shoot up in the air.

Fuck.

We're so fucked.

56

BRYONY

I'M ONLY VAGUELY AWARE of what's happening around me. Valen's hands are on me, instead of a dagger. All my men are here, crowded around me, each one wearing different expressions. None are what I would categorize as good.

Knox's anger radiates off him. Heavy waves crashing through my insides. But why?

And Graham and Pierce, each with a hand reaching in my direction. Individual palms held open for me to take, beckoning me toward them. But why would I leave the press of Valen's finger against my center? I wouldn't. Not when lust soars through my body.

Around me are the four pieces to complete my simple puzzle. Or maybe my complicated puzzle. Four pieces I want to be bonded to me. Buried so deep inside me they may never find their way out.

The fog slowly clears as my essence leaks from me, merging with one I know so well. My eyes finally flutter completely open to reveal Knox in front of me. His thick brow furrowed as he lazily brings me back to life.

"There you are," Knox releases a relieved sigh his thumb stroking my cheek.

Unable to help myself, I launch my body forward into his arms. His hold is tight. Our essences immediately calm as our skin touches. The ghoul's dark magic forced to sit in the corner and wait to be summoned.

"What happened?" Knox pulls back his eyes searching mine. A hand stroking my wild hair back from my face.

An uninhibited flow of words funnels out of me. "We found the Azukeen. It, uh, obeyed me. Valen thought it might." A factual repetition of tonight's event.

"That's impossible," Knox mumbles.

"It's not," Valen clucks behind me, no longer straddling the stone where we'd just been.

"You took her out there to find a fucking Azukeen?" Pierce roars. His long strides put him in Valen's face in a matter of seconds. Pierce, the sweet boy, can become one of violence in Valen's presence, always because of me. A part of me hates myself for changing him. A bigger part is proud to see him stand up to his supposed best friend.

"She fucked it and it seemed to submit to her, so yeah I wanted to test my theory." My back is to him but I have no doubt there's a careless shrug. A dagger finding its way into his hand, endlessly twirling between those long digits.

"Guys, we have other problems," Graham cuts in.

"Yeah, we do," Pierce growls. "Bryony, what the hell is going on here? You don't even like Valen, but you're letting him feel you up."

My mouth opens to answer, with what I'm not sure. I have no good excuse. Sure, I could blame it on the post-ghoul lust soaring through my veins, but something tells me Pierce won't buy that answer this time. Honestly, I'm not convinced he did the first time.

"She let me fuck that sweet pussy again too," he laughs. Pierce's eyes go wide and then narrow. "And don't forget, she's with Professor Wynston Knox, too." The British accent used to accentuate Knox's name, obnoxious, but oddly fitting, too.

"I kissed her," Graham blurts as if those three words will do anything to help the situation.

My groan is long as I plop back onto the stone, my face buried in my hands.

"Good job, man. Didn't think you had it in you," Valen chuckles from his new spot against the wall.

Pierce collapses to one of the stones, his hands working through his hair. Long strokes leaving the strands standing at odd ends.

"You have to choose," he whispers. "I can't be strung along."

It never occurred to me that the relationships I had with each of them meant anything to the others. I figured we were having fun. Knox and I, nothing more than an experiment orchestrated by my elders. Valen ... well, we won't analyze that. Graham, the person who's become my best friend. The one who understood me so well without knowing my secrets. And Pierce, a man I would make a home with if someone like me could.

"No," I blurt.

They all look up at me. Each expects to have their desires torn from them. It hadn't occurred to me that I needed them all. That each of them has proved to be of importance to me, although killing Valen might still happen.

"Choose, Bryony. You can't be with all of us," Pierce begs. His body jerks to stand as he paces toward, then away from me. The heartbreak and the anxiety written on his face nearly destroys me. "But more importantly, choose me. We're great together, aren't we?" The plea in his voice shatters my heart as a finger glides beneath my chin, tilting my gaze up to meet his. "Please." His last attempt at making me see his reasoning.

There have been so many times in my life where I stood in a room and had no idea what to do. No idea who to be, other than the light wielder my family perfectly curated me to be, both in public and at home. But for once, there's no hesitation. There's no question about what I want, or who I want. What I currently wish for.

"No. It's all of you or none of you." The words come out low. Only a hint above a whisper. The room remains silent. Then I say it again. "It's all of you or none of you." My voice is strange, but mine. Strong, but not pronounced.

Four sets of eyes stare back at me. Each with scrutiny and confusion in their features. I am a bit shocked I dared to voice my choice, but what else am I supposed to do here?

Valen has the knowledge I need. Only Knox has the power to control my essence when I lose it. Pierce is just the epitome of good and hope despite being a dark wielder. And Graham is the only person who has seen the real me, without *what* I am being of importance.

No one says a thing. All four of them forming a line in front of me. Faces void of expressions, just blank stoic stares.

"Well? Are you in or are you out?" I move directly in front of them, hands on my hips.

I don't want to lose any of them and the bonds we've formed but I have too much other shit going on to worry about some men crying over their feelings.

"In." Knox steps forward.

"As long as I get to fuck you and still threaten your life, in," Valen snorts. My eyes roll in response. The corner of my mouth twitching as I fight a grin.

Graham releases a loud sigh, his body curling in on itself. "Okay," he breathes. "Me too."

My gaze falls on Pierce, his locked on me. It hasn't shifted a bit. So many thoughts whirring through his head. Hesitation written in the tension holding his shoulders high.

"Please, Pierce." I move toward him, my hands winding around his waist. With my cheek pressed to his chest, I listen to the rapid beat of his heart as it calms my own. "Please."

What seems like hours pass. Me holding on tight, hoping it won't be the last time I get to hold him like this. To inhale the cedar wood of his body wash or feel his muscles move beneath my palms.

"Alright." The single word spoken so softly I hope I didn't imagine hearing it.

I don't release him right away. This new dynamic we've just agreed to unsettles him. The hope for me to finally give myself over to just him was destroyed when I made my own choice.

There will be time to talk about it later. Just him and I.

"I don't mean to spoil the moment, but seriously Bri, I have things you need to hear," Graham announces before clearing his throat.

Releasing Pierce, I settle back onto the stone bench, Knox settling in right next to me, his fingers weaved with mine. Our essences automatically release in unison, a thin cloud of pewter fog covering the floor up to our ankles.

"Let's hear it." Exhaustion begins to wash over me again. My body needs rest after siphoning so much from the Azukeen. But sleep will have to wait.

"Headmistress Milgren isn't pure," Graham starts.

Valen laughs loudly. "Yeah, okay."

Graham sneers at him, but continues, "I went to the library tonight to find information on Grisyms. You know ..." he pauses as he rolls his shoulders back, as if uncomfortable, "...to learn more about you, and I found this." He displays the book he's referring to. A thin tome, with aged lines across the leather cover. "Then I found this letter inside from Gavin Milgren Von Tavern. He has to be Milgren's grandfather."

"You've decided that she isn't pure simply based on some old love letter?" Valen scoffs over Graham's shoulder as he and Pierce read it.

"No. I looked him up. He had a son. A Grisym son. Said son supposedly died in a fire with his wife and child. Conrad Milgren."

He pulls his phone from his pocket. Fingers pinching the screen to make the image bigger.

Valen takes a step back, his brow scrunching. A confused gasp comes from Pierce.

"That's Professor Johnathan Tillerman. He's been our liaison with Jordden for the past three years," Pierce asserts. His voice sure, but confusion knitting his brows low.

"No, that's Conrad Milgren," Graham insists. His finger jabs at the screen.

Knox gestures for the phone. Recognition flashes across his face. "That's definitely Johnathan. Teaches *Advanced Siphoning*."

Valen wears a pointed smirk as if Graham should have never corrected him.

"Wait, hold up. You're telling me Janelle is a Grisym and she and her family supposedly died in a fire but clearly didn't because her father is here, teaching under a different name, and works with my father?" I all but gasp. How had I not known? How did I never see it?

"Sounds about right," Graham nods with a nervous swallow.

My fingers rub at my temples. The information makes sense now. Why Janelle always accepted me. There are other Grisyms here. That must be the only reason she was so willing to have Knox and me here. She's one of us.

The most important question should be why her father faked their deaths. But for me, it's not. It's obvious. It's been centuries of Grisyms being executed just for being born as they are. Why not erase yourself from the earth so they never come looking?

But the question of how he faked three deaths wears on me. A likely answer is the fact that forensics weren't what they are now back in the 1960s.

"Well, since we're revealing shit, as you know, Bryony can control ghouls," Valen drawls. His focus suddenly on his short-clipped nails as if the whole conversation is a bore for him.

"False, I commanded a single Azukeen that I've now fucked twice." The words sound funny on my tongue. The set of muscles moving inside my mouth as I try to determine what the foul taste now invading is.

"Bri, do you understand what you just said?" Pierce sputters.

I nod. Starting to repeat it.

"Azukeens are the most volatile and particular ghouls known to man. Not only did it seek you out again, I remember it spoke to you. If you can command an Azukeen, there's something far bigger at play here." Knox faces Valen. "What's your theory?"

"Bri is different. We've all established that. To attract a talking Azukeen that submits to her speaks to the power she has or the blood she holds. If she can control it, then she can control them all," Valen announces, his chin cocked a fraction higher.

My eyes go wide. There's no way. It can't be.

Then the Azukeen's words come back to me.

More. Come.

An omen. A promise.

57

BRYONY

IT'S WELL AFTER TWO in the morning when we funnel out of the Vault. My ass is numb from sitting on stone for hours. My mind racing with the shit show this year has become. So much for a quiet existence and a little sleuthing.

My world has suddenly turned upside down, resituated, and then torn itself off its hinges once more. It's as unnerving as it is exhilarating. My fear for my life and those that are important to me sits heavier on my shoulders. A weight I'm questioning if I'm strong enough to carry.

I want to believe this is all coincidence. Now. Here at this school. I'm losing the fight convincing myself no one planned this. It's not the work of someone coming against me. But I can't seem to force myself to believe it. There are too many moving pieces for our current situation to be nothing more than chance.

Knox escorts us all back to Valen's room. I know mine is empty, Camilla spending the night with her now girlfriend, but it's easier sneaking one girl in rather than four guys.

The wave of exhaustion I'd felt after the ghoul and then Valen fucking me senseless rushes through me, my body curling in on itself as I slide into Valen's bed. Pierce is the one to climb in behind me, snuggling close. His familiar scent and warmth are exactly what I need to finally relax a little. To let my muscles uncoil from the contracted state they've been in all night.

"We need to get Jordden back here. Too many things don't make sense," I mumble, eyelids fluttering slowly as I fight sleep.

Mental notes bulleted to be sorted through tomorrow.

"I already reached out. He'll meet us down in the Vault on Sunday and Tillerman too," Valen states plainly, his back against the edge of the bed as he sits on the floor near my feet.

It's odd how much a single proclamation so drastically altered our dynamic. I honestly thought I'd be walking out of those forgotten catacombs alone. Of course, I would still have to call on Knox. On paper, he is my advisor, but anything beyond that would cease all because Pierce wanted me to choose. A desire I can't fault him for.

How could I?

They've all infiltrated my life and accepted what I am. Graham is the only one who carries fear in his eyes when he looks my way. He still doesn't understand what I am, but he knows me. The real Bri and that's the only reason I can think he chose to step forward.

He keeps his eyes trained on the books in his lap. Scanning over the words at a speed far too quick to assume any of the information sticks.

Knox is the only one to sit apart in the desk chair on the far side of the room. He is the one that's different from us, though, isn't he? He's a professor. A thirty-eight-year-old man—his age only known to me because I caught several professors wishing him a happy birthday last week—who shouldn't be sexually involved with his student. He shouldn't be camped out in another student's room planning a next move that he shouldn't be part of in the first place.

Yet he's here. His focus stays on my face as I try to communicate my thanks to him with nothing but my eyes. A single look meant to convey what he means to me, likely failing as another yawn breaks free.

"Wynston." His eyes go wide at my use of his given name. "What happens if more rogue ghouls get on campus?"

He rubs the short stubble of his chin. My brain only now computing that he's wearing his glasses. Usually, he only wears them in class or while reading. The dark tortoiseshell frames a complement the faint golden hue of his skin.

"Other than with a Red Moon, they shouldn't be able to once the wards are reconstructed this weekend. Even then, whoever is deemed keeper of the wards will have to allow the gates to form between their world and ours. Without it, they aren't supposed to be able to enter the mortal world, Red Moon or not."

"Valen, your dad studies this. How are they getting past the gates when they're not supposed to be open?" I hate that I'm exposing myself to knowing anything about Valen, but I'm desperate for answers. I think we all are.

Valen's father and his position at the GCP are just as well known as my parents. Their organization has become more and more vocal over the years about its stance on the treatment of rogue ghouls. Each plea for the dissolution of ghoul hunters pointedly ignored by the Council.

For once, Valen looks defeated. He says nothing as he stares off into space, another knife dancing through the air.

"The GCP looks at the ghouls themselves, not the Hell Gates. The Department of Magical Realms would know that information, but I doubt we would get the truth. Light wielders love to keep to themselves what the masses should know," Valen snarls.

There's no hiding his disdain when it comes to his feelings regarding how light-wielders conduct themselves against the dark. He shouldn't. He's right. Something I would have never admitted before coming here. Light wielders harbor information from the public, so they can maintain control of institutions like the Council and the Magical Realms department.

The longer I've been at Beauxgraton the more I've come to realize how wrong the ways of the light can be. How much harm we've done over the decades. A "we" I can't pretend to identify with anymore. For them, it all boils down to control. For me, I don't think I can stand behind those ideals anymore.

For the first time I can recall, I consciously remove myself from the class of light wielder. I've never felt as though I could proudly and confidently hold myself apart as who I am. So, I molded myself to fit in with them like I was told to. Expected to. Warned to.

"So, we've got nothing, is what you're saying?" Pierce huffs as the point of his chin digs into my shoulder.

I let my eyes flutter closed again. Fatigue pulls at the shell of my body, while the ghoul magic twirls with life inside me. It itches to break free, to be used. A menacing pulse within me wanting to wreak havoc.

"Knox," I croak. In mere seconds he's across the room. Hands cradling my face. "I think ... I think it's going to happen again. I feel it stirring."

His forehead presses to mine our essences swirling together between our necks, the speed much faster than it normally is. "Knox ..."

"Shhh." The soothing brush of his breath over my face is calming. My lips part as more of my essence flows freely. Black as the night, littered with stars. It leaks out into the room, into Knox's mouth, twisting around each of my guys. Yet there's a calm to it as it releases this time. Not like before, when the rush threatened to tear me apart.

The tips of each wisp of power flicker across the skin of each guy. Testing. Teasing. Learning. I hope my thoughts convey they are safe. They are mine. They are to be trusted.

"Oh shit, Bri. Your eyes!" Graham bellows.

I don't need a mirror to know what has happened. The white sheen and the black rim.

The moment Knox's mouth touches mine, I know his eyes have changed, too. My body longs to move with his. Against him. To have him inside me. Filling me.

"Look, I get that we're all on board, but please don't have sex in front of me," Graham groans.

"What's wrong pretty boy? Upset that she hasn't fucked you yet?" Valen quips. The dagger ticking back and forth like a pendulum between his fingers.

Graham goes silent his mouth opening then pressing shut when he realizes he has no retort for that. It's simply the truth. Graham and I are friends. He's never had that interest in me, or I in him. Our two shared kisses were nothing of note. A convenience and then a shared emotional moment.

"I think I'm going to try to get some sleep. Let's all meet back here after breakfast," he says. The books tucked back under his arm. Eyes downcast.

I move to stand, Pierce and Knox releasing me. Our essences still cycle through the room. On wobbly legs, I shuffle my way to him. Throwing my arms around Graham's neck, I pull him close.

"Thank you," I whisper. A quick peck pressed to his cheek. "If you find more, let us know."

He nods and then he's gone.

I've only just sat back on the bed when Knox pulls me back to my feet. "You should get some sleep too." I nod, not willing to argue.

I'm exhausted. The warring magics inside me are using up every bit of energy I have left.

Pierce is quick to kiss me. A deep languorous endeavor while Knox and Valen watch.

"Night guys," I wave as I make my way to the door. Valen barely acknowledges my departure. A non-surprise for me. I never expected my claiming him would bring out his warm and fuzzy side. Pierce shoves him in the shoulder when all I get is a grunt.

It's fine. Our having sex didn't trick me into believing the two of us would suddenly warm up to each other. He was there both times to deal with the post-ghoul lust. It's as simple as that. But I *do* need him.

Valen's unique perspective on the world and wide range of knowledge will only be helpful. Plus, I think he might be the only one more obsessed with ghouls than I am. His father's role with the GCP and that notebook he keeps tucked in his pocket, which he thinks I don't know about, may be an invaluable tool to help us navigate executing my connection to those misunderstood creatures.

When I said all or none of them, I didn't mean it as some sort of twisted five-way relationship. I meant more than that. I need them all by my side. I need them all to respect each other. Each of them is a complement to me in some way. With one wheel missing, the vehicle falls apart and I'm left stranded. Exposed. Vulnerable.

It might be a selfish mindset, but I kind of have to be. We Grisyms must be if we want to survive in this world.

Knox and I are quick to get to my room. No one in the halls to spot us as my professor follows me inside.

"What are you doing?"

"If you think for one second that I'm leaving you alone, you're more delusional than I thought. Where are your pajamas?"

I throw him a wry look.

"I don't wear them." A partial truth.

"Fuck," he groans before tossing me onto the bed.

Sleep can wait.

58

PIERSON

THE ANNOUNCEMENT CAME AS a blaring text message this morning, the siren jolting me from my bed. The mandatory simple charm added to our alert messages with a mission to blow out our eardrums. My body is tired and achy as if I'd done too much physical activity. Working out is not my thing, so I can only chalk it up to the mountain of revelations and Bri's proposal last night.

Students and Faculty,

Classes are canceled for the remainder of the week. Students are to remain indoors but are free to roam the Beauxgraton Residence and use the underground tunnels to access Buckingham Proper.

Any student caught outdoors will be reprimanded and put on probation.

If you have questions, you may send them via email to Secretary Windhaven.

Sincerely,
Headmistress Janelle Milgren

We figured the announcement would come, but what I can't stop staring at is Milgren's name. Rerunning what Graham told us last night. Conrad Milgren is Johnathan

Tillerman—at least that's who we're convinced he is. Our confidant. Mentor. Liaison to Jordden's initiative.

Another Grisym hiding in plain sight. Not once did I ever suspect. Would I have ever known he was anything other than a dark wielder like me?

I think back to Bri. There is nothing to truly give her away, either. Sure, her physical characteristics are off, but that's not something unseen or unheard of.

What bothers me is how young he appears. Conrad looks no older than fifty, yet Milgren must be on her way to sixty. Maybe we're wrong. Maybe Conrad and Johnathan's faces just resemble each other so much that we are seeing what we want to see.

Throwing myself back onto the pillows, I search Conrad Milgren online. A slew of pictures come up. Each one is a spitting image of Johnathan, just a younger version. He would have to have a twin out there. Even doppelgangers don't resemble this much. It could be spellwork, but it takes a lot of finesse and skill to duplicate another person's features. To make them so identical they could be clones.

With a loud breath, I climb from bed, combing my unruly hair from standing straight to the side with my fingers. Today is not a day I am going to care about my appearance anyhow. There's plenty of other shit to deal with.

My thoughts wander to how impeccably Graham dresses every day. How Bri admires his choices and compliments them. Sudden inadequacy settles in my gut. She'd chosen all of us because we all give her something the others don't.

That much is clear, even without her voicing it.

I don't know how to do this. My mind fails to coach me on how to mentally, emotionally, and physically handle that green monster of jealousy that is sure to pop up over and over. Bri was made for me. Me for her. She is the fire that burns my soul and the air my lungs need to breathe. The oxygen particles that make my brain function. A beauty I never knew the world could possess.

She is mine and I will not lose her. Not for anything or anyone.

I hadn't left Valen's room until five this morning. The two of us sat in silence more than we talked. When we did speak, most of his questions revolved around me having sex with Bri. What I thought were necessary details at the time, sit differently with me now.

He'd asked repeatedly if it felt different with her. If I felt different after. I told him no. It's not the truth about what he's asking, but I'm not sure I could put into words what it's like. How my insides churn chaotically as if the pieces of me are being suctioned straight into her. It's probably just how overwhelming my feelings are for her. That's why I said nothing.

I've always loved quickly. Loved hard. It's who I am. My mom always warned me that I have a heart too open. A heart too willing to let someone own it. With a single look, Bryony Avalon—or is it Guthrie?—stole mine. Became my every thought. My every action and impulse.

There was no stopping giving that lump of muscle to Bri. I just won't tell her or the guys I'm not completely comfortable with this situation. Unsure that I want her staking a claim to all of us or none of us. My agreement was delayed because I fought myself. I had to tell myself that I would take her this way or have her no way. In the end not having her simply wasn't an option.

When I finally got Val to talk about anything but sex with Bri, it still made it back to her through Jordden. A man he has idolized since our high school years, maybe even longer. Valen has an attraction to the idea of doing whatever it takes to get the outcome you want. It doesn't matter who you hurt, maim, or lie to along the way. The end goal is the only thing of importance. That is how Jordden has lived his life. The public eye remains zoomed in on him. Many don't agree with how he goes about pushing the New Order's agenda. They accuse him of all the things the New Order is guilty of, but can never be proven. They ridicule him for having the balls to bring about change. Only the light side would rather see him behind bars or dead.

Neither Valen nor I actually know exactly what he has planned at its true core. That's clear now.

We thought we knew what we were fighting for. What we were trying to accomplish. A dimming of the light to cast away the shadows they hang over the dark. Yet, it seems it's not the light or the dark he wants in the forefront, but both. His children and the others like them.

I admit I feared an association with Bri when I found out. A weariness that quickly changed. My attraction toward her only grew by the day. Attraction to the woman who could understand the dichotomy that lives within me. I was born of the dark. I wield of the dark, but my soul, the heart of me, belongs to the light. Only someone like Bri can truly understand that inner turmoil. Or at least that's what I first told myself.

Then I see her and Knox together. How they blend and mold as one. A mixture that is meant to be just as much the light as it is the dark. No dichotomy lives within her. She is who she was always meant to be, and I'm not what she needs to be that woman. Not on my own.

My phone rings, the caller ID unknown.

"Hello," my voice is a hoarse, croaked rasp.

"My office, ten minutes."

I nod, even though the caller can't see me. Hanging up the phone, I'm quick to change into sweats and a hoodie. I slide my bare feet into my sneakers as I shuffle to the bathroom to brush my teeth and do something to keep my hair from standing up on the top of my head.

I quickly stalk through the hallways, hands tucked in my pockets, head down as students wind past me toward the dining hall. Frankly, I'm pissed. I'm going to miss the food, but whatever. As I turn down the hallway with windows lining one side, a gray hue casts over the floors. Eerie shadows lingering against the wall in a taunt.

The steel-gray clouds violently roll across the sky. Reminiscent of Bri's essence when she lets it free. Thick snowflakes fall past the crystal-clear glass to the ground, already covered in a soft glow of white. White that reminds me of Bri's terrifying stare when her eyes change. Funny, I'd been annoyed Valen always found his way back to her last night, but it's no different than the thoughts that swarm me every day since meeting her. With a shiver, I continue to the administrative wing.

When I get there, I find the door to the office cracked open. Figuring it was intentional I step inside to find my best friend.

Valen tends to be an early riser, so I'm not surprised to see he's already here. His ass is planted on the arm of one of the leather chairs, boots propped along the edge of the desk as if he owns the space. Despite his parents being refined, it's as if he has no concept of good manners.

We clasp hands before I slide into the chair next to him. Professor Tillerman arriving only minutes after I do. A dark glare pointed our way.

He sits behind his desk, adjusting the collar of his shirt. His gaze never quite finds us until he's ready. It's a typical tactic for him. Let's you stew and won't even acknowledge your presence until he is ready to waste his breath on you.

"Are you both pleased with yourselves?"

I honestly have no idea what he's talking about. More than likely it's some shit Valen did again, which automatically pulls me under because I'm forever associated with his dumb ass. For the umpteenth time this year, I am questioning how this friendship made it this far.

"Which part?" Valen sucks on a tooth as if this whole meeting is a huge inconvenience for him. His expression, nonplussed by Tillerman's pointed anger.

"Oh, let me see Mr. Greer. Putting Bryony in danger with that Azukeen. Involving a light wielder in our business. Continuing to fornicate with Jordden's daughter." He clears his throat as if uncomfortable with that one. "And my personal favorite ... you've blown my cover with that same light wielder."

"Johnathan." Valen's tone is just as condescending as using this man's first name is. "I didn't put Bryony in danger. Not really. I proved she can command ghouls." He leans back in his chair, resting an ankle atop the other knee. "Second, involving Graham wasn't intentional. Not to mention he's here to stay per Bryony's choice. And third, that same light wielder—Graham—is who figured out who you are. If you want someone to blame, blame yourself for not being more careful with your identity and your father for being a pussy-whipped bitch, leaving his business lying around."

Tillerman roars to his feet, brushing back his coif of hair. Usually perfectly styled.

"Boy, don't think because you're foolin' around with Jordden's daughter and he's allowed it that you've got the upper hand here. You don't."

Tillerman has always been the type to go from zero to one hundred at the drop of a hat. His temper is a raging fire that's sure to burn should it find unlimited oxygen. His face reddens as he leans down close to Valen, those crystal blue eyes darkening. Val's smugness seeps out of his pores. That typical smirk, firmly in place.

"Calm down, old man. The guy is just curious about who you are and where you and your daughter fit into this mess, but he's also wrapped around Bryony's pinky finger. If she tells him to back off, he will."

Tillerman calmly walks back around the other side of the desk. His mouth pressed into a tight line as he smooths back the sides of his hair with both hands. Each strand laid back in its proper place. The gray, streaked throughout, is the perfect highlight to his near-black strands. Only now do I realize just how out of place he seems. A man from another time in a younger body. I never noticed before. I didn't care. I had an assignment alongside my best friend, and that's all I needed to know.

"See that she does. I don't need to remind you how much is at stake here."

"No, Sir. You do not," I cut in. My spine a bit straighter. Val might walk around with the swagger of someone who doesn't give a shit, but I'm not that person. Plus, if this has anything to do with keeping Bri safe, then I'm ready and willing to fall in line. To lead the charge, even.

"On another note, explain to me what happened with the girl and that Azukeen."

Valen suddenly straightens in his chair, his gaze laser-focused on Tillerman. "Exactly what Jordden predicted. She commanded, it obeyed."

Somehow, I'd convinced myself that it was an exaggeration last night.

It wasn't.

And Jordden knew she could.

I'm speechless.

59

Bryony

I've never seen a ward broken down to its most basic parts and then rebuilt into something stronger. Something indestructible—supposedly.

The closest I've seen is reinforcement. Back when I was sixteen and still traveling the world with my dad. When his presence was required at any institution around the world, he allowed me to tag along. Years of front-row seats to the good and the bad that goes into maintaining and elevating these places of education.

At sixteen, I saw my first reinforcement. The colors of the ward magic alive before my eyes. Vibrant shades swirled together before the light wielder in charge of strengthening each source of power, rearranged them. His large hands wound through the air in a pattern only he understood as those pieces of power strung themselves together. I've never seen anything more breathtaking.

I always loved those trips for Dad and me. Even though I understood that man wasn't my father early on, it was quality time that was always precious. Always ours. He never treated me as anything but his blood. Never considered me anything but his to protect, love, and care for.

We'd gone to Greece that summer. One of the new wielding schools, Nyriah—only in operation for about three years—was having issues with wielders approaching from the sea. They needed their wards reinforced to keep travelers and others who had no business in their metropolis of a campus, out.

It's a beautiful place. Every backside of the campus buildings has large windows that look out over glistening water. Sparkling azure sea spreading far and wide. Bright sunshine illuminating the gold and white interiors and the sandstone that covers every outdoor surface. The architecture, a copy of what you would see in Santorini.

It was the last light school to open and the first to close. Memories of my dad crashing down into his seat when he got the news assault me now. The way his face dropped. His long fingers pulled at his features as they dragged down his face. The school in Greece had been a major win for him. It took years of fighting to build and then open it. Only the historical Erobus School of Wielding for dark wielders had been there. Hundreds of years of history sequestered into that cave, its entrance only by water.

Standing at the large windows at the rear of the main building, I and so many of my classmates watch the invisible ward that should have been protecting us turn shades of blue and purple. Tiny cracks spider out along the surface like broken glass. The shards suddenly shattering into a million pieces, as tiny particles float to the ground, absorbed once again. The magic of an essence, reused once expelled back into the earth. An immediate power source for the new ward or an extrinsic or charter that borrows from nature.

Pierce comes to mind. He mentioned pulling from the earth is the most effective way for him to channel, but I've never seen him do it. I've never seen anyone channel from an in-ground well of endless power in person. From what I've heard, it's a life-changing thing to witness. Just seeing it via a recording doesn't compare to the feeling of being present for that type of power exchange.

The wielder they'd asked to come here stands tall as she stares off into the distance. Shoulder-length fiery orange hair billows out behind her. Her eyes like shining emeralds even in the distance. I admit I was a bit unnerved when Janelle insisted I meet her last night. It made no sense for me to, but it was something Knox and Janelle both dug their heels in over. There was no answer for them but yes. The both of them clung to the dumb, unfounded notion that something about me might aid her in constructing our new set of wards. Maybe it's because of the whole "ghoul boss" thing, but either I didn't see anything about me that would benefit more than harm us or I was missing something entirely too important to be ignored.

The two apprentices she brought with her flank her on either side. A male and a female I haven't yet met. One a light wielder and the other dark. Even now we call together the two sides, yet someone like me isn't allowed to live.

Something inside me burns. The few private conversations I've had with Jordden since our covert meeting, are alive in my mind now. His passion for bringing those like me and Vincent into the light, so to speak, is inspiring. If both sides of wielders are important for such things as this, why shouldn't me, Knox, Vincent, Janelle, and the thousands more Jordden says are out there be able to exist? Why aren't we accepted?

I hadn't been sure I would willingly join his cause until now. Until I watched the tendrils of essence stream free of the three of them. Their unique colors mix in thin air and swirl high as a new barrier begins to form. Once joined, the combination never strays from a perfectly neutral gray until a split second shifts to peach, and then pink becomes a deep red as it reaches the sky. The same crimson as the Red Moon.

I wonder if that type of gateway magic was necessary to source into the wall. A piece of that force needed to ensure that rogue ghouls can no longer get in.

Another pang vibrates in my chest. There was something different about the last experience with the Azukeen. I had only thought Valen was being his normal sarcastic self when he brought up how it was taken with me. How it yielded to me. But now I see the submission that was there. The wanting and willingness that it exuded as if its only desire was to please me in all ways possible.

More. Come.

Those two words ring in my head now as the ward walls stretch higher and further, blanketing us in a green haze. The neon sheen casting an eerie glow over us all.

I never considered what the different colors represented. A blend of various sources, forming variations of purpose. It's not something my family taught me. Nor is it something I came across in a book. My fingers tremble as they press against the glass in front of me. Eager to reach out and touch it. To call it to me. Pull it inside of me, tasting its true nature. A tiny space inside me, clearing to make room for this foreign entity.

Pierce scoots in closer so his front molds to the curve of my rear. A comfort I wasn't sure I needed until his arms wrapped around me. A distraction from the thoughts rippling through my tired brain.

The pieces I'd either willingly ignored all these months—more like years—begin to form a picture. One I'm not sure I am ready to accept. Truths that will forever change how I choose to live the rest of my life.

As a Grisym.

Free.

But always still bound to the fear of being "other", misunderstood, and hated.

I fear why I was able to command the Azukeen. I fear that I can do it again, with other ghouls. No wielder has ever been able to do such a thing, as far as I know. But I also know there's so much knowledge I'm lacking. So much my family restricted because I was supposed to pretend the dark half of me didn't exist. Maybe that's why it rages stronger. It would not be stamped out and forgotten.

I'd already decided to stay away from the next Red Moon. Swore I would not put myself in the pathway of ghouls again. Then we found that Azukeen and my plans were trashed. My magic hadn't rebelled against me so violently this time, but I'm not sure if that was familiarity, or tolerance, or the fact that Knox was right there when I first started to feel that overwhelming burst of every essence inside me trying to break free.

Knox's essence and practiced control were there to reel me back into myself. The force to center the two of us, as our essences crave. The dominating forces strong enough to control everything inside me.

You read in books about fated mates and souls connecting, but in real life, you never expect to feel something so potent. Something so jarring. Something so right. Yet I imagine what it's like when Knox and I touch, or are even in close proximity, is the same. We were meant to find each other. Our essences meant to mingle. The question is why. Was it by design or fate?

The trio disappears as they round the side of the school. Their work done in what seemed like minutes but had been over an hour.

Something warms and tingles within me and I know Knox is close. My body senses him. Feels his nearness. Anticipation fluttering in my lower belly.

I don't need to turn around to know he's standing right there. I can feel every bit of him. Our magic calls to each other. Wanting to mix and be one.

But not here. Not in front of half of the student body.

"Ms. Avalon, Headmistress Milgren needs to see you in her office," Knox urges. I turn with a sigh. I had hoped I would have the day off from managing my secret identity, but it seems not.

Pierce links his fingers through mine as I start to weave past my classmates. The stares I'd once gotten in dedication are now nothing more than passing glances as they watch the shimmering new ward outside.

From what I know, the color will remain for a few hours while the new combinations of power settle. A beautiful sight I'll never forget.

"Not you." Knox's hand is on Pierce's shoulder. His face is blank, except for his eyes. There's an apology there. One I hope Pierce sees and can understand.

We may be unraveling every secret as of late, but there are some things Knox wants to keep to himself.

There are things I do, too.

He leads me through the halls. A few students whispering behind their hands as we pass. That rumor—which is no longer a rumor—that Valen started has stuck with some people. I hear their comments and feel their stares. I honestly don't give a fuck. I have way more to worry about than a bunch of twenty- and thirty-somethings trying to figure out who I'm sleeping with.

Janelle's door creaks open as we step inside. Edina and her two assistants, Professor Tillerman, Janelle, and Valen fill the space. Each with their eyes focused on me as I enter. I swallow loudly as Knox quietly shuts the door behind us.

The office is a decent size, but not when you have so many bodies crowded together. So cramped, everyone's presence seems larger than life. Infiltrating and filling every bit of space the tight quarters have to offer.

A swipe of Tillerman's finger flips the deadbolt lock on Janelle's door. My body involuntarily jumping at the thunk. No one has spoken yet. Nor taken an eye off me. As if Knox can sense I am moments from panicking, his fingers weave through mine. A small squeeze of reassurance.

My chin lifts. Just a fraction. I have one man at my side. I can handle whatever shit is coming our way now.

The room rumbles around us as Edina puts up a ward sealing us in the room. Her method is so different from my dad's. His brute force, but hers, an intricate design made from the wings of butterflies. I'm in awe.

"My dear, we have a problem," she croons.

Shocker.

60

Bryony

My pulse thunders at my throat and wrists. Despite not being surprised we have another issue on our hands, my body still reacts with fear. My heart still thumps loudly in my ears as every bit of blood races through my veins. Sweat droplets slithering down my spine as I collapse into the one open chair.

Coming here to Beauxgraton was supposed to be easy. I was supposed to be safe and hidden, and there was supposed to be nothing of note that happened here. That's what Janelle promised my parents when she insisted on me being here, where she could keep an eye out.

That's what my brother Merrick promised when he hugged me to his side the night before I left, his newborn baby fast asleep in his other arm. His perfect light-wielding child. She will be nothing like her aunt. Nothing like *me*.

I never considered how my siblings felt, having to grow up alongside me. A creature that isn't allowed to exist. Harley was very vocal about how much he hated me, but Merrick and Sicily always treated me with love and compassion. I'd always thought it was genuine, but now I wonder if they, too, feared what I am. If they played a role, ensuring they'd never have to find out what a Grisym that matured ten years early—seemingly out of nowhere—was capable of. Whether they wondered if my dark or light tendencies would win out that day. Each falling into bed at night, hoping for the light.

"What's wrong?" I croak, speaking to no one in particular, but turning my body to face Janelle.

I don't want the answer, but they might as well come out with it. Another reminder of what my presence here does. What my conglomerate of gifts—ones I've yet to fully identify—has done to uproot our world. It's always me, inadvertently bringing destruction to those around me.

"Well, we were successful in building a stronger ward. We attempted to shut out the gates that allow ghouls entrance ..." Edina's words drift as her large eyes stare at me expectantly. "I assume you watched." I nod. "When you saw the wards flash red, that was meant to be us accessing magic to keep those gates closed except during the Red Moon."

"And you couldn't ..." I meant to voice it as a question, but comes out as a drawn-out conclusion. It's the only logical explanation for how softly she is attempting to deliver her message.

"Correct. We could not." Edina takes a deep breath. Her eyes drift to Janelle before floating back to me. "My dear, something about you is keeping them open here on the campus."

"That's not possible," Conrad—or is it Johnathan—barks.

"It is. And it's the truth," the male of the trio chimes in. "My particular gifts allow me to hear an essence, or any surrounding magic, if you will. It speaks to me. Tells me its secrets and truths. The way my presence works, it's almost like a truth serum if you will, the answers pulled unwillingly from the essence. The magic that should be holding the gates closed spoke to me. It fought us. It will only answer to you. It said you are its keeper."

I don't know how to respond to that. How to make sense of what this man is saying to me. I've never heard of anything like this. I search the faces around the room, looking for confirmation that something like this has happened before. That these people made some sort of mistake.

My gut tells me everything happening is tied to my father. Tied to how he forced my early maturity. What other explanation could there be? That potential truth sits as a solid boulder at the base of my stomach. Viscous bile threatens to shoot up my throat in response to my thoughts. I can't know that for sure, but the voice in the back of my mind tells me it must be true. Just me shooting darts in the dark, trying to figure out why I am the way I am since no one will tell me the complete truth.

"How can that be?" My words are a whispered rasp. Barely audible for everyone to hear.

"Bryony, when you were with the Azukeen, did it ever feel as though there was an exchange between you?"

I think back to both of my encounters. The first time stands out now. That moment right before I orgasmed, my essence streamed from my mouth, the Azukeen quickly inhaling that tiny swirl. Just for a second. I hadn't watched it take my essence in, but I felt a tug inside me. As if a piece of me suddenly went missing. I chalked it up to nothing more than the experience of being with a ghoul for the first time. Of my body acclimating to having this new power siphoned into me that I would then have control over.

"Yes," I breathe.

The man nods. "What I think happened was, the Azukeen took from you that night of the Red Moon. Even then—from what I've been told—it answered to you. So, it wanted to keep a gateway to you. A way to always access you, if you will." He clears his throat with a fist over his mouth, immediately returning it to the position behind his back, hands clasped tight.

"This is fucking insane," Knox blurts. "You have to be wrong."

"Professor Knox, I am not wrong. I have never been wrong about things like this." The assistant's tone is calm as he responds to Knox. His face betraying nothing about his emotions.

Knox growls from behind me. A possessive sound that has me resting a hand on his forearm, hopeful it helps him calm down for just a second.

The last thing we need is tempers flaring in this room. For us to turn against one another when there's too much at stake.

"I—I don't know where to go from here. Have you already told my dad?"

Janelle's eyes narrow, but it's Johnathan who responds. "Yes, Jordden will be here in a matter of hours. Until then everyone in this room is to remain silent about what has been discussed here."

The room nods. But I don't. "No, I meant my *real* dad."

Johnathan's face darkens. Valen's mouth pressing into a tight line of disgust. "Your mother and Jordden made you. He is your '*real* dad.' Roman is just the man who pretended to be on your side."

The words sting. I want nothing more than to retort. To defend the man who raised me, but something about that statement gives me pause. Throws the gears in my mind into an agitated halt.

"Pretended how?" I question, squaring my shoulders.

Johnathan barks a laugh, Janelle shooting him a pleading look, before speaking up, "Don't. Please."

I'm so damn tired of everyone keeping secrets from me. Of deciding, for me, what I can and can't handle. My glare levels on Johnathan's face. A challenge for him to reveal whatever it was he was planning to say. His bulbous nose wrinkling before he speaks.

"Know your place," he growls at Janelle. Her lithe form steps back from him, not out of fear, but her version of respect for her father.

"Yes, father." Her hand retracts, both clasped in front of her.

I've never seen Janelle cower at anything. Never seen her back down from any challenge, but when her father spoke to her, ordered her, she fell in line in seconds.

Fuck, this is way too much to process. My temples throb with all this newfound information. A fresh mountain piled on top of the one from only a few nights ago.

"Roman has been using you. Do you think he kept you alive out of the goodness of his heart or his love for your mother? He is the man she was *supposed* to choose, but she settled for your father. She chose Jordden and has done so every day of her life, but things were different back then." Johnathan smooths his already perfectly styled hair, the small comb he'd used slipping back into his wool suit jacket. "You are only precious to Roman because you are a bargaining chip. A prize he can use to dangle in front of your mother and Jordden."

"You're crazy!" I'm on my feet in seconds ready to defend my dad. He has been nothing but good to me over the years. He kept my secrets. Kept me safe. Kept my mom and siblings safe. He's worked tirelessly to improve the educational system for wielders alongside the Council. He's a good man. I know he would never use me. He would never do that. "He would never," I roar.

He *loves* me.

But even as I tell myself those words, as I fight to believe them, a tiny morsel of doubt weasels its way in. Creeping into the deepest parts of me, determined to stay put, sprouting unmovablq roots if I let it. Johnathan planted that tiny seed. There's no undoing the damage he's done.

My chest heaves. I'm so overwhelmed with all of this, but I will not sit here and listen to this stranger talk badly about the man who raised me.

"Oh, he would sweet child. And he has been, for twenty-five years." He steps out from the side of the desk, moving to stop right in front of me. Hands in his pants pockets, his face twisted with anger. Who he's angry at is beyond me. "Your *dad* ..." those three letters, a curse on his lips. A mockery of the man I continue to cling to as Dad, "is a spineless man," he spits out, face contorted as if he drank spoiled milk. "He doesn't deserve the good that has come to him. What type of man would dangle another man's child's life in front of him? Hmm?"

I rear back as if slapped before the warmth of Knox's arms wrap around me from behind.

"You're wrong," I shoot back at him. Hot tears build behind my eyes, but I won't let them fall. I can't.

"I'm not. Ask him about the day you were born."

Then he's gone, the door creaking shut behind him. Edina had to of dropped the ward keeping us all in this room. My emotions are so wild I hadn't noticed her and the apprentices had already left, too.

Knox's strength is the only thing keeping me from crumbling to the floor at his feet. The roots that only started growing minutes ago, thicken, becoming an overgrowth I'll never be able to trim back.

He's wrong.

61

VALEN

IT TOOK EVERYTHING INSIDE me not to smile with glee at the chaos Tillerman let loose in Milgren's office this afternoon. The doubt he built within Bryony by telling her what a piece of shit Roman Avalon actually is: *Glorious.*

Sure, Bryony has claimed me, or whatever you want to call it, but she's still a liability. There are still parts of me that want her dead. More importantly, I know that urge won't go away until she willingly chooses Jordden's side. The chinks that would put in Roman's armor would be magnificent to watch him try to repair. If what Tillerman has said is true, then maybe it wouldn't change much. Whether Roman cares about his "daughter" or not, she is a priceless commodity he can't afford to have used against him.

Yet I know her death can never be part of the plan. Her life has always been the center of it all. Everything Jordden has molded his life around. She is the reason he breathes. If only he'd trusted us from the beginning to know that! Not that it would have made me trust her more. At the end of the day, I still believe her heart lies with the Avalon family. If push comes to shove, I'm not convinced she would choose us. No matter how much we would want her to. How much *I* want her to.

"What's your deal?" Kaia kicks at my foot as I lie sprawled out on one of the couches in the lounge area of the sixth floor.

"What are you talking about?"

She throws me a wry look, as if to say I'm not fooling anyone. "You're thinking about that light bitch, aren't you?"

I know she's talking about Bryony. Except for Pierce and me, no one in our group knows the real plan. They don't understand how important she is. Jordden made it very clear that they are not to know.

"And if I am?"

She groans, sinking back into her chair. Sean glances up from the journal he carries around, his every memory stored, not only in the globe he keeps in his room, but on those pages as well. I've never seen that thing out of his sight, not even in the ghoul pits or the shower.

"I never thought you would be the one to fall for some light ass. They're not like us, Val," venom coats her words. Disgust laced into each one. He knows she is more than that. Jordden already divulged she is his daughter in front of them, yet they still treat her like an Avalon. Like a pure light wielder.

I wonder if Kaia's hatred of light wielders goes beyond the fact that her mother left them for one. I've never asked. Never really cared, to be honest.

Anger and resentment only take you so far in this world. The nature of those emotions is the anchor that keeps you locked in place. The things you were meant to do, left abandoned to the derailment of the instability of those emotions running your life. It's better to plan. To use those emotions to fuel your actions. Not live in them. That's why Jordden would never pick someone like Kaia to lead us, because when all is said and done, she's shackled to those emotions. A storm of negatives raging inside her.

Kormoran is different. He hates light wielders, sure. There's no doubt about that. But he refuses to waste any energy on them at all. His ability to detach from anything more than what is right in front of him is what makes him good "muscle" for Jordden.

"Kaia, I am only going to say this once, so listen close." I sit up, my boots thunking to the floor, elbows resting on my spread knees. "You speak one more word about Bryony—good, bad, or indifferent—I will slit your throat myself."

Her eyes go wide as she scans my face. No doubt searching for my sarcasm, for the joke to be made clear. I hadn't meant to defend Bryony with such gumption, but Jordden wants her protected and that's what I will do. She is mine, and everyone here will damn sure respect that. Mine to protect, that is. The rewards that Jordden will give me for keeping his little girl completely safe are endless. I am not jeopardizing that for anyone.

Kaia snatches her bag from the seat next to her, storming past me. "Understood," she snaps, then she's gone.

"What the fuck was that?" Sean asks. "You fuck the girl once and now you're her knight in shining armor?"

"You really shouldn't speak on things you don't understand."

"Then explain it to me. Because a few weeks ago, all you wanted was that girl dead."

Sean has always been the level-headed one of our group, always looking for the most logical path for the situation at hand. He's not easily riled and, generally, can find reasoning we can all agree on. So, it doesn't surprise me that he wants me to explain it to him now. A memory he'll no doubt capture and save for later.

"That hasn't changed."

"You sure about that? Pretty sure your nose just grew." He slaps his journal shut and then he's gone too.

With the lounge finally empty, I can be alone. Free of my friends planting stupid shit in my head for me to brood over. A loud sigh leaves me as my tired body falls back onto the leather cushions of the couch that I've been on for the last hour. My fingers toy with the short beard at my chin, the coarse hairs a comfort. A fixture on my face since the damn thing started growing in during my late teens.

I let my mind go blank. Attempt to will myself to stop thinking about everything that's happened this year. Tell myself to focus on the fact that everything has always revolved around Bryony. Every decision and alteration to the plans will be based on her and her alone. The fact leaves me grinding my molars.

That damn woman is the center of it all.

A new due north none of us were anticipating. But how could we not? Jordden has made her the beacon in the night meant to light the way to a world none of us have ever imagined coming to fruition.

She controls the Hell Gate. She commands ghouls. She's a Grisym with power like I've never seen before. The one with two fathers—both influential in their own right. She's the one that sets my insides on fire just by existing near her.

That last one I'll ignore. It was nothing more than the ghoul magic coursing through her as I sunk into her heated core. Nothing more than the lust that overwhelms you after fucking a ghoul. I could lie to myself and say that's all it is. That I'm not itching to be alone with her again. To see if she'll fuck me just because I want to.

Because she wants to.

Before I had a chance to be with her, I only wanted to fuck her to destroy daddy's little girl. To taint what he deemed to be his perfect little angel.

As if my very thoughts summoned her, she appears. A messenger bag on one arm and a book cradled in the crook of the other. Her thick-rimmed glasses—ones I've never seen her wear before— slip down her nose as she begins to sit in the armchair directly across from me. An O forming on her lips when she spots me for the first time.

"Sorry, I didn't realize anyone was here." She immediately snatches up her bag to go and something about that grates on me. It's not her nerves that have her bolting, but it's the fact that she would rather go back down two flights of stairs than be anywhere near me. It makes me wonder if she really wanted me as part of her clan, or if she only took me because of Pierce.

I shouldn't care one way or the other, but I do.

"It's fine Bryony. Sit down. I'm napping anyhow."

She sits again, giving me a scrutinizing glare as I settle further into the cushions, fingers woven atop my stomach. My eyes press closed, but I can still feel her staring. Cracking one eye open, I gaze over at her.

"I heard you snore," she snorts.

I don't do it often, but I laugh. A deep rolling laugh that has her eyes stretching into cartoonish saucers. My booted feet hit the rug again as I sit up. A sly grin quirked her way.

My bun bobs at the top of my head. I somehow forget its weight until I'm around her. Damian, the bastard, has taken to calling us the bun duo. My gut tells me it's just to piss me off. It's a dumb fucking name, but every time he says it, something burns deep in my chest. I swear if I'm getting heartburn before I turn thirty, I'm going to be pissed.

Sauntering toward her, I squat at her feet, knees wide as my elbows once again rest on them.

"And who told you that my Little Forbidden Fruit?"

She waves me off, opening her book in her lap. Her spine straightening just the slightest.

"I asked you a question," I growl as I snatch it away, tossing it behind me. My body ignites being so close to her. Wanting so badly to run my fingers up her thigh and over the generous curve of her hip.

"Damian," she shrugs. Another of those pesky laughs escapes me, as I reach out to grab the back of her head, pulling her face close to mine. She winces slightly but doesn't move to pull away. The sage of her eyes twinkling in the sunlight.

"He should learn to keep my secrets better," I purr. My mouth brushes her cheek as I speak, just after wetting my bottom lip. Her body shivers under my touch, a heavy sigh breaking free in response to my tongue skirting along the edge of her jaw.

"I would prefer if he told me better ones." Her breath hitches as my lips wrap around her earlobe. "Darker ones," she hisses in response to my teeth.

She pulls back slightly, our breath mingling in the space between us. Her eyes searching mine, wondering what I'm going to do next. We're not alone together often and frankly, I'm not going to waste this moment.

Drawing one of my daggers from my pocket, I release her, her body scooting as far back into the chair as it will go. The tip of my dagger lightly digs into the divot at the front of her throat, just above her collarbones. The skin depresses beautifully. An invitation for my blade to push further, slitting it open to reveal the soft tissue beneath.

Bryony has never shown fear in all the times I have threatened her. Never shown anything at all, but right now her eyes burn bright with lust. Her breathing heavy, those palm-filling tits moving up and down beneath her baseball tee. The lace of her bra is obnoxiously visible through the white fabric. Fabric, I want to shred with my knife. Or my teeth.

"You have two options: either remove your clothes yourself, or I will do it for you."

Her brow quirks. "No thanks." That defiance she carries like a shield makes my dick rock hard in my jeans. Fuck, how did I go from wanting nothing more than to murder this woman every second of every day to a prepubescent teen that can't control his erection?

Shooting to my feet, I fold my body over hers, the dagger never moving from its spot. The pressure only increasing slightly as my nose runs along her cheek.

"I must insist. The Azukeen is not the only one who wants to please you."

A heavy gasp escapes her, her face pulling back to search mine again.

"Valen." My name whispered on those pouty lips connects with the twitch of my dick before my mouth crashes into hers.

Her body arches into mine, fingers curling around the fabric of my henley. A moan parting her lips so my tongue can slip inside.

"Valen," she breathes. "Either fuck me or get lost. I have studying to do."

My grin quirks, hands already tearing her joggers down her thighs. Her fingers work at my belt before she shoves my jeans down my legs. The tips of my fingers run over the soaked lace that's keeping her pussy from me. Her core is soaking wet for me like it's always been.

"Oh baby, this is going to be fun."

Yanking her up by the hair, she groans as I spin us around so that she's falling to the couch. I should be a good guy and warm her up, allow my fingers to swirl inside her, driving her to the edge, but not letting her tumble over it. But I don't. I won't. Tearing her panties clean from her body, I drive into her.

A loud moan vibrates my ear drum. Eyes rolling back in my head, I seat myself deep in her pussy. The remaining siphoned magic inside me stirs. Beating at the barrier of my skin, eager to exit. An eagerness to mix with this woman in front of me, tightening my stomach muscles. I let just a bit escape, the thin swirl disappearing into her gaping mouth as her eyes change. But not the normal whites they go after a ghoul.

They go black as a demon. No white to be seen. It only eggs me on. My hips pumping into her as her nails dig into my naked ass, her pelvis meeting mine thrust for thrust. The clap of our flesh reverberating off the walls.

"I hate you," she breathes.

"No. You don't."

"I hate you," she says again, shoving at my chest, so I'm kneeling. In a single swift motion, quicker than I would have expected, she rises with me, her chest instantly pressed to mine. My dick never leaves the tightening walls of her sweet cunt as she begins to ride me. Her body relentlessly rolling against mine. Only seconds of our new positioning before she throws her head back, exposing the column of her long neck. Thick curls bounce behind her, her casual bun coming half-loose. A single hand gripped behind my neck as her nails scrape along my flesh. The pain is the best mix to go with our pleasure.

My fingers dig into the ample flesh at her waist and hip, keeping her there with me. The grip so tight I'm not sure I'll ever be willing to let go. I need her body to stay flush against mine. Need her heat to radiate through me as if it's all I need for survival.

"Bryony Guthrie, you are mine."

There's no denying it. I need her. I need this delicious cunt wrapped around my dick. I need her moaning my name and playing our wicked games of daggers and rough sex.

I. Need. All. Of. Her.

She smirks, her eyes drifting closed for mere seconds, allowing me to forget that her eyes changed. "Only if I decide to keep you."

Her hips move faster, her continuous moans and noises, only she makes, filling the space. There's no doorway here, so anyone roaming the halls beyond will hear us. Let them. Let them know who makes her scream like this.

Too bad Graham isn't here to witness it. Maybe watching Bryony with another man might light a fire under his ass. Then again, it's fine if he doesn't. More for me.

"You will," I growl my palm flat on her back as I hold her close, filling her with my release. Her walls milk me dry, her orgasm only seconds behind mine.

"You will," I breathe again.

62

Bryony

You would think a magical school for wielders would operate differently than a human school or college, but it doesn't. We still have finals week before the Christmas holiday like everyone else, even though only a few of us acknowledge the holiday anymore by the time we mature.

Once we've passed the age of human schooling, we stop pretending as if Thanksgiving, Christmas, and New Year's mean anything to us. They don't. Celebrating those customary holidays is just part of the facade so we blend in during our most visible years. Most wielders will tell you by the time they turn eighteen their parents stopped decorating for the holidays. Stopped buying trees and presents. The human holidays forgotten as if they never existed.

Those that do still give any merit to the human holidays are either part human or have married one. Even then wielding rituals and tradition tend to dominate. Without a close connection to the human world, we don't bother celebrating. No more gifts given or joy-filled parties revolving around bringing the families together. We don't leave after our finals the way humans do.

Our holidays are the four Red Moon Festivals for dark wielders. Then celebrating the holiday for light wielders called New Sun. A shift in fresh energy and magic coming into the year, the way the Red Moon does for dark wielders.

I will not be traveling home to see my family. We decided, before I came here, that it would be safer to stay on campus, even if I had access to two of the people who could sign off on my leaving. Not to mention I am being battered with every lie I've been told my entire life, so I am not sure I want to see them to begin with. My mother is the hardest one to forgive in all of this.

As before, my spellcasting final will not take place with my classmates. The fear that I might actually kill someone this time is still alive in their minds. I have apologized to that girl countless times, but she still looks at me like she wants to shove me down the stairs for almost accidentally murdering her. Thankfully, it'll be the last final I take.

Today is my wielding final. One that Knox has practiced with me for countless hours. Our time spent in the cabin is the only place we can be alone; fortunately, that luxury remains secure for us. We'd gone extra early this morning I thought to practice, but we just ended up having sex, with him holding me afterward on the pull-out sofa bed. His fingers stroked my arm as he whispered a reminder that I knew how to control my essence. The leash I've learned to put it on is *mine* to control.

My responsibility.

My burden.

He did his best to reassure me that today would be fine. There would be no mistakes. Swore I wouldn't bring this place to the ground as his thumb stroked my cheek. His beautiful pine eyes locked with mine, filled with silent promises. He'd kept his tone light but firm. A final attempt at making me believe the words that came out of his mouth, but they did nothing to slow my racing heart or remove the clammy moisture from my palms.

Somehow, I think that messing around was his plan the whole time. It puts my body and essence more at ease after our sessions. Usually, it's itching to get back to him as soon as possible, but just giving ourselves to each other this morning left our insides sated. For the time being, at least.

As I enter my classroom, his touch still lingers. His deep voice ringing through my head. My consciousness does everything it can to hold on to it. To remember his words and believe them. Internalize them so that when it's my turn, I don't expose us.

Graham is already here, his body just sinking into the seat that he always occupies next to me. Yet he stands the moment he spots me. A hand comes to my arm as he places a quick kiss on my cheek. He's only given me the gesture a few times. The press of his lips so brief, it's as if he's burned or testing our touch.

In my mind, it's his way of warming himself up to me again. Of erasing the fear of knowing what I am.

A snicker sounds from behind me. A group of women from my hall, all staring my way. I can't make out their whispered words, but I hear Pierce's name. The rumor mill will be hard at work again. They always are each time they see me embrace another man who isn't Pierce. Like the entire student body is only on his side, waiting for me to mess up so they can have another reason to shun me. You would think the older we get the more we would grow out of this shit but we don't. Some never grow up. Some never learn to be kind. Some never learn to just let shit go.

"Everyone in your seats," Professor Pollin bellows.

The room quiets as the assistant places objects on the display table at the front of the room. Enough for each of us to receive our own for our demonstrations.

"Today, you will be handed an object at random. Each has stored foreign magic within. It is your task to properly channel it, control it, and then return it to the object. You will each be timed. You will have only five minutes."

I shift in my seat. That ghoul magic still swirls inside me, alongside Knox's and mine. A calm combination of rolling clouds as if telling me they will behave today.

In theory, this is simple.

In theory, we should all be able to channel or siphon even though innates don't need to.

In theory, we should all be able to control the small amount of power each of these objects holds. Whether that magic is from the light or dark, it shouldn't matter.

In theory, we should all be able to return that magic to the object it came from using the collars our essences have willed upon it.

I am not a theory. I am an experiment. I am a mixture of essences. My magic doesn't always respond predictably. The source of that foreign magic will dictate whether the combination of essence within me accepts it. I've seen what happens when it doesn't. I've seen what I can do when what's inside me rebels and I have no choice but to submit to it. To let it run its course or to allow Knox to save me.

Professor Pollin runs through the names. Dismissal only granted once we've had our turn. Graham is long gone by the time Pollin croaks my name, but the classroom is still half full. Plenty around to see my potential downfall. Or my success.

I let Knox's voice fill me again. Coach me into calm. I wish he were here. The sight of him is the security blanket I wish I had here in front of me. But I don't. He's not here. I am on my own and I need to keep my true self hidden.

Professor Pollin withdraws a slip of parchment from the carved wooden box on her desk. Slipping me the tiny sliver her lips purse into a crinkled tight line.

The Scepter of Anuk Shu Ra.

My eyes scan the table. There's only one scepter there. The very one I'd once seen Knox piecing back together. And for a moment, I wonder if this was planned. If a favor was called in, or if this is just a coincidence. Looking at it now, it is whole. No signs that it once lay in pieces. The jewels lying on his desk, missing their spots in the ornate, gold carved piece.

My arm trembles the moment I pick it up. The magic fights to get free while my essence sniffs it out to determine if it's what it wants to mix with. My body jerks forward. The beat of my essence behind my tightly pressed lips nearly impossible to keep contained. I have to control the release, or everyone will see the black smoke funnel from my mouth. They will know my secrets in an instant.

With a deep breath, I will my essence and the channeled power to calm. I promise our mixed essence that I will reunite with Knox in a few short hours. As if it were listening, it returns to a soft simmer. Finally soothing my inner turmoil, I release what is inside the scepter. A billowing light pink smoke exits in a seductive wave. The tendrils quickly forming sharp spikes.

I've never seen anything like it. Each spike points at me. A threatening quiver as they sit directly in front of my face. Still, I will myself to take another deep breath. Remind myself *I am* in control.

My head cocks to the side as I let my essence come to the surface. As I let it unfurl its way through me. My split focus is on the coloring as it escapes. I only gaze down for a second. A shimmering gray flowing from my fingers as it slithers up my body, forming a shield against the pink spurs pointing in my direction in threat. Yet it doesn't move to control it. This stare-down will either end in submission or disaster.

Yield.

The single word rings in my mind.

My essence begins to swirl around me and the deadly rose barbs pointed my way. The scepter is still firmly gripped in my hand, level with the tip of my nose, as its surface heats in my grip.

Yield.

The spikes begin to change, reaching out to lace into the swirl of my essence around us. The calm rotation becomes violent as it absorbs the foreign power. A power that I can now feel within me. It's old. Ancient. And it's angry. I blink several times, knowing the feeling I have now. My eyes are changing. To the white or black form, I'm not sure. The black only happened when I fucked Valen a few days ago in the lounge.

Calm.

A plea for my essence to quiet around me. The vortex quickens, the coloring shifting a few hues darker. I shut my eyes, my breathing quickening.

"Control it, Ms. Avalon," Professor Pollin calls in an insistent tone. But it's distant, as if her voice is distorted and I can't quite find it. "Control!" she demands.

Calm.

The voice in my head is more adamant this time, begging me to keep control.

"Everyone out," Professor Pollin bellows. I hear the shuffle of feet. The whispers are a deafening boom in my ears, with small gusts of wind as students race past me.

Just before the door closes, my palm opens to call back every bit of power and essence; all of it sucked back inside me within seconds. My body lurches as the final tendril snakes back into my finger. A tendril black as night.

The scepter clasped in my palm is suddenly ice cold. There's nothing left in it at all. I took it. All of it.

I turn to face Professor Pollin, her face alive with shock. Something like apprehension and fear shines behind her dark brown eyes.

"What have you done?"

63

Wynston

For what seems like the millionth time this year, Milgren has summoned me. This time to Pollin's class. My class left with an apprentice in charge, as I was told this was urgent.

I enter the room to find Bryony slouched in one of the student desks. Milgren and Pollin in the corner, whispering in panicked tones. Pollin's hands move with animation, as they do when she's worked up over some injustice.

With a sharp clearing of my throat, I announce myself, "Headmistress, you called for me."

I'm careful to lace confusion into my tone. The moment I saw Bryony sitting there I knew something bad had happened, but I can't let on that we have a connection. Publicly, people can only know that I am advising her at Headmistress Milgren's request.

"Wynston, do you recognize this?" Milgren questions.

She holds up the scepter I pieced back together what seems like a lifetime ago. The very one I had locked away in the archives. The usually restricted section, where artifacts like this one are meant to be kept. Subject to be looked at and never used. A mixture of glass cases and iron cages to keep the items locked away.

Even after I pieced it back together, that gold glow washing down its length once the last jewel was glued in place, I wasn't sure it was stable enough to hold the power it was meant to harness. A power of ancient times that allows a wielder to recreate any object into a vessel for channeling regardless of the ability to hold power or compatibility. That type of power is long gone. It was prevalent in ancient civilizations, such as Egypt and Persia, but never came to the Americas or Europe. The release of that destructive power was outlawed as it was deemed too dangerous for even the most good-intentioned to have access to.

"I reconstructed it at the beginning of the school year. Why is it here?"

Professor Pollin steps forward, her bottom lip pulled between her teeth. "It was part of the items set out to be used for the final today."

My chest seizes. The erratic beat of my heart skyrocketing in seconds. "How did that happen?" I breathe.

"And who pulled these items for you?" Milgren presses Pollin.

"My assistants." Pollin waves her hand as if they are still there, but the room is empty except for us four. "They retrieved them from the attendants that guard the artifacts the way they always do."

It could have been several people who snuck it in, but there are even fewer who have access to restricted archives. Why would someone pull this particular scepter out?

This object once belonged to an Egyptian pharaoh. A man who'd committed acts as vile as the forgotten God it's named after. Their works heinous enough that both have nearly been erased from history. That pharaoh's dark magic could bring down entire kingdoms should he have chosen to do so. That very scepter was his favorite trophy.

"Okay, I'm guessing this isn't the only reason I am here, though." I wait for the inevitable. For them to tell me what this has to do with Bryony.

"Correct, Mr. Knox." Milgren steps forward, her usual stern expression in place once more. "Professor Pollin instructed Bryony to control the magic that was channeled into this artifact. Then return it."

"Okay ..." I drawl as confusion knits my brow. It's a typical assignment in any wielding class. One that's tested over and over again with different types of foreign essence and your own throughout your schooling years.

"So, my first question for you is, where did you find the ancient magic to infuse into it?" Milgren questions.

A choked cough leaves me. Several blinks hoping I misheard the question she asked me. She can't possibly think I would risk putting foreign magic into an ancient artifact.

We have a whole team of professors here who specialize in that very task. That's not my expertise. I simply like to put old artifacts back together to clear my head.

"It was an empty vessel when I finished with it. Empty when I stored it, too."

"You are sure?" she presses.

"Positive." I am full-on panicking now. My body tight with tension. My essence wanting to wrap itself around Bryony. But I sense there's something different about her. There's something there that's not the mixture of us, or even just her or the ghoul.

"Do you know what type of power this can harness, Wynston?" Milgren's voice is softer. Motherly like. A probe gently searching for answers she thinks I am keeping from her.

"Yes. Why?"

"Because Bryony did not put it back." Her pause seems to last a lifetime. Deep down I know I don't want to hear what she says next. "Her essence absorbed it."

I stumble backward, ass hitting the desk right behind me. That can't be. Sure, it's a rare gift that some wielders have. But not at a level that would require someone to absorb power like that. To keep it.

"You're sure? The scepter is empty again?" Milgren tosses it to me. The metal is as cold as if it came from a freezer. A depleted vessel. Nothing is left behind.

"I watched it, Mr. Knox," Pollin clucks. Impatience fortifies her tone, intolerant of me questioning everything they are saying to me now. How can I not? None of this should be true. Shouldn't even be a topic of conversation.

Shit. This is the worst thing, but maybe now I understand better what has happened between Bryony and me. Why my essence is so insistent on filling her? Of slipping inside and staying with her.

"She's an Eistiab," I breathe. The words escape me in a huff of disbelief as I sink into a seat, hands running through my hair.

"I believe she is," Milgren sighs. "Professor Pollin, please reschedule the rest of your students for their finals. If you would allow us the privacy of using your classroom that would be appreciated." An uncomfortable grin pulls at the corner of her mouth.

It's clear Milgren nor Bryony knew. Did her parents know what they let loose in this school?

Pollin is quick to exit, taking one last look over her shoulder before shutting the door behind her.

Milgren keeps her back to us. Long minutes of her gaze focused on the front lawn of the campus beyond the large oval windows.

"What were you thinking?" she asks as she suddenly turns back to us.

At first, I think she's talking to me. My mouth opening and closing repeatedly, searching for any answer as to what I may have done other than fix an ancient relic.

Bryony clears her throat while shifting in her desk, making me realize she's the one Milgren is speaking to.

"I tried to keep it out. I told my essence to calm down so I could put the magic back, but it absorbed it, and then when I opened my palm to call my essence back, it retreated inside me with it."

It's a simple recap of what took place. Her gaze is downcast as she searches for something she missed. Something she did wrong.

"Have you done this before?" Milgren moves closer. The frustrated, yet motherly voice she'd used only moments ago softening at the edges. Bryony's shoulders instantly drop from around her ears.

"Yes." Her shoulders shrug, body curled forward as her forehead hits her forearms. I assume she is going to review what has been happening between us for months, but Milgren already knows that, so why ask again?

"Other than Knox and the ghoul?" she presses.

"Yes," she sighs again. The word mumbled, head still down.

"Who?"

It's then she looks up. "Harley and Valen." Her eyes are sad. Apologetic. "Maybe Pierce too."

None of this is her fault. I blame her parents for choosing to keep her but never helping her. Before me, I wonder who has ever really helped her. Has anyone ever taken just a moment to care for her?

I don't know how to respond. Maybe there isn't anything good to say in response to what is happening here. Maybe there isn't anything that could have prevented this. But I can't help but believe there might have been, as Bryony sits there with her shoulders hunched forward, disappointment in herself so potent I feel it inside me. Defeat keeps her chin tucked into her chest while her soft sniffles tear at my insides.

"Was it given willingly or taken?" Milgren's fingers press beneath Bryony's chin, lifting her gaze to meet hers.

Bryony sits quietly for a few minutes. Her back is straight but those shaking fingers coil around each other atop the desk. Still, she refuses to meet the headmistress's stare.

"Valen was—uh—well, we'll say it was in the heat of the moment."

Something tightens in my chest. I rub at it, but it doesn't fade. It's not like I don't know she's sleeping with more than just me. I've known about Pierson the whole time and I figured she'd continue to see Valen. He can pretend like she's nothing more than a task given by Jordden but I see the way he looks at her. I *hate* the way he looks at her.

I've heard of how he protects her from others but then shoves a dagger at her in the next breath. No one is allowed to threaten her but him. It's a fucked-up dynamic, but it's who the two of them are together.

"Pierson?" Milgren presses.

"Um, him I'm not sure of. I think maybe a bit of essence went up my nose in that first class with Knox," Bryony exhales. "But I don't know for sure. It was ..."

"And Harley?" I ask.

Her eyes find mine. "Taken." A single tear streams down her cheek. "I was nine and he was being an ass to me. All I wanted was for him to play with me. And he cast his essence to slam me against the wall. I remember the moment my back hit it. The bones cracking. I was so hurt, but for the first time, I was angry too. So angry that he couldn't just love me like the rest of my siblings. I remember uncurling my fists, my chest puffed out, and every bit of his essence absorbed into my skin. When he kicked me out of his room after that, it was by hand. Shoving me face-first into the hardwood floors outside his door." She recites the moment as if she's there, reliving it again.

New cracks threaten to shatter my heart. We all know there's no love lost between Harley and Bryony, but to hear of him purposely hurting a child hits differently. Violence burrows itself into me, and I want to tear him apart myself for hurting her. For continuing to hurt this brave and beautiful woman.

There's no stopping my feet as I come to her side, scooping her up out of her chair I plant my ass on the desk as I finagle her into my lap. Should I be acting like this in front of Milgren, like I'm in love with the hurting woman in front of me? *No*. But it doesn't stop me from cradling her to my chest or pressing a single kiss into her hair.

"Knox, it's okay." Her fingers sweep my hair back from my face.

I get that we are not creatures that the world loves and accepts but at the end of the day, Bryony is still his blood. They are still family, and she at least deserves his respect. He can keep his love. She's better off without it.

"Bryony, dear. I am going to need you to ensure that doesn't happen again. You can take from Knox and even ghouls if you choose, but no one else."

Her gaze stares off into the distance. Focused on nothing. Seeing nothing.

"Am I dangerous?" Her words are small. So unlike the firecracker of a woman I know. The one who bleeds snarky remarks.

"Yes." Milgren steps closer, her hand draped over Bryony's. "You are. Do you understand what an Eistiab can do?"

She shakes her head. Not many do. They're a type of wielder that's lost to ancient times and other continents. Many history books ignore them. Other texts write them out of history as extinct. Something we no longer need to learn about or to focus on, yet this woman is sitting here as one.

"Bryony, look at me," Milgren urges. She does. "Not only can you take someone's essence, their power, but you can store it. You could choose to give it back once mastered, but more importantly, you can become what those gifts are capable of producing."

My eyes close. I'd known this. Yet to hear Milgren state it so plainly brings down a mountain of impending doom on my head. It makes sense why she was always so greedy to have pieces of me and siphoned so much from the ghouls. I thought it was nothing other than a Grisym function. A side effect of what we are.

"Furthermore," she continues. "we do not know if a Grisym has ever held this gift. You are unchartered territory, my dear."

Her declaration is the final straw before Bryony's face floods with tears. Her sobs break me apart from the inside out.

And in an instant, I know.

She can't stay here.

We can't stay here.

64

Graham

Unexpectedly, Knox called us all down to the Vault. I'm the last to arrive. Pierson and Valen are reclined next to each other on the stone bench. Bri across from them, curled up in Knox's lap. Her eyes are a puffy, red mess. I'd tried to find her after the final, but it was hours before she resurfaced in her room. Headmistress Milgren had excused her from the rest of the day, and it took both Camilla and me begging her to eat before she'd finally nibble some pretzels.

I hadn't stayed long, Collin and I needed to work on a spellcasting project that's due in two days. So, when the text came in our group chat to meet down here, my heart did a flip. I couldn't pack up my things quickly enough. Nothing good could come of Knox insisting on an emergency meeting.

"What's going on?" I ask as I slip onto the stone closest to Bri and Knox. I may still be terrified of her, but she's the only one I wholeheartedly trust in this room.

"Jordden will be here shortly. We'll talk then," Valen responds in a flat, definite tone. His word meant to be law. Authority I am not to question. Bri might accept the guy, but I'd be perfectly fine with never having to stand in a room with him again. I can't simply forget how horribly he's treated her since we got here.

I nod, allowing myself to sit in the silence this room holds. The stones seemingly creak around us. That dank smell that always lingers just a bit stronger tonight. Each sconce that lines the perimeter of the wall dances with quivering flames that are both light and delicate, casting out our shadows against the walls and floors. There's no electricity down here, so this is all the light we ever get. It's desperately ominous if you ask me.

My focus shifts to the compact box Pierson holds in his lap. Its surface is a smooth, solid wood with an intricate metal design along the top exterior edge. His lips move at a quick pace, but his voice does not cast out from them. Only a moment passes before a pale blue haze escapes through the cracks as the lid pops open.

The cloud forms a small sphere, floating just atop the surface. The edges distorting as he runs his fingers over and around it. His lips never stop moving. Not until the sphere settles in front of Bri's face. Transparent fog morphs into rolling waves and the chirp of ocean birds fills the room. Some exotic place brought to life right before our eyes.

She smiles up at him. His little scene, a creation to make her feel better. And in an instant, I like the guy just a bit more.

Jordden saunters down the steps, interrupting her tiny morsel of happiness. A moment she'd only barely grasped. The image instantly evaporating into nothingness.

"I leave you kids alone for five minutes and you completely let everything unravel," Jordden grumbles as his feet land on the last step.

We all stare back at him. I honestly have no idea what he's talking about, but that seems the case with everything that happens around here as of late.

I'm never privy to the biggest secrets unless I happen to be there when they are coming out. Despite the trust I imagined existing between us, I'm not granted access to the same information that's available to the inner circle. Even though she chose me, I'm still in the dark. An outsider.

"Jordden," Bri pops out of Knox's lap. Her arms wrap around her father's neck, a sigh of relief breaking free. From the talks we've had, she's never spoken about him with genuine affection. So, to see this now is weird.

The way she holds him is as if he is the lifeline she has always needed. As if they've had a relationship all this time.

He sags into her, his arms looping around her back with a tight squeeze. His contented sigh bringing a content smile to her lips. "Tell me what's happened, sweetheart."

We all sit in silence as Bri rehashes the revelations of the past few days. Things I knew nothing about. More and more, I feel my best friend slipping away. Now I realize all the things she told me before were what she chose to tell me. A week ago, I was hurt by her not sharing all of her with me. But now, I understand why she keeps these things to herself.

It's not just for her, but for all of us. The more we know, the more we become accomplices to the things that may go wrong. To the pitchforks that will point her and Knox's and Jordden's way once those truths become known.

"Bryony, I have some things I should tell you," Jordden says. His hands cup hers in a way that traps her beside him. "Do you want them to stay?"

One by one, she makes eye contact with us. Her choice is not about whether she wants us to stay, but whether we want to. Only when she finds what she is looking for in each of us does she take a deep breath returning her focus to Jordden's face. With a single nod from her, he continues.

"I am the reason you matured early. I took what wasn't mine from a ghoul and gave it to you. Your body couldn't handle staying in an immature state as you were. I knew what you were then. An Eistiab, so I knew you could take the power. I'd hoped it would help level you out over time. Make your gift more," he pauses, "manageable. I wasn't sure what that would mean for you and ghoul interactions, but I did suspect you would have some sort of control over them. Hence what we've seen."

"Okay, that's not too much of a revelation," she eyes him. "Well, it is and isn't. Mom told me you're the reason I matured early, but she made it sound like you just wanted to experiment on me, so I could be like Vincent." She sniffs a loud, long sound.

"Roman, your mother, and even Janelle may treat you like an experiment, but my sweet girl, I have never, nor would I ever. Frankly, your mother is lucky I cannot live without her. I'd gut her for what she has allowed Roman to do to you."

"You can't mean that," she breathes.

"I do. But, Bryony, you may also not understand what all this means for you. You are quite unique in what you can do. More importantly, what that means for the essence coursing through your veins, as well as any other essences and gifts you've taken. Tell me has it ever felt like any of it has left you?"

"Only that moment," she hesitates. "The first time I—ya know— with an Azukeen."

It's almost cute that she reverts to being a little girl when talking about stuff like sex with a ghoul—something so normal among dark wielders. Something that no one even blinks an eyelash at. Yet here she is dancing around the act.

"Yes, I've been made aware that you're the reason the gates will no longer close. I had an inkling that this might happen. I am happy that I was right. It means that you are capable of so much more than we could have imagined."

She snatches her hands away from her father. Her features scrunching in frustration.

"Jordden, I am *not* a pawn."

"No, my dear. You are *my* daughter. Are you not?"

She nods. "I am, but this is a lot to process. This has been the craziest several months and I don't know what I'm doing or how much danger I am putting everyone in. My parents," his gaze darkens as she continues, "never explained any of this to me. They only told me I am a Grisym. That I am powerful, and I'm supposed to hide my dark side at any cost."

"Well, in that regard your mother told you to do one thing right. She doesn't know you are an Eistiab. I only figured it out after several instances she described to me of you snatching essences that weren't yours." He moves toward her again, taking her hands in his once more. "Fear not, Bryony. Soon you won't have to hide anymore. You are with me now."

Now I understand why Jordden asked if she wanted us to go. This moment is so intimate between a father and his lost daughter. A woman and the man she only recently found out is the other half responsible for her birth. It's not something we are supposed to be part of, but I am so grateful to be here. Grateful to see my best friend have this moment.

I take a casual look around the room at Knox, Pierce, and Valen, suddenly remembering I am not the only one witnessing this conversation. They each sit with stoic expressions. Nothing given away as they listen in. How can they be so calm right now?

Just as the thought flits through my mind, Knox opens his mouth to speak.

"She can't stay here, Jordden. That's why I called you." Jordden's gaze flicks over to Knox, making his back stiffen under the older man's heavy focus.

"And why not?" her father retorts.

"Her magic is unpredictable. You heard what happened today. You know there have been other times, both in and out of class, she hasn't been able to reel it back in and I wasn't there." For once, I don't think Knox is bragging about him being exactly what Bri needs. There's tenderness in his voice, sure, but more importantly, he cares for her well-being. Even for him, her safety has become priority.

"Did my daughter not pick you to protect her? Are you now telling me that you can't?"

Knox swallows, running his palms down his thighs before he responds, "I'm not saying I can't. I'm saying I can't properly do it *here;* with everyone watching."

"Because you are too cowardly to let others know of your relationship. Too scared to lose your position teaching here?"

My eyes go wide. I hadn't expected Jordden to lay into Knox. The only one of us that has ever truly been able to help her.

"You know the position I'm in," he swallows.

Jordden stands before barreling toward him. "And I know my daughter picked you to protect her. I trusted you to protect her. So can you do it, or not?"

Knox stands too. They are equal in height, causing the tips of their noses to nearly touch.

"Yes," he growls in Jordden's face, the sound vibrating off the walls.

"Then see that it's done. The next time we have this conversation, I won't be so understanding. You'll be nothing more than a forgotten memory. Have I made myself clear, Mr. Knox?"

Knox slips around Jordden, his body sliding behind Bri's as she just stands there, watching the entire exchange.

His essence seeps out of him, calling to hers as the smokey curls loop together. His lips are at her throat as both their eyes go white.

"Is this clear enough for you, Jordden?"

His words are the last thing I hear before the whole world turns to blaring sirens.

65

Bryony

IT TAKES ME A moment to shift out of the haze that being in Knox's embrace sometimes gives me. With simple touches, I remain clear, but the moment his essence caresses mine, my mind goes fuzzy. Our essences are always intent on becoming one. I wonder if that will ever happen or if it is something that our bodies will fight over for the rest of our lives.

I question if mine will always need to remain dominant within me.

"What is that?" Graham bolts to his feet. He clutches his bag to his chest as he spins in circles as if the old walls will give him the answers.

"Someone knows I'm here." My father brushes a thumb over my cheek. "I am only ever a call away. You have me inside you, too. Think of me. Call for me and I will be here, regardless of the consequences."

As if he were never there he disappears in a shimmer of black essence. *He can teleport.* My father teleports and my mother transports. *This is insane.* Two rare gifts coming together like this makes me wonder if my mother got the gift from him. If he gave her "more" the same way he did to me.

The five of us bolt up the stairs, emerging into the hallway that is teeming with students.

Some roll with laughter as they speed walk to the large windows that look out over the front lawn of the school. Others are frantic, sweat dripping down their brows. Their mouths gape wide open as they gasp for air, running in confused directions.

I don't know where to look or who to focus on as I try to figure out what is going on. Jordden seemed to think this has something to do with him, but why would they set off the alarms instead of just quietly retrieving him? Why draw so much attention?

The school is already under enough scrutiny. This has to be something else. A bigger threat than a single dark wielder.

"What's going on?" I yell at a girl who runs past us. She pauses for only a few seconds, eyes darting every which direction before storming off again.

"They're here!" someone else screams in the distance.

Knox grabs my hand and takes off. The five of us jog through the halls and down the main staircase, right out the main front doors. The warmth of the residence startlingly replaced with frigid cold. A shiver immediately runs through me. None of us with coats, gloves, or hats to combat the winter weather.

We'd been down in the Vault so long I hadn't even considered that the night had found us. Only the lights from the front pathway of the residence and the moon illuminate the grounds in front of us.

A horde of shadows stands strong at the gates. None of their forms are distinct from here. Just blackened outlines, chorused by growls and shouts that become muffled in the wind. But the tone is clear. They are here for revenge. The fury is palpable even from a distance.

"What the hell?" Pierce breathes.

"Come on," Knox tugs harder.

Still, I resist. Inching closer to the enraged people at the gate. Something tells me I need to see them up close. That if I do I might understand why they are here.

Knox tugs at my arm again, refusing to let me get any closer, but it's too late. I've already seen what I needed to. *This is bad.* With a final pull, we take off running. My legs have trouble keeping up with his long strides. His direction is clear as we angle toward the woods, away from the crowd gathering behind our gates. Their palms strike the iron, clanging loudly, drowning out our heavy breathing. Each beat making me internally jump with fear.

He suddenly stops, my front crashing into his back. The unexpected halt nearly causing me to topple backward only for Graham to catch me.

"What the hell Knox?" I groan, gasping for air. My body hinges forward at the waist, hands braced on my knees. The fight to suck in lungfuls of crisp, winter air is more challenging than it should be.

"You need to teleport us out of here," Knox demands. The panic in his tone is enough to draw me back to standing.

"What! I—" I look back at the three guys staring at me. Pierce is the only one with brows raised high.

"Do it. Now!" Knox barks.

I snatch his hand and then Graham's. Pierce urgently grabs Knox's and Valen's.

Eyes closed I will enough power to the surface to take us all to the cabin. It's the only safe place I know. The only haven I can think of outside of the school's main grounds.

Our beings split. Every tiny particle funneling through space to place us at the steps of the cabin.

I pray no one saw us. Hope that no one followed us. If they moved fast enough they could latch onto the trace that stays when you teleport. It only lingers for seconds, but that's all it takes for someone else to use it. To follow you to where you've gone. Valen's method of following us on occasion.

The moment my feet find familiar ground, I allow my eyes to peel open.

When all remains quiet around us, the tension finally releases from my coiled muscles. My breaths evening out to a natural pace. It's been too long for someone to have followed at this point.

"Where are we?" Pierce asks. His focus sifting through the darkness nestled between each tree trunk.

"Someplace safe. For now," I cough on a choked inhale.

As a group, we make our way inside. My ass is the first to sink onto the couch. Exhaustion works its way through me. So much has happened in four short months and I don't know how to process it all anymore. I don't know how to make it all make sense in my head because none of it makes sense. The things I thought I knew, I didn't. The abilities I thought I had are so much more devastating than I could have imagined.

Someone like me is bound to destroy everything.

If there are more Grisyms out there like me it's no wonder they want to kill us off. I am unpredictable and a danger to so many. And let's not forget my particular gift is one that is supposed to be long lost. My father stole from a ghoul, which now leaves me with the ability to command them, all while inadvertently keeping the Hell Gate open.

Fuck my life.

When did things get so out of hand?

I can't take much more of this. I can't keep running. Can't keep hiding. I won't.

Yet, it will only endanger the people I care about most if I reveal what I am. Unimaginable harm will knock at the doors of my parents and siblings. And ... my father. I have no idea what Jordden sacrificed for me, for his cause, but I saw what he lost as I looked into his eyes when he talked about my mother. The love he holds on to for her is what keeps him steady. Yet still, that love is somehow secondary to the love he has for Vincent and me.

In their hearts, they may have never parted, but they haven't been together for a long time. I still don't know the story there. The scenarios I've concocted in my head are far-fetched at best, but I hope that someday they'll tell me. I hope that someday everyone stops hiding shit from me and can just be honest from the jump. We could have prevented so much of this if they had been from the beginning.

I could have kept everyone safer.

I'd never questioned coming here, specifically. Never questioned attending a wielding school period, but now I wonder if we made the wrong choice. I've jeopardized the safety of so many just by being here. But I've also found my father and people I don't think I could live without. So truly, am I winning or losing here? Are *they* winning or losing?

"Bri?" Pierce slumps down next to me. "Are you okay?"

"Honest answer: no."

He nods, pulling me against his shoulder. My head rests there as I just breathe in his scent. A comforting aroma that allows me to relax, even if only for a moment.

"Who were all those people?" I ask, suddenly remembering we just broke out of campus even though we weren't supposed to be able to. At least the new wards were holding and, keeping them out. They could only be wielders, though. They could clearly see the school and knew we were there.

Any human who came across the gate would see nothing but an abandoned mansion falling into disarray from years of not being occupied. Those wards also alter what humans can hear, smell, or see. Any one of us could have been standing directly in front of them on the other side of the gate, singing at the top of our lungs and they would never know we were there.

That revelation doesn't erase the ghostly stares in their eyes. How blank and lifeless they seemed as we drew just close enough that I could make out some of their features. I can't put my finger on what was different about them, but they were not "normal."

"I honestly don't know," Knox groans, his hands running over the back of his neck.

"Dormants," Valen whistles.

Each of us looks his way. "They don't exist," I mutter, furrowing my brow, convinced he is confused.

"Bri, you're more ignorant than I would have ever thought," Valen replies with a snicker. A growl rumbles through Knox's chest in response. "Dormants do exist. They hate your father as much as they hate dark wielders."

"You have to be wrong," I breathe. If one more revelation comes out today, my head is going to explode, my finger massaging at my temples accomplishing next to nothing.

My essence rages within me, wanting to break free. So I let it. Let the vortex of dark waves run free of me, the glittering stars dimmer tonight. Even my magic is tired. Many wielders do have limits on how much use they can withstand in a short period. I don't know the depths of mine. Or if they even exist at all.

"I *am* right. They are the product of dark wielders siphoning magic that wasn't theirs to take in the first place."

"Don't sound so prideful about it," I sneer.

"Bryony, get off your fucking high horse. You think you're someone special. That you're not the result of this?"

"What are you talking about Val?" Pierce snaps.

"The same technique dark wielders have used to strip away a light wielder's gifts is what Jordden used to take essence from that ghoul and give to you," Valen shrugs.

"How could you know that?" I'm searching my mind as if I will somehow be able to come up with an answer as to how Valen would ever come up with that explanation.

"I don't for sure, but it makes sense. It's truthfully the only thing that makes any sense," Valen's voice low. The confidence he usually speaks with suddenly missing as he chews on his bottom lip.

"So why are they here, genius?" I cross my arms over my chest in petulant defiance. I hate that Valen is making me regress in how I feel about my father. A small step back toward believing Jordden is the bad guy in all of this.

"Hell if I know!" Valen snaps.

"I think I might have an idea," Graham announces. He turns his phone to face us. The news article zoomed in on the screen.

The daughter of the most notorious dark wielder this world has known has been confirmed to be a first-year student attending the Beauxgraton School of Wielding. It's not enough that he has a son of equally dark tendencies roaming the streets, bringing back to life those who deserve to rest in peace, but he now has an unknown daughter infiltrating what should be safe places for our children. It has not been confirmed who she is, only that she did, in fact, start as a first-year this September, an inside source states.

"She is wildly dangerous and unpredictable," a source says.

What has this world come to where we have allowed such dangerous wielders into our schools? Have we digressed so far down into the depths of hell that we will allow our children to sit beside such a person?

We can only hope the administration, including Headmistress Janelle Milgren, will be able to identify this individual and remove her from this prestigious and historical institution.

Light and dark wielders alike will appreciate removing magical folks like her and her father from having free reign around the world.

I shove his hand away from me, unable to stomach any more of the article. The fear it's spreading because of me isn't completely unfounded, but it still burns to see those words printed. Sadness consumes me knowing Jordden may have already seen it. The attention that will come to Beauxgraton because of it. It will make it impossible for Knox and me to continue to hide.

My breath hitches, not understanding how this happened. Only a handful of people know who my father is. I can't imagine a single one of them outing me. Not a chance they'd expose me to the world. But someone did.

An enemy is lurking close. Close enough to know our secrets and play this game of cat and mouse. They are toying with us. For what gain? I don't know, but I don't want to wait around to find out, either.

No one can be trusted. Anyone who would move against the people in this cabin is no friend. My mind drifts back to the punishment I promised to bestow upon Valen earlier this year. I never did get to deliver on that promise. It's no matter. I have a new enemy to destroy.

I'm suddenly consumed by thoughts so dark and overwhelming I can no longer sit. I trace an anxious pattern back and forth across the old floorboards. Adrenaline, or maybe something more dangerous, courses through my body. I can't sit still. Can't sit here and wait for us to be found or allow these guys to continue to treat me as if I'm seconds from shattering into a million pieces. I might be, but I won't let them see it.

Sucking my essence back within, I bolt out the door, sprinting out into the night.

Sprinting to nowhere in particular.

Running from everything and everyone.

A dark cloud of essence breaks free as I clear the cabin. My roar shattering the tranquility of the woods.

I scream and scream and scream, my feet never stopping their punishing pace. But it's not enough.

It will never be enough to outrun what I am.

66

Bryony

The crowd is gone by the time I return to school. The campus deathly silent. Even the outdoor poled lights simmer low for the night.

The hallways are just as empty as I shuffle to my room.

Just like the rest of campus, our room is empty, too. I assume Camilla is with her girlfriend. I've barely seen her lately. So wrapped up in the boys and my shit that I haven't been there for my friend. She has stood by me from day one and I haven't done the same.

The only reason I am even debating making amends is because I know she knows nothing about me, other than I sleep with multiple men. To her, I am nothing more than another first-year student who wields innate light magic.

I'm thankful I've been able to keep her out of this. That the Council will spare her any of the repercussions of what may come of my existence.

It's no surprise I lose the fight to change into my sleepwear before I collapse onto my bed.

My phone buzzes, Knox's name popping up on the screen.

"You're back," relief thick in his tone.

"Yeah." I am seconds from asking how he knows before I remember our growing connection. Since we first mixed our essences, we've always been able to sense each other. The more time we've spent together, the more the mixture alerts us to anything going on with the other.

"Where'd you go?" he asks, skepticism drawing out his words.

"Does it matter?"

"Bryony, don't pull this shit with me. I don't care what that article says."

"I just wandered around for a while. Go to bed, Wynston."

He goes silent before answering, likely analyzing what crawled up my ass, irritating me enough to call him by his first name. "I sent Graham to your room. Let him in when he gets there."

I end the call with a sigh, the hand still holding my phone, flopping out to my side. My eyes focus on the ceiling. The blank slate above me is something I wish I could have for myself.

Graham knocks several minutes later. No doubt he hears me groan as I heave myself from bed. Concern likely pulls at his handsome features, deepening the laugh lines around his mouth.

I expect him to be dressed to impress. His slacks and dress shirts and cashmere sweaters, only to find him in the same pajamas any of the rest of us would wear.

Flannel bottoms, thin t-shirt. One that shows off the mold of his frame. His hair sticks up at odd angles, telling me he'd at least been lying in bed, even if he wasn't asleep.

Letting him in, I allow him to settle on the edge of the bed. Knowing it is about to become a sleepover, I grab my night shorts and tank, shuffling into the bathroom to freshen up and change.

I don't have the energy to argue with him to return to his room. If I do, they'll all be here at my door, and I just can't handle it tonight.

Haunted eyes stare back at me as I splash cold water on my face. The sage green of my eyes holds my attention as I stare at my reflection. The color appears dimmed, just like my spirit. Just like my energy. It's a cumbersome shuffle through the motions, applying oil to my hair and brushing my teeth. My dirty clothes are left in a pile on the bathroom floor. A tomorrow problem.

He says nothing as I signal him into the bed. His arm extended straight as he holds the comforter high for me to climb in first before scooting in behind me. Immediate warmth drapes around me.

Besides hugs, this is the closest I've ever been to him. Through countless movie nights, I may have rested my head on his shoulder, or our thighs may have brushed, but he's never held me. We've never cuddled. These arms around me now are the exact comfort I need as emotions flood me. As I let those feelings consume me. Here in the dark, where no one can see my tears, I freely let them fall. The quiver of my hands or the uncertainty behind my eyes only witnessed by the dark.

"I've got you," he whispers. "You're my best friend and I've got you."

I snuggle in closer, my cheek on his chest. The beat of his heart contrary to the calmness of his words.

"Graham."

He hums in response. A low melodious sound.

"When did you stop fearing me?"

He pulls his head back as I tilt mine up. "I'm still terrified of you, Bri." His thumb strokes my cheek. "But you're important to me, and I know you would never intentionally hurt someone."

Our eyes stay locked for long moments. Both of us long since adjusted to the dark. I act before I can take it back, my lips pressing to his. There's no hesitation on his part as he kisses me back. Where his thumb once stroked my cheek, his hand now cups the side of my face.

"Bri, I—" he pauses.

"No, I'm sorry. I know it's not like that with us. I just—" *I wish.* "You were my safe place to land just now."

"Bri, I should tell you something." I stare into his eyes. His hand still curving around my cheek. "I—" he clears his throat, "I really like you and not in a just-friends kind of way."

This time when I kiss him, he's more eager. His body rolls on top of mine. My legs instantly falling open to allow him to sink against me. The length of him hardens as I tilt my pelvis against his, my sensitive flesh seeking the friction it needs.

I've kissed Graham twice. Both times with a tentativeness. We never explored each other. But we do now as his tongue slips across the seam of my lips, encouraging me to open for him, the mint of his breath invading me. His hips grind down as he groans into my mouth. "Bri."

One hand fists into the pillow next to my head while the other yanks down the neckline of my tank, exposing my naked breast to him. His mouth latches onto my nipple without hesitation. A swirl of his tongue, before he lightly tugs.

"Graham, I—"

"Should I stop?" he breathes, both hands now shrugging the tank down my body. The slight chill of the room further pebbling my hardening peaks.

"No," I breathe.

He smirks. One so reminiscent of Valen. Not what I would expect from Graham at all. His mouth travels down my soft belly, peppering me with soft kisses. A single hand gliding up the underside of my shorts, the gaping thigh width giving him easier access than the tight waistband.

"You're so wet, Bri."

I blink, unsure how to respond to the switch in Graham. He's an academic. He's refined and put together. So for him to say something like that to me throws me for a minute.

"Have you ever been wet for me before?" His mouth trails down my inner thigh, my back arching when he sucks at the skin along the crease between the limb and my pelvis.

"Yes," I breathe.

I won't admit that I found him attractive from day one. I've always thought he was handsome, but I needed a friend and I needed to be careful about my identity. Then everything started with Pierce, and it seemed a moot point.

A girl can just enjoy the view of her best friend, right?

"Good. That's very, very good."

Long fingers loop into the waistband of my shorts, pulling them down. My naked core now left exposed to him.

"Fuck, Bri. I've been dreaming about this. About you."

"You, what?" I pant, unsure if I heard him properly.

"Shh," he breathes over my swollen flesh. The tip of his tongue flicking up through my folds. Lips latching onto the bundle of nerves with a soft tug, pausing only long enough for the tip of his nose to press against me as he takes a loud, boundless inhale of my center. Then, he runs his nose along my arousal-drenched flesh before he chuckles, "Precious."

My hands are in his hair, further mussing it. The strands long enough for me to grip. The number one thing I love about all my men. Hair that I can pull on and play with.

"Graham," his name a labored groan on my lips.

His palm flattens on my lower belly, holding me in place as his finger enters me. That mischievous tongue of his following right behind.

Fuck me sideways.

Shock waves shoot through me, my essence breaking free as I stop fighting for control. The leash holding my true self abandoned. Allowing myself to satisfy the parts I kept dormant for so long.

"Mmm, my girl is close," he breathes against me. The ridges of his face rub against my wet, heated flesh. What the fuck! Why is that even hotter than his tongue inside me? Peering down, his face glistens, covered in me.

He's back inside me in moments. Fingers swiping and tongue licking along my slit. Teeth nipping at me in earnest. My orgasm builds. A violent torrent to match the vortex of my essence swirling above us. The onyx so dark there's no seeing through it.

My release hits me like a freight train. A bucking of my body counteracted by his forearm pushing me back down into the mattress. Relentless torment dished out by the man I thought would be a sweet, caring lover, keeping my body from coming down from its high. Slow, lazy roaming licks of his tongue over me, drawing more and more out of me. Every part of me entirely sated.

Tugging at his shirt, I pull him back up to me, my mouth crashing against his. The taste of me on his lips an intoxicating drug I know I'll need more of.

"Your turn." I use my hips to flip us, his pants gone in an instant as I sink my mouth onto his thick cock.

Everyone needs a best friend like this.

67

BRYONY

THE NEXT DAY COMES as if the previous never happened. Finals administered like none of last night's revelations nor the dormants even matter. Not a single word uttered by anyone remotely mentioning our unruly visitors. It's odd. Unnerving. An unease leaving my intestines in intricate twisted knots.

I'd woken tucked into Graham's side, the both of us naked. The endless pleasure we'd both taken and given to one another left us exhausted. That obnoxious buzz of a phone against a solid surface was the only thing that kept me from going back to sleep. My only defense against sinking further into his warmth. A smile pulled at the corners of my lips as contentment settled into my bones knowing that choosing Graham too had been right.

For as filthy as Graham spoke to me last night, he thought it best we didn't have sex. His insistence that we take this one step at a time tugged at my heartstrings. He assured me he's not threatened by my relationship with the others, but rather that he wanted ours to be just that. *Ours*.

It was Knox that woke me with a phone call. I'd been so out of it that I missed my alarm to meet him this morning. I'd left him waiting at the gate, much the same way he'd once left me. I feel like an ass, but he also understands that my body is attempting to acclimate to all that's going on within it.

There was nothing but relief in his tone when I croaked into the phone this morning. I imagine the lines of worry that must have creased his forehead were likely to permanently dent his skin. Not to mention he's already taken too many risks showing up in my room to do so again. I don't care that my father challenged him to throw caution to the wind with our relationship. I won't let him. Here at Beauxgraton, we have a modicum of protection. We need the dust to settle just a tad before being cast out into the real world.

There was no sneaking Graham out this morning as Camilla barged in. Her white-blonde hair a matted rat's nest atop her head as she fell face-first into bed.

"Good morning, you floozy," she'd groaned.

I laughed as I let myself fall back into bed for another hour. Deep, blissful rest claimed me.

As I enter my *History of Wielding* class, it's impossible to miss the eyes on me. I'm used to them gawking at me. But after that article, my insides prickle, wondering if maybe they know. If it was one of them that outed me. Yet no one says a thing, so maybe they don't. Maybe I'm imagining things. Or maybe there's a visible hickey on me or something. The mirror was not on my list of long-winded stops this morning.

I slump into my seat, ready for the only written final I have. I've been looking forward to this one. Nothing can go wrong during a written test. We're not allowed to use spelled writing materials during them, so it should be smooth sailing.

Graham enters a few minutes after me, his perfect image firmly back in place. So different from the man I woke up next to this morning. I wouldn't mind starting more of my mornings that way. My brown skin against his pale torso. It was perfect.

The bells chime and Professor Duster is nowhere to be found. The murmurs fly through the room as we all grow curious about where he is. He's always been early, so this is unusual. Each morning, he's seated in his desk chair, sipping piping hot coffee from a "Coffee First" mug.

It's fifteen minutes into class when Professor Tillerman enters the room, his briefcase slapping onto the desk. "I will be administering your exams today."

The room sits straighter, as if his authority is the most terrifying thing they've ever known. It might be. Apparently, he's ruthless to his classes. A professor I wouldn't have to cross paths with until my final year. Only now, I know I will see more of him. He's Jordden's right-hand man here at the school. Likely the eyes I'd almost convinced myself hadn't been on me the whole time.

"Unfortunately, Professor Duster failed to pull together what I thought was an acceptable exam, so I created a new one. Let's see how many of you actually paid attention."

With a wave of his hand, test packets flutter through the room. Each one landing on all of our desks at the same moment. "Begin."

He sinks into the chair behind the wood-carved monstrosity, his eyes trained directly on me, mouth pursed with an expression I can't quite place.

My nose scrunches as I read through each prompt. Obscure questions that play no real role in the majority of what we've studied. Chancing a glance in Graham's direction, his expression is a match for mine. A quick scan of the room reveals the same on the faces of my classmates.

Pens flip through fingers in concentration. An in-depth search through our minds for where this information was noted in the text or our lectures. An exam many of us are likely destined to fail.

I don't know what this shit is but there's no way I'm doing well on this exam.

Hunching forward, I try to work through the answers. I'm five pages into what must be a thirty-page packet when the classroom door bangs open.

Sobs reach me first, my gaze drifting up to find my mother and Dad with Janelle at their heels.

"Please, Roman," Mom whimpers. Her thin fingers reach out for him, but never quite touch his sleeve.

"Bryony, let's go," he roars.

"Roman, you are not permitted to be here," Professor Tillerman booms as he stands from his chair. He works the small plastic comb through his hair as every pair of eyes dart between the intruders and me.

If no one knew I was hiding things before, they do now. It's right there in the narrowing of their eyes and the press of their mouths into straight lines. Small smirks quirk on the faces of others who have never found me to their taste.

"Now, Bryony!"

"Roman, let's discuss this in my office," Janelle pleads, her hand reaching for his arm, only to pull it back.

"Discuss what? How you have failed to protect my daughter?" Dad booms.

I stay in my seat. I have no idea what's going on. I'm not sure I want to. Every eye is on me except my mother and Janelle and I can't take it.

"Roman," my mother sobs again.

"Bryony, I won't tell you again."

Gathering my things I make my way down the aisle, my partially finished test left on the desk.

I don't have to look back to know Graham is following me. My dad grabs me by the arm as he shoves me and Mom through the doorway before Janelle tells Graham to return to his seat. I can't look back as we nearly sprint down the hallway. But I know Graham didn't as Tillerman's shouts filter down the corridor behind us.

My dad drags me back to my room. His silence weighing heavily on me. The only reasonable explanation for this kind of out-of-character outburst is that fucking article.

Pulling my suitcases and trunk from my closet, Dad shoves my belongings into open bags. The only items purposely left undisturbed are my uniform pieces. His way of making it clear he has no intention of letting me return here.

I hate that I feel like I have no choice but to obey. Loathe that I still feel like my standing up to him now will somehow tarnish my family's name. A name that, in truth, isn't even mine to have.

"Dad, what is going on?" I keep my voice soft. I hope that maybe it will allow him to pause for a moment. To breathe and consider what news like this will do to us. To him.

"Bryony, get your things," his voice low. The tone a clear threat.

My mom continues to sob, her face in her hands as she slumps into my desk chair. Graham just stands there, the vibration of my phone indicating several texts coming through. It'll likely only be a matter of moments before the rest of them show up here. The group chat is something we put into place after the last time with the ghoul. A way for them all to keep tabs on me or quickly reach Knox as needed.

My dad grabs my arm again shoving me forward. Not once, ever in my life, has my dad been rough with me. He has never touched me with anything but care. He rarely ever even raised his voice. The man standing in front of me is now crazed. His world has become a frenzied panic. I don't know this man and I don't want to.

I shuck free of him, standing at Graham's side. My safe place.

"You tell me what you're so upset about and I might pack."

My dad whirls on me, something sinister in his sky-blue eyes. "You are not safe here. Clearly, I made a mistake allowing Janelle to watch after you." My jaw drops at his accusation. Janelle has been there for me this entire time. How dare he march in here pissed at those who have been helping me control and understand what I am. Something

I can't be mad at him or Mom for because they didn't know the most important truths about me.

"I am just as safe here as anywhere else."

"You are not!" he roars.

"I am!" I shout back.

"Tell that to all the newspaper articles running stories on you. Those vultures broadcasting the details of what you can do, of what you are." That last sentence almost comes out as if laced with disgust. I don't understand my dad's reaction to me. Dare I say, it's more like having Harley screaming in my face than the loving man who has always cared for me. "They haven't said your name yet, but do you think they won't figure it out? Your constant faux pas in class has made you quite visible here at the school."

I step forward, ready to retort, but I honestly don't have one. He's right.

But I am reluctant to just up and leave, set to stay locked up in our mansion forever. I can't go back into hiding the way I've always done.

"Dad," I keep my voice calm as I wrap my arms around his middle. "I need to stay here. Don't you think it's more important that we find out who is telling my secrets instead of causing the scene you just did?"

My mom finally looks up from her hands. Her face streaked with dark mascara. The brown of her skin appearing stained. Tainted. Skin splotchy for all to see.

"Bryony, I can't risk you being discovered."

"Dad, listen to me. That has always been a risk. From the day you guys kept me. We always knew there was a chance somewhere, someday, someone would figure out what I was. Sure, there's more at stake now that we know more about me, but this has always been the inevitable."

He drops his head. A heavy breath puffing out his chest, then sucking back in before he relaxes again.

"Look at me, Dad," his head rises slowly. "I am safer here. The wards here keep me safe and ..." I wonder if I should say the next bit as I chew on my bottom lip. "Should real trouble ever come for me, I have others I can call on. I believe they'll protect me." I refuse to name those others as ghouls. I know Jordden has communication with my parents, but I don't know if that's something he would tell them.

"Bryony, you don't know that."

"No, you're right. I don't ... But I have a feeling. I trust Janelle and Wynston, Valen, Pierson, and Graham." I gesture behind me as if they are all standing there. Their presence felt without them actually being here.

"Are you sure they can be trusted?" I nod, patting his cheek.

He drops to the edge of the bed.

"I'm sorry," his words come out choked, as if he is keeping himself from crying. "You were always my little girl. Even if you're not mine, not really."

I sit next to him, pulling him to my side. It's the first time he has ever truly admitted that I wasn't his. Something about it sits wrong in the pit of my stomach, but I let it go.

Another of those problems for "later."

Graham and I have an exam to get back to.

68

PIERSON

WORD TRAVELS QUICKLY THROUGH the halls of a boarding school. Where people normally whisper about rumors and he said she said, today they're speaking loud about it. Conversations of speculation at every corner, in every classroom.

Recaps of Roman and Geneva Avalon busting into Bri's final and yanking her out. Even more, question if I knew she was cheating on me with Graham since he followed her out. The people who saw him walk out with her and her parents seem convinced of it.

I have no time for the rumors. For hours, the five of us sat in her room before Camilla waltzed in while we were mid-conversation. And now she knows, too. All of our secrets, laid bare for yet another person to carry around with them.

Where Graham and I feared what Bri was, Camilla leans in with keen interest. She's asking every question under the sun, although it has no bearing on the importance of finding out who betrayed Bri. Because if they betrayed her, we're likely to be next.

It's a miracle the fucking Council hasn't shown up yet. They hold their decrees high as they search for the daughter of the man they deem to be a traitor. Fortunately, no one has mentioned Jordden's daughter being a Grisym. Those on the hunt are only looking for a dark wielder.

Just the same, the Council coming here would also bring in multiple divisions of the Wielding Bureau. Investigations carried out exposing more than they bargained for. If we can help it, we can't allow that to happen. At least Jordden seems to have a plan—one he won't give us the details of. Our video chat with him ended just minutes before Camilla showed up.

"So, what's the plan?" Camilla leans forward, genuine interest shining behind her eyes. The four of us guys lean our backs against the wall while Bri leans against the headboard, her legs stretched over the tops of ours.

"Cammie, I need you to stay out of this," Bri sighs. The plea in her voice nearly breaks my heart. She cares so much for her friends. It would kill her for anyone else to be in danger.

"No way! There's no way I'm missin' such a dangerous adventure." A gleam of mischief beams in Camilla's eyes. Eagerly shuffling her knees to the edge of her bed, she stares wide-eyed at the five of us.

I groan. This girl has no idea what she's trying to get herself into, and I hope Bri doesn't cave. It's bad enough she now knows Bri is a Grisym. There's too much at stake now to let someone else in. Not to mention Jordden might lose his shit if he has to be around a light wielder as perky as Camilla for an extended period.

"Cammie, please. I have enough people to worry about. You can't be one of them." That's enough to make the pixie of a woman slump back against her headboard, arms crossed.

"We need to be more careful," Knox chimes in. "Our sessions are being noticed amongst the staff."

Bri's hands tug at her bun, a loud sigh leaving her. This isn't something he's already told her. Just more cherries on top of this overcomplicated cake. I think I know Knox well enough to understand why he said nothing to keep her from worrying about it. He seems to do that a lot. Carry burdens for both of them so she doesn't have to.

"How?" Bri asks.

"I don't know. I heard it mentioned on my way here."

"Whoever is running their mouth is going to be on the other end of one of these daggers," Valen chimes in.

As if to prove a point a single dagger flies across the room with the swipe of two fingers. A small sprinkle of black smoke streaks through the air as it lodges into the opposite wall. The handle wobbling back and forth a few times before it stills.

"Please, don't throw knives in my room," Bri groans, her hands scrubbing against her face.

He's the closest to her face, and he leans in, tongue licking at the corner of her mouth before kissing it. "Do you prefer them at your throat?"

She throws him a wry grin, but there's no missing the glow behind her eyes. A pulse of her irises at the possibility.

"I will ask around. See who knows something," Val supplies. The dagger he'd thrown across the room wiggling free of the drywall, shooting backward to his hand, only to be twirled as he thinks.

"Well, what if we got away? The holiday break starts on Saturday. What if we went somewhere?" Bri suggests. "I'm sure I could talk Janelle into signing off on us leaving."

"And your dad?" Graham quirks a brow.

"I can figure it out," she mumbles, tucking her bottom lip between her teeth.

"Me, too! Right?" Camilla raises her hand, her little body perking up again.

I swear, if this girl doesn't let this go, Val is going to lose it. There's no way he could tolerate Camilla's upbeat personality on the daily.

"Well, I actually just meant us." Bri coughs. Her gaze pleading with Camilla to let this go.

"Well, fine then. Go off and have your group fornication for three weeks." Camilla's arms cross her chest again as she drives her tiny pointed chin in the air.

Graham coughs. Bri chuckles.

"Cammie, we're not having an orgy," I roll my eyes.

"Well, that's even less fun." Her eyes dart from me to Bri. "Missy, you have all those man parts, and you don't even use them all at once?"

Laughter bubbles out of all of us. This girl is a riot. Her lack of profanity or dirty language only makes it that much funnier.

I look down the line of us, I'm at the end, mindlessly massaging Bri's feet. Her mention of them throbbing prompted me into action. That run through the woods wrought havoc on her body, so I was all too happy to take it away.

We're an unlikely bunch, yet somehow, we all work together. We all work with her. I never thought I would be okay with sharing my girlfriend with another man, yet there's no one I would trust more with her than them.

"So where should we go?" Bri snuggles further into her pillows, eyes closing.

"I have a suggestion," Graham pipes up.

"Out with it," Val snaps.

"When I was twenty I found this abandoned house. The owners happened to be there. It had been their home once, but they left it after a murder. Said they didn't want to take care of it anymore. They asked if I wanted it. I didn't know what to say, but they handed me the keys and asked for my address. A week later, the papers came, and it was officially mine."

Only Graham would have some long-winded story about stumbling upon an abandoned place that's likely in shambles. A place covered in filth that I can't even imagine him entering with his designer clothing and million-dollar smile.

"That won't work," Knox says.

"Why not?" Graham questions.

"Don't you think if someone is looking for her, they won't look for us too? It's no secret who she associates with. Not to mention Valen and Pierson bear his name. His supporters are no secret, either. If they find out she is Jordden's daughter, then they will eventually be looking for his sympathizers, too."

Knox has a point, so we all sit in silence. The idea is not dead, just tabled.

"What about a foreign country? Kind of off the grid," I supply, clearing my throat.

"That's better, at least," Camilla snorts.

"Like where?" Val snorts.

"I don't know," I shrug.

"I'll call my dad," Bri yawns.

"No offense, sweetheart, but I don't think calling your daddy will be helpful here," Valen grunts.

"Why not?" Her yawn is wider and louder this time. I swear this woman is always exhausted. Sleep dragging her under quicker than she can fight it. Maybe I would be that worn, too, if I'd done nothing but hide and run for my life for twenty-five years. I've never had to pretend to be something I wasn't. I only chose to so I could pretend to fit in somewhere I never felt I belonged. "I'm sure Jordden has plenty of hiding places."

The room goes silent. Each of us holding our breath waiting for her to realize what she just said.

One eye cracks open as if she can sense us all staring at her. "What?" she quirks a brow.

"You called Jordden, Dad," I breathe.

Her eyes go wide before narrowing as if trying to roll back the moment. Trying to recall if that's what she actually said in her sleepy state. She's always so careful to only refer to him by name aloud. It makes me wonder how long that transition has been taking place in her head.

"Anyway," she continues. "We can ask him," she yawns loudly again, her eyes darting away from Camilla's shocked stare.

Bri curls onto her side, tucking her hands under her cheek. Valen maneuvering behind her and Knox shifting to press in front of her. Graham and I left with everyone else's legs draped across our thighs, knees, and shins.

"I guess that's lights out then, huh?" Camilla chirps.

She's quick to turn out the lights. The breathing of every person in the room evening out in minutes, except mine.

I sit awake, my fingers rubbing at my girl's calf.

Every moment since I first met Bri plays through my mind. Every word, every look, every touch. So much has changed. So much has come to light.

I am different now and I know deep down it's because of the woman breathing heavily next to me. Just like Knox helped bring her into her own, she did the same for me. A kindness I can never repay. Gratitude I can never accurately show her.

I allow myself to obsess over the mess we've fallen into. Until now I never questioned what being involved with someone like Jordden would mean for me. I blindly followed Valen because he assured me of our safety. And now, I know I've bitten off more than I can chew. But there's no turning back. Not with Bri involved.

Wherever she goes, whatever she does I know I'll follow.

She is my home now.

69

Bryony

I WAKE SURROUNDED BY way too much body heat. Not only had all of them stayed, but each one is curled around me in some way.

I know this isn't normal. Four men at once. None of them fighting over me. Each accepting what I've chosen for myself.

Knox has his face in my chest, while Valen's chin digs into the side of my neck. His light snores tickling me with each rumble.

I almost don't remember falling asleep—our plan to get away stalled. A plan that won't do us any good if the wielding world knows who they are looking for. I'm already too recognizable. So is Valen to an extent.

It takes far more energy and prowess than should be necessary to uncoil my body from all of theirs. I'm surprised none of them wake as I slip into sweatpants, a hoodie, and boots, edging out the door. Valen releasing a high-pitched snore as it clicks shut, but none of them follow, as I stand there, holding my breath, hand cradling the handle.

I haven't spent a lot of time alone lately. Someone is always around to witness the shit that has been going wrong in my life. There always seems to be a shoulder to cry on or a body to lose myself in. I miss the time I used to have alone.

With all three of my siblings grown and my parents living as influential workaholics, I'm used to having a lot of time to just sit in the quiet. To dream of a life that I hoped to have someday. Or work through the countless fears that have taunted me ever since I understood what I am and what that means for my future.

Those same scenarios I obsessed over in my younger years fill my head now. The possibilities I had always hoped for, but knew they would never be my destiny. Whips of wind spiral powdery flakes through the air as I make my way to the lake, doing little to distract me from those thoughts. Even the pristine fresh layer of snow that lines the ground can't hold my attention with its beauty. The lake is my last option to clear my head; it's the only place of solitude I've found here.

The surface of the lake is a frozen mass, the way I expected it to be. Ridges of solid, white-capped miniature waves texturize the surface with moments captured in time. It reminds me of the illusion Pierce made for me the other night. The memories of chirping seagulls make me smile now. The cerulean blue waters creating heavy splashing waves right before my eyes. I've seen similar illusions created all my life, but none were as beautiful as the one he created specifically for me. It's a fond memory I won't soon forget.

A beach vacation is definitely in order after the year I've had so far. No matter if anyone joins me, I'll be digging my toes into the sand come June. Assuming I live that long.

"Ms. Avalon, I hadn't expected to find you out here."

I turn to find Tillerman behind me. A long thick wool coat, not of this time, drapes over his body. His hair is a picture of perfection. Cheeks and the tip of his nose ruddy from the cold.

"Why's that?"

"It's not safe for you to be alone."

A chill runs down my spine. Tiny pinpricks that drive the urge to roll my shoulders, as my only way to erase the lead boulder sitting uncomfortably at the base of my belly. But I hold still, features structured in such a way that his presence seems like nothing more than an annoyance, instead of allowing him to see the alarm bells ringing inside me.

Tillerman has done nothing to make me question his trust. Yet, there's something behind the clear, crystal-blue eyes that's a warning. A blaring red siren buzzing directly in front of me.

Janelle's supposedly dead father. She's supposed to be dead, too. But here they both are, living and breathing. Carrying on with their lives and no one has given any thought as to how. Not to mention they never changed their names—well, Janelle didn't. How did no one catch that?

"How did you fake your deaths?" I probe.

"Who said mine was faked?" He steps closer, hands in the pockets of his knee-length coat. The flaps at the bottom part as they billow in the wind.

"Right ..." The single word drawn out as I take a step back. "I'm going to finish my walk. It was nice seeing you."

Everything within me tells me to run. Tells me to call the boys or for my dad. Milgren or Tillerman—whatever the *fuck* his name is—sets me on edge. His piercing stare leaves my skin crawling and my heart racing. Every twitch of his brow makes me feel like he's learned another secret about me. Each secret stored away in an arsenal he will use to bring about my destruction at some unknown point in time.

"Ms. Guthrie." My father's last name on Tillerman's lips stops me cold. A frigid tingle that sets my nerves on edge is now a full-blown anxiety attack in the making. No one has so openly used that name with me. No one has mentioned who my father is when we're not behind closed doors. Hearing him do so now has my hackles thrown high. "I would advise that you stick close to those whom you trust. Someone is clearly out to get you and Jordden."

He tips his head as if he's going to go, but he doesn't move. He just stands there, watching me. A single tilt of his head into one last nod before he turns away from me. No last words. No goodbye.

The entire encounter has me more on edge than any other moment since arriving here at Beauxgraton. My insides scream not to trust him, but my logic reminds me my father does. So maybe, for now, I can too.

I will myself not to run. Not to show panic as I all but jog for the tree line at the opposite end of the lake. Thankfully, my phone was already in hand, so if he's watching me, it won't look like I pulled it out in response to him.

Opening our group chat, I shoot off a text to the guys.

Me: ***What if it was Johnathan?***
Wynston: ***Where are you?***
Me: ***Lake***
Wynston: ***You could have woken one of us up***
Me: ***Wanted time alone***
Valen: ***You don't get to be alone anymore***

Me: ***Fuck off, Valen***
Wynston: ***I'm coming to you***
Me: ***Ok***

Tucking my phone back in my pocket, I lean against a tree trunk.

Less than ten minutes pass before all four are stalking toward me. I do my best not to roll my eyes as three of the four hit me with unforgiving glares. The fury of angry bulls burning bright behind each of their unique-colored irises. Pierce is the only one who doesn't look pissed. Instead, he appears heartbroken, as if he thought he lost his puppy.

"Save the lecture. I'm not in the mood." Palm up and head turned to the side before I get another lashing in less than twenty-four hours.

"We're just glad you're okay," Pierce mutters as he steps forward, wrapping me in a tight hug. I swear if this boy was any sweeter, I'd have nothing but cavities.

"What did Tillerman say?" Valen asks. His usual nonchalance on display as he leans against the tree next to me.

"Just that I shouldn't be out here alone. That it's not safe, blah blah. Stick with the people I trust. It's not what he said though, it's how he said it. There's something off about him."

"Nah, he's harmless," Valen insists.

I want to brush it off, but I can't, so I tuck it away. Something to analyze later if I'm lying awake staring at the ceiling.

Knox gives him an "or else" look, and I struggle to hide my chuckle behind my nearly frozen lips.

I hate that it's unclear who I can fully trust and who I can't. I hate how much the men in front of me are still holding back secrets. That there are things all of them aren't saying. Whether it's for my protection or their own, it doesn't matter.

"Look, I need full transparency from all of you, or this isn't going to work."

"And what is 'this' exactly?" Graham circles his arm, indicating our group of five.

"You're my guys. Simple."

"Yeah, okay." He nods a few times but doesn't seem appeased with the answer.

"We've told you everything we know so far." Pierce steps forward, taking my face in his hands as his eyes search mine. As if questioning if I believe him. I want to, but the pit at the base of my stomach tells me not to. Not entirely.

"Look, we better head inside and grab some breakfast. We have two more days of finals. It's probably best we don't flunk out," I say as I grab Pierce's hand, linking our fingers together. My other arm looping around Graham's middle.

Knox's gaze darkens. I never wanted to believe we were anything more than the experiment everyone thought of us as. A way to explore what Grisyms can do together, and for him to help me learn to control the storm that constantly rages inside me. I've never been able to convince myself of anything else, despite the countless times he's told me there's more to us. Then tiny moments like this happen, and I don't know how I don't believe in him. In *us*.

Somewhere along the way, he became the one person I could trust with all of me. The good. The bad. The ugly and the undesirable. People laugh at the dumbasses that fall for their teachers, knowing full well it's not going to happen, but I became one. And I barely even noticed.

At first, the sex, cuddles, and talks may have been nothing but an obligation to him. An order given to him. But that's different now. He means a lot more to me. A tiny voice nudges me to stop pretending the same might not be true for him. Something I need to accept and keep in mind.

I train my eyes on him, hoping to catch him sneaking a glance my way. But his gaze is cast downward as he looks away from me, tangled with two other men—a third at my back. Maybe I can believe I mean more to him, too.

I want so badly to wrap my arms around him. To press my mouth to his in reassurance, but we're still out in the open. I can't.

The moment we cross through the back entrance to the residence, Knox splits off. Hands in his pockets, he doesn't say a word with his departure. Doesn't even look back. Not once. Only a few students catch his retreating form, none of them double-taking as he parts from our group. Their imaginations are likely not drifting past the assumption that the four of us were caught doing something we shouldn't have been, and Knox was simply reprimanding us for it.

I keep myself linked with Graham and Pierce as we enter the dining hall. Loud chatter reverberates off the walls as silverware clinks off plates, and trays thunk onto the spell-powered conveyor belt. All is normal. The same as it has been since the day I got here.

The hall looks no different than it always has, yet it feels different. It's in the way that people's eyes scan us. The way they take an extra step back as we enter.

I'd expected Valen and Pierce to lead us to the table with their friends. Kaia and Kormoran's grimaces making me want to dig my heels into the stone floors rather than go any closer to them, but the men veer left toward my friends. Collin, Whitney, Frankie, Camilla, Mailee, and all the others who always line our obnoxiously long table watch us approach. Each silent as Valen sits on the bench next to Collin, dragging me down onto his lap.

His lips brush the shell of my ear as he whispers to me, "Tell Pierce what you want to eat."

My insides heat. Suddenly, food is the last thing on my mind as his erection bulges under my ass. The shift of my weight drawing out the vibration of his groan against my spine.

"Move again and you're not going to like what our classmates get to watch," Valen's breath brushes across my neck as he speaks.

"Graham, you know what I like," I cough just as Valen's fingers get a little too close to the apex of my thighs.

Pierce and Graham stalk off grabbing trays and multiple plates.

Valen's teeth graze the lobe of my ear. "I said, stop moving." His grip on my upper thigh tightening to the point of pain. My panties growing damp in response.

"Bite me."

"With pleasure," he snickers before his teeth sink into the flesh of my throat. My yelp drawing more attention than we already had.

"Damn girl," Whitney fans herself.

"I thought you were dating Pierson," Collin quips shoveling a fork full of pancakes into his mouth. The gaping hole wide open as he chews. *Gross.*

"Pecket, mind your business," Valen warns. His arms shift me again. This time sliding me onto the bench next to him, his body a barrier between Collin and me.

It's not long before Graham and Pierce return with trays piled high. Enough for all four of us. More than I think my churning stomach can take.

The conversation flows as it always has. Barbed jokes and sarcasm are in ample supply as we consume our mounds of breakfast. I would have never expected Valen to blend with us. Never imagined he'd want to share space with anyone other than his crew, but it is as if he's always been one of us. As if we've always known one another.

This feels normal.

A normal that I know won't last.

70

Wynston

I slump into my desk chair, running my hands over my face. Finals weeks are always draining. The number of students who haven't mastered the manipulation of their essence is mind-blowing. The countless hours we spent on them were either wasted or lost in a ball of nerves.

With first years, I get it. Many of the students have just reached their maturity, some within just a few months before classes start. Many don't have parents with the right expertise to help teach them control. I know I must work harder with those students. Mold them into what they should be based on their talents. Help them discover their gifts, whether they are innate, charters, or extrinsic. It takes so much out of me some days, but the first years are my favorites.

Memories of when I first matured flood my mind. I was so scared during my first year attending The Kellerman Institute, in the northwest corner of the country. My dad and stepmom couldn't handle me. My dad clueless as to what type of power I would hold as a Grisym. As far as I know, he never told my stepmom what I am. They shipped me off to school early, because my gifts ran wild at the most inopportune times. I was the problem they didn't hesitate to rid themselves of.

One professor there, Tomas Opperman, took me under his wing. It took my first two years, but he taught me to control it. I think he always suspected what I was, but he never said anything. He simply taught me what I needed with the patience of a saint.

He's the reason I wanted to teach. My desire to pay it forward still steadfast to this day. What he did for me became the driving force behind doing well in my studies. I remained determined to keep my head down and my nose in a book. There were many late nights of practicing every spell known to man, simply to ensure it conjured the way it should in front of my classmates. I spent my evenings, late into the night, in his office; often long after he'd retired for the evening. I need to bestow that same hope on those young wielders coming behind me. I also thought an institution might be a great place to hide. He's the one who introduced me to Milgren. I hadn't even been in my interview with her for five minutes, a fresh graduate from Kellerman, and she'd hired me.

Thinking back now, I recall her words.

"You are special Mr. Knox. You will be safe here."

How had I not realized then that she knew exactly what I was? I was so blinded by gaining such a prestigious position with impractical ease that I never even considered how transparent of a being I was. The way I've always been.

It's well after dinnertime, and my mind drifts to Bri, wondering what she's doing. We've both been so worn down this week that we haven't had a single session. My body misses hers. My essence craves her. Sleeping next to her last night wasn't nearly enough.

At this point, I'm not sure I give a fuck who knows about us. Let the education board fire me. Let them kick her out. Our safety as Grisyms is so much more important than the political bullshit.

I love my job. I love what I do, but I love being alive more. It would be even better to live without having to look over my shoulder. Although I'm not sure that's something I'll ever be able to stop doing. Unless the world decides to accept us, it will always be this way.

My phone buzzes on my desk. Our group chat lighting up.

Bryony: ***Headed to the library***
Bryony: ***None of you need to ride in on white horses to save me***
Graham: ***Sure you don't want company?***
Bryony: ***Nope. Hoping the place is empty***
Me: ***Text if you need me***

Usually, I don't contribute much to the chat, but Bri insisted I join it. Just in case any of us ever needed each other. From what I've determined, we men don't need each other, but we all need her. All for our unique reasons. Whether good or bad, that's to be determined.

More than anything, I pay attention to Valen. I don't believe just because he's sleeping with her now that he won't endanger her. I see the way he twirls daggers in front of her face for sport. An act I was hoping would dwindle the closer he and Bri became. Alas, it won't surprise me if one day he actually stabs her with one if she says the wrong thing.

Leaning back in my chair, I let my eyes drift shut, hands resting atop my stomach.

It's the few minutes of peace I'll get tonight.

While the students hunker down, practicing and studying for their finals, the staff parties in Beechum. Loud music and laughter blaring down every hallway. They will consume enough booze to drown an elephant tonight. I've always hated the tradition. Only when Fiona and I were hot and heavy did I ever attend, because she would drag me into our various apartments. Each one filled with different groups of us, either drinking away every memory, dancing on tables, or bitching about whichever student has them wound up.

It's not my scene. I'm a quiet guy. Give me a book, my couch, and a beer and I'm happy. Bonus if there's a sports game on. A pastime my parents never allowed me to participate in for fear of what I might do to the other kids. Maybe that's a product of always having to hide myself, or maybe it's truly just who I am. I honestly don't know.

My body finally begins to relax when a jolt shocks my insides. My essence thundering to life. It only does this when I am near Bri, or when something is happening to her. My heart races as I get to my feet, darting down the hall.

I let my essence guide me. A black coil of smoke floating above the floor as I run like my life depends on it. She said she was going to the library, but I have no idea which one. That tendril weaves faster and faster as if racing to get to her. To save her.

Just as it slithers under the main library doors, I shove both open, a palm to the edge of each door with a grunt.

The place is empty. Even the librarians are nowhere to be found. Likely at Beechum partying already, figuring if the students aren't ready for their last finals tomorrow, they simply won't be. It's sound logic, especially since the majority of the testing here doesn't require reading a ton of literature the night before, and no spellcasting is allowed in any of the libraries for fear of accidentally destroying the many tomes.

I'm peering down every row of books, my breathing rapid. My focus solely on trying to find her. My essence has long since slunk off somewhere. The time it took me to push open the doors proved to be enough for it to sneak off.

I stop when I finally find her in the middle of one of the stacks. There's a book open in her hands as a ghost of a smile curves at the corners of her lips.

She's fine. Safe. So why did that hammering response happen? Why did my essence call out for her?

"Bri?"

She turns suddenly, her brow dropping. Concern pulls the corners of her mouth down. The clap of the book closing does nothing to calm my racing heart.

"Knox? What's wrong? What happened?" She reaches me in seconds. The metal of the ring she wears on her pointer finger cool against my cheek as her palm rests there.

"I—I felt something, and I thought you—"

Her brow scrunches for a brief moment. "I'm okay." She reaches as if she's going to hug me, then pulls back. Her eyes jerkily scanning the room for anyone else.

I should be doing the same, but I don't care anymore. Let them see us. I want her and she wants me, so fuck every consequence that comes with my mouth slamming into hers.

The book falls at our feet, her hands looping around my neck as she pulls me closer. Our height difference curving my body down over hers. My hands brace against the shelf on either side of her head as her back settles flush against it. The solid surface balancing us. Only then do I touch her. The rounded curves of her ass fill my palms before I allow my hands to rove over her body. My strength enough to easily hoist her into the air, those thick thighs looped tightly around my waist.

"Knox. We can't. Not here."

I ignore her. My mouth crashing back into hers. Any protest effectively silenced.

Our essences surround us. That light gray shielding us from view. Its way of agreeing to this coupling right here and now.

"I don't care," I groan against her mouth. "You. Are. Mine."

She nods, tugging at the hair at the nape of my neck, sucking my bottom lip into her mouth with a grin. It makes my knees go weak, the two of us tumbling to the ground with a laugh. *This is better*, I think as I undo the button on her jeans, shoving them down her full thighs.

I've always loved touching her. I love the way her body curves out, unapologetically taking up the space she deserves. Her hips roll against mine, gaze drifting up to my face as she scoots down my body. Lifting my collared shirt and sweater out of the band of my slacks her tongue flicks along the dense line of hair that starts under my belly button and travels down to my pelvis. Her lithe fingers deftly unbuckling my belt before sliding the zipper down, freeing my dick for her pleasure.

The tip of her tongue runs along the underside of my shaft, causing my head to slam back into the hardwood floors beneath us. A long, wet stroke as she swirls around the tip before sucking me into her mouth. Her cheeks hollow out as my hand finds its way into her loose hair. A soft tug at her roots drawing out her grin around my length. I love it when she wears it down and allows it to curl the way it's meant to.

She's gorgeous with it straight, but like this, it's like she's completely naked for me.

I'm lost in the sensation of her swallowing me deep into the back of her throat. The combination of her hand and mouth drawing me closer to the edge. One I'm happy to tumble over with her for the rest of my days.

Yanking her by the arms, I pull her up my body. "I'd prefer not to get caught with my pants down."

She grins as she climbs off me, lying face down on the floor, her legs spread just wide enough for me to slip into her. Our magic goes wild as I thrust home. Our bodies moving at a frantic pace. She does nothing to quiet her noises. *Fuck,* her favorite word in the English language.

I drive into her, my chest coming down to meet her back, our fingers twining at the side of her head. Her squeeze so tight she may break them, but I don't care. The gyration of my hips into her drives her wild, my name the only one on her lips tonight.

"I'm gonna come," she moans, licking her lips. I can barely reach, but I capture her mouth with mine. Our combined tastes unforgettable on my tongue.

"Not yet."

She nods, a pained expression on her face as she closes her eyes. That familiar white flashes up at me when they reopen. Mine adopting the same change, as my essence streams out of my mouth into hers our orgasms become pronounced roars of passions drowning out the silence of the empty library.

Always together. Always a team.

"Think anyone heard us?" she pants.

"I hope so. They should know who you belong to."

71

Bryony

WITH FINALS DONE, I am ready to relax. A movie night equipped with endless pizza, ice cream, and beer is the exact type we all need. It didn't take long for word to spread that Camilla and I would be hosting yet another epic movie night in our room. Classmates classified as friends and those who are nothing more than acquaintances confirmed their attendance, no invitation needed. Our room is always open to everyone.

I try to be excited about it, but Knox won't be here. Despite us fucking in the middle of the library yesterday, where anyone could have found us, I convinced him nothing like that should happen again. We already have too much attention on us as a pair. I am a walking billboard for "What the hell will happen next?" No need to tempt the devil with our forbidden sex life.

I've only just showered and changed when our friends begin to file in. Camilla is already three sheets to the wind. The poor girl never sipped alcohol until she came here, and she doesn't know how to handle her booze well. Her girlfriend slips into bed next to her, the two of them seconds away from making a porno right in front of us.

"Knock it off, you two," Collin mumbles as he drops onto Camilla's bed, effectively splitting them up. We all knew Collin had a thing for Camilla so it was difficult not to feel for him when he ended up disappointed he wasn't her type.

He seems completely over it as he begins recounting some ridiculous story that leaves us all rolling our eyes. Comfortable conversation and laughter fill the room as we wait for the rest of our attendees. One by one, they trickle in. The noise level growing exponentially with each new face. Bean bag chairs, pillows, and blankets litter the floor, but my boys line my bed.

"Okay, let's get this Scream-A-Thon going!" My voice deepens to sound like those announcers at a sporting event as we all cackle with laughter. Valen pinching my ass, making me yelp in response. His wink drawing a deep flush up my cheeks.

I'm pressing play on my phone when a knock comes at the door. Camilla's slurred speech reciting a spell to have it open on its own. The words come out just clear enough between hiccups for the door to creak an inch away from the doorframe.

Sean and Damian enter, each with their pillows in hand.

"Why are you here?" I ask. It comes out nastier than I expected, but other than Damian, none of them have even tried to pretend they tolerate me. Kaia and Kormoran likely want to kill me as much as Valen wanted to, but Sean almost acted as if I didn't exist at all. Damian makes an effort to speak to me more often now, but the conversation is usually so mundane I'm sure the things I've said to strangers in passing are more interesting at times.

"We invited ourselves," Damian huffs, snagging a spot on the floor at the far edge of my bed while Sean picks the opposite side of the room next to Whitney. A small giggle escapes her as he settles in close, his arm wrapping around her shoulders.

Well, I'll be damned. I did not see that one coming.

I make it through the first three Scream movies before I pass out. Movie five halfway over when I finally groan and stretch awake.

I'm surprised no one has left. Nearly everyone is awake except Camilla and Frankie. That one isn't a surprise. Frankie always passes out first and poor Camilla had three shots while applying lotion after her shower alone. Who knows what she consumed while in Mailee's room.

"You okay?" Graham whispers.

At some point, the boys changed positions. My legs still cross Valen's but I've got Graham against the headboard on one side and then Pierce on the other, his finger mindlessly twirling one of my stray curls.

All at once, our phones start buzzing. Each of us yanking them from our pockets or the spots on the floor next to us.

"What the hell?" Damian grunts, standing from his spot to tear open the blackout curtains. We all follow, both sets thrown wide open as the glow hits us.

What should be that bluish-gray moon shining bright above the treetops is quickly shifting from soft pink to deep crimson.

It's another two months before the next Red Moon. There are only a few cases ever documented in history where it turned out of cycle. Those instances were nights of bloodshed and turmoil. My insides turn cold as I watch the last sliver of gray go through its transition to red. The glowing orb a pulsating mass in the sky. Sunken dark craters visible as the sphere seems to shift closer by the second.

"This isn't supposed to be happening," Whitney whimpers. Sean pulls her to his side, placing a kiss on her temple. Her face instantly burrows into his chest, hands fisting his shirt.

For a moment, I ignore what it means for this unpredicted Red Moon to appear. I look at the couples around the room, including myself. The world worried that merging light students with dark could be disastrous. That we would tear each other apart. And yet, here I see nothing but mixed couples and friends. Just wielders coming together and giving themselves to one another without thinking about what color essence lives inside them.

For the first time, it gives me hope that maybe someday my kind might become acceptable to the rest of the wielding world. That this merging of wielders at a base level may bring about the rise of Grisyms. Just as Jordden wants.

"Does this mean the ghouls will be released?" a voice comes from behind me. My focus was distracted enough I'm not sure who asked the question.

I'm snapped back to the present. I'd nearly forgotten that the gate never closed. If the ghouls wanted to, they could enter at any moment. All because of my supposed link to the Azukeen.

"I don't know," I breathe, doing my best to hide information I'm not willing to share.

Pierce's grip on my waist tightens. "I texted Knox," he whispers. The slight jerk of my head enough of an acknowledgment.

"I think we should hunker down in our rooms," Collin's quivering voice sounds through the room. The pitch is higher than normal as his nerves get the best of him. He should be nervous. We all should be.

"I think we should stick together," Whitney counters.

"No, he's right," I add. "We should get back to our rooms. Just until we know what's going on."

I just need them all out of here when Knox shows up. Camilla can stay, but I bet she'll go with her girlfriend. An outcome better for us all.

Everyone hugs as they make their way out into the hallway. Their whispered words carrying through the doorway until Camilla closes the door behind her. My roomie the last to leave with an unfocused, but pointed glare over her shoulder.

Me: ***Coast should be clear in ten***

Wynston: ***Got it***

He waits twenty minutes before knocking, wedging himself between the barely wide enough space to accommodate the girth of his body.

"Have you talked to Janelle?" I ask.

Knox shakes his head. "I tried calling her—repeatedly—but there's no answer. The majority of the staff are making their way out to the pit to see if any ghouls show up."

"Something tells me that's a horrible idea," I mumble.

"I agree, but what are we supposed to do?"

I turn away from them all, chewing my bottom lip between my teeth, finger cupped around the bottom of my chin as I think.

There are no good choices here. No real answers. At least not ones I know of.

"What about Jordden?" I suggest, spinning back to face them.

My gaze falls on Valen. He's always been the primary point of contact.

"Nothing," he confirms.

Fuck, why does shit suddenly seem to be hitting the fan, and none of the elders I can trust seem to be around?

Pulling my phone from the nightstand, I make the last call I would ever want to make. I'm still upset about how he acted, but I have no other options.

He answers on the first ring. "Bryony!" My name is a roared growl, a manner my dad has never taken with me. "What the fuck have you done?"

The phone is on speaker, and I sense the guys freeze behind me. The heat of them closing in at my back. Sweat rivulets beginning to soak into the fabric of my shirt.

"What are you talking about?"

"You and that dark magic you hold did this, didn't you? You can control ghouls and so you brought the Red Moon early," he snarls.

"How do you know that?" I gasp. I'd never told him. But maybe Janelle did.

"Your *father* answers to me. I know every dirty thing about you," each word spit with venom. "You. Did. This!"

I'd known there was some sort of contact between Roman, Geneva, and Jordden, but not to the point they shared such detailed information about me. Especially the things that could mean more trouble for all of us. Part of me is disappointed Jordden didn't keep those secrets just between us.

Just the same I can't believe what Dad is insinuating. I would never purposely put any of us in danger. "Are you listening to yourself? How would I even know how to do that?" I retort.

"I should have listened to your brother years ago. You're not meant to be part of this world." His voice is maniacal and harsh as it blares over the speaker. "But don't worry, it'll all be over soon."

The line dies as my dad hangs up on me. I'm at a loss for words. It feels as though Roman Avalon ripped my heart from my chest. He has always loved me, just the way I am. So, to hear him speak to me that way hurts. My heart in shattered pieces scattered across the floor.

With a single, deep inhale, I throw my shoulders back, straightening my spine.

"Get whatever you guys need from your rooms. Meet me at the back entrance of the residence. We're on our own."

"And what is it we plan to do?" Graham questions.

"I honestly don't know because I don't understand what's happening."

There are too many moving parts here for me to understand what is happening. I pace my room for several minutes after they've all gone attempting to put any of my thoughts into a configuration that helps bring us some clarity. Only Knox remains. The silence welcomed as I think.

From what I know, even the strongest wielders that use earth magic can't do things like change the moon. Terrain sure, but this is different.

My insides twist and turn, the pit at the bottom of my stomach telling me something big is coming tonight. That everything I thought was bad is about to get so much worse.

Our group gathers at our meeting spot within ten minutes. Valen with a bandolier of knives strapped across his body and cargo pants covered in more pockets and straps than I've ever seen. Shining ebony daggers fill every free space. His favorite, onyx and silver, sitting at the center of his chest.

Pierce only has a coat.

Graham, with only a backpack, the edges jutting outward in sharp points.

The campus is silent as we creep out into the night. The moon casts an eerie glow over us. A glow that was always beautiful to me now causing my insides to churn with anxiety.

"We should check the pit first," Knox suggests.

I nod. It had been my first thought too, so without another, I lead us directly to it.

It's empty when we arrive. The curved posture of tension I'd moved with since we stepped foot outdoors loosens. The pit holds no one. Not a single wielder or ghoul. The ground undisturbed as if no one had ever been here at all.

It seems odd that the campus is so quiet. Even Beechum sits dark and silent in the distance. Only the glow of hallway lights from the residence greets us through the hundreds of windows that grace every floor and exterior-facing room.

Changing course, I head for the spot where I first met Jordden. The small clearing is just as I last saw it, only the ground is a bit softer. Mud sucks at the bottom of my boots from the recently melted snow. But it too seems undisturbed.

I close my eyes and think of my father. He told me that's all I would ever have to do to call on him. That the bond of our blood would be enough for him to feel me. To hear me.

I focus.

There's nothing.

No answer.

No sense of him.

Just silence.

72

VALEN

IT SHOULD BE GIDDY anticipation that fills me, but it's uncertainty that finds me instead. Tonight should have been the night that Jordden's ultimate plan came into play. The changing of the moon was the signal for it, but something isn't right. His people aren't here. His followers, meant to be stationed around campus, are nowhere in sight.

The plan only changed slightly with Bryony coming here. The priority, should all hell break loose, is to protect her.

I eye Pierce. We left him out of what was supposed to come next. He's just as confused as the rest of them.

It will be near impossible for me to find Damian, my partner in this, for what needs to be done next. There will be no explaining why I need to find him specifically. But I believe he can handle the next phase alone.

It's better that we found none of the professors out there in the pit. This pseudo Red Moon was planned to bring the ghouls back to this side of the plane. Only Jordden, Damian, Tillerman, and I know that the illusion cast as part of this Red Moon is meant to incite them. To drag on the anger and untapped rage of the ghouls. Any dark wielders out there looking to siphon would likely die without the protection of the power that comes with an *actual* Red Moon. It's the source of energy that keeps the ghouls from losing themselves.

There's a reason Milgren picked the ward builder she did. Edina returned the next day, adjusting the spells she'd cast with her two assistants so that when tonight came, the moon would appear to shift. The normal hue it carries, hidden beneath a façade.

Yet, it may have been fine. Having Bryony, there would have been a quick fix for all that. Her ability to control the ghouls should be enough to keep them from attacking. At least that's what we believe in theory. Technically, we've only seen her with that single Azukeen. But that was enough for Jordden to believe she can control them all.

If we're lucky, every staff member and student will stay locked behind their bedroom doors. Jordden's followers won't hesitate to dispatch of anyone who impedes the ghouls surfacing. It only occurs to me now that Jordden never explained the purpose of the ghouls—not in its entirety. Without the Red Moon energy, it's dangerous to approach them. It's a potential hazard to siphon magic from them, which is what I would assume we would use them for.

I laugh to myself. I always thought I knew every detail of what was meant to happen here, but I didn't. I'm just another pawn in a bigger picture that only Jordden has the final print of.

As we reenter the residence, we head down to the Vault. *My suggestion*. The safest place that came to mind while we wait for our leader. While our plans unfold around us.

Kaia, Kormoran, Damian, and Sean are already there. The four of them in attire matching mine.

Propping myself up against the far wall, I listen for any sounds coming from the cavern that runs alongside the Vault. The space is enormous enough to fit hundreds comfortably.

It was a small blessing Bryony didn't want us around last night. Her insistence on time alone served me well. It gave me time to sneak off with Damian, allowing Jordden's followers entrance. Each one funneled into that underground cavern to wait for tonight.

All I had to do today was wait for the panic to set in. Having everyone in Bryony's room to see the moon change like that only made it better. So many witnessing it happen as one was enough for that fear to uncontrollably spread. Many are likely making phone calls to family out of confusion. Others posting photos on wielder social media channels.

It will only be a matter of time before the Council has to step out of the safety of their homes and offices to address the world falling apart. They couldn't explain school closures. They sure as hell can't explain this early Red Moon. As Jordden said, "*Creating chaos will make them realize they are not in control the way they think they are. The world will see that. The world will change with that knowledge.*"

"It's done," Sean murmurs.

Bryony goes stiff at my side.

"What is?" Her eyes are wide as she backs up until her back hits a chest. Her gasp is audible as she turns to find Jordden. His body having just formed into its corporeal form after teleporting—or rather his version of it. Technically, Jordden was born with the gift of a transporter. It took years of him coupling spells with his transport abilities to accomplish moving his body over short distances the way he can an object. I've asked how he did it, but Jordden isn't the type to reveal secrets that set him apart from the norm.

"It's time." He runs a thumb over her cheek as he locks eyes with us.

"Someone better tell me what the hell is going on, right fucking now!" Her finger points at her father, then me, then Pierce, her expression changing to heartbreak as their eyes meet. He reaches for her, but she steps back.

"Sweetheart, it's time for you to rise."

I expect another freakout, but she simply stares at Jordden like he's the most breathtaking piece of art she's ever seen.

"How?" her voice low, in question.

"Chaos, my dear. We are revealing the weaknesses of those who think they are above us. A new world order is in store."

I finally let the grin spread across my face.

The years of dark wielders being looked down on are finally about to change. Time for the light to bend to our will. To accept us. To accept *all* of us.

"Why come here to do it?" she asks.

"Because the only gate that sits open is here. You are here," he coos with one last stroke of her cheek. "Now," he addresses us all. "You know your roles in what must happen here. It's only a matter of time before they see what they should."

"Cut the shit, Jordden. What happens to her?" Kaia throws a nod in Bryony's direction.

Jordden looks back at his daughter as if contemplating the question.

"What do you mean?"

"Does she get to die with them?" Kaia snarls, teeth bared. She's been waiting for the moment to choke the life from light wielders that refuse to embrace us, that refuse to bend to the world Jordden wants to create. Not to mention, there's extra animosity toward Bryony for stealing Pierce's and mine's attention.

I almost berate her when I remember the conversation Kaia and I had weeks ago. She'd heard Jordden call Bryony his daughter, but refused to accept it. To Kaia, she is nothing more than a filthy light wielder, with the last name Avalon tied to her. No matter what Jordden says, Bryony will only ever be seen as her enemy.

Kaia doesn't want to believe what Bryony is, and I should be able to forgive her for that because I didn't want to either, at first. I should be able to let the comment slide, but I can't. Rage barrels through my chest. I've never been a possessive man, but Bryony sets me on edge. She is mine. No one threatens her but me.

I charge forward, my favorite dagger drifting up into my hand before the point digs into the flesh just above Kaia's heart. "You touch her, and I will kill you, very, very slowly."

Kormoran throws every threat at me as he's held back, by whom I don't know. Nor do I care. I'll kill him too. If the twins won't fall in line, they are nothing more than a liability to me. And dispensable.

No one is going to threaten Bryony.

I will fillet anyone who even remotely thinks about it.

"Enough," Jordden roars. "Kaia, I can assure you that should you suggest something like that again, I will enjoy watching Valen tear you apart."

She shoves me away. "I followed you because you told me the dark would reign. You told me we would rid the world of light wielders!" Kaia screams. Her outrage fills the room. A heavy blanket of smoke choking the life out of it.

Kaia's body quivers with unfettered fury. Jordden's simple declaration in favor of his daughter destroying every wish she ever had. Death to light wielders was never part of anyone's plan; unless it was necessary. But we let her believe and cling to what would keep her a faithful supporter of the cause.

"That is not what I told you. That's what you wanted to hear." Jordden steps forward, his approach threatening as he stalks her down. She retreats until her back hits the stone wall again. "You are so focused on hating the light wielders that you can't see we need them. I have no intention of murdering anyone—so long as they don't get in my way. There has been enough of that."

"You. Promised," she snarls.

"I promised a new and better world where no one would have to hide. You interpreted that how you chose to."

"If not the dark, then who?" Sean finally steps forward. I can't believe the little genius hasn't figured it out yet.

I knew the moment I found out what Bryony was, and that she was Jordden's daughter. Those truths revealed this had nothing to do with the dark versus the light. He wants a blended world.

Jordden moves to the center of the room. His eyes focused on Bri and Knox. The two of them side by side like royalty overlooking their subjects.

"The Grisym, of course," I announce as a wide grin spreads across my face.

73

GRAHAM

I CAN'T BELIEVE WHAT I'm hearing.

But at the same time, I do.

Jordden has made it no secret how much he values Bri and what she is.

Why wouldn't he want his daughter to live in a world where she doesn't have to hide? But that's not all he's suggesting. He wants them to be at the top of the food chain. A superior species to the rest of us. At least that's what I think I'm hearing.

I will always put Bri on a pedestal, but announcing something like this will send the world into an uproar.

It will destroy the balance. But as I sit here and ponder the world we live in, I can't say that there *is* a balance. The light wielders are revered. Its light wielders that sit on the Council. The same individuals that set our laws and dictate how every wielder lives. There is no balance in that. It shows that our society favors one above the other. I just never saw it because I sit on the favored side.

When school is done, I will have the best opportunities. My name is one they will speak about with praise versus a dark wielder who might hold the same or similar job. My children will be shining lights in the world, while the dark ones get brainwashed into becoming the villains we've turned them into.

Realizing all this now, I want to stand behind what Jordden is fighting for. What he has always been fighting for, despite the world calling him a demon that is filled with nothing but evil intent. But his radical nature might also destroy everything I hold dear.

I might lose my best friend because of it. The woman I love.

"You will all stand with me." His eyes track to Kaia, Kormoran, Pierson, Valen, Sean, and then Bri. When his eyes meet Knox's and then mine, it's clear he doesn't mean to include us.

Bri steps forward. "Then I want to bear your name."

Her father's eyes glisten. His pride shining through at her declaration. At first, something like panic finds its way into my chest. If Bri does this, there will be no turning back from that decision. But the love that shines behind her father's eyes has me stepping forward, too. I intend to ask for the same. To beg for it if Jordden says no because there's no world I will exist in where I don't stand by my best friend's side. With two quick steps, I come up beside her. "Me too."

He nods, drawing his essence out of him. "Where?" is all he asks.

Rolling my shirt sleeve up, I present my forearm.

Jordden meets my eye one final time, confirming this is what I want. A single nod before his gaze returns to my exposed flesh.

A burn runs over my skin. As if a fiery brand is being dragged over it. The cursive loops are elegant. Refined. Something I would have never picked for myself, but somehow, fit perfectly. My skin flares bright red as he finishes the N. His lips moving in quick succession before the essence that had carved into me absorbs into my skin.

I feel it moving, ingraining itself within my very being. In seconds, it becomes a permanent part of me.

"You now bear my name. You are now one of us." I nod, blinking back the tears of pain. *I did this for her*, I remind myself.

Knox steps forward, holding up his shirt, turning to the side, and quickly running a finger down his rib cage. Another sliver of essence breaks free, pressing against his golden skin. His are strong letters. Their appearance is plain to an outsider, but in my opinion, speaks to the simplicity of the man. The quietness that he would prefer to live in. "Fuck," he barks as the essence absorbs.

Bri rests her hand on my forearm as she steps forward. Her sweatshirt is torn over her head, revealing the scoop neck tank beneath. Cleavage, exposed, stealing both mine and Valen's attention.

"Over my heart," she says, her chin rising just a little higher.

She winces with a hiss as the essence carves her father's name into her chest. Her fists clenching at her sides, trembling with the effort of enduring the tattoo of her father's name. Fat tears coat her irises in a glassy sheen. Unshed tears, she refuses to let fall, pooling. I want to reach out and take hold of her hand, but I don't. Bri is strong on her own. She doesn't need mine.

My. Girl. Is. Strong.

Where all of our tattoos are nothing more than his name, hers has an extra symbol. What appears to be a star or depiction of the sun just below it. Each pointed edge is sharp but appears as if it sinks into her smooth skin. Like prongs digging into her flesh, embedding themselves into her. They'll forever be there. Always a part of her.

"You are my family," he says as his tendril seeps into her skin, her chest pulling upward as if being yanked by an invisible cord. When she releases her breath, her essence flows out. A lazy swirl of black as Knox's follows suit.

I've learned this is their thing. Every time she touches foreign magic, their essences need to relearn each other.

"What the fuck?" Kormoran breathes behind us in unison with Sean's audible gasp. I can only imagine they hadn't taken the time to think about what it means for Bri to be Jordden's daughter until now. That they hadn't been privy to witnessing what I've now seen so many times. For them, this may be the first time seeing Grisyms interact. I can only hope the display is enough for them to recognize they can't fuck with her.

The way she and Knox combine has always made me wildly uncomfortable. An intimate moment that should be just for them. He shifts directly in front of her, the tendrils of their smokey essence dancing between their open mouths. The two drawing so close their mouths brush. Knox's closes first, Bri swallowing the last of what flows between them.

The room goes silent as Jordden watches. His arms quickly wrapping around his daughter, cradling her against his chest. There's a gleam in his steel eyes just before they press shut for a few brief seconds. The quickness with which they burst back open making me flinch back several steps.

"Ahh, right on time. Our guests are here."

Guests?

There's no need for conversation as we make our way out of the Vault. A line of mixed wielders stalking out into the hallways as a united front. Following Jordden's lead, we head toward the main stairwell in silence. Our footsteps thunderous claps through the empty halls. Something tells me tonight is going to be so much more than we bargained for. When the sun rises in the morning, everything will be different.

It's already different. The searing pain in my forearm is a reminder of that. If tonight goes to hell, Bri might not come back here tomorrow. And though I am still somewhat scared of her, I'm not sure I am ready for that goodbye. But I've decided. If she has to run, then I'm going with her—at least for a few days. An adventure I've had no time to prepare for.

Something tells me whatever we may encounter tonight could destroy Beauxgraton as a safe haven for Bri. Jordden won't let her stay here if she's not protected. That much I know for sure. I can't stand the thought of her needing to go into hiding elsewhere. Can't stand the possibility that she will have to hide again at all.

A mental list of everything I wish I had ready to go on the run bullets in my head. The research I've been collecting still sits in my room, tucked away in the bottom of my drawer so my roommate wouldn't find it, comes to mind first. Scrawled notes floating through my mind on an endless loop. Many of the words reviewed so many times I've memorized them. The information may be helpful. That is probability enough to encourage me to grab it now.

"I'll meet you guys out there. I need to grab something from my room," I call, already backing away from the group in the opposite direction.

Valen scoffs, not even pausing to see if I was still following or had already turned away. I don't know that we'll ever get along, but would it kill him to be a little kinder to me because of Bri?

Probably.

Yes, definitely.

"Don't take long," Bri waves over her shoulder.

Back to them, I take off as quickly as I can. Darting through hallways and bounding up the stairs two at a time toward the men's wing, with a newfound purpose. One that curves the corner of my mouth into the slightest grin.

74

Wynston

We're vigilant as we make our way through the halls of Beauxgraton. My side still burns. The tendrils of my essence flicking at it every so often. Abrupt touches, as if testing if that magical ink may stay. Bri's essence grabs hold of mine within my chest, tearing mine away from her father's. A silent promise that it will be okay. An assurance that his essence is safe to hold on to.

It's eerie how quiet things are. I would have expected more students out and about. Yet, they don't need to leave their rooms to see the Red Moon above. Each likely huddled in their beds, unsure of what something like this means. It's likely we only have a few scant hours before parents arrive, demanding answers that none of us have or can give.

It will be a madhouse of confusion and worry we as a staff won't be able to quell.

I've never heard of anything like this being possible. There shouldn't be a wielder out there that can change the moon. Many of us hold unmatched power in certain areas, but nothing like this.

I search my mind for some old text I've forgotten. Maybe something I overlooked. Nothing comes to mind. Not a single inkling or morsel of information to cling to that explains this phenomenon.

This isn't normal.

Janelle comes racing down the hall. Her hair, normally twisted at the back of her head in a chignon, loose at her shoulders. Pin straight strands swinging freely with her every movement. Matching silk pajamas cling to her thin frame. I can only assume she has been sleeping in her office again. She'd done so for weeks before the light wielders arrived instead of traveling back to her off-campus residence each night. "Endless preparations," she'd said, but knowing what I do now, maybe it was the unknown of all we're experiencing these past few months.

"I have been looking for you." She grabs hold of my arms but immediately lets go, as if burned. Her eyes drift down to her reddened palms, the pads of her fingers rubbing together in wonder.

My new essence combination angrily shocked her, just for daring to touch me. The slight tingle I still felt from Jordden's mark is now a raging inferno.

Milgren slowly raises her gaze, a delayed reaction in noticing everyone else around her. Her eyes slowly track to Jordden while nervously rubbing her hands together. Another attempt at alleviating the sting from her moment of contact with my body.

"How did you get in here?" she asks, taking a small step back from Jordden.

Isn't she supposed to know he was coming here tonight? I thought for sure Milgren held a role in Jordden's plan, if for no other reason than her relationship with Bri. Then again, are any of us really in the know regarding the intricate design of Jordden's grand plan?

He chuckles darkly. "Janelle, you continue to underestimate me."

"Clearly." She clears her throat, turning to face us all. "We have a problem. Someone has told the Council about Bryony. They are on their way."

She doesn't have to say the next part. They'll be bringing executioners with them. Those that can strip wielder gifts before inducing permanent death, such spells exclusive to a small group of light wielders that live in Italy. A similar technique to what Jordden used to create dormants used for their practice.

"Janelle, the plan was always to bring the Council here. You know this." Jordden's voice is calm. His expression blank as he recites his words. "You need not worry."

"Jordden, they know about *our* girl!" Janelle snaps, her face twisted with the agony of the meaning behind her words. Bri may not be her blood, but she loves her as if she is. Janelle—just like the rest of us—would give her life to protect Bri. And I know that fierce, impulsive woman would do the same for us without a second thought.

"Mine!" he barks. A reminder that Milgren is to know her place when she speaks to him or about his daughter.

After receiving Jordden's letter, I thought for sure Milgren had an intricate role in his plans. Why wouldn't she? Milgren is here. She has protected us. She is a Grisym too, as is her father. As is Jordden. I let myself be so blinded that I've missed so many obvious things.

There's no time to linger on everything I should have known. Our focus needs to be on protecting Bri. The Council is coming. With executioners. Their advance too quick to not have been pre-warned.

I catch her eyes, searching them. Wondering if the Council knows about me, too.

"They are only coming for Bryony." Milgren angles to face Bri, a sad smile cresting her thin mouth. "You shouldn't be here when they arrive," Janelle urges. A quiver to her tone I'm not sure I've ever witnessed.

"Janelle, I am not one to run. Should they choose to murder *my* daughter, it will be through me." The emphasis on his words is another reminder that Bri is his to love, protect, and call his own. Not Milgren.

Her mouth opens and closes several times as she searches for a way to fix this.

"Who told them?" Bri moves forward as she takes hold of Milgren's hands, waiting for the answer.

"I wish I could tell you. There are plenty who have learned about you. A handful more have always known. Who knows who may have caught the wrong glimpse of you while you were here and figured it out?"

Bri's lips press into a straight line. Her hands shaking Milgren's once, then twice before letting go. There's nothing to say.

Someone made sure the Council knew there was a newly matured Grisym here. Jordden's daughter. This means if they didn't know before, they will piece together that Vincent is one too.

"Jordden, we can protect Bryony. You should go to Vincent," Milgren tries to dissuade Jordden from staying once more.

"He is protected," he waves her off, turning to continue down the main staircase as if the conversation never happened. "Not that the demon needs any protecting at all." His throat clears loudly as he pulls at the collar of his coat. There's a smugness to his tone. The pride laced between the words is almost imperceptible if you're not paying attention.

My insides are raging. Fear attempting to bring me to my knees. If anything happens to any of us tonight, I'm not sure I'll be able to forgive myself. We had a chance to get away after finals today and I talked the group out of it. Assured them we were going to be safer here behind the school wards than anywhere else in the world. Out there, where we would lack the protection of this administration, is too much of a risk. The possibility that anyone could figure out what Bri and I are, too great.

I was wrong and anything that goes poorly tonight is on me. Every death. Injury. Secret revealed. It's. On. Me.

"Janelle, get somewhere safe," I whisper, hugging her close to me. Genuine gratitude blooming in my chest. "Thank you for everything."

"Oh, let me go Wynston!" She swats me away. "Do you truly think I will let you all face this alone? I am a Grisym, too, and I will always stand with you." She throws Bri a small smile. "I promised your grandmother I would always be by your side."

As one, we make our way down the main staircase.

The beginning of the end looms before us, and I hope I am ready for it. I hope we all are.

One final deep breath flows free as I tear open the massive front doors of Beauxgraton, the chill of the outside air no match for the pit of ice I'm carrying in my gut.

Here we go.

75

Graham

I rush through the hallways with intention. Everything that has happened since the beginning of this school year swirling through my head so fast I can barely focus. I'm so lost kicking around every detail, I almost miss the man standing outside my door.

"Oh, Mr. Ava—" I cut my address short remembering I should be using his title. "Apologies, Director Avalon."

Bri's dad smiles at me. Closed-lipped and tight, but genuine, I think. Yet, the stretch is so wide his grin still unnerves me. "Roman," he nearly coos, "if you please. Why are you in such a hurry?"

"Oh, uh." My hand rubs at the hair at the rear of my skull, unsure how much I should tell him. I assume he knows about Jordden being here on campus. Bri mentioned her three parents all having conversations and not including her. A reality that frustrated her when she brought it up. Roman will only want to help. I only want to help.

Then, the way he'd spoken to her only hours ago rings in my head. None of us were happy about it. Who would say such cruel things to their daughter, especially when not long ago it appeared as if she was his whole world? His favorite gem to hoist into the air and allow the world to gawk at. I know now that he hid her, but it never seemed as if he made her feel that way.

I may have pledged myself to Jordden, but I only did it for her. Because I have my best friend's back. The woman who has become something more than a best friend to me. I will do anything to protect her, even if she's pissed at me for it on the back end.

"Actually, we could use your help. Come in," I flag him inside my room ahead of me.

He lingers by the door until I've entered and allowed it shut behind me. I don't hesitate to rifle through my things. My breaths coming in hot bursts as I stuff random items I might need for a few days into a backpack I never used until tonight.

"What can I help with, son?" I turn to face Director Avalon, papers crumpled in my hands as I decide what I should and shouldn't say.

I choose to trust the man I've seen look at Bri with nothing more than adoration. Maybe he just had a bad night and lost it on her. It doesn't mean he meant what he said. He loves her. I've seen it.

"Um, Jordden is here. And he seems to have some sort of plan going. I'm scared Bri is going to get hurt. He mentioned guests being here," my words come out as a nervous blurt. I think I've said enough, but then wonder if I've said too much as Director Avalon's mouth turns down into an intense frown, his sheer blue eyes darkening.

Instinctually, I take a step back and then another, realizing I must have made a mistake. I shouldn't have said anything. Comprehension becomes clear as his features stiffen and veins throb at his temples. The quivering curl of the corner of his mouth into a sneer forces me back several more steps. Anything to put distance between me and the raging bull in front of me.

"What's the matter, Graham? You look pale."

I'd been so distracted by all this shit that I hadn't stopped to notice obvious things. Like, why would Bri's dad be waiting outside my bedroom as if he expected me or maybe was looking for me? Or worse, looking for her with that same venom in his stare. The face of the man staring back at me now is not the same as the one who laughed with us for hours in her room or took us out to breakfast the next morning.

This is not the loving man Bri has talked about so often. Rather, this is the man who yelled hours ago. The one who yanked her from class in a rage. This man terrifies me more than Jordden ever could. More than those twins or Valen's flying daggers.

"Mr. Avalon, why were you at my door?"

A wicked grin spreads across his face as I retreat another step, the backs of my thighs hitting the edge of my roommate's bedframe.

Where is Jordden when I need him?

Director Avalon only continues to stalk toward me, his face unchanging, until we're no more than half a foot apart. "Where is my daughter?" And now I know I've made a grave mistake telling him anything.

"I—" My breaths come in stuttered pants. I brace my hands on the edge of the bed as I lean back, attempting to put extra space between us. "I-I don't know."

"Don't lie to me. If you think Jordden Guthrie is bad, you'll loathe what I can become."

I swallow loudly, trying to formulate a plan. Some way for me to warn her.

I'm sorry, Bri.

I pant searching for a solution. My phone would be too obvious. That new tattoo tingles and I'm thankful my clothing covers it. There's no way Director Avalon can know I swore myself to Jordden, too.

I am just now wondering how it works. I know he mentioned it was similar to a blood oath. We're bound to him by this sliver of his essence, but what benefit does it serve me now? There's a way to somehow signal him, but does it require a spell or my deep thoughts? I hate that I didn't ask the questions that could save me now. But I also know if I summoned Jordden to this room, Bri would be with him and every bone in my body tells me she needs to stay as far away from her dad as possible tonight.

Pressing my eyes shut, I call his name anyhow. Over and over, that two-syllable word repeated. A silent prayer, hoping he hears me. Maybe he'll sense my distress and keep her away. Keep her safe. Someone needs to save Bri because her dad surely isn't here to do that.

"I'll ask only once more, Mr. Mayer. Where is Bryony?"

I'm terrified and out of time and options. But maybe if I give up that they've gone out to the pit, it will be enough. At least that's where I assume they are going since I heard Jordden whisper about it to Bri, as we climbed the Vault stairs. He'd said that the ghouls were waiting for us. Somehow, I don't think those are the guests he was referring to, though. A shudder runs through me, thinking about being so close to those beasts. I've always wanted to see them, but if they are here tonight, it's not under the protection of the Red Moon.

"The pit," I blurt. "They're going to the pit."

I press my eyes shut, hoping I haven't just done something awful. Breathing heavily, I wait to hear the sound of my door opening and closing behind Director Avalon as he goes off on his mission to locate Bri. My new prayer becoming one of hope that their head start will give them some sort of advantage. A prayer that my out-of-shape ass will be able to run fast enough to beat Director Avalon to her if I sneak out of the rear of the residence.

Enough time has passed he should be gone, but I still sense him there. Slowly, my eyes peel open. His glare focuses on my face in disgust. I'm unsure what his plan for his daughter is, but it can't be good. It's there in his eyes. He knows that I know Bri's secrets. When this ends, I have no doubt he will resign me to the same fate he has planned for her.

"Thank you. Grab your things. We need to go find that daughter of mine." None of the fondness he'd held for her remains. The look on his face is now a copy of the disgust Harley holds so tightly to.

There's nothing but silence between us as he leads me from my room, his fingers curled around the rear of my neck. Suddenly, the school feels like a ghost town, and the knots in my stomach torque a little tighter. Bile threatening to creep up my throat and further dirty my clothing.

I'm grateful I grabbed my long winter coat while in my room as we step out into the night. Roaring winds further drop the already frigid temperatures. I am not made for this mountain life. Not meant for the forever frozen noses and fingers and the wind that throws my hair in the wrong direction.

"Come on," Roman chuffs.

We head around the side of the residence only for a horde of shadows lurking just beyond one of the many alcoves created by the architecture of this place. Bodies. Lots of them. From where we are, I can only make out silhouettes. Both men and women of all sizes.

Only as we draw closer do I realize how many of these faces I know. Faces we all know in the wielding world because they are our leaders. The trusted ones we look to for right and wrong. Those responsible for our laws and justice.

"Laurent. Michael. Grab him," Director Avalon snaps, pulling at the lapels of his coat before sauntering off in the direction of the pit.

Strong hands grab me around the arms. My fight against them is a worthless use of energy. The heels of my most prized casual loafers digging into the hardened ground, likely ruined now as they drag me forward.

“Hey, calm down. I’m coming. I’m not fighting with you,” I grit out as I try to get them to loosen their bruising grips. They don’t.

One of the men grunts. Michael, I think. His face is not one I recognize. Short-cropped wavy blonde hair to go with his pastel green eyes. His thin lips press into a line so straight it appears as if he doesn’t have them at all.

The group travels in near silence as we navigate through the woods. A few of the leaders occasionally whisper amongst themselves. Their voices never quite high enough for me to capture much more than tone. If their tone is anything to go by, it sounds as though many of them are skeptical about why they’re here. The intermittent growls of the ghouls in the distance repeatedly drawing them back into silence.

Suddenly, we come to a stop. My view obscured by the crowd ahead of me. They were careful to keep me toward the center of their mob as we trekked across campus. Director Avalon never more than a few bodies ahead of me.

His voice broadcasts clearly through the night now.

“And there you are.”

76

BRYONY

I'M NOT SURE WHAT I expected when my father engraved his name into my flesh. The moment pledged my unwavering support to him. Bound to him with more than just my blood.

We bring up the rear as we march through the foyer of the school, his arm draping over my shoulder, stopping me just before we exit the front doors.

"You are my daughter. I will make it so you never have to hide."

Tears well behind my eyes before spilling down my cheeks. "You are my dad."

He pulls me close. The words he always wanted from me are finally there for him to hear.

"Let's go change the world."

The night is almost as quiet as it was when we were out here hours ago, except for the growls in the distance. Vicious and angry. Defiant. Terrifying.

The ghouls have come. Their attraction to the Red Moon pulling them from their homes.

My fingers tremble at my side as our shoes crunch over the partially frozen ground. Part of me is terrified about what lies ahead. The Council coming is not likely to make for a cordial visit.

The roars grow louder as we tramp through the woods. Energy sparking between us, fueled by the hatred and misunderstanding we've all endured. I'd been so focused on the path ahead that I hadn't noticed more bodies falling into step with us. Faces I've never seen. Dark eyes glistening in the glow of the Red Moon.

"Who are *they*?" I whisper to Valen.

"Yours to command." He tosses me one of his daggers. "Make Daddy proud."

I want to be frustrated with him for cryptic messaging, but that's something I'll worry about later. I can only assume they are Jordden's followers. The men and women who have stood behind him and his fight for all of us to just be wielders, regardless of what type of magic we feed off of.

I've grown up believing this man was the worst villain the world has ever seen. I believed he did many of the despicable things they say about him. I still do, but now I understand the purpose. His sacrifices are there for all of us to see. The glint in his eye is a reminder he's unafraid to continue to sacrifice for the bigger picture.

I admire him for that. Many don't have the balls to do what needs to be done. I always thought my dad—Roman—did. Maybe in his way, but after what he said to me on the phone tonight, I also believe what Tillerman said about him. He has never been on my side. I was just a pawn to use whenever it became convenient.

One day, I will find out what he did to dangle me over my real dad's head, and I will make him pay. I will make him suffer for pretending to love me. For pretending to care. But mostly for encouraging me to believe that being different was wrong. That I was meant to be hidden. That their mercy in keeping me alive, living as someone else, was a gift I should show unquestionable gratitude for.

I don't deserve that. Knox doesn't. Neither does Vincent, Janelle, or anyone else who falls under the Grisym umbrella. But neither do light wielders or dark, or extrinsic or charters. We divided ourselves into such fine categories, there is no way to equal the god-like prestige of being an innate light wielder. The exact being I pretended to be for twenty-five years.

The beginning of the end comes tonight. My men beside me prove that. My friends and their mixed relationships prove it. My parents, Geneva and Jordden, and their endless love prove it, too. The Council and executioners coming here solidify it.

We break out of the tree line into the pit. Several ghouls sprawl across the open space, their snorts and low rumbling growls are by no means loud enough to account for everything we heard making our way here.

"They're loose," I pant.

"They are being hunted," a hoarse male voice comes from behind me.

I turn to face the Council, other world leaders at their back.

I fight to find some of their faces in the shadows. Looking for the ones I recognize. I have known council members and wielding world leaders since childhood. A consequence of my dad holding a position of prestige in our community. They've watched me grow up. They've given me advice and come to birthday parties. Many attended my maturing celebration, too. I know them, but they only *think* they know me.

These four months at Beauxgraton have opened me to so many things I left buried within me over the years. I'd grown accustomed to being alone. To being different. Part of me believed it was wrong to be what I was. I now know that my mother and father not being together has nothing to do with me and everything to do with appearances and law.

"And there you are," Roman grins.

I know I am worth being loved, and the way Harley treated me all my life isn't acceptable. I shouldn't have to beg for someone to love me. I found people who do. Genuine souls who know who I am, and who don't care. The man grinning at me doesn't love me. He likely never did.

My father and I step forward between Valen and Knox—Knox to my right and Valen to Jordden's left. Our breath forming clouds in the air in front of us.

This stare-down feels like some epic moment. This will either go very well or very wrong.

It only takes a few minutes for my dad—Roman—to shove to the front of the pack.

His eyes find Jordden standing next to me. Then dart back to me.

"You didn't."

Somehow, I know he means bearing Jordden's mark. That name now permanently woven into my chest. Pulling the neck of my sweatshirt aside, I show him. His eyes widen, followed by seconds of sadness before hatred replaces any trace of it.

"You are here for my daughter," Jordden says plainly.

"So, it is true?" a woman with short brown curls, coiled tight to her scalp calls. Catroina Ebbers, Council Chair. She had been one of my favorites throughout my childhood. Allowing me countless days of sitting on her lap and typing on her computer. I was always her assistant. And now she sees what my brother has always called me, an abomination.

"It is. Can you not see it in the woman standing next to me?" Jordden proclaims.

She does. They all do. My chin lifts a little higher.

"It can't be. She is a light wielder. She is Roman's daughter." Catroina fights to make sense of the lies she was told. She'd held me. Nurtured me. Only now to realize she should have been reporting me and my family.

"She is not," Jordden announces. "Neither her nor my son are light or dark wielders."

"You can't mean," another leader breathes. His voice is familiar, but I can't quite see his face to know who it is.

Jordden's voice booms over us all, "I do. My children are Grisyms and they will no longer hide."

The crowd silences a moment as if contemplating if this is the truth.

No one speaks a word. No one seems to so much as exhale.

Suddenly, the roar of a ghoul breaks the silence. My insides shifting, knowing exactly which one it is.

Come to me, you beautiful beast.

77

PIERSON

THE COUNCIL AND WORLD leaders' magic sparks to life. Essences dancing at the ready. Prepared to defend themselves against the ghouls. Other than ghoul hunters, light-wielders never interact with them. The one lie we've told them only benefits us now. Their fear keeps them hesitant.

Light wielders believe fucking a ghoul will kill them. It won't. Nothing at all happens. Unless there is dark magic within them that's incompatible with said ghoul. A ghoul's magic doesn't understand the makeup of light and therefore can't siphon to it, in most cases. But we pedal the lie. We tell the light the ghouls only want their heads should they come near. It works.

A grin spreads on my face as the crowd takes several tentative steps forward, immediately falling back when her name is called.

"Bri," a voice wails from the center of the Council pack. "Bri! Bri!" Each shout of her name is more insistent. The plea breaking even my heart. That voice. *Graham's voice.* For a second, I glance behind me, expecting to see his shoes shining brightly in the moon's glow above. Only now do I realize he never caught up to us.

"Shut him up," Roman orders, before turning his focus back to Jordden.

"I can assure you, should any of you attempt to touch my daughter, there will be deaths here that I will show no remorse for," Jordden sniffs. His voice is even. Unaffected, as if these people didn't come to murder his baby girl.

As one they take another step forward, her fake father leading the charge. "You couldn't just do as you were told? Couldn't just lie low and be a talented student?" he spits.

Bri takes a step forward. "No, Roman, I couldn't."

His eyes go wide as she uses his first name. She has abandoned this man as the dad she knew, and we all see it. I should pay attention to this exchange, but I'm busy scanning the crowd for Graham. If we don't get him back, there's no telling what they'll do to him to punish Bri.

Once again, they move as one. A choreographed synchronization that has me wanting to drop to my knees. Our friend will have to wait. For now, I need to save us. A command rushes through me, the message repeatedly broadcasting to my brain. Jordden is the only one that could be the owner of that command, so I yield.

My knee slams into the dirt, my palms pressing into the cold earth. Moisture soaks my jeans and my palms as I call on the earth. Call on its power to fill me. Possess me.

A rumble starts beneath us. The ground shaking in a tumultuous tremble as the first traces of earth magic absorb into my palms. I grit my teeth as that burst of ecstasy hammers into me.

It has been so long since I channeled this way, I'd forgotten the feeling. How it feels to have something ancient and deadly fill my veins. Earth magic is the purest form of power. Even purer than what an innate is born with. It rolls through you like a thunderstorm, a violent tornado ready to destroy anything in its path.

It's a fight to pull away. To not take too much. To not allow it to consume you as your body takes in more and more. Its purity is an addiction that can be hard to walk away from. So old, so powerful, so tempting.

A loud groan flows out of me as I take more than my fill. A bellow as loud as the ghouls vibrating the tense muscles of my chest. The seconds tick by at a rapid pace. Soon, our enemies will be too close for me to throw up my spell. I need to move.

Several council members already throw cheap shots at us. Spells that will do more damage than we have time to repair should they hit us. The men and women behind me strike back in force, as bolts of light and essences dart past my face.

I should have stopped already. Should have broken the connection.

But I can't.

I won't.

I need more.

Want. More.

I will protect the family I've made here. The people I love and care about. I will not let another person harm Bri.

My head is thrown back as my eyes go black as a demon. Finally, I yank my hands away as I jerkily find my feet and then stalk forward. My movements are uncoordinated and stiff. There's no consideration left here. Anyone in my path may or may not make it out of the trajectory of the barrier spell I shoot at the ground.

My mind only sees those trying to get past us. Trying to get to Bri. They know what she is now. They will kill her.

They will kill all of us for standing with her.

They will let Roman fight by their side tonight, but tomorrow they will turn on him. No need to waste another thought on him now. Angry faces come into view. Some light, some dark. I don't care. They are coming after us. After her.

My lips move in quick succession. The spell coming to me on its own. Earth magic will do as it pleases. As it feels is best.

My lips move faster and faster and faster, my palms straight out at my sides. A ferocious power ready to burst free.

No one notices me as I move forward. Right toward the throng of those that are ready to attack. Those behind me block the spells well, their grunts and screams minimal.

I latch onto the distinct voice I recognize.

The cackling laughter of the twins. Their joy over finally having the opportunity to kill a light wielder without repercussions here in front of them.

Tillerman and Milgren's orders.

But Valen's barked "Fuck!" is what nearly makes me look back.

With one final mumble of the spell on my lips, a wall of cobalt flashes to life between them and us. Those that had picked up the pace, running for Bri, slam face first into the solid surface, landing on their asses on the cold ground.

My black eyes stare at them as their mouths gape open.

The blue shade of the wall evens out, becoming more translucent. Their shocked faces and continued spells bouncing back toward them, easy to see. My spell holds. They always do.

It takes a moment to realize it's not the wall they are staring at.

No, their gazes rise to something higher than their line of sight. The tremble of the ground beneath us now is not because of me.

My girl's friends have come.

78

BRYONY

I'M SO FOCUSED ON the shimmering blue wall in front of me I don't notice the change of my essence inside me. It rages. Fighting to break free.

I let it. Knox's essence shoots from his fingertips, immediately mixing in the space between us.

"How?" another council member breathes. One of the youngest. "That isn't possible." Her words are clear despite the wall.

"It is. We *are* Grisyms." I shout the words, determined to broadcast them to the entire crowd.

I chance a glance out to my side, watching for Knox's expression. He didn't need to be outed tonight, but the words broke free. Still, he looks just as defiant as I do. *Good.*

The only response I receive comes from Graham as he shouts my name again. There's a hoarseness to it now, fueling my anger. A screech of pain following, echoing into the night. They will all burn for touching him.

A growl bursts through the trees behind us. My essence shifting again, a small sliver reaching out to the Azukeen. I don't have to turn around to know it's behind me. Just as Jordden gave a piece of himself to me, I'd unknowingly done the same with my ghoul.

Gasps sound from the Council as they back away from the barrier that would keep the ghouls from them anyhow.

"Do we run?" a female voice whimpers.

"No!" Roman barks. "I didn't give up my child to you for us to run scared now."

He glares my way with a sneer.

It was him. He's the one that made this night what it is. He's responsible for me and my friends praying we make it out of this. That bastard is the reason we may have death on our hands tonight.

"I hate you," I whisper.

His eyes go wide as if he heard my words. I hope he did. I hope he knows they're the truth.

The ground continues to shake beneath us, heavy footfalls and growls closing in. I close my eyes, choosing to trust my true father's theory. Choosing to believe I can do what he says.

I can feel the ghouls at my back. Hear the shuffle of all those who stand with us. They part to let the ghouls go through. Hundreds of beasts here, for me. My essence wanting a piece of each of them.

"Pierce, drop the wall," I command.

"Bri!" Knox is at my side, his breathing ragged. There's no hiding his fear. I pull him to me, placing a kiss on his mouth.

"Trust me. Pierce!" My order is simple. I need the barrier gone.

His lips move in quick succession. His eyes still black as night. One moment, the wall is there, and the next it's gone.

The horde of light wielders still stare at us. Their magic poised for an attack or maybe to defend themselves. One council member has an orb of light that illuminates all their faces, casting enough of a glow to bring out the features of every person.

"Go." As I speak that simple word, each ghoul lunges forward. Their large bodies slipping between ours with ease as they stalk toward those who have come for me. Those that would kill me for being a mixture of the light and the dark.

Our world leaders shoot their most potent spells at the ghouls. Their thick, leathery skin protects them from extensive damage. Even still, viscous ruby-colored blood runs down their legs and chests. Their howls rattling the trees as they reach the front line of the retreating crowd.

A Virideist immediately plucks two council members from the ground, their throats captured in its claws. Their spells and curses are worthless as it roars in their faces, forcefully tossing them into the trees beyond. The sickening crack of bone meeting bark reverberating back to us. The volume not enough to drown out the ghoul rampage before us as they continue to maul the light wielders attacking them. Nothing will drown out the sounds of dozens of these beasts defending their master.

"Please. No! Stop!" someone cries.

"Bryony," Roman screeches.

I only cock my head in his direction, unwilling to stop my creatures from protecting my family. Maybe it makes me no better than him, but Roman Avalon will know he can't fuck with us again. He will know the consequences if he does.

More cries and pleas sound as the crowd retreats. They don't run, but their steps hasten to keep time with the stalking pace of the snarling ghouls. White eyes shining bright against my cloud of onyx.

I focus my thoughts on the Azukeen. Focus on directing it to Graham. Willing it to find him via the image I'm conjuring in my head of my best friend. The way he was that morning, with messy hair, in bed beside me. I need more moments like that.

I can only hope it understands me as well as we think they do. Understands that I want Graham returned to me unharmed. Only a few more seconds pass of me holding the image before voicing my last command.

"Come."

As if frozen in place, each ghoul stops, turns, and returns to the spots they were in before. A wall of demons standing tall at my back.

"How?" Roman breathes as his head rolls back on his shoulders, watching my Azukeen lazily move past him. Claws latched onto the collar of his shirt trap Graham's dangling body. His mouth wide open as he stares down at the wielders below.

It's my turn to step forward, hand raised to keep any of them from following me.

"Roman, I am a Grisym. I am an Eistiab."

His eyes narrow, but he's not surprised.

I stop directly in front of him, looking up at the man I idolized my entire life. A single tear slips free. The last one I will shed for an Avalon. "And I control every ghoul in this world and the next." One more step closer, every set of eyes watching me. "And we will destroy each and every one of you."

My jaw stretches as I allow my essence to release from me anew. The cloud, so thick and violent, we're draped in a darkness so pure that others may fear we will never find the light again. Only that glowing orb floating just above the palm of the councilwoman's hand illuminates the space around us now.

Locking eyes with Roman for what I know won't be the last time, I smirk just before my eyes find that glowing sphere.

"Mine," I whisper.

Also by Britton Brinkley

Misfits Trilogy (with L.A. Scott)

Misunderstood

Misfortune

Accepted

Night Life Duology

Night Life

Night Life 2: Will to Fight

The Company Series

The Tournament

The Target (COMING 01-19-26)

Disavowed Birthright Trilogy

Rise of the Grisym

Dimmer of the Light (COMING 7-14-25)

Fall of the Phoenix Trilogy

Feathers of Truth

Feathers of Destruction

Feathers of Change (COMING 12-19-25)

Scarlet Hearts

Scarlet Hearts

Boulder Ranch

Ride Me

Buck Me (by Ashley Willow)

Want Me (COMING 11-15-25)

Love Me (by Ashley Willow – COMING 11-15-25)

Save Me (COMING 04-20-26)

Hunt Me (by Ashley Willow – COMING 04-20-26)

Dagger & Sword

The Shadows That Shackle (COMING 9-25-25)

Baudelaire Blood

Venetia (COMING 10-13-25)

The Loyals

The Loyals (COMING 10-17-25)

New Coalition Novels

Crux Duology

Don't Scream (COMING 2025)

About the Author

Britton Brinkley was born in New Jersey and now lives in Northern Virginia.

Growing up an avid reader, the sciences and ancient civilizations mesmerized her. She has always loved immersing herself in new worlds. Britton now enjoys creating her own with her writing buddies Jay Gatsby and the little psycho Artemis Prime (the cats).

When she isn't writing, she's likely either reading, watching Criminal Minds, or some other true crime show on Investigation Discovery.

Learn More at BrittonBrinkley.com

www.ingramcontent.com/pod-product-compliance
Lightning Source LLC
Chambersburg PA
CBHW020918310726
48980CB00011B/936/J

* 9 7 9 8 9 9 2 9 5 6 5 1 1 *